The Wages

The Wages

FANNY HOWE

Grid Books
BOSTON

The first edition of *The Wages* was published in 2018 by Pressed Wafer.
This edition was published in 2020 by Grid Books.

ISBN 978-1-946830-07-4

FIRST GRID EDITION
Printed in the United States of America

Contents

THERE was a child went forth every day;
And the first object he look'd upon, that object he became;
And that object became part of him for the day, or a certain part of the day, or for many years, or stretching cycles of years.

WALT WHITMAN

Charles McCutcheon and Fanny Howe in 1977.

A Note on the Reprint

by FANNY HOWE

THIS BOOK is a work of many hands over time. Its first pages were passed from one person to another across a century. From the beginning they were plain-spoken but urgent words on fragile pages that should never have survived, given the violent events that took place around them and the obscurity of their origins. They start with a baby and a grave and end with a grandchild at a graveside.

The account was never typical of slave narratives because of its blend of fiction with fact. From bits and pieces of paper hauled out of a basement just recently (2016) and all but one photograph of the people involved lost—the original story (always called *The White Slave*) was a double act of bravery and secrecy. It has, by now, the quality of a folk tale.

In the back of this volume I have put fragments of the versions that we have. The novel itself, now a revision of the one I wrote in 1978, is built out of incomplete accounts of what happened to a certain child in 19th-century America. The tone of voice in which it is written is somewhat formal, even out of step with contemporary fiction. It reads almost like a translation because in many ways it is a translation from a variety of texts that were spoken or scrawled.

THE GRANDSON of Peter McCutcheon, Charles McCutcheon, is the one who researched and saved and articulated the original manuscript. The story of his grandfather was an essential part of his own identity. He first heard it in Kansas as a child, and then when he was thirteen, his father asked him to transcribe what he remembered into a nickel tablet under a kerosene lamp. Charles did this, methodically, and asked his grandmother, Charity, to help him with some of the facts. She did, and he carried this tablet with him from one part of the country to another, through five floods, and a variety of storms. Charles lived from 1911 to 1979 and died in Wabaunsee County where he was born.

He worked as an ironworker in Colorado and Kansas, settling near his sister Agnes with his wife and children. Over the years he copied out the scenes and dreamed of making a publishable book out of them. He could think of little else. He could envision the entire life of his grandfather Peter like a work of embroidery that would reveal a hidden edge of the slave tapestry, and would be a contribution to American history. He and his sister Agnes huddled over the pages together and talked about the story to people they met, and finally a professor, Lee Steinmetz, from Eastern Illinois University, heard about it and came to interview them.

Steinmetz spent months researching plantation history in Kansas and Arkansas and looking through cemeteries for McCutcheon family members. With the help of a colleague, Roger Whitlow, he took Charles's manuscript and turned it into a fifty-page presentable summary for publication purposes. This was during the early nineteen-seventies. It was rejected by magazine and book publishers as being too familiar a story, too unlikely a story, too lucky, and too inflammatory. The names had been changed—all but McCutcheon, that is—but still it had a dangerous aura. Secret and suppressed facts about property and race, during the 19th century, were kept that way well after the Civil War.

Finally Lee Steinmetz gave the outline to a literary agency that said it was interested. And soon it came to me, in 1977, a document that pulled me into libraries to study the Antebellum period in the Midwest.

For two years I studied the ordeal of American slavery and the foul dishonor it generated (and still does) in all parts of this country and globally. I took every little act and detail as far as it could go in logic, and tried to understand the psychology and soul-life of each character. The great advantage was that the "plot" itself was complete, a credible and shocking structure that I could work inside. This was, for me, an adventure with reality and storytelling.

In 1978 I went to Kansas to meet Charles and Agnes McCutcheon. I drove to the town outside of Sterling where they lived and near the lake where the movie *Picnic* was made. I was shaken by the overlap of fiction and reality, the breadbasket farmland of L. Frank Baum and the stretch of road before me, and by the characters in the McCutcheon story and the two older people waiting for me on a wooden porch of the tidy house belonging to Agnes. They had both been through personal ordeals, were sensitive and well spoken, kind and hopeful.

We sat together under the receding glow of the Civil Rights Movement and the passage of the Civil Rights Act. Jimmy Carter was president and *Eyes on the Prize* was being developed in a basement in Boston. I promised them that I would do my best for their family history. We parted as friends.

IN RETROSPECT, I deeply regret that I had not seen the documents that only in 2016 came to light, through the generous intervention of Roger Whitlow, because they supply so much life and character to this strange story and show how closely Charles McCutcheon was involved in every stage of its creation. I am so glad I had the new material to deepen my original narrative.

In the beginning Charles used pseudonyms for his family and for the slave-holding people whose real name was Rankin. He called Peter "Sam" and Charity "Millie." He was rightfully afraid of retaliation. It was 1979 when Avon Books first published the book with some of the real names, the same year that Charles died and before he got to see the story in print.

Forty years later I was asked if I would agree to print a new edition of *The White Slave*. I re-read it and faltered, embarrassed by the dated language, uneasy with the word "slave," and especially by the title, which was given to the very first version of the story. Basically, I re-translated my own first version of the story and changed the title to one that is my own, *The Wages*, for reasons that must seem obvious.

RIGHT AFTER the original publication of *The White Slave* I heard from a stranger who knew Charles and Agnes personally and their grandfather's history, just as they had told it to her, and she said to me, "It was much worse than what you wrote." This comment has stayed with me. Surely it was much worse, so much so, that it was unspeakable among family members, their children.

More recently a stranger called me from Kansas to say he was a friend of one of the "white slave's" great-grandchildren. He was trying to help this man understand that he was not white, though he insisted he was. The stranger on the phone said this young man was "obviously black" and deluded by thinking otherwise. He asked me to send the original manuscript I received years ago to prove it to his friend. I did, and never heard back.

IN DECEMBER of 2016 I got an astonishing message from the great-great-granddaughter of Peter McCutcheon. She told me she had read the original book more than once, with great enthusiasm, and wondered if I could ever meet her to talk about her family. I told her I was in the process of revising *The White Slave*. And within minutes we realized we were in the same city, working on the same material. So we hurried to a café in Los Angeles.

Eden McCutcheon Tirl is a tall former model and actress, light-skinned black and proud, and in her bag she carried family photographs and clippings and lists of family names. It seemed supernatural that we were there together and I asked her to write an Afterword for this new edition of *The Wages*. She was my ideal reader for this book, as a McCutcheon heir, as a young person of this time, and because of her insightfulness. I am very grateful for her part in continuing the story of Peter so readers can see flesh and blood behind and ahead of this true, all-too-American story.

As Willa Cather wrote of the Midwest, I can say of this book: "There was nothing but land; not a country at all, but the material out of which countries are made."

The Birth of a Slave
Missouri, 1832

On a warm April night in Missouri, a girl lay on the floor of her cabin. She lay exactly as she had during the nights that a man forced himself on her. One, two, three, four times, her face hidden in sackcloth.

On this night in 1832 John Howard, that man, her boss, snatched the baby away from her. It was a sickly infant girl, born too soon, with soft black curls and a pinched face. Betty had nursed and rocked her hour after hour until the man stamped in.

When he twisted the baby from her arms, Betty screamed and tore at him, but he knocked her to the ground and marched to the hill where the burial ground lay. There was a hole already dug and a pine box no bigger than a fiddle case already built.

The orange rays of the sun glowed on his hand over the infant's wailing mouth as he pressed down till she cried and seemed to breathe no more. Then he buried her in the box under the dewy grass as the morning birds sang and a tiny voice cried from under the ground.

For three days after Betty sat on the floor, not moving, not eating. The blanket drooped over her shoulders. From time to time her friend Ruth would come to see her and rub her back and wash her face.

At dusk Ruth came and whispered to Betty, "Now they are bringing you another baby—Miss Nora's baby. They won't kill this child, one of their own, like they did yours, but they will send it away from its mother—just because she did what she did. To keep her a lady. Get ready, Betty."

Then Ruth slipped away, back to the big house, to Nora, whose contractions were beginning.

Betty did not move, but the expression in her eyes changed as she absorbed Ruth's news. She had hoped to sit there alone, dying. But now she would be forced to keep on moving, working, living. She had no choice. Had she ever?

A low moan came from Betty's throat, and she rocked slowly from side to side. Across the yards of silent livestock in the night she heard, like an echo, Nora's birthing cries and the baby's cries at being born.

IN HER NARROW childhood bed in the big house Nora Howard writhed and cried. Labor took a long time. Nora was only sixteen and small, the baby large. It took hours of straining. By the time he was born, Nora was drenched in sweat and half delusional. Her father Will stood over her.

"Here, drink this," he said. He held a small glass of brandy to her lips and the girl consumed it, choking.

Ruth washed the baby in a tub of warm water. He didn't bellow, but emitted small whimpers. Cupped in her hands, he was very pale. "Wrap him up, Ruth," Will Howard whispered, "and bring him downstairs as soon as you can."

Then she left the room. Nora was moaning her way into sleep, blood still flowing, her body sore.

Nora's uncle John would not touch the baby. But her mother Mrs. Howard stepped out of the shadows and followed Ruth out to the slave quarters to Betty, who sat on the floor.

The baby was wrapped in blankets and was howling hunger cries. They pierced the air in the little shack, where one candle burned. Nora's mother kneeled down beside Betty while Ruth handed her the new baby.

"Now child," Mrs. Howard said, "I want you to take this baby and raise him as your own."

"No," Betty said, her shoulders hunched to reject the infant.

"Yes, Betty, you have no choice," said the woman coldly. "Take it. Now."

"No. He's white."

Mrs. Howard looked at Ruth for help.

"Betty," Ruth said, "it's just a baby. Didn't do no harm to you or anyone else."

And she pried apart Betty's arms to settle the baby in. The milk in Betty's breasts automatically prickled and streamed at the feel of the warm infant, at the sound of his close hungry cries. But she turned her face away, grinding her teeth.

"Do as Mrs. Howard says," Ruth whispered and kneeled to draw back Betty's chemise, so the infant could find her breast.

Betty drew her breath, for in spite of her emotions, the feel of the baby's gums on her nipples was a relief. She stared with stone-cold hatred past Mrs. Howard to where John Howard stood on the darkened threshold.

"Now listen, Betty," said the woman, "Ben is going to take you, tonight, in the wagon, about fifty miles south. There's a big plantation there. Your new master's name is Collins. He owns many slaves and keeps them in good health." She looked around the shack with disapproval and disgust. "This is an opportunity for you, Betty, a good chance to improve your lot. The Collinses are a great deal richer than us, and you won't have to see Master John again. Understand?"

Betty did not respond. She gritted her teeth, angry at the way her insides melted as the baby's gums clamped thirstily on her breast.

"Call him your own," Mrs. Howard said. "We told Mr. Collins he was yours by a foreign railroad man. Name him whatever you want. Make up a story. He's yours now, your son, and will be put to work as a slave, just like you. He was born in disgrace and will live out his fate."

Her face, thin and tense in repose, now crinkled as she spoke. For the baby was, after all, her flesh and blood. As she rose to her feet, she staggered and grasped hold of Ruth.

"No one will believe a word of it, of course," said Mrs. Howard.

"Look how fair he is! But we have no choice. We are a Christian family. Betty, Ruth, you must never, never tell the child the truth. You understand? If you do, John Howard will come after you. There are plenty of light-skinned Negroes in this world, thanks to the men who are making them so."

And she left in a rush, disappearing without a look back. Ruth kneeled beside Betty. They looked at each other with mirrored expressions of outrage.

"Someday they'll pay for this. Someday. Just you wait and see," Betty said.

"Well, like they say, the knot in the plank will show through the whitewash," Ruth agreed. "You might not have to lift a finger to see them get what they deserve. Now I'll pack up your clothes. And I brought you a pack of food for the journey. Share it with Ben. The baby will pull your milk down all right. I just hope he makes it through this world."

Betty and Ruth gazed at each other in the light of the flickering tallow. The only sound in the room was that of the suckling baby.

A Boy's Story
1844

1

PETER SQUINTED as if he could see the future. The hatchet had fallen from his hand. He gazed down the long incline at timber, split, broken and ready to roll. Below was the big house, the slave quarters, and the peach orchards. Beyond was the silvery sky. The farm steamed in mud and dung, the neat grids of the fences held in cattle and plough horses. He could hear hammering from every direction, some shouts. The sun beamed down on his long hair that fell wild and unkempt below his ears. His face was flushed from his labors and he breathed hard. But he kept his dreamy, distant expression.

"Get to work, boy," shouted a man from behind. Morgan, the overseer, moved down the hillside from his concealment and reined in beside Peter. Morgan was rough with little experience in fieldwork. "What you doing resting this time of day? Only ten o'clock. Long way to go." Morgan's features nestled in a thick beard. He wasn't smiling even though his lips were split apart. "Think you're special? You're special, all right." Turning his horse, he trotted east, beside a line of timber.

Peter picked up his ax and moved on to the next tree, which he hacked at halfheartedly. He was very thin and muscular for a twelve-year-old boy, and he had a defensive posture. His eyes were bright, as if he was trying to see beyond his place, and because he rarely spoke. For another two hours he knocked out little chips in the side of the hemlock, while its dark green boughs trembled and shook their shade around him. He didn't enjoy cutting the boughs from the trees; it seemed to hurt them. If he paused, he could hear the sound of other axes echoing around the hillside and birds singing. He had had this job a couple of weeks; before then, he worked with the livestock. He was happy enough with the animals, but then he was moved to this position because the boss wanted more muscles on him.

Solitude was familiar to Peter. Even though he had been on the plantation since infancy, he was now ignored. The boys and girls he had played with as a young boy had gathered into gangs and turned against him and each other, as if they could foresee a battle ahead and needed to practice. The boys had learned from the masters. They had learned to fight and instill fear in anyone weak or strange.

Over the years they had noticed and listened to the way Peter was discussed and treated, and the older he grew, the more stories increased around him. About who his father was and his mother Betty who kept him out of sight when he was a baby. When he grew older and his color didn't darken the taunts and questions grew more frequent. People tried to stroke his blond hair; they made fun of his freckles and red sunburn, even the ones who were indifferent to his birth story.

Betty told Peter she had found him in a cave between Texas and Arkansas—and that was that. Two years after her arrival on this plantation, carrying the infant in her arms, she married the driver, Robert, a man she loved, and she had his children, all of them dark-complexioned like herself and she turned all her attention on them. One of them, a boy, died early of a cough. Betty was moved from the field to the kitchen afterwards.

She always said Peter would leave her as soon as he could although he had acquired, naturally, the mannerisms and speech patterns of his companions and was sensitive to the insults thrown his way. His naturally shy temperament held him in check and silent. But when he turned twelve, and was handed an axe, he changed and a fury grew in him and often broke out uncontrollably. Whippings were common for him. Morgan, the overseer, teased Peter, and the boy then refused to do his chores or argued back and would look the man in the eye with open hatred.

At twelve he could no longer believe that he was found by the roadside, or was Betty's son at all. He believed he was a "blended" child of someone white and someone black. A vague dread grew in him alongside his own potential for violence. He didn't know who he was, and he didn't like it. If he came from nowhere, he was also going nowhere, and nothing much mattered. Betty said he was asking for it when he got whipped, but then so were the other children. Their ribs were cracked and healing, their thighs streaked with welts both open and healing. Flies followed them.

Her lack of an honest response to his questions frightened him and made him sad, for then it seemed she had lost sight of him. When he came in contact with Morgan, he forgot everyone else in the world and focused all his outrage on the man. He was almost testing him to see how far Morgan would go before striking. So maybe he was "asking for it," and if he was, where would it get him? He acted as if he wanted to go somewhere else.

He and his family and the other adults were not allowed to learn to read, so during breaks they made music, worked on clothing, quilts, utensils, fiddles, strainers, and garden plots, designed lattice-work, nails, houses, and porches, and figured out what was happening in the outside world from inside the house or from passing strangers. Many of them coughed while they worked, hacking and spitting phlegm and blood; many cut themselves but had no cloth to bind the wound. Their noses dribbled no matter how many swipes they took at them.

LIKE PETER none of the other children entered adolescence without changing. Many of them, boys and girls, fought fiercely and plotted and got caught and punished. They seemed to have been born with an idea of justice that had to be beaten out of them till they became resigned like their parents. They all expected Peter to bolt one night or be killed. Like his childhood friends, he was beginning to plan how to escape, a sudden dash into the wilderness. Always at night, beautiful night.

2

"PETER!" his mother's voice called from the kitchen of the big house.

Peter's head was bowed, his hair shading his face, his motions reluctant. Betty pulled him inside the door, where the smell of cooking was heavy in the air.

"The master wants to see you, boy. Don't know why. Go on in the front room. He's waiting." She pushed at his hair quickly. "Now don't give him one of your looks, you hear? You just keep your eyes down and your mouth shut. Listen to what he says and say nothing but thanks and please, according to what he wants. Understand?"

Peter did not respond but passed by Betty and out the door into the front hall. He quickly appraised the staircase, table, rug, and the comfort and elegance of each object. Then he rapped on the doorjamb outside the living room and, head bent, waited.

"That you, Peter?" called Mr. Collins. "Come on in."

Peter stepped into the large room. Way across from him sat Collins, a man with a tan, healthy face and soft yellow hair. He wore rough clothes, which gave him a pioneer's rather than a planter's appearance.

"Now, Peter," said Collins, "don't look so scared. I'm not going to whip you. Didn't call you in here for any kind of punishment." He rose from his lounging position and stood smiling with his chin up. "Why, you look for all the world like a normal child, but you move and talk and act like a pick-a-ninny gone to seed."

His smile disappeared, and he added, "It's not a very pretty sight. But," sighing, "I don't suppose we can change all that now, can we?"

Peter said nothing.

"Can we, boy?" Collins repeated.

Peter, again, did not open his mouth.

"I've heard you've got an insolent streak, boy. We'll have to take care of that. But I didn't call you in here to scold you. I want you to take a little trip with me." He moved to the front window and looked outside, while Peter stole a look at him. "I'm a footracer, as you probably know. And I need someone reliable to travel with me. Someone to rub me down, get my ankles strong. Someone I can trust. And I trust you, Peter. For two reasons. You want to know what they are?"

Peter said nothing, but looked at the floor.

"That's right," said Collins, "because you don't open your mouth is number one. I like that. But more important, I don't really care what happens to you because there's no wage for such a creature. Do you have a value? And I've been around. Never saw such a clear example of rape and run. Someone brought you from somewhere else, to sell, maybe from the DeWolfes of Bristol . . . How Betty got hold of you is anyone's guess. But we got you both for free. And now you're old enough to be of use to me. So come on with me tomorrow. You could prove yourself."

Collins moved to Peter's side and stood near, looking him over.

"I'll have Betty clean you up and get you in shape. We're leaving after lunch," he said. "Now, Peter, you may go."

Peter, turning, made a grimace for his own benefit. Then he shambled back into the kitchen.

Betty asked, "What did he want, boy?"

"Wants me to go with him on one of his races. Rub him down, and all that." Peter lifted his eyes to Betty's. "I don't want to."

"Well, that's just too bad. Now get on back to work."

She handed him a piece of cake, and watched him go outside. He was greeted by two of the Collins children, soft, round, eight-year-old twin boys, who ran around him shouting, "Peter needs a whipping! Peter needs a whipping!"

"Is that why Daddy called you?" cried one. "'Cause you were bad again?"

"I want to watch 'em beat you."

Peter made a threatening move, which caused Betty to open the door and step out; but then he quickened his pace and moved up the hill to the timberline.

Betty returned to her flour and dough that covered the long kitchen table. Her hands were covered with the pale spots of dough and they hurt from her harsh grinding motions. Peter was always good and obedient where she was concerned but the ridicule and abuse he had taken since early childhood had made him uncommunicative. She knew how cruelty grew harsh toward outsiders and slower people; it was a weakness that all human beings seemed to share. The children were free of it until around eight or ten, and then they too kicked the afflicted, killed birds and mice for fun, and pushed around the children who were now smaller than them. Betty watched while Peter grew from a commonly accepted friend with the other children into a solitary ten-year-old, and she grieved.

"One of these days, he'll be gone," Robert would say, "and maybe that's as it should be. If he got away, he could fit right in and make a life for himself."

"What you say is true," Betty would reply, "but I still think of him as my own, and it hurts to think of him going into such a hard world. What do we know of it, out there?"

Her daughters might never make it to freedom but had, as she saw it, no possible chance of free choice; if she thought about it too hard, her eyes would burn with resentment. Her infant son found the easy way out: die. Someday Peter would run free and forget her. So a part of her stayed aloof, waiting, as a kind of self-preservation. She had done her duty in raising him. He grew more independent daily. She would never tell him how he came to be hers. She would never tell him, or anyone else but Robert, the secret of his origins.

As she wiped the flour off the table with a damp rag, she did not see Collins come to the door. He leaned there, watching her for a few moments, and then spoke.

"Did Peter tell you what I told him, Betty?" he drawled.

"Yes, sir, he did," she said, startled. She leaned down and washed her hands in a bucket at her feet.

"Maybe if we give him a little responsibility, he'll begin to shape up."

"I hope so, sir."

"Betty, I like Peter, he's quiet, and seeing as he's so—you know—and all, I can use him. They say boys his age can be a real problem, but they never said nothing about a bone-white slave. I mean, I never heard of one before myself. And I consider myself fortunate, Betty, to have someone who looks like him for these excursions." He moved to the table and ran his finger around the edge of a bowl full of sweet dough. "Yes," he went on, "I always believe in taking advantage of problems. Seize them, before they surprise you, is my way of doing things.

"Now when my daddy left me this land to take care of, it was nothing but grass. Grass and trees. I was twenty years old. You came here, with Peter, a few years later, as I recall, and since then we've worked hard, all of us. Haven't we?"

"Yes sir, real hard."

"I had twenty slaves, now I have more than forty. That's a lot of property. And what I'm getting at is my plan for Peter. If we get him in shape, he'll make a fine overseer someday. He'll know you folks as well as he knows himself. That's an advantage. People like Morgan, they're worse than dogs. Mean, money-grubbing trash. No humility. No class. Slaves and aristocrats, like myself, have got one thing in common. We know what we are. People like Morgan think they can move up the social scale just by barking under the table. But give them some money, and you'll see they're dogs then, just like they always were."

Collins often came into the kitchen to talk like this, so Betty was not taken aback. She pounded the dough, while he rambled on. She knew that he and his wife did not get along. He spent more nights with one of the slave women than he did with her. He had children by this woman, who loathed him. Betty knew about that. He never talked to his wife because she turned her face to the side every time they sat together. As a result, he hung around the kitchen more than most men would. He was a vain man who worried about his health and dressed in rough, outdoor clothes. He exercised regularly and would neither smoke nor drink anything stronger than wine.

"Now I don't want too much sugar with my dinner tonight," he instructed Betty, "for I have a theory that sugar is the cause of indigestion. The children are too fat anyway. It's ugly the way their clothes are so tight. Of course it comes from Joan's family, not mine. They all run to fat. I wish I thought of that before I married her. You know how I feel about fat."

Betty nodded and tried not to smile. She turned her face away momentarily.

"Well, now, I better go take my ride. I'll be taking Peter early tomorrow morning, so see he gets a good sleep. He's going to need it."

"Yes, Master Collins."

"And clean him up!" he shouted over his shoulder.

3

"HE SAYS I've got to clean you up," Betty told Peter that night. "I got some scissors to trim your hair. Now, start washing."

Peter, stripped to the waist, did as he was told, rubbing his arms and torso with a cold wet cloth, dipped in a pan of water. They were huddled in their quarters now: a one-room cabin with a stone fireplace and a table with two chairs. Pallets of rags and straw served as beds. Betty's children were playing with stick dolls on the mattress they shared. Robert, at the table, was rubbing his bow with rosin. Small, and lightweight, he had a kind of elfin appearance.

Peter admired him and his beautiful handiwork. He wanted to make fiddles too! Robert glanced at Peter washing in the light of a tallow candle.

"Now if you be a good boy with Master Collins, I'll start making you a fiddle, Peter, and you can watch. How's that?"

"Just fine, Papa."

"But if you act up, it'll have to wait."

Peter looked from Robert to Betty anxiously.

"I don't want to go," he said.

"It's your first trip out into the world," Betty said, "and you're bound to be scared. But nothing's going to happen. The boss will take care of you, and you'll be home before you know it. Besides, we want to hear all about it."

"That's right," Robert said. "This is a chance for you to see something new. And if the boss likes you, he'll give you more chances like this."

"Why he doing it? He hates me."

"He don't hate you, Peter," Betty said. "Why, he told me he wants to make something of you."

"Why?"

"Well, I can't honestly say. I don't know how that man thinks. But it's what he told me."

"I hate him!" Peter said vehemently. "He makes me sick. The way he talks to you and Papa. The way he makes you work on Sunday. No rest, nothing. He's mean, and proud of it."

"You be quiet, boy," Robert said firmly. "We know all that."

Peter sighed into silence, while Betty clipped his hair around the edges. He watched the two little girls playing and his burning eyes narrowed. He loved his sisters and little brother, and he dreaded leaving them, even for a few days. It made him want to cry to think of sleeping somewhere strange, far away from his family.

That alienated feeling came over him again, and mingled with the panic he already had. His mother's long brown fingers passed across his face. There was a snipping sound, and his curls dropped down onto her lap. He loved the way her hands had many shades and colors in them, from pink to pale yellow to brown to black and back to pink under her nails.

Their eyes met briefly, and she seemed to read his mind in a glance. She nodded her head in a way that told him she understood what he was going through, and that she was there for him, whether she said so or not.

4

THE EARLY MORNING LIGHT dappled their trail. The air was pleasantly cool and spring's pale green leaves fluttered, damp and shiny and newborn, in a soft breeze. The horse moved quickly, goaded on by Joe, the driver. Peter sat up front beside him while Collins lounged behind. Around noon Joe stopped the wagon at a neat white farmhouse and picked up another man, who joined Collins behind. This man was a friend of Collins, a farmer about his age, with a Southern accent. As they traveled, the two men talked, giving Peter his first opportunity to listen to the conversation of white men. Their subject was slavery.

"Now I don't know about you," said the man called Sloane, "but I think these abolitionists up north have a point. I can do without it, myself, without the whole damn problem. I don't need it! I'd just as soon pay the nigra's like I do when I hire them for harvesting, and have them live somewhere else. I don't need it around my neck, night and day."

"Maybe you have this opinion for a reason," said Collins in an easy voice. "I mean, your property is small. You stick to raising the staples, you don't come from the sort of family I do. My whole life has been spent on acres and acres of land belonging to my family. That's a responsibility, and there's only one way of dealing with it. And that's with the system we've got. Hell, on a small farm you might not need it. But, where I come from, there's no way of doing without."

"Doesn't it bother you?" Sloane asked. "I mean, speaking honestly, doesn't it get you down having all these folks running all over the place? It would make me sick, just dealing with all them Negro problems, day in, day out. If I had my way, I'd ship them all back where they come from. And I'm not the only one."

"Then who would do the labor?"

"Why, we got hands. It's good for a man to earn his own wages. Makes him strong. You think they do it better than we could, if we had to? Because that's where you're wrong. They interfere with production, they stop to make something new and hide it. They act stupid but they know more than you think."

Collins laughed.

Peter glanced at Joe, who might have been deaf for all you could tell from his long face. Peter's face burned. He wanted to turn around and spit. He clenched his hands together in his lap, trying to swallow his words for the sake of that fiddle his father was going to make for him. But his mind was racing. There was no shortage of talk, at night, about the plight they were in. But he had never heard it, brazenly, from the mouths of white men. He hummed a tune in order to control his distress.

"What you singing, Peter?" Collins called.

He stopped humming, but didn't reply or turn his head.

"That's just about the first time I ever heard your voice," Collins laughed, and said to Sloane, "I guess you've heard about this boy."

"Sure, most everybody has," said Sloane.

"Someday I'm going to find out where he came from," Collins said, "because there must be a real story there."

"Who'd you buy him from?"

"Uppity family in Missouri about fifty miles. He came with his mammy. Just a newborn. They wanted to get rid of her and him, fast. Know what I mean? So I got a good deal. She's turned out fine. But I bet you there's a story there—incest, rape, kidnap. Something skewered in his first family. Howard. But that's okay with me. He's a pretty boy, isn't he?"

"Don't know about that," said Sloane.

Then the two men began to talk about the race. Collins was going to race an Indian who was said to be the fastest runner along the border.

"I'll believe it when I see it," Collins said. "I never heard of a speedy Indian before. Always think of them moving real slow alongside a pack of buffalo."

"Well, from what I hear he's not called Chaparral Charlie for nothing. Comes from Santa Fe. He knows the countryside. He's packed away a lot of cash in his travels, just from racing."

"I'm not doing too badly myself," Collins said, as he automatically rubbed the calves of his legs.

"Well, we'll see. Should be interesting anyway. I plan to throw away some cash on booze tonight, but you'd better stay sober."

"I wouldn't drink, even if I could. Bad for the brain and the kidneys," Collins said.

Peter watched the trail emerge on a large meadow with a view of a cool blue lake and distant blue hills. He wondered what would happen if he jumped out and started to run. Was he really surrounded, night and day, by mobs hidden in the leaves, waiting to kill him or sell him? He moved around in his seat, restlessly, and then he heard Joe speak in a low voice, for the first time.

"Calm down, boy, calm down," he said gently.

5

TOWARD EVENING they entered the town where the race would be held. Peter had never been off the farm before, and though this one was thinly settled, including only a saloon with rooms, a trading post, and a few board houses, it contained enough activity to be interesting. He and Joe were left in the wagon with food packed by Betty, while the two white men set off on foot.

Peter had never seen an Indian before, though he had heard plenty of tales. Now, seeing them in the flesh, mostly men at the trading post, he was fired with interest. He knew they were hounded, pursued, ambushed, lied to, and slaughtered by white men. He saw now they were freely moving about. Never before had he seen dark-skinned people doing what they wanted to do without the oppressive figure of a white man around. Guns hung all over those men, hung down around their crotches and leather belts, creaked when they walked. The Indians didn't flinch.

"Where do they come from? Where are they going?" he wondered.

And Joe, as if he had read his thoughts, said, "Those Cherokee people come from all over. Like families they have tribes they belong to, but they roam free. This is their land. So long as they don't make the white man mad, they can deal with him on an equal basis. Still, I think they want to see him gone."

Then he shut up, for he saw the boss returning. It was growing dark and the lights in the saloon were on, voices and music pouring out into the night.

Collins stepped up to the wagon. "Come on, Peter, grab my bag and come with me. Joe, you wrap yourself in that blanket there and get some shuteye."

"Yes, sir," said Joe.

Peter followed Collins through the saloon filled with smoke and the smell of liquor. They went up some wooden stairs to the floor above and entered a small room done in red.

"Put the bag on the chair there," said Collins.

Peter did as he was told, but he felt a thickening in his chest, a sense of unease. Collins sat on the edge of the bed and removed his jacket and boots. Then he rolled his pant legs up to his knees and lay back on the pillow. Peter stood in a corner looking down.

"Take the liniment out of that bag, Peter. I want you to rub me down."

Peter didn't know what he meant.

"Liniment. It's in a yellow jar." Collins yawned and stretched, wiggling his toes. "I just conferred with the man I'm going to race, Peter. A young fellow with white hair. Tall, well built, but proud. Like you, boy, he doesn't talk much. Talks with his eyes. Too proud for what he is. Covered with beads and seashells. Don't know how he's going to run in a getup like that. But they say he's a fast one—Chaparral Charlie.

"Come on, now, sit down, boy. Put some of that stuff on the palm of your hand. Then you rub it in, real hard, from the knee down to the ankle. Press your fingers in deep. Got to keep the blood strong in the legs. He wants to bet eight hundred dollars on this race. You got to rub me down for a good two hours."

Peter spread the cream on his hands and rubbed one hairy leg, then the other, doing as he was told, digging his fingers in deep. He pretended the man was a beast, a horse, or a heifer he was working on, in order to swallow the disgust he felt. A fat candle burned beside the bed. Peter did not look up from his task, but his thoughts were racing.

Words the boss used in the wagon, about Peter's past, the place he came from, some people called "trash," kept returning. His mother Betty was being insulted, and he wanted to whack the man in the face. He didn't dare lift his eyes, for fear they would meet Collins's gaze and tell him all he felt. Collins carried a gun on his hip, even as he lay there on the bed. Peter imagined the man falling asleep, and being alone then with him and the gun. Would he be able to resist killing him?

"Not so hard," snapped Collins, withdrawing his leg, "you're going to put some bruises there, if you're not careful. Now watch it, boy, just take it easy."

Collins's eyelids drooped, but he was carefully watching Peter. The boy's long eyelashes, like his curls, fluttered shadows on his cheeks.

The muscularity of his arms and hands was a contrast to his youthful face, as hairless as a girl's. His full pink lips were pressed tight. His gestures were deft, easy, and slow, and he said nothing.

"I just don't get it," Collins said in a low voice. "You're a strange specimen, Peter. No question that you're different, but you've got all the manners of a nigger. The expression on your face, the tone of your voice—even the way you smell. Just goes to show, blood can be turned into water, given a chance."

Peter clenched his teeth and continued rubbing the leg between his hands.

"Ha, I'm making you mad, now, I can see it. I've learned. I can read a slave's mind, just by the way he moves or blinks. That's right. You're sitting there thinking I don't know what's going on in your head. But I know every line of it. Because you're waiting your turn, you want to spring, no question of it. Makes people want to play with you. That's right. The more you go inside yourself and make plans, the more they want to hurt you."

He turned his head to the side on his pillow, still looking down at Peter.

"Ah, but you have good hands for this rubbing. You're doing just fine now, Peter." He lay in a kind of sensual trance as Peter massaged his legs. He raised one knee, while Peter rubbed the lowered leg, then lowered that knee and raised the other.

Peter's hands were aching and he felt a sickly sensation in his stomach. The air in the room pressed hot against his skin and he wanted to ask when he could go out and join Joe in the wagon. He didn't want to speak into that air, and the man's deep sighs now scared him. He glanced up at the gun lying on Collins's hip within easy reach, but Collins caught him looking.

"What you looking at?" he shouted and lurched up, grabbing him by the hair. "What you want to see?" He jerked Peter's head up and down, and swung up into a sitting position. He knocked Peter across the face with his hand. "You dirty-minded rat. Don't you look at any part of me like that. Understand?"

Then he shoved him down onto the floor. Giving him a kick in the side, he said, “Stay there, dog, and sleep. I don’t trust you out of my sight.”

He blew out the candle and lay down, undressing in the darkness. Peter listened to his motions from his place on the hard floor and heard the belt and gun being stashed under the pillow. For a long time he moved restlessly around on the bed, and Peter waited, motionless, until at last the room was quiet. The light of the moon gave silvery substance to the few articles of furniture in the room.

Peter contemplated the leg of a chair and imagined smashing it down on the boss’s face, not just once, but again and again. He turned over on his stomach and began to reach for it, holding his breath, caring nothing for the consequences.

“You make one move, boy,” said the boss’s voice out of the dark, “and I’ll whip your mother’s ass and sell her down south soon as we get home. And not only that. I’ll bet your skin against that Indian tomorrow. He can have you, boy, if he wins. That’s right. Make one move tonight, and you won’t see your mama again.”

Peter’s limbs relaxed; he dropped. With his cheek pressed against the splintered floor, he lay still. Tears burst from his eyes. He didn’t dare move to wipe them away. Silently he lay there, and he didn’t sleep all night.

6

THE NEXT MORNING, before dawn, they walked to the racetrack outside of town. Sloane and another white man came, too, and they were carrying shovels. Joe was left behind, which alarmed Peter, who depended on Joe being nearby, he was so steady, quiet, and kind. Peter had to go because Collins wanted to have his legs rubbed again before the race.

The track was part of an abandoned corral and had been pounded down originally by horses. The grass was moist with dew, but the earth on the track was hard.

"Come here, boy," Collins said to Peter. Then he smiled slightly and touched the side of Peter's face. "Why, where did you get that blue bruise? Looks painful."

Past the boss Peter saw the other men digging a trench at the far end of the racetrack, where it curved around.

"That's right, Peter, they're going to help me win this race. Seeing as I didn't sleep too well last night, I need a little boost. Now, you sit here. And when I want you to do my legs, I'll tell you. It may be the last time we talk, boy. I'm holding to my threat last night. I'm betting your ass against the Indian's eight hundred. If he wins, he gets you and keeps his money. If I win, I get his money and keep you. Maybe not. Maybe let the Indian have you."

Collins gave Peter a long solemn look, tainted with irony. "I know how much you love your master, boy, so I'm sure you'll be rooting for me, all the way."

Then he turned and walked away. Peter leaned against a cottonwood tree. He drew his knees up and chewed a blade of grass. He watched the men at work. They dug a trench about fifty yards long in the right side of the ring. The Indian would be given that side to run on, and the uneven ground would slow him down. It didn't surprise Peter that such cheating went on, and he yawned and dozed for a while in the warm sun.

7

PETER JERKED AWAKE at noon. A small crowd of men had gathered to watch the race. Collins wanted him to rub his legs down one more time. He stood over Peter, who spread the liniment thick, while stealing glances at the Indian they called Chaparral Charlie. He was, as Collins described him, tall and young with straight white hair. But he wore no beads or seashells, only a pair of buckskin pants. His chest was bare, as were his feet. His hair was held down by a red band. He stood apart from the white men, with a kind of confidence that Peter admired.

Collins wore special soft leather shoes for the race, his feet being too tender to run bare. But he did as the Indian did, and removed his shirt. As the crowd moved over to the ring, Peter moved back to the tree and closed his eyes, praying that Chaparral Charlie would win. He prayed he could go away with the Indian and never return to the Collinses' plantation.

"Oh Lord Almighty," he said as his mother would, "let that Indian win! Let me be sold to him! Let me be free!"

Then he opened his eyes in time to see Collins pointing in his direction, as he spoke to the Indian. Peter stood up automatically as the man approached to look him over. As they stood there under the tree, in silent appraisal of each other, Peter said in a low voice, urgently, "Run on the inside, run on the inside," and his eyes blazed the importance of his message. The Indian looked straight into his eyes, and then he turned and walked back to the track. There was some debating going on, Peter could see, and a lot of gesticulating in the direction of the track. But when the race began, Collins was on the inside, where he had planned to be.

Peter sank down under the tree, and covered his eyes. He didn't want to watch the injustice being carried out. But then when the gun went off and the men began to run, he jumped up and saw Chaparral Charlie speeding along the outside ring, several feet ahead of Collins. He ran easily and gracefully, while Collins seemed to be pushing the air to get through it. Peter ran forward to the side of the ring, where the men were shouting in favor of Collins. Now they were approaching the end where the trench had been dug. Collins moved alongside the Indian, then farther by several paces ahead. The broken ground helped Collins as he took the lead by a couple of paces. Chaparral Charlie was a faster runner, and no one who knew about the trench could deny it.

Gasping and self-satisfied, Collins threw Peter a look of triumph. His friends gathered around him shouting congratulations. Peter watched as Chaparral Charlie turned back and walked around the ring the way he had run, examining the ground. When he discovered the trench, he turned, his head held high, and pointed down, silently. The white men, bunched together, fell quiet, watching him.

"You did this?" the Indian shouted. "I will not pay. Give me your boy."

And he walked forward again toward the crowd. Peter held his breath. His heart pounded. He saw his boss move back into the mob and the mob moved forward, as one body, to meet the Indian. Two of them pulled guns.

"You give this man his money, Charlie," one of them shouted.

"Don't you try cheating a white man with one of your Indian tricks," another cried.

"Pay up, Indian."

The Indian pointed at Peter. "Pale boy try to warn me what you did," he said. "That your son?"

"That boy's a slave, Charlie," Sloane said.

Peter's face burned. His mouth was parched. He could see Collins looking at him with rage.

"I won't pay," said the Indian.

"Then you'll pay with your life."

They raised their guns, all of them, and Peter ran forward, recklessly, to stand in front of the Indian. "Let me go with him!" he cried out.

But in a flash he was dragged away and hurled on the ground.

The Indian went to his pack under a tree and removed from a small brown pouch the money he must pay to Collins. He threw it on the ground and, raising his pack to his shoulder, walked away to the east.

Peter's hands were tied around a tree and Collins ripped down a branch and whipped him, while another man held up his shirt. Panting violently, Collins beat him till the branch broke on Peter's back. Some of the men turned away, disgusted, and some left the scene altogether. The few who remained were more interested in Collins's extreme passion than in what he was doing to Peter.

"He's just a kid," they murmured.

"Didn't do that much harm."

"Man must be a little crazy."

Sloane finally calmed Collins down, giving him a couple of shoves along the road, heading homeward.

"That's what I mean," he said to Collins, "about this business of owning people."

"Shut up," said Collins.

One of the men untied Peter and pushed him along the road. At first Peter dropped his head, cowering in pain, but then he recalled the Indian's posture, and he lifted his head and held his back straight, looking directly down the path he was traveling. It was the first time that he knew he was a slave, down, down into his heart, and only when he lifted his head.

8

THE TRIP AWAY from home continued to haunt him for days after. He could not shake off his memory of the town, the race, Chaparral Charlie, and above all, his master's behavior. Collins, who had before appeared a mere representation of a human being, not real in any complex sense, now was composed of many parts. And while Peter loathed him, he could not ignore him at this new level of discovery. His knowledge of Collins was a kind of possession. Peter felt he owned a part of his master's spirit, and it made him uncomfortable as if he had eaten something bad.

"There's another kind of world out there," he told Betty and Robert one night, "and I want to know it, especially the Indians."

"Maybe you will, Peter," Robert said, "but not for a long time."

Betty gave Peter an anxious look. "You're too restless for your own good, honey. Master Collins has big plans for you. Told me so himself. You just take it easy."

"I don't think he'll take me nowhere again—after what happened," Peter remarked. "And that's just fine with me."

"Well, you sure ain't getting no fiddle till you shape up, boy," said Robert.

"Why are you so mean to Peter?" one of the girls called out. "If it was me, I'd've done the same thing myself."

"Don't you say that, Georgia, don't you say that again."

Peter moved outside, not wanting to be the cause of any trouble. He felt sometimes his parents were just waiting for him to make that final mistake, which would cut him off from them forever. Maybe it would be a relief to them.

He roamed along the edges of the slave quarters, a row of small multi-toned shacks, where people stood around outside, breathing in the sweet evening air. The smaller children were asleep already, and only the soft tones of adults speaking quietly came across the air. A small group of boys and girls his age were ringed in front of one cabin rolling pebbles. They paid no attention to him, passing. He might have been a ghost.

So he sank down, alone, under a tree and went over in his mind the days away from home. Those things his master said about his parentage worried him. He thought he had been born—or found—right here. Not what Betty had said about a cave. He thought maybe his color was the result of a meeting between Betty and a white man years before, but that man would have to be minus white, a ghost, given how dark Betty was and how pale he was. There was no other explanation. Not even an Osage Indian was white enough to make his arms so white. Because he knew himself to be black in his deepest self, just like the people he lived with. He had never seen his own face.

He knew all about the woman with whom Collins had his children. She had been given a cabin apart from the others. A small dark-skinned woman with surprising pink lips and large hazel eyes, she lived like a pariah. She was in charge of laundry and her chemise was always sparkling white. Graceful, quiet, she still exuded a mood of depression. Like Peter, she rarely spoke, but he felt connected to her, at some intuitive level, as he watched her bear three children, inseminated by the boss.

Now he thought, "I'll go see her," and he got up and headed for her cabin.

He could see her candle lit inside but there was no sound, so he approached stealthily, afraid the boss might be there. Her door was ajar to let in the evening air, and as he peeked around inside, he could see she was alone. Her children slept in one pile together on the straw.

He called, "Hey, Jessie."

She looked up quickly.

"Oh, Peter."

She smiled and stepped outside. Between her fingers she idly rubbed a stone arrowhead, which she carried everywhere. Now she leaned against the doorjamb.

"What you doing here?"

"Just checking, you know."

"Training to be a boss?" she smiled.

Peter frowned and looked at the ground. He could see pink between her bare brown toes.

"I'm just teasing, Peter," she said. "I know you wouldn't turn on your own folks."

She sank down on the stoop and patted the space beside her. Peter sat down. He had always thought she was the prettiest woman he had ever seen, and he thought that she understood him deeply all the way through. Confronting her, he had no words to say. They sat comfortably in silence, looking at the moonlight on the meadows and listening to the cicadas chirrup.

She said, "Master Collins wants to make you overseer someday, Peter. That's what he told me."

Peter's stomach turned over.

"Why, don't look like that," she said softly. "It wouldn't be bad. You'd make some money, have a little freedom. It's the only reason he's keeping you around, what with all your bad attitude."

Peter sighed more deeply.

"I'm only telling you, so you'll know what he's got in his mind, honey. So don't be mad at me."

"I'm not mad," he said.

"Why, you might even get your freedom someday, Peter. No one'd be surprised at that."

They both gazed at the big house through the trees. Windows glowed upstairs and down. Peter felt that her saying that to him was a rejection of all that he wanted to say to her. But it was such a familiar feeling, it was as if one more pebble had been dropped into a heavy load of stones he carried with him.

"We haven't been off those ships, we haven't walked in chains for that many years," Jessie told him. "We're still fresh and strong. Africa. Our ancestors still walk among us. Now whatever skin you got to start with, Peter, you already have the rebellious soul of a free people. But you can go, we can't."

"Everyone expects me to run," he said, "so maybe I will someday soon. Maybe I will. Out there, they will know what I am. Whites I mean will know I'm black and try to kill me anyway."

They stood up together.

"Listen, Peter," she said, "I want you to know one thing. It's not such a big world as you think out there. Most everyone knows about Collins's boy. Even if you do take off, chances are they'll find you. I tell you, Peter, we're surrounded. What this evil brings out in men is lust, and the urge to hurt. It goes deep, deep into the most secret part of the master, his sex, and his property. Slavery makes men curdle like buckets of milk with flies floating in them, their women too. . . . You take care, Peter."

"Well, we'll see about that."

"You be a patient boy," she said, "and you'll do fine."

He gazed at her soft dark face and couldn't help imagining what Collins had done to her. It was, he thought, just what his natural father, if he had one, had done to Betty, and the thought filled him with a nauseous rage. He was glad he wasn't white.

"If I ever get away," he told her, "I won't forget you. Or him. I'll be back. And I'll save you, all of you! Or else I'll burn down the house and let all the animals go."

"Time will tell. Goodnight, Peter."

He waved his hand and walked home, quickly, full of thought.

9

IN A COUPLE OF DAYS Peter was summoned to the big house from where he was rolling timber. Collins wanted to see him outside on the veranda. The day was heavy and gray. The wagon was hitched in front of the house. Joe sat at the reins.

Collins said, "I'm sending you to town, Peter. I want you to pick up some mail and a package they have waiting for me there. Carry this letter and show it to the man in the store." He gave Peter a long, condescending look. "I see you're right back where you started. Hands dirty. Hair a mess."

Peter silently looked up at Collins, with contempt in his eyes.

"I've instructed Joe to keep his eye on you, boy. If you step out of line, there'll be hell to pay. And you know I'm a man of my word. Wipe that look off your face. You think too much."

Then he handed Peter the letter and went inside. Peter got in the wagon with some excitement. He could see Joe was not happy to have him as a traveling companion, but he didn't care. Joe was a person who liked to do things his way. Peter knew this and kept to himself.

It was not a long journey. Much to Peter's surprise, there was a small town only ten miles from the plantation. It was a mining town, and the walls of the hills around were checkered with wooden shafts.

The post office served as general store. There was, also, a small saloon and a row of shanties for the miners. Joe told Peter to take his time about his business.

"Ain't in no hurry to get home," he said, unwrapping his lunch and a small flask. "But be back so we can get there by sundown."

Holding the letter, Peter got out of the wagon. He didn't know what to do with himself. He decided to walk down the road a way out of town, just to see what happened. He was glad about the emptiness of the place because no one was out staring at him. He was nothing but some farmer's boy walking through town.

This time it felt wonderful, being alone and unguarded, white. Though the sky was gloomy, his spirits were high. He could hear hammering sounds from the mine areas, and as the road spread ahead and the shanties lay far behind him, he heard a new sound—horses, a man's voice. He slowed his gait and uneasily turned a bend in the road.

"Hey there, give me a hand!" someone shouted.

A small bowlegged white man, wearing an oversized hat, waved at Peter. Beside him stood a wagon train packed with goods. Four carts, six horses. Peter stopped, not knowing what to do with himself.

"Come on, kid, I need your help," the man said again. His voice was high-pitched and rasping. He was holding onto the horse in front, whose foreleg was lifted off the ground. "Just hold the horse for me, will you?" the man shouted.

Peter did as he was told, moving forward and taking hold of the horse's harness, while the little man squatted on the ground and began to twist rocks out from inside the horse's shoe, using a knife. The horse didn't like it. He bucked his head and moved around restlessly as Peter held on tight.

"Every ten miles I've got this problem," the man said. "If it isn't one horse, it's two. Rotten goddamn roads. At this rate, it'll take me a year to get to Santa Fe." His face was gnarled and weatherbeaten and brown from sun like cuts off a mahogany tree. He looked up at Peter. "What's around the bend there?"

Peter had never spoken casually to a white man. He didn't know how to respond, and so he said nothing.

"What's wrong, fellow? Dumb or mute or something?" He dug out the last stone, and the horse, relaxing, dropped its hoof to the ground. "I asked you a question. Am I anywheres near a town, or no?"

"Yes, sir," said Peter to the ground, "right up there. Right around the bend."

"I thought so. That's good. Hope they have a blacksmith. Need new shoes." He moved around to the other horse, checking its hooves for rocks, while Peter stood where he was, as if rooted to the ground.

"You mighty polite for a boy your age. Saying 'sir' and all. Where you come from?" the man asked.

"South. A farm, sir," said Peter.

"You a farmer's boy? Then you'd know where I can get myself a blacksmith."

The man moved directly to Peter now and scrutinized him with a wrinkled little smile.

"You can let go of the horse now," he said.

Peter did as he was told. He was red in the face, not knowing what to do with himself.

"Now you can lift your eyes and talk," said the grinning man. "My name is Walls. Harry Walls. What's yours?"

"Peter, sir."

"Peter what?"

"Peter—Collins."

"What you doing walking around like a lunatic? Look like you've done something bad. Running away from home? Had a fight with your daddy?"

Peter couldn't help smiling, but he didn't reply.

"Well, you're a good strong boy. Come on, sit down, have a bite of mutton."

Peter followed Walls to the seat of the wagon and climbed up. He was given a large leg of mutton to eat. He had never had so much before, and he hungrily ripped into it. Walls gnawed on a bone beside him and plied him with questions.

"A farmer's boy. Is that so? Must be familiar with animals, eh? Know how to feed the pigs and butcher them? Know how to groom the horses and shoe them? What *do* you know how to do? How old are you, anyway? About fourteen, thirteen, fifteen?" Walls was a flexible character. As soon as he discovered Peter was not much of a talker, he fell right into line, and began to answer his own questions. "Yeah, I'd say thirteen," he said, "and easy with the livestock. Done a lot of chopping, too. I'd say you've had some trouble at home and want to hit the road. Get some experience out in the Territory. A regular boy, full of adventure."

Peter said nothing, sucking on the bone, as he looked straight ahead at the gray skyline. Collins's letter was tucked in the waist of his pants. As the man rattled on, the letter seemed to burn a hole in Peter's side. He was conscious of his role, the chains binding him to Collins.

"How about you come with me, Peter Collins? I'm heading for Santa Fe. Lost one of my fellows back aways. You're just what this man is looking for."

Peter glanced at Walls, unable to believe what he was hearing. He threw his bone into the bushes and slowly licked his fingers, figuring how he should talk to this man, how much he should tell him.

"I got to spend a while in this town, get some supplies, and have myself some fun. Then I'll be leaving late tonight. If you want to come with me, come back here around midnight, and I'll be waiting."

Walls hopped out of the wagon and walked to the rear of the train. Peter sat still, unable to comprehend this sudden blast of good fortune. Nothing in his life had prepared him for such a chance. His jubilance was so intense, he suffered. He couldn't move, but only attempted to contain his excitement by breathing slowly.

Walls hobbled up beside him.

"Well, I'm heading into town, Peter. A fellow in the rear is keeping guard. Want to come with me?"

Peter got down, and began to walk at the man's side. He realized his chances might be ruined if he was seen with Walls, so he paused.

"Think I'll just lie down here for a time, sir," said Peter, waving toward a grassy hillock.

Walls scrutinized the boy again, his eyes winking and twinkling like a small sparrow.

"Why, I never met someone who talked like you who wasn't a nigra," he said. "Strangest thing I ever saw. But you'll do just fine, if you are willing to come. Now, lie down there, Pete, and snatch some winks."

Peter sat on the grass and watched the little man disappear around the bend. He decided to lie low for about an hour, then go to the post office with his letter. He would, he decided, have to return home with Joe, and then steal away by night, later, if he wanted to escape. It would be impossible to hide out now, waiting around till midnight. They would quickly track him down to Walls's wagon train since Joe was willing to have him caught and whipped.

As he lay back, large drops of rain began falling. Now he had no choice but to run to town fast, take care of his duties, and pray all the way he wouldn't run into Walls.

JOE, who was usually mild, was mad. "Where was you? Get in this wagon and let's get going."

The rain fell cold on their faces. Peter put the package and mail under the seat to keep dry as he settled down beside Joe. The horses moved at a fast clip down the road homeward, their heads bowed against the windy showers. But Peter's face was lifted and radiant, as if the sun was shining down on him.

He carefully noted their route and tried to imagine how long it would take him to return that night through darkness. He reckoned a couple of hours, which meant he would leave the plantation as soon as his family was asleep. None of it seemed impossible. Nothing could interfere with his plan. He had never felt so happy or full of hope. To run away alone was one thing, but to go in the company of a man like Walls was quite another. From Walls he would learn white ways and manners. He would be on the other side of the hill country, the free side. His blue eyes glittered and his posture straightened, as the rain poured down his cheeks.

Collins instantly noticed Peter's strange attitude. When Peter handed him his packages, Collins looked at the boy before examining his mail.

"You got a glitter in your eye, boy, and I don't like it," he said. "I'm trained to notice these changes, you know. I'm no fool, as you might think."

Then Collins called out to Joe, shivering in the rain, "What's this boy been up to, Joe?"

"Nothing much, master."

"Was he talking to people in town?"

"No sir. Not so far as I know," Joe called back.

"Well then, there's no explaining it. But I'm keeping my eye on you, boy."

Then he moved inside, perusing his mail. Joe returned the horses to the stables, and Peter went to his cabin to dry out his clothes. His whole body seemed to be pulsing visibly, for he knew his master as well as his master knew him.

10

COLLINS WAS RESTLESS that night. The dismal weather made him feel trapped, and he roamed several times around the house, before looking for his wife. First he went to the kitchen to talk to the women there, then to his children's rooms to see how they were doing, and then while sipping Madeira he wandered around the sitting room. Raindrops spat up from the fire. He stared at the flames for a few minutes.

Then he went upstairs. His wife was seated, as she often was, with a book and candle beside the window. Her straight, dark hair fell midway down her back. Her soft round face was naturally placid and sensuous, but when he entered a frown and tension crossed her features. She stared at her open book, obviously not seeing the words.

"What do you want, Ed?" she snapped.

Collins crossed over to where she sat and peered out the window.

"Wondering if you can make it from here to Jessie's cabin without getting wet?" she asked.

Reddening, Collins looked down at her.

"When will you learn to keep your mouth still," he said. "I never knew a woman who had to talk so much. Have to say everything the minute you think it."

"At least that way I speak the truth," she replied.

"The truth! You don't know anything about the truth—reading all those books. Stories and lies come to the same thing."

"You're just jealous because I'm not bored. Not like you, anyway." She closed the book and sighed heavily. "I try to keep my mind occupied. You just think of your pleasure."

Collins yanked her hair quickly.

"Shut up, Joan. I mean it, now."

She stood up and crossed by him to her large, ruffly canopy bed. Collins watched her pink nightgown trail behind her.

"What are you doing now?" he asked.

"Just moving away from you."

Collins smiled. "I love it when you walk away from me," he said.

She grimaced, rubbing her face hard with her hands.

"I wish I could leave here and go home!" She threw him a look of anguish. "I hate it here. It's not natural to me, this kind of life, out in the middle of nowhere, surrounded by nothing but miserable darkies. I feel sorry for them—and me. I even feel sorry for Jessie!

You treat us all the same. What gives you the right? Three of your own blood offspring running around in the dust."

"You knew about it when you married me," he said, "and you didn't say anything then."

"I didn't know. I was ignorant. You can't hold me to that." She rubbed her hands together, head bowed. "I'd rather be alone than live like this."

"Too bad. You thought you could change me, and I thought I could change you. I thought I could make you into a natural woman instead of a thinking bitch. My father told me I was a fool. 'Never marry a Northern woman,' he said."

"What about you?" she cried shrilly. "The only thing you ever read is a newspaper and you call yourself cultured. You only think about your bodily needs. I'd rather have a man who smoked cigars and got drunk every night and at least had a heart than one like you!"

Collins self-consciously smoothed down his jacket as she spoke. Sometimes these angry verbal scenes with her would arouse him and he would force her down to have sex with him. Sometimes it seemed like a form of seduction on her part, too. He knew she feared him physically, but she was a passionate woman who needed the contact of flesh, and having no option but him, she fought in order to be held. He wouldn't do it tonight, however, his will was weak.

"Thought you wanted to live alone," he said, "and now you're talking about some man who smokes and drinks."

"It was just an example," she said quickly.

But he walked over and pulled her face up as if it were made of clay.

"Better not be another man behind all this," he said, "or else there'll be hell to pay. Understand?"

She twisted her face away, cowering and nodding at the same time. He swatted her back quickly and left the room.

COLLINS WENT BACK downstairs to the fireplace, and poured himself another glass of Madeira. He examined his face in the mirror hanging over the mantelpiece. A look of anger still hovered there, creasing his naturally smooth features, and he rubbed his skin as if to erase the flaws which age would soon reveal. The clock chimed nine.

"That boy's up to no good," he muttered aloud.

And he went to the front hall to put on his hat and jacket. He walked through the now-empty kitchen and stood outside on the back veranda looking at the slave quarters. The rain had let up but no one was outside. He saw a few candles still lit in the cabins.

His boredom made him feel lonely and then his loneliness made him suspicious. It was a pattern he followed frequently. He had never made any choices in his life, except the one to marry Joan. All the rest was decided by his father. He would be a planter, he would tend this land and manage these people for the rest of his life. That was it. His father had raised and trained him from boyhood to do this one thing. He had done what he was destined to do and rarely thought about the implications. His arrogance and vanity were based on nothing but fear.

On nights like this, when he had nothing to do, the fear came to the surface. He realized he didn't care if his wife left him. He wouldn't miss her and would even be relieved at her absence, so long as she didn't insult him in the process. As long as the people who knew them both could blame her for leaving, he would be all right. But what if she went around broadcasting his private life? What if she went off with another man? She was unpredictable, and adhered fiercely to her own moral code, which was not based on a social structure, but on personal preference. She was capable of justifying anything she did, because she had the power of language. And education.

He bent his head and stepped into the rain. His normal course in his present mood would be to Jessie's cabin, where he would work out his restlessness on her. But tonight he headed elsewhere. He had been haunted all day by the look on Peter's face after he returned from town. The boy filled him with conflict. On the one hand, Collins hated him for acting subservient; on the other hand, he hated his look of independence when he had no rights in the world.

11

THE CANDLE was not burning in Betty and Robert's cabin. They slept early and deeply. As usual the family spread out across the straw dragged in from the barn. Their bodies were warmly pressed together. Peter, on his own pallet, was the only one awake. He sat upright, alert, watching the others in sleep. He could make out their features through the darkness and could tell how deeply they slept from the modulated tones of their breathing.

Their ignorance made him hesitate. If he ran after Walls and onto the trail with him, when his parents awoke, he would be gone, never having said goodbye. They seemed like his victims more than his parents.

At the same time they would all be better off if he got away and could make his place in the world. He would confront Collins and take them away. His mind swarmed with adventures on leaf-dappled trails leading to Santa Fe and back again.

He saw himself as a handsome free black man with two guns in his belt and a fortune in gold as he rode over the mountains on a fine stallion.

It was a wonderful dream, full of detail, and as his mind traveled through time, Peter crawled to the cabin door on his hands and knees, quiet as a mouse. He felt as if he was racing through space toward that final triumph: freedom for his family.

Outside, he rose to his feet and shut the door. The rain, cold on his neck, jolted him out of his vision. He looked around quickly and anxiously. He knew which way to go and darted quickly in that direction.

Collins grabbed him from behind.

"Ha!" he shouted in Peter's ear, his arm pressed around his throat. "I got you that time!"

He squeezed hard, nearly strangling the boy. Peter struggled wildly, kicking his legs and beating his arms back against Collins. But the man was taller and stronger and seemed to enjoy the fight. He stood still, while Peter, gagging and twisting, tried to wrench free of him.

Collins laughed.

"I'm going to lock you up, boy."

He pinned Peter's arms behind his back and shoved him along ahead of him. Peter kicked back at him, twice, three times, but it was useless. Collins only laughed. And as they passed the slave cabins, a few faces peered out and saw Peter being roughly pushed into the smallest shack on the plantation.

This was the room where pork was cured. It contained the smoke oven and great lumps of raw meat in storage. A thick fleshy smell suffused the air. Peter was thrown inside, and the door slammed and bolted behind him. Darkness shrouded the boy, as he huddled, breathing hard on the floor. He had never known such darkness or smelled such dense odors. The smell was of death, the dark was the dark of a grave. So deep was his terror, Peter couldn't cry, but stayed motionless, trying to pretend he didn't exist.

The rain ticked like thousands of clocks or armies of vermin marching in his direction, but he did not move. Time was his only oppressor now, and if he could just stay still and blend into time, he would no longer exist. He would be a shadow, a part of the black air, a ghost in a tomb. This was what he must do and not conceive of the red hunks of meat hanging close to his face. He strained to forget everything, all the possible creatures he could not see. He breathed only through his mouth, attempting to cancel the awful smell.

He breathed high, in regular sips, without stirring a muscle. His consciousness of time was all he had to go on, but he couldn't still the thoughts that came with it. Why go on at all? What was the point? Why should he care? Who was he? His own identity seemed to fall away from him there in the darkness; he clutched wildly at the thought of his mother; but then that thought, too, failed him as he wondered if Betty was in fact his mother. Maybe not!

He almost cried out, then regulated his breathing again, only anxious to become a nothing, a nobody, something erased. He felt in some way this was his true condition and he had only stumbled on it by chance. He briefly held his breath in an effort to kill himself, but his body would not allow it. He tried again, and again, and the more he did so, the more light-headed he became. He would gasp for breath against his will. And little red and white stars showered around his eyes. He was dizzy.

He lay his head down on the cold earthy ground at last, and his mind swirled out galaxies of stars, as he inhaled, held his breath, and gasped involuntarily. Finally he slipped into unconsciousness. It was a long deep sleep and a kind of blessing.

12

THE SUN slowly rose on a clear sky. Before the light had become more than a distant glow, Jessie left her cabin. She slipped along the silent rows of shacks till she came to Betty's, where she tapped gently on the door.

Betty came out, rubbing her arms against the cool air.

"You know where Peter is?" she whispered at once.

"Sure do," said Jessie. "Master locked him in the curing shed last night around ten."

"What for?"

"Caught him running away."

Betty looked aghast. "Running away? He didn't act different last night. Where did he think he was going?"

"I don't know," Jessie said, "but I feel real bad for him—being locked up like that."

Both women looked in the direction of the shed, and Jessie leaned closer to Betty.

"I think we ought to help that boy get away, I really do. I know it's taking a chance, but he's the only one of us who's got that chance." She looked anxiously at Betty. "Do you mind if I interfere, just a little?"

"How would you do that, without getting yourself in a mess? I mean, you couldn't do it now. People's about to get up."

"No. Tonight. I mean tonight."

Betty quickly examined Jessie's features, in the gray light. She shook her head disapprovingly.

"No, Jessie, don't do nothing about Peter. Not now, anyway. He's still too young to be out there on his own. If he was your charge, you'd understand."

"I don't know about that," said Jessie. "If I had a child with any chance, I'd be glad to see him free."

"Free? Or dead?"

"Amounts to the same thing, sometimes. This might be living, but that's as far as it goes."

"Don't talk that way, Jessie, and you leave Peter alone. I want to give him time. Then I'll worry about freedom."

Already Jessie was drifting away, not listening. Her pink lips were pressed tight.

She could clearly imagine what Peter's emotions must be, for she had been locked in there more than once herself. The effect of the experience could not be measured or expressed because it was worse than physical suffering. It made her shudder to imagine his feelings. Betty, both stubborn and obedient, could not think this way.

Jessie knew Collins would leave Peter in the shed for two or three days, without looking back once.

Now she couldn't resist the idea of having Peter escape without breaking the lock. This would give the master real cause for fear. He would not trust any locks again, if she did it right.

So she meandered around the curing shed, while the sun climbed higher into the sky. The rooster began to crow, and she hurried, examining the structure and strength of the shed. She gazed up at the stone chimney alongside the back of the oven and smiled. She bet to herself a boy with enough willpower could claw his way up and out through that tunnel. He would need some coaxing, but she could take care of that when night came again.

If Peter had known she was out there, he would have been happier. As it was, he automatically woke, at daybreak, but could not tell whether it was light outside or not. There was a hint of light in the room, but not enough to indicate complete shapes. The stench was heavy and nauseating. He thought he heard crunching sounds, as from some large insect, but blocked his ears rather than make it out.

His stomach was empty and his mouth dry. All day he waited and prayed that someone would come to release him. If only they would, he vowed he would be good and obedient. He would not talk back again with his eyes or his body, but would submit, as his parents had, to the life they were given. He would play the fiddle! He would sing! He would work all day, just to have that joy at night.

If only his body could be given back to the light of day, given food and water, given a function again. But, no, he had been forgotten. Nobody seemed to care if he entered the sun again. He was like one buried alive.

13

AT TEN THAT NIGHT Jessie slipped out of her cabin to the curing shed.

"Peter," she whispered.

And she tapped gently on the wooden door. It was the knock, and not her voice, he heard. Startled from a light doze, he stiffened inside, listening.

"Peter," she said again, "it's Jess."

He crawled on his hands and knees toward the sound of her voice. She knocked again and he groped for the noise, finally touching the wood of the door. He knocked back, leaning his ear against the wood.

"It's Jess," she said again. "You all right?"

So grateful was he for the sound of a human voice, he could not respond with more than another light knock on the wood.

"You've got to get out of there," she said urgently. "I've got some food here for you. Now, listen to me real carefully. You can climb up through the chimney."

She listened for a minute but got no response. "Are you listening?"

"Yes," he said.

"Okay, now, you just move in a straight line, toward the back of the shed, about fifteen feet. When you feel the stone of the oven, reach around till you find the hole there. You can squeeze your way up and out onto the roof. I just know it. I'll be waiting for you in the back."

"Jessie," he said hoarsely, desperate that she would leave. "Just talk to me."

She slid down and leaned against the wood and spoke in a low voice: "You've got to get out of here, off this land, away. You're the only one who has a chance. Take it. My kids are all stuck like me, but I see their father's features in them, and I think to myself it's their fate to stay here and stare him in the face every day."

She hauled herself up onto her feet, and there was nobody there to see the long anguish etched into her features, nobody there at all.

"Go on, boy, you just get all your strength together and do as I say. I know you can make it."

He listened for her voice and another word of encouragement, but she must have gone around back. He turned around to the blackness behind him, and heard her knock from that direction. So he followed it on his hands and knees, as the stench of the meat thickened and almost made him sick. He counted his paces, approaching the sound of her knock, until he found himself touching the back wooden wall. He knocked there, and she transferred her own response to the left of him. He groped his way over when his head banged against stone.

Now she was silent. He felt her presence scant inches out of his reach and he heard rats shuffling around.

His hands moved downward in a circular motion over the cold stones until he found the opening in the oven. It was not a large hole, no more than a foot wide and two feet high. He was terrified to think of squeezing inside its dark confines, but he could not stay as he was, given Jessie's guardianship and the thought of escape. So he crawled in backward and stood up inside the narrow stone tunnel. He peered upward. The chimney bent outward, and he reached up his hands to pull himself onto the platform of stone he felt there. He still saw nothing.

He twisted and turned and pulled with his hands. Choking on smoke, he nearly wept with the char and frustration. But, finally, with total exertion, he managed to haul himself up onto the flue, balance there, and stretch up again to the top of the chimney. Feeling cool air there, he looked up and saw one star in the black night sky.

He was flooded with joy. Using his feet as supports, he was just tall enough to haul himself up to the rooftop, where he swung out into the fresh air. Jessie stood below, smiling up at him. He jubilantly jumped down beside her. His face was stained with ashes, his hair gray.

"I knew you could do it," she whispered, and quickly put a package of food in his hands. "Now is your chance to get away from here. You've got to stick to the woods and rivers. Follow that star, there. Sleep when the sun is up and move by night. If anybody asks you a question, answer right back, with your chin up, and eyes straight. You might make it if you act white. Understand?"

With a nod and a hasty goodbye and thank you, he fled into the woods with Walls, the wagon train, and Santa Fe on his mind.

14

PETER MOVED through the thickets along the edge of the road that led to the mining town.

Never before had nature been so beautiful. Spring leaves, thorns, branches, the melancholy whistle of an owl, and above all the air itself, floated from inside him all the way up to the starry galaxies. He felt he was loved by the sky, safe and protected by the arcing trees. He did not feel, as his mother would, that the Lord was guiding him. Instead he experienced a blissful connection with the spirit of the natural world.

As he darted through the trees, he envisioned himself in a part of the country warm enough to allow him to live out of doors. The thought of confinement terrified him, reminding him of that shed. He imagined a nomadic life, stripped of all human contact. He would not look back; he would try to forget his family completely.

His package of food was the last reminder of home, and he almost feared opening it although he was weak with hunger. As he approached the town, he slowed his pace, and listened for sounds of human life. It was not fox or wolf he feared, but a human face. But the town was quiet. Even the tavern doors were closed and darkened. It must be well after midnight.

He paused quietly, noting a road that led off to his left, west, and wondered if that was the road the wagon train would follow. Would Walls, by any chance, still be there, one night later than he was supposed to be? It was Peter's only hope that he would be, and so he slipped around to the rear of the shanties and ran in the direction of the place where Walls had been.

When he got there, the wagon train was gone, and only the remnants of an outdoor fire, ashes and coal, remained in a cold heap by the side of the road. Peter sat down there and opened his package of food. He slowly ate a part of the food and savored the taste which returned him home. His eyes burned; he felt his spirits drop.

"Don't look back," he told himself, "just don't look back. Keep going, while it's dark."

He stuffed half of his food back in its package and stood up. He examined the track marks on the ground, which the rainfall had embedded deeply. They passed toward town. Peter lowered his head, following them, and discovered that they did, indeed, branch off on the road heading west. He walked along the edge of the road, ready to leap into the underbrush should anyone suddenly appear. But there was no sign of human life.

As he walked, he noted how black his hands were from the soot of the chimney and realized his face must be ash-covered too. He was flooded with a strange sensation he had never had before. Alone now in the world he was a free soul, and he must not forget that. Could he make such an adjustment? In his soul, he felt he was owned. His skin was an aberration, a freak of nature, as happened, sometimes, with livestock. For he was not foreign in the way people meant it. A black sheep in a white flock was still a sheep. A slave of any shape or color was still a slave.

And he felt like any other fleeing slave. The stories he had heard—from Robert, Betty, and many other adults, on Saturday nights, around a fire in someone's cabin—came back to him now. He had heard about people who had escaped, successfully, as far as anyone knew, and about others who were caught and returned, sold back home, and beaten insensible, or not sold home, but were taken to a new plantation and enslaved among strangers. "Might as well just stay put," Robert would say, and Betty would nod in agreement. They had faith that sooner or later someone would liberate them and their children; but like all prisoners before and after, they also feared freedom among people vile enough to enslave them in the first place.

Peter stepped up his pace, recalling all the stories he had heard, and once again tried to believe that he was going to get by, to pass. No one would know he was a slave, he told himself. Walls didn't know it, so why would anyone else? As Jessie had said, he would just have to learn new manners, hold his head high and look people in the eye. He would have to converse like a free person.

Now he saw a light rising on the horizon over distant mountains. The wheels of the wagon train were still clear, but Peter, exhausted, decided to sleep for a time in the woods that were thinning out. The landscape was changing already. He could see less woodland ahead, and more flat meadowland stretching to those low mountains. Where would he hide? And how would he eat when he ran out of food? He realized that people on the plantation would be rising now. But when would they find out he was gone, and what then?

He crawled into a dark green thicket and made a bed for himself there. He covered his eyes against the rising sun.

15

THE SUN CLIMBED warm and orange over the Collins plantation, and the roosters responded with their usual cries. Work began with the women baking in the kitchen, and the field hands preparing to eat mush before heading out to sow the crops. They were undernourished, ribs showing.

Morgan was the first one up and out, and his high rasping voice, like one of the roosters outside, could be heard from the kitchen.

"The boss told me to let the boy out yesterday," he said into his steaming porridge, "but I plumb forgot. Plumb forgot. Now I'll have to do it right away. Wouldn't want to let him starve in there."

Betty's face tightened, but she hid her expression, depositing a plate of hotcakes on the long table. The two other women were silent too.

"It's real dark in that shed," Morgan said, "so I bet he couldn't tell what color he was after a couple of hours. Ha. Well, we'll see—maybe this has done the job on him. Make him settle into things better. A little shock never hurt no one."

He gulped down his coffee, stood up, and slammed out of the kitchen. Betty went to the door to watch him depart. Then she said, "I hope my boy's all right. Two nights is a long, long time to be alone."

"And in the dark, too, like Morgan said," remarked her friend Mary. "If it was me, I'd never come out alive."

"Lucky Peter's young and strong. But I don't know what this will do to his mind." Betty touched her head, adding, "You know how that affected Jessie. Being locked in there. She was never the same after."

"More than *that* affected Jessie," Mary muttered.

And they quietly returned to their tasks.

Morgan could not believe his eyes when he found the shed empty. He moved stealthily through the small space, now bright with sunshine. The key dangled from his fingers as he leaned down to peer up the oven flue. He felt as if he had entered an empty tomb! It was more than he could believe, and he fled from the place, his hat in his hand, to the big house.

His boss still slept and he dared not wake him. He didn't dare, in fact, tell anyone what had happened, so he took his horse into the fields instead. He felt responsible because he had been instructed to release Peter the night before and hadn't done so. Now he knew he was in deep trouble, for he was sure Collins would fire him.

He wondered where and how the boy had gone. Seated in his saddle, staring at the rows of brown, freshly tilled soil, he felt a cold draft pass through him. Maybe the boy was some kind of supernatural creation. Peter always struck Morgan as a freak, and he called him "a pearl and a swine" or "a swamp lily." But now in confusion and fright he wondered if the boy wasn't an emissary from God—or was it the Devil? Morgan had gained a modest mixed education in Christian religion and paganism from his travels.

Finally he rode back to the house and, full of dread, tried again. This time Collins was awake and seated at the dining-room table alone. His wife and children were in the kitchen.

Morgan, his hat in his trembling hands, stood at the door.

"Sir, Mr. Collins, sir," he stammered.

"What now, Morgan?"

"The boy—Peter."

"What?" Collins gave Morgan a contemptuous stare. "What about Peter?"

"He's—uh—gone. Flown the coop."

Collins's face paled. He stared hard at the bearded man.

"You let him out, like I told you, last night?" he asked.

Morgan's eyes darted here and there. He longed to lie, but he already knew, when he entered, that he couldn't. Peter's parents would tell Collins the truth, and he would believe them.

"Well?" asked Collins, rising.

"No, sir, I didn't."

"So where is he?"

"Gone."

"How gone, if he was in the shed? Huh?"

"I just went to let him out this morning and, uh, the shed—was—empty."

"You fool," Collins spat out, "You!—Wait here."

He rushed into the kitchen and grabbed Betty's arm. Seeing his mood, his wife and children moved quickly out the back door. Betty tensed, bending at the knees.

"Where's Peter?"

"I don't know, sir. Ain't he in the shed where you put him?"

"He's gone. Morgan says he's gone."

He threw down her arm, seeing from her expression that she was shocked. No sign of wile.

He marched from the kitchen to the outside and rushed to the shed, where the door stood ajar. Like Morgan, Collins was for a moment scared. Although he considered himself a rational man, when confronted with a break in his usual conception of himself as being in control, he fell apart inside. A deep concealed fear, like well water, rose cold and clear in him.

He moved anxiously about the hollow room. He peered at the walls for flaws and stooped beside the stone oven. The space and construction of the oven was so unfitted for a twelve-year-old boy, especially Peter, that Collins put it out of his mind. If Peter had been one of the ordinary black slaves Collins would have imagined at once such an escape. His evaluation of his slaves was based on his expectation of their being able to perform unnatural feats, and so he could imagine one of them twisting a way out through the oven—but not pale-faced Peter.

As Collins paused at the shed door before leaving, he realized that Peter occupied a special space in his consideration simply because of the boy's looks. That was not all, though. Peter brought out in Collins certain sadistic emotions for he was a sensuous man and his strong feelings were generally tied to sexuality. He enjoyed the idea of subjecting Peter to various humiliations, which in turn humiliated him.

For a moment he thought, "Don't follow him. Let him go, let him go." But he had been trained since youth to pursue a runaway slave. When one of them got away a man was supposed to go after him or her. Not to pursue Peter would be like letting his wife run off with another man.

So he set off for the house within minutes, prepared to send Morgan north and south to post notices of a reward for Peter's return. The notice read:

> *Ranaway, on the 1st of May, a slave boy named Peter. He is as white as any white boy with yellow curly hair and blue eyes. He is twelve years old. He wore brown pants and a dirty shirt. I will give a $20 gold piece for his apprehension and delivery. He has no respect.*

By noon Morgan had several copies of the notice, and he set off at high speed.

16

SHORTLY AFTER NOON, Peter woke up and ate half of his last piece of bread. His mouth was parched, but he dared not leave the trail of the wagon train. The trail cut through fields stumpy and pocked with reddish earth. A few bushes sprang up to his right and his left, but he would have a hard time hiding. He constantly looked behind him and walked as fast as he could.

Low-flying birds blew up from the bushes before him, and the air was full of spring fragrance. Peter imagined the trail eventually would lead him to a brook, where he could drink. His mind raced as he strode along the trailside. The changing landscape made him feel newborn. He might have been walking on the moon, the desolate territory was so strange to him.

He was free! But he was also filled with anxiety. Now, no one would be familiar. His growing rebellion and anger would be useless emotions now. They made no sense in the midst of all this emptiness. He occasionally broke into a run, praying that each rise and fall of the ground would lead to a view of water, or, best of all, of Walls and the wagon train. There was nothing. The trail skirted the sparsely forested edges of the mountains shadowing the flat expanse of prairie grass he traveled.

The sun began to drop when he had gone about twenty miles, and he ate half of the last piece of bread. What remained was about half the size of his fist. A couple of bites and his palate was like dust. From time to time, a rabbit or gopher would shoot across his path, but he had no weapon to kill one with.

At dusk he came to a mound of coals and ashes from a recent fire by the trailside. He looked down at it with wonder for it assured him that he was not far behind Walls. The coals were not warm but they were firm, undisturbed by wind. As he stood there, he heard a faint gurgling sound. Water. Almost dizzy with delight, he followed the sound and discovered a spring, cold and bubbling up in a thin stream from underground. It ran in a narrow line toward the mountains. Peter fell to the ground, threw the water into his mouth, and then eagerly washed his face and hands.

If only he had a container to carry some away with him, he would be fine, but he believed, now, that if he just followed the trail through much of the night, he again would come to a stream. So he moved on reluctantly, leaving the sound of the water behind.

By nine, the darkness was nearly complete, for clouds had moved up from the south to cover the moon and stars. He could no longer see the trail, and the mountains made a looming mark far off to the west. He lay down, curling in on himself, exhausted and afraid. The earth was the closest thing to a mother he now had. He moved around, tucking his limbs into her hard, cooling curves.

When he at last fell asleep he encountered a terrible vision of himself pursued by white riders on white horses approaching with guns and lassos in a strange white light. His legs were paralyzed. He woke up with a leap and sat upright in absolute darkness. All he could see was the clouds moving fast overhead, and all he could hear was the wind whistling over the prairie grass. The cool evening wind made him shiver.

His voice did not come to his rescue as he tried to talk to himself or sing. He couldn't make a sound and lay down conjuring up images of his family sleeping in their cabin back home. He wondered how he could go back to them without being murdered by Collins. He couldn't. And who would care anyway what happened to him? The suspicions planted in him over the years by others took hold of him. He didn't belong anywhere. Those whom he called mother and father were not his mother and father at all. But who was?

He hugged himself tight against the cool breeze, and shuddered at coming to this realization alone out here. Who did he belong to? Where did he come from? Why was he alive? And where was he going? He was like an animal, he thought, a speechless creature that roams and scavenges for no reason at all. He remembered his older childhood friends falling in love, being partners, helping each other, and knew he had no such future because he was a blank. He rubbed his arms hard, and rocked back and forth, waiting for the sun to come and erase these bad night thoughts and visions. No, he realized, not an animal. An object. A tool.

WHEN THE SUN finally appeared, Peter was so glad he ran for two miles along the trail, as if he could leave behind the self he was at night. It made him so thirsty, he thought his mouth would break open and bleed. Finally he had to slow down and suck on his last piece of bread.

The sun was still cool and almost orange when he saw ahead of him over the prairies a herd of buffalo. He stopped and watched them move in a thick dark clump, hundreds of them, heads down, at a slow clip. The rocks seemed to thunder from underground. Peter crouched down, clutching the grass around him. The buffalo were not coming in his direction, but moved with mysterious precision in a crowd toward the east. Whether they were heading toward something special or away from something special, Peter could not guess. But they had a purpose.

The earth jiggled as they passed, and dust blew up in clouds. Peter wondered if they were heading for water, for that was the one thought in his mind. Filled with awe for their size and motion, he followed their passage closely with his eyes.

Then, as they thinned out and moved farther to the east, Peter saw why they were running. An Indian and a boy on horses were following, riding bareback, at a slow canter. They reined in about fifty yards from where Peter crouched. He was fully exposed on the wide prairie, and there was no way they could miss seeing him. Peter knew it, but he stayed stock-still.

He heard them talking in loud voices. Although they spoke in their own language, Peter understood by their tones that they were in good spirits. The boy looked about his own age. The man was about as old as Collins. The boy wore only a loincloth made of bearskin and his straight black hair was encircled by a strip of plain cloth. The man was more elaborately dressed in bead-embossed bearskin leggings, moccasins, and loincloth wrapped with a long trailing strip of skin. His hair was braided.

The man spotted Peter. He stared at him in the rigid way a hunter stares at prey for several seconds before the boy noticed. Peter stared back. There was nothing he could do but stand up and expose himself completely, at their mercy. Besides, he felt he was dying of thirst. Nothing could be worse than the pain behind his lips.

The man boldly rode forward after signaling the boy to stay behind. Unsmiling, cold, he looked down from high on his horse at Peter.

"Where you come from?" he asked.

Peter gestured weakly behind him. His knees were trembling as the man could see.

"What's your name?"

Peter could not reply because his mouth was dry, his voice lost. Then the man waved the boy over and ordered Peter to climb up on the horse behind him. Peter could not make the right motions, so the man climbed off his horse and shoved him up behind the boy.

"Hold on my son," said the man.

Peter obediently closed his hands on the boy's waist, as the horses turned and trotted west.

Peter relaxed into the sway of the horse's gait. Somewhere in his burning brain hung a feverish feeling of relief that it was Indians and not white men who had found him. But then, his head turned to the southwest. Through blurry eyes he saw, like a mirage that mocked him, the wagon train moving slowly along. He blinked several times, trying to test his vision. Could it be true that he had just missed his one hope of freedom by a mile or less?

THE INDIANS reined in near a narrow gully, where wild flowers grew in profusion. This was their campsite, where they were greeted by a woman and child, a little girl in a long brown skirt and beads. Various articles of trade—blankets, fur pieces, pots, and bottles—littered the ground around the fire. In the gully lay the carcass of a buffalo, neatly slaughtered and stripped.

The man spoke to the woman and gestured toward Peter. He then pulled him off the horse. The boy leaped down after him. Peter's blistered mouth and dry tongue stated, better than words, his misery and thirst. The Indian man, his smooth brown skin crinkling in a grin, folded his arms.

"Agwa?" he said. "Boy want agwa? Water?"

Peter nodded limply. The boy was watching him from beside his horse, as were the little girl and the woman. Sounds of crickets, dry as old leaves, crackled up from the gully. Two black hawks circled the sky overhead.

"We find you water," the man said, without kindness. He didn't move. "You come a long way. You need water. White boy come long way."

Peter's knees buckled and he sat on the ground. His head was bowed and burning.

"You settler boy? Young soldier?" the man asked, squatting to look in Peter's face. He got no response. "You from fort, hunt my people?"

Peter did not respond. In the man's voice was a familiar, sharp tone of anguish and desperation. It was the voice some of the people at home used, late at night, after an unusual abuse had been aimed at one of them by the master. The Indian man put out his hand and shook Peter's shoulder.

"No speak?"

Peter shook his head without looking up.

"Want water? Get water. There," the man said, pointing across the gully.

Peter stood up and moved through the tangle of flowers and leaves and up the other side of the gully. He listened acutely for the sound of water, but only heard the voices of the man and woman behind him. He half crawled up on the ledge of loose soil, and there saw another gully, but this one contained a thin trail of water. He rushed toward it, and was throwing himself down on the ground to drink, when he was snatched back from behind.

The man pulled him up by the hair.

"No drink water," he said loudly in Peter's ear.

He dragged him back to the campsite and knocked him down on the ground. Weak as he was, Peter was filled with anger and leaped up to struggle his way back to the water. He shoved at the man with all his might, but was pressed down firmly, flat on his back.

Panting, he lay there, while the Indian man called instructions to the woman. She ran over with strips of cooked buffalo meat in her hands, and squatted down beside Peter's head, holding the meat out. The man raised the boy's neck and back up, saying, "Eat."

"No, no," Peter cried, "water!"

"Blue-eye boy," said the man, "squaw say she know you. Trading post. Free boy like black. Run away?"

Peter's mouth was too dry to say more than *water* again, and this time the woman came with a gourd full of lukewarm coffee and held it out to him.

Peter gratefully drank the bitter liquid he knew only by its smell. The man stood up, handing him the meat. Peter, eating, discovered in his clenched fist the last piece of bread given to him by Jessie. He swallowed that, too.

The man and woman talked in cheerful voices to each other, and now their son came over and sat down beside Peter. He stared with rapt attention. Peter glanced at him and saw he had a friendly face, almond eyes, and a full generous mouth. They could not speak to each other, having no common language, but they were the same age. The boy was sympathetic to Peter and curious.

He called questions to the man and woman, who answered from where they sat by the fire, without hesitation.

The boy took the cup from Peter's hands and ran to refill it. Peter had enough energy now to wonder what his fate would be and to mull over the possibilities. His knowledge of the world was limited. He could only envision violent acts. They would feed and then kill him, whip and enslave him, or they might leave him there, alone, to rot like the carcass in the gully. Nothing good could come from this encounter.

He knew Indians hated white people from the stories he had heard at home. There was no other way they could view him, in spite of what the man said about his being "like black." His veins seemed to sing a song of despair.

"Blue-eye boy," the Indian called, "we take you home. Get money back." He stood up slowly. "Show us way."

Sinking back, Peter stared at the man and saw he would do anything for money, and Peter was a piece of good fortune that had befallen them in their travels. What could he do? He was trapped! He would almost rather die than go back to the plantation, but these people cared nothing for his desires. He was a piece of property to them now, as he had been to others for so long before. He took the second cup of coffee from the boy and began to drink slowly.

The man called out. "Drink! That good water. Bad water there," he pointed over the gully, "much poison. Make person die."

Peter looked slowly at the man, and realized he might have died had he drunk that water. The Indian had stopped him not out of kindness but for the reward the woman implied he could get for Peter's life. If she had not recognized him, he would be dead.

Peter sobbed and smiled at the same time. He was struck by the random way in which events were resolved. His smile was rare, but it was infectious. The Indian boy smiled, too, where he sat beside Peter. But the man and woman were busy packing, and didn't smile at all.

17

THE NEXT TWO DAYS were the happiest in Peter's young life. The woman was preoccupied with the little girl, named Rainbow, and the man rode his horse in a kind of trance. So Peter and the boy, whose name was Nine Bears, were free to communicate as they could, and to hunt and fish together.

They did not follow the trail Peter had taken, but moved in the same direction on a different track. This way they were concealed. The horses were loaded with objects for trade and moved slowly. The family stopped frequently to set up a fire, relax, and eat. Nine Bears taught Peter hand signals, while they lounged beside the fire, and drew him into the underbrush to scavenge for edible plant stalks, berries, and fat roots. Nine Bears always carried a bow and skin quiver containing arrows with points of sharpened bone.

Many of Peter's earlier fantasies about Indians were being realized. The boy was an expert marksman, shooting rabbits and spearing fish. But more than that, he and his family had an attitude toward the world around them that Peter shared. They revered the moon and sun and stars, fire and water, and showed it in their attention.

Sometimes they paused, taking note of the position they occupied, and suddenly broke into song or prayer. Peter sensed that these songs were intended both to praise and ensure a feeling of security in the family, as they wandered solitary over the landscape. He dared not ask the man why they were alone like this, and not part of a tribe. The clutter of objects they carried on their horses indicated disruption and desperation.

However, Nine Bears was a cheerful companion, the best Peter had ever had. He was a patient teacher who enjoyed sharing his knowledge and skills with Peter. As they left the prairie behind and entered verdant, forested areas, Nine Bears had an opportunity to show Peter how to fish and hunt. The sun-flecked forest contained many secrets for Peter: which herb and berry were edible and which were not; how to uncover a sweet root; how to tell which way a rabbit or elk was traveling. Arrangements of twigs and stone, which to Peter appeared purely accidental, to Nine Bears were writings left by others before them. At first he couldn't understand why Nine Bears crouched in concentration over a flat stone covered with leaves and pebbles, but when Nine Bears used his hands to explain that he was reading them, Peter understood.

His body pulsed with excitement. He longed to be able to read those signs himself. But there was no way Nine Bears could explain it, and Peter had to follow him silently to the next discovery or activity.

Two nights were passed sleeping under the stars. Peter was given a blanket. He curled up, watching the man sit in tranquillity, smoking a pipe in front of the fire, while the others sank into sleep.

"If only I could stay this way forever!" he thought.

The family moved on the next day, and now they were crossing through those mountains Peter had seen from the trail below, and from where he sat on the horse behind Nine Bears, his woeful expression was hidden. What was most familiar was most horrible. A whiff of the air, its bittersweet fragrance, filled him with grief.

His friend seemed to sense his tension, and sang a couple of songs, smiling back at Peter. Peter wondered if he knew what was happening, where his parents were going, and why. He seemed sublimely unconscious of their plans, so used to a nomadic life, it didn't matter where he was going.

When they paused for a midmorning break, Peter approached Nine Bears's father where he squatted arranging sticks for a fire. He stared down at the man's long, able hands. But the man did not look up. He wore his usual reserved and distant expression, which only changed to warmth when he spoke to his family directly.

Peter nervously cleared his throat.

"Where we going, sir?" he asked in a near whisper.

"Take you home," said the man, still looking down.

"But," said Peter, "can't I just stay around?"

"Take you home," the man repeated.

"Oh."

"Pale boy bring money." The man looked up then and smiled at Peter with some triumph. "Pale boy slave."

Peter wanted to cry, but his mouth felt clogged and his eyes burned. Ashamed, he turned away.

Nine Bears watched with a bewildered expression from a distance. He waved Peter over and led him deep into the woods to shoot a rabbit for food. Peter, following him through a gloomy cluster of evergreens, suddenly thought of running. He gazed deep into the forest where beams of sun glowed gray with pollen. Nine Bears moved ahead in his loincloth, his brown back bare. Nine Bears moved stealthily, almost without a sound, and Peter hung back, trying to avoid making a sound.

It was strange, he thought, how the boy's father let Peter move so freely away from the camp. Didn't he think he would try to bolt? *If I ran into the forest and mountains*, thought Peter, *this time I might get away. Nine Bears has taught me how to fish and hunt. I could survive*. Nine Bears was crouching now, several yards ahead of Peter, fully concentrating on his game. Peter thought, *this is my chance*.

He began to move southwest across the soft blanket of pine needles, silently, his heart pounding. His eyes never left the still figure of Nine Bears. He was amazed at his own silence, and continued to glide sideways under the low branches. But then, when he had just lost sight of Nine Bears, he saw him rise up out of the branches, his bow and arrow pointing at Peter.

Nine Bears said something in his own language, sharply, and Peter moved back to where he had been standing before. The two boys looked at each other steadily, speechless, until Nine Bears lowered his weapon. Then the Indian boy returned to his former crouch, his back to Peter, waiting for his first prey.

When they returned to the camp, later, with two rabbits in hand, Peter watched to see what the boy would say to his father. But it appeared that he said nothing unusual, for the family went about preparing the meal in its ordinary way. Not a glance was thrown in Peter's direction.

18

WE RETURNED. I was taken back, on foot at the end, to my place, the plantation and the people there. I was twelve years old and didn't understand. I should've run, should've escaped, that time, out there on the prairie. I could've survived and made it to Santa Fe and freedom, could've been absorbed, easy, into the general run of things.

But I was young and afraid. I let myself be taken back. I was a true slave by then. I couldn't see over the rim of the ground, east, west, north, south. Couldn't see those miles expanding into cities. Couldn't see my face as it was, or my hands, for what they could do. I was a true fool.

I let the Indians take me back, and my feet dragged, and I hung my head. All I could see was pebbles and dirt. The walls of the mountains contained me. The smells of spring were bitter in my nose, the taste of the dust gritty. I followed the Indians and their horses, slowly, as we moved up the avenue of cottonwood trees. I didn't look up, not forward, not right or left, but dragged my way dreary along.

My heart was like a hornet's nest when I heard the master's voice.

"Hey hey! You got him!" he shouted from the porch. His voice was high and gay.

The Indians said nothing, I didn't look up to watch their transactions. I was already half broken, before I was beaten. The horses whinnied and the little girl chattered. Nine Bears was silent on his horse in front of me. It was a warm and humid day.

"That's done then," said the master. "So get along with you. And thanks! Never thought I'd see this boy again."

The horse's flank was slapped, and the three of them turned. In their shadows, I glanced at the boy beside me, up on his horse. He was looking down. His eyes were large, and I saw he felt sorry for me, and confused by what was happening. So we said goodbye and he rode away with his family. The packs on the horses' backs clanked and creaked as they moved away back down the avenue.

"Well, Peter," said the master, planting his hand on my back, "the treat's on me."

I felt where he touched me my skin take on a life of its own, and I clenched my fists and gnashed my teeth.

"Your mother will be real happy to have you back," said the man, shoving me along toward the slave quarters, "but first I'm going to reward myself for my labors. Looking for you cost me plenty, boy."

All around I heard the familiar sounds of chickens, horses, sheep, axes, and voices, but they came into my ears as far away as rain on a roof. I, myself, was somewhere deep inside, crouching and attentive. My body was like a house made of wood. Snow, rain, and lashes might fall on it, but they would not move me. So long as I focused on the fact of myself, curled inside, small as a bee in a sunflower, I would feel nothing that he did to me. I heard the voices I knew well, calling out, "They got him!" "Peter's back!" "Now, look what the master drug in." But I didn't look up.

I was jostled instead, past the small shacks, and pens of livestock, leaving those voices behind. I was pushed by my master to a somber hidden place, where no one could see what he would do to me. This place was a kind of cave in the side of the mountains, a cave made of roots and rocks and dirt, all dripping down around a deep hole, just big enough for a couple of men.

"Strip, Peter," directed the master.

I didn't do as he said, but stood like wood, looking down.

"Do what I say, boy."

Again I didn't move, for my limbs had turned into another element and wouldn't move according to his or my will.

He cracked his whip across the backs of my legs. I inhaled the moist odor of the cave, and peered into its darkness; then I closed my eyes and held my breath. I would seal myself off completely from him, if I could. He took me and swung me around and ripped the shirt off my back. He ran his hands quickly over my skin. I could hear his hard breathing and his words, in a continual babble, coming mean and soft at the same time, the pitch of a wild turkey. To me, they had no meaning I had gone so deep inside. He bound my hands with a small coil of rope. He rubbed my arms and stomach and back, pushed me to my knees and stood, for some time quiet, over me. I leaned over. Spots flashed in front of my eyes. I was dizzy. But the walls of my house were wooden and numb.

The whipping began all of a sudden. To me, it came like the curl of a tornado down over the roof of my house. I lay myself down against the walls of my body, waiting, while lash after lash tore at the outside. In this way I felt nothing. Yes, nothing.

Blood poured down my back, under my armpits, dripping around my spread hands on the floor of the cave. The whip struck my cheek and the warm blood came down. But it might've been rain on glass. I kept my eyes closed, my breath shut up inside, and sensed the end of the storm only when I realized the master had dropped the whip and was standing beside me, leaning down, his hand knotted in my hair. He pushed my face down, swung his leg over my back like a child trying to ride on a dog, and it took all my powers of concentration to close in further away from him, and the pain he was causing me.

I was too young to know what he was doing, but not too young to feel humiliation. The shame I felt was a hundred times greater than the pain, as it invaded the house I had constructed for myself, and seared me inside. I covered my face with my hands, my eyes squeezed shut, waiting only for the time to pass. If the time would just pass, I felt I would be saved from committing murder. For he had gone too far and come too close and I was ready to kill.

Luckily for him, he stopped and removed himself from me. I could hear him like a rat scratching around, building himself up to return to the sun outside. I listened to him sighing loudly, his boots scuffing the ground, uneven in his gestures, as one is uneven when woken too soon from sleep. I listened and knew he was in there still, for some time, hanging around, tired, against the cave walls. His sighs came to me like the wind traveling off to the east, to break up and rise into the sky. Go, go, I begged silently.

And finally he did, he did go. Without a word. Nothing to me. Nothing aloud. And as he went farther and farther away, and the time extended longer, I felt the wounds in my body awaken to pain. I saw that I was dripping blood, and I smelled a sickening smell around me in the cave. I straightened myself, reaching for my shirt, and groaned aloud at the pain. The sound of my own voice surprised me, consoled me, and I groaned and whined again and again, trying to pull the shirt over my shoulders. But my hands were still bound in a knot of rope.

As I twisted around, trying to free them, I saw, at the cave's opening, four faces watching me. They were crouched there, in the sunlight, staring silently—Dan, Isaac, Lucy, George—slave children my age and older. Faces I knew. I stared back at them. My stomach burned, and I felt I might be sick. Their presence filled me with a strange emotion, entered my house, as if I had thrown open the windows to let in the light.

I only wanted them to go away. But my voice was still groaning of its own accord, so I couldn't say nothing to tell them to go, and I saw the boy Dan crawling toward me. I jumped back, at once, and tucked my body, hard, into the curves of the cave's wall. It hurt.

"You a mess," he said. "Get out here in the sun."

My mouth filled with bile, and I was all fear.

"Jessie wants you," he said.

My eyes must have asked what for?

He said, "She's going to fix you up."

He reached out his hand, as a person does to a vicious dog, real slow and careful. I looked in his eyes and felt like a dog. I tried to warn him, but was speechless, and his face seemed to melt a little. His eyes and mouth started to smile.

"A rabbit in a hole is what you is," he said, "and the fox done got you. Ripped you up. But you'll be okay."

I looked past him to the others stuck by the cave entrance. Their faces expressed only concern for me, but I was hanging over that big hole where you don't trust no one. I was near crazy, like as if a wind was sucking me down, down into a dark tunnel, and all I knew was fear. Dan kept his distance and I turned on my hands and knees around to retch and heave, my stomach empty but gasping. All I wanted was to be left alone. Couldn't they see that and go away?

I retched and groaned and finally, exhausted, keeled over, scraping my back on the wall. The pain was a spear, and I cried out "Mama" and at last they fled from the cave, running, like lambs across a meadow, leaving me at last alone with my pain and shame.

When, at last, my mother came I was nearly unconscious. She kneeled beside me in the cave, begging me to stand up and come home. She was crying. Her face swam before me, doubling, like a picture in a pond, all wetness and glitter. I looked at her and tried to gather together the scattered lights and make them whole. She had her hands on my face, and the well-known smell of them filled me with a kind of hunger.

"Peter," she said, "you got to get up and come with me. You got to let me wash you off."

She said this over and over many times, but I couldn't make a move. Instead, I asked her through a kind of thick wall, as the walls of a buffalo are thick and woolly, and the sounds they make are like horns made of wool, so was my voice like that.

"Is that Mama?" I asked her.

"Yes, honey, it's me."

"You sure now?"

"I'm sure."

"That's good," I concluded and the words sounded strange, a lowing from a head of cattle. I felt her head drop on my chest, as lightweight as a small stone, and while she continued begging me to come home, I felt hope return to me, just a little drop of it responding to her own.

She called to Dan, George, and Isaac where they stood vigil outside the cave, and they came inside and helped lift me, supporting me as gently as they could. Inside the cabin, she washed me, but had to return to work in the kitchen before she could begin to bandage me, so Jessie came in and soothed and dressed me, and between the two of them, I was restored to health. I became what I had been before except for the scar on my face. And I felt I was the boy I was before, although I could rarely open my mouth to speak, and only did so when it was absolutely necessary. I preferred silence to anything else from that day on. I saw the boss do it to other boys, too, whispering, "At least you won't get pregnant."

19

PETER STAYED on the plantation four more years. He remained silent, but his friends sat around him talking. Now he was just a good listener, a receiver of secrets. People moved up to talk to him, where he drove a team of oxen dragging timber down the hills, and they would tell him their dreams, hopes, disappointments. They could tell he was listening by the way he bent his head to the side and looked off into the middle distance, his blue eyes sharp but dreamy, absorbent and sympathetic. He would nod a little, shrug, maybe smile, then return to work in silence.

He grew taller, thicker, and his face became downy and square. A scar ran down his left cheek, left over from the beating that day, and often he thoughtfully ran his finger down it. No one had any more doubts about where his heart lay.

The whipping and assault by his master had little to do with the change in attitude Peter inspired now. That he had failed in his effort to escape was a greater influence on people than a whipping. His failure brought him down to the common level. Like a rite of initiation, failure was a mark of membership in the family of the enslaved.

A survivor, like a slave, he realized, is just a person who died and went on living.

He kept to himself, as before, but in a different way, for now he seemed to need the company of his people in order to feel secure.

He sat close in the circle at mealtimes; he joined others around a bonfire at night; he played the fiddle to make others dance. He listened attentively to conversations around him, and it was clear he was interested in all that was said, although he said little himself.

Sometimes, when he was sent off to work alone on a far slope by the new overseer, O'Leary, and found himself in the company of that white man, he became so agitated he couldn't perform his tasks correctly. His hands jerked uncontrollably on the handles of the yoke, or he broke into a sweat and grew dizzy. He would look wildly from right to left, gnashing his teeth and muttering prayers in a low voice in hopes that one of the other slaves would appear out of the woods to be near him.

His hatred of white men was something he could not conceal for long. There were times when he was in the presence of black friends and the master or overseer would call him away to some task. His physical reaction was out of control, then, and his friends saw his body jerk, as if cramped, and his shoulders automatically stiffen, his back tensed over like a bow. Often one of his friends would conjure up an excuse to accompany him. He hated their skin, their dainty hands, the cracks in their faces as they aged, their nasal voices and conceits. One look of recognition and sympathy from one of them, usually a woman, melted his hatred, but the rage stayed.

Betty fretted over him, but that was about all she could do for she was driven to the limits of endurance by Collins. She labored in the kitchen from dawn till after nightfall and rarely saw her own children. By the time she came to her own cabin, she was broken with exhaustion.

Enough was known in those days of slave rebellions and abolitionists to have an effect on even so isolated a sector of the black world as those who lived on the Collins plantation. Word seeped in, mainly through the arrival of the enslaved people bought by Collins, people who had lived in both the South and North. They did not tell tales of individual escapes, so much as tales of internal revolt on large plantations and social movements initiated in the North, about long marches, forced migrations, chains. These tales chilled and thrilled the younger boys and girls, mainly those Peter's age and older.

Betty, watching Peter grow toward manhood, realized that his intense need of her would be transformed soon. He had been emotionally fragile since that whipping, but was now physically large and strong. What would it take to drive him to violence? After her influence was gone, which way would he turn?

20

THREE HARVESTS PASSED. Then there was an event at the plantation that altered the course of his life. It was at the height of the harvest. Hog killing and corn shucking were the order of the day. Spirits were high, for the crops were abundant that year. There would be more food for everyone during the winter months.

Plans for the feast included the usual baking of all manner of breads and pies, the shucking of the corn, and butchering, curing, and roasting. It was a beautiful fall, and the trees were tinged with the bright colors of October. A light mist suffused the blue sky, turning all that the sun touched a pale gold.

When the shucking was done, the workers would be given whisky and a huge feast to enjoy at dusk. Then there would be dancing and singing around bonfires in the slave quarters, while the Collins family watched from the veranda. Those who were content grew more content; those who were discontent grew bitter and even hostile. So O'Leary was instructed to move guardedly, here and there among the slaves with his gun and whip ready for action.

As the night sky deepened into a starry dome, the festivities got into full swing. Peter played the fiddle for the children by one fire, while Robert did the same for the others, at a distance. There was lots of shouting, laughing, and passing of bottles, and only the pale specter of the overseer served to remind the people of their limits. O'Leary was not as mean-tempered a man as Morgan. Short, squat, and bowlegged, he moved with some timidity behind his gun and whip. He knew all the slaves by name, and was friendly in the way of a keeper of vicious animals. He called no one names of a low kind, but was generally soothing and polite.

Whenever his figure moved by Peter, the boy would stiffen and his fingers stumble on his bowstrings. But Peter went on playing while the children danced in a circle, inventing from his tune long and elaborate fantasies which they acted out cooperatively. He and the children were gathered near the end of the row of slave cabins where Jessie's cabin stood set off in a circle of hemlocks. Her light-skinned, light-haired children leaped about, while she watched aloofly from her stoop.

Peter was conscious of her presence there, as the night wore on. He noted how still she was. Some of the children dropped off to sleep on the hard ground and were carried away. Two of hers stayed up, but one curled in sleep around Peter's back and sucked his thumb.

Toward midnight, Peter was taking a break when he saw the tall figure of Collins emerge from the darkness. Peter's face, near the fire, broke into sweat, and he twisted his hands together to keep them from shaking. Collins had never spoken to him directly when they were alone. There were no more privileges for Peter. No drives into town with Joe, or talking to his mother in the kitchen. Collins barely looked at him, but he still visited Jessie in her cabin. The children were always frightened of Collins and now dispersed toward home. Peter was left alone with Jessie's sleeping child, whom he drew down on his knees.

The master shouted, "Go on, scram! Get away!"

Peter jumped involuntarily.

Jessie's other two children had scampered back in terror to the fire. Both girls threw themselves down against Peter and their little brother.

"He's going to bother Mama," said the eldest.

The little one cried.

"Shh," said Peter, indicating the sleeping boy, "go to sleep now."

The girls twisted around him, thrust their thumbs in their mouths, and stared dreamily into the flames. Sounds of singing, laughing, and dancing came from the adults at the other end of the quarters. Peter stared into the faces of the little girls, thinking of their origin. Then, through the sounds of celebration, he caught the sound of Jessie crying. It was nearly indistinguishable from all the other noises, but Peter recognized the sound at once. He turned his head and saw that Jessie's cabin door was shut, and it was dark inside. He found himself trembling all over, clenching his teeth, his body out of control.

Visions of his attacking Collins filled his head, and it was only the weight of the three sleeping children that kept him still. Now Jessie was shouting and the master was shouting back. Peter whirled when he heard a crash and twined his arms across the children's bodies.

The boss stepped out of Jessie's cabin and yelled, "You're finished, wench. Sold. You're gone. It's all over. Done! I've had it with you. You're as good as dead. Sold. Gone!" And he strode quickly in the direction of the big house.

A stillness came over the plantation at the sound of Collins's angry voice. The singing, laughing, and dancing stopped, as if on command, and dark figures hurried into their cabins. Within minutes Peter was alone with the children. He gazed steadily toward Jessie's door until she emerged at last. She appeared unmoved and unshaken as she walked toward Peter and her children. Her pink lips were pursed, her eyes luminous and moist.

"Help me carry them, Peter," she said in a soft voice.

She lifted her son and Peter helped the half-sleeping girls into their cabin, where a chair lay shattered in pieces on the floor.

Jessie looked tenderly at her children, covering each with a blanket and kneeling beside them quietly. Peter turned to go. His body trembled, his legs were weak. He knew he couldn't speak.

"Thanks, Peter," she said in a low voice and lay down with her children.

He stepped outside and sobbed, alone, into the palm of his hand.

The next day Jessie was taken away in a wagon. She did not look back once at those waving goodbye, and she never reached her new destination. On the way south she quietly cut her wrists with her arrowhead bone in the back of the wagon. The driver discovered what she had done at nightfall over the Arkansas border.

JESSIE'S DEATH made Peter want to kill someone as white as himself. He went off alone for hours the night after her body was returned to the plantation. At dawn when he came home, he was a changed person. The fears that had consumed him were gone, but they did not leave a vacuum. A new energy was in him, and he viewed the world differently. His eyes, red-rimmed from sleeplessness and emotion, burned intensely. He saw that he was alive, and she was not, and the simplicity of that fact gave him a destiny. He remembered vividly the words she had said to him when he was locked in darkness, and how much she wished her children could avenge Collins just by staying there.

Collins seemed conscious of Peter's hate at Jessie's graveside, where all the slaves collected, during a gloomy funeral in the rain. He furtively glanced at Peter. He seemed to see in the boy a judge, a moral reference that intimidated him. He looked abject, pale, and guilty, standing with his hat in his hands, looking down at the simple pine box splashing off drops in the dark muddy hole. His knees shook.

It was a Sunday, the hour approaching dusk. Robert led the slaves in singing, as they circled Jessie's grave three times. Peter was conscious of the hate he felt as something he had been given, like a flu, from someone else. He had learned it, caught it, been taught it. He had not been born with it, not felt it when he was a young boy, but it had grown into a sickness with his years of witnessing injustice and cruelty. Children do not understand or accept injustice. If they see enough of it, they adapt to its being part of human nature. The deals that were being made, all around and away from Peter, in the new country where he was born, were constructed out of this acceptable injustice and its sister, rage.

Collins stood aside, rain in his hair, watching uneasily as the people in a large group shouted their song. Tears and rain melted together on their faces. O'Leary stood behind him, his rifle and hat in his hand, his eyes lowered. Peter, his expression merciless, stared directly and continuously at Collins. In the singing and mourning there was an emotion threatening to the master and his overseer, if only because they were outnumbered many times over by the large crowd. Both looked anxious and impatient for the service to end. A white preacher quickly conducted the service and finally the slaves returned to their quarters and a feast of tears.

Collins paid the minister and hurried O'Leary away. For a few minutes Collins stood in the rain beside the grave and chills flooded his body, his trembling knees.

21

PETER WAS LOADED with heavier work as he grew older. He drove a team of oxen up and down the mountainsides, chopping and dragging timber back to the plantation. The heat in August was insufferable, and Peter, working alone and shirtless, often cursed aloud, calling his master names under his breath. He thought about Jessie. Rage swelled in his chest till he thought he would break open. He wanted to be free of the anger that was poisoning him. But all he could do was vow to no more cowering and trembling when O'Leary or Collins came upon him while he was alone. He stared at each of them with open hatred. He vowed to stay there, to let them see his face watching them without mercy.

One day in the heat the oxen were moving all wrong—getting twisted around trees, no matter how much of a path he tried to clear for them, and, in a burst of anger, he struck one of them on its head with a large branch. The aging beast groaned and sank on its knees to its death. Its nostrils dribbled watery blood as it lay inert beside the standing ox. Peter stared down in horror at the creature. He tried, wildly, to revive it with slaps and loud words, but the breath was gone from its body. Nothing in the world seemed to move for several minutes.

Peter had never hurt an animal nor had the desire to do so. He was horrified by his own strength, by what he could do in one blow. He kneeled beside the ox and cried for what witlessly he had done in such a quick and final act—the creation of death. He closed the animal's eyes and brushed the flies away. Hating himself, he jumped up and ran into the woods.

He moved swiftly ahead as the shadows of pine trees flashed about him and lashed his cheeks. The animal was innocent and clumsy and he had killed it, confusing it with others who were not innocent. His feeling of hurt and outrage at himself was so intense, he couldn't think of where he was going or how he would be punished. He only stopped running when he found himself at the edge of the dirt road outside the plantation.

Gasping and transfixed, he stood there. The road made him realize how far and blindly he had come. Now he must turn back or move on. Breathless, he sat down with his head on his knees and half hidden by the underbrush when a white man on a dappled horse emerged from the bend in the road.

From on high, he saw Peter at once, and drew his gun.

"You, boy!" he shouted.

Peter jumped up defensively at once.

"The slave boy, eh?" the man said grinning. "Trying to run away again?"

Peter stared with eyes burning up at the man.

"Okay, boy, I got you covered. Start walking. Home."

So Peter was returned to the plantation where the ox had already been discovered by O'Leary. The overseer shackled Peter and set him down, chained to a fence by the pigpen. He sat there, his head up, waiting for over an hour as the sun beat down on his head.

At last a smiling Collins appeared in elegant dun-colored clothes. He swung a whip.

"Well, Peter," he said, "you've done it again. This time you've killed one of my oxen. Almost worse than trying to run away from home. You know, I've just about had it with you, boy."

Peter did not lower his gaze, but stared straight into the boss's face. Collins, averting his eyes, turned Peter around, and gave him countless lashes. He didn't stop until he was bored and Peter was bleeding profusely. Then he stood back, panting. Peter pulled himself up, as far as he could go. The chains clanked like bells. He looked, half smiling, at Collins.

"Master," he said serenely, "this is the last time I'll take a whipping from you."

Collins glanced into Peter's face, then looked up uneasily at the sky.

"That so, Peter?" he queried. "What about tomorrow, when I do it again?"

"You won't do it tomorrow," said Peter. "You won't do it again."

"That so?" Collins repeated.

But now he looked directly at Peter, moving backward at the same time. The chained and bleeding youth wore an expression of such fury that Collins felt a shot of terror pass through him. He had never been confronted openly with the hatred of his slaves. It was unmistakable in Peter, and he didn't want to see it again. Whirling, he walked homeward, his body tense as if he could be shot from behind.

He wanted to eliminate Peter from his field and from his sight, but he feared letting him go in case he returned free and murderous.

22

Over the next two years Peter grew into a tall, strong young man, with the heart of a boy. The more manly he became, the less he liked his appearance. He dressed sloppily and let his curls hang limp around his face, as if to conceal it. In an effort to develop some color in his skin, he rarely wore a shirt, but he was fair-skinned and only reddened or freckled. His mannerisms and speech were indistinguishable from the other black youths, but he was still uncomfortable in his body. The kids who were half white were nowhere near as white as Peter, and even they were teased for being stuck-up, proud, too near to master.

Something must be Betty's! His ears, nostrils, eyelids, lips—why didn't one part of him copy one part of her? At one point he thought his hands were the same shape as his sister Georgia's—but then he realized her hands came directly from Robert. He watched his friends, who were beginning to fall in love. Romantic liaisons occurred in the moonlight or out in the fields, but Peter didn't dare experience passion for anyone. He squelched his desires before they could grow strong and continued to spend his spare time with his sisters or Jessie's children or others younger than himself.

Often alone in the woods where he drove his oxen, he would steal time to examine and identify wild flowers and roots, harking back to his time with Nine Bears four years before. He expected to live out his life where he was and always in the same manner. He would labor not for his friends or family but for those who despised him. He would receive no rewards or profit from his labors. It was abnormal. People should take care of themselves, period.

Collins knew that Peter was as valuable as any other slave on his plantation who knew how to plant and build. Collins needed his labor but sickened at the sight of him close up and often tried to explain this to his wife without supplying the details. He just said that Peter was dangerous. He feared him being free and coming back.

"Why, I can't imagine," he told his wife. "I've done nothing to harm the boy out of the ordinary, nothing he didn't ask for and deserve."

She smiled cynically from her perch on the edge of the sofa, where she was sewing. "You are a law unto yourself, Ed, so what's the use of talking to you?"

"Well, tell me, I'll listen, if I did something wrong."

"There's no point," she sighed.

"Come on, Joannie, speak up. I'll listen."

"You started to make something of him. Then you stopped. That's enough of a reason for him to hate you."

"He ran away. That's breaking the rules. How could I trust him with my hands if he'd do that?"

"He was just a boy then," she said. "He's not any more."

"No," said Collins, "I want to get rid of him."

"That's what I mean. What's the point of my saying anything?"

Collins snapped, "Well, what are you saying? You want me to keep him around, make him overseer after O'Leary?"

"Not yet. But, as you once said about Peter, he's something to take advantage of. He's so—well, odd. Sometimes I watch him," she said, laying down her sewing, "and I see he has a kind of power about him. Curious."

Collins eyed her coldly. "You'd better not be watching him too much."

She laughed. "Well, he is a mighty handsome specimen."

"He's a mess."

"Of course. He has no vanity," she said with a pointed glance at her husband.

"Well, that settles it. I'm getting rid of him." The tall man's face burned at the ridges of his cheekbones.

"Nobody wants an albino, honey, nobody. Either you take advantage of him yourself, or you let him go. Set him free."

"Free?! He couldn't survive more than a couple of days. Only reason he looks strong to you is he's got all the protection here he needs."

"Maybe."

"I have one other hope, anyway," said Collins, turning his back to her, "and that's to send him back where he came from."

"Same people."

"That's right. They deserve him." He glanced at her over his shoulder. "Besides, they're poor folks, plain farmers, they could use an extra hand from what I hear. I'd give them Peter for nothing."

"You got him for nothing. The missus is supposed to be pious," said Joan. "She thinks she's some kind of martyr because of her arthritis. Truly she talks about suffering all the time from what I hear."

"No fooling. The men, her husband and his brother, are cut from rough cloth. Not the most efficient farmers, either. And they've got something like five or six children, only one of them married so far."

"Still. Why would they want Peter?"

"I dunno, I just have a feeling I could force him on them. As I said before, they gave me Betty and him in a real hurry. No auction, nothing. I just bet I could force Will Howard to take Peter back. That man has no power, no social standing. All it would take would be a couple of hints, or threats, call them what you will, regarding Peter's blood origin, and they'd be ruined. I could do that."

"I know you could," said his wife coldly, "just like I know a lot else you could do. Maybe Peter is some kind of throwback, like Jessie's children right here. Soon you'll have a slew of Peters on the plantation. Isn't that so?"

Collins averted his face, as he always did when Jessie's name was mentioned.

"Why don't you just set him free?" his wife said quietly.

"I don't want him loose on the land, that's why," he replied. "He's capable of insurrection. He'd come back in the night. I don't trust him."

"Then see about the Howards," she sighed and couldn't help adding, "My Lord, the blood history of this nation will be one of a kind. So much hate and fornication. Never heard of anything like it before, not in all my reading."

23

FOR WEEKS Peter had no knowledge of his future, but labored as usual on the mountain slopes. He never dreamed he would leave the plantation; he had made his adjustment as everyone had hoped he would. His attention to the trees, fields, stones, and animals kept him fit for the day's work.

But then, during a January thaw, when there was some flooding in the fields and the cattle gathered in clusters on the hillsides where grass could be found and water ran in rivers around their legs, Collins found Peter chopping wood. It was before dusk, out behind the curing shed. The air was moist, chill, and steamy. Peter, seeing the boss approach, stood erect with his ax in his hands. Collins stood at a distance.

"Peter," he said, his voice quivering slightly, "something to tell you. We've got a new home for you. About fifty miles north of here. Small farm. They need a hand."

Peter gazed at Collins through the gloomy light.

"They'll be good to you. People name of Howard. Small farm," he repeated. "You'll be going there tomorrow. Now you can go in the kitchen and tell your mammy."

Collins stepped backward a couple of paces, then turned on his heel, and strode away fast. Motionlessly, Peter watched him go and tried to absorb this information. He rolled the words around in his head but their meaning appalled him. Here was where he and his family lived. He knew the land and every tree. How could someone just come along and tell him to go somewhere else? What gave the man such a right?

He finished chopping and piling the wood, until it was too dark to see, and then he walked to the big house to find Betty.

She was preparing dinner in the kitchen when he came in.

"Peter!" she smiled, and it was clear she had not yet heard the news. "What you doing here?"

He silently looked at her, and felt he couldn't bear to tell her what Collins had said.

"What's wrong, boy?" she asked with sudden concern. "Are the girls all right?"

He said, "Girls are fine."

"Then what's the matter?"

"Hungry, I guess."

"That all?"

He lowered his head and she stepped closer, looking up into his face inquiringly.

"You tell me what's wrong," she demanded.

"Boss going to sell me."

Betty gasped and staggered, and Peter grasped her arms to steady her.

"Told me so himself. Tomorrow," said Peter. "Well, probably give me away."

Betty sank into a chair, her knees weak, and shook her head unbelievingly.

"Maybe he's just going to hire him out," suggested Mary from the table, "you know, just for a short while."

"He said," Peter murmured, "I got me a new home."

"But you didn't do no wrong for a long time!" cried Betty.

"He knows I might.... Guess he don't find me useful no more."

"Where's he sending you? Did he say?"

"People name of Howard. North of here."

"Howard?" Betty said sharply. She stood up quickly to return to work. This was her way of handling crises. "Wonder if it's the same Howards I know."

"You know them?"

"You leave me alone. I want to think," she said.

Peter watched her hack energetically at lumps of red meat. He shrugged and stepped outside. His sisters, passing him on their way inside, jumped and swung on his arms. He pivoted, throwing them onto the porch, watching them run inside.

For a time he stood by the lighted door. Chill after chill passed over his skin as he tried to cope with the humiliation of this situation. He couldn't help but think of Jessie and how casually and brutally she was sent away from her home. Now he understood how she had done what she did. He moved on toward his cabin, when he heard Betty calling him back. She approached him, speaking in low tones.

"Now listen, Peter, I want you to listen to me. Won't be another chance after this, most likely." She gently put her hand on his arm. "If these people be the same Howards I know, and if my friend Ruth is still there with them, she'll look after you. I know that. She's a good bit older than me, but not by much, and she's a good soul. They call her Grandma, as if she was one of their own. Put yourself in her hands, do your chores, and keep quiet, and you'll do fine.

"And one thing more," she added softly. "No matter where you go, or for how long, I'll find you again. We'll be together, even if it's only for a little while. Understand? The Lord is good."

Peter nodded, blindly looking into her face. She squeezed his arm hard.

"Robert will help me write you a letter, don't you fear," she whispered.

She was not a demonstrative woman by nature, but now she gave him a quick hug before going inside again. Peter cried and cried, covering his face and voice, and wanting to say many last things to her.

As she had warned, they had no other opportunity to speak to each other alone. Night came, and sleep. By the time the other slaves learned of Peter's fate, the dawn was already light on the plantation. Collins forbade his slaves to come and say a formal goodbye to Peter, but each stood up and turned his and her face to the north, listening acutely, when Peter was driven away in a cart in the early morning frost.

The Home Place
1848

1

PETER'S ARRIVAL was delayed by the storm. The higher the wagon climbed, the heavier the sky became, and he and Joe were overcome by the whirling flakes. They kept on course as far as they could, but finally had to stop at the first farm they could find. This plantation lay only twenty miles east of the Howards'. Gusting winds made the snow nearly blinding. The horse could barely drag the wagon through the rising drifts. Joe and Peter were frozen to the bone. Their lips were numb.

The owners, Bart and Nancy Williams, were hospitable and at once sent the two men into the cookhouse to get some hot coffee and food. One of their farmhands took care of the horse.

"What kind of master would send you on a long journey this time of year?" asked the cook, a heavy woman tied up in an apron. She folded her arms in outrage. "Here. Drink your coffee. There's more in the pan. You must be frozen right through."

"Down where we come from," said Joe, "there was a thaw. We thought it'd last a few days."

"Must be mighty eager to get rid of you boys, your master."

"Not me. Him," said Joe, pointing at Peter. "I got to ride back alone. He stays."

"You going to have to wait awhile for that. I just can't imagine what kind of boss would do a thing like that."

"You just try and imagine, and you'll come up with what we've got," said Joe. "Cold master. Now this boy here, he's a slave like us. But you wouldn't know it, would you?"

She looked Peter over critically. "I don't know about that. My master Bart, now, he told us about this boy. Said he's a white boy all right. And a one of us too. Never saw such a thing in my life. Not a little white. A lot white. Completely white."

Joe looked around the warm kitchen with wonder. "You got a nice setup in here," he said. "What kind of master you got?"

"As they go, a good one. Just Master Bart and his wife Nancy and a couple of kids. She's a Howard from up there where you're going to. They all pretty good. Treat us kind. Feed us well. Give us good cotton wool to make our clothes from. I have no complaints. Where this boy is going to, that's another story."

Peter held his hands around the warm cup of coffee and stared silently and attentively into it.

"Peter's got a temper," said Joe. "That's why the boss is getting rid of him. Real mean." Then Joe patted Peter on the knee and laughed. "Still and all, I've gotten kind of fond towards him. Sticks up for what's his. Takes care of his own."

"Well, he better do all that, and more, over on the Howard farm," she said, settling down heavily across the table from them. "Master John there, he's a devil in the flesh. Talk about mean? And the missus goes about moaning for God, acting all Christian, saying her prayers under her shawl. And they don't take good care of the folks up there. Poor food, thin clothes. They're no good farmers. Only Miss Nora has a heart, and she gets pushed around just like us."

"Uh oh," sighed Joe, "poor boy here—nothing but trouble coming. But, I always say about Peter, he can find his way to freedom one day, being free-looking. Wait and see. He'll leave us behind."

Peter said nothing but let his gaze travel around the small room packed with cooking utensils and foods. He wondered how long he would have to stop at this strange place before moving on to the next one. He stopped listening to the talk and as the chill passed from his bones he was conscious of the mental pain he felt. There was a delayed reaction to saying goodbye to Betty. Outside the wind blew and made whistling sounds in the cracks between planks of wood.

All he wanted now was to be alone with his sudden depression, to crawl under a blanket in a shack somewhere, to think. The drifts of snow blanketing the outdoor world only intensified his sense of loneliness. He no longer had reason to behave himself according to the old set of rules. He was halfway between masters and in a sense free. If it weren't snowing outside, he would make a run for it. He had lost everyone he loved already. Why go on to the next place? He was young, sixteen, and could now adapt to the outside world, as he couldn't four years before.

The weather was determining his destiny. It seemed that even nature was conspiring against him. If only he could have the pride of blaming himself for this journey. That would be a small shaft of liberty, to be able to say to himself, "I made a mistake in coming this way." But he couldn't say that. He felt too connected to the fate of all the people he had known and who had suffered so much. He couldn't just run.

"Here comes Master Bart," said the cook, as the door blew open.

Peter looked up and saw a man bundled from head to toe in furs. He had a pair of watery blue eyes, a small nose, and full friendly lips. His cheeks were rosy, and he smiled when he entered.

"Hello there, boys. Did Annie give you something to eat?"

"Yes, boss," Joe and Peter said in unison.

"Well, then, come with me. I'm going to set you up for a couple of days in a cabin nearby. Got a chimney. You'll be warm enough. When the weather clears, I'll take you, Peter, by sleigh up to your new home. We'll have to fit up some vehicle for Joe. Come on now."

Peter and Joe put on their thin jackets and scarves and, with Annie the cook clucking after them, they followed Bart Williams out through the snow. He led them directly to a small cabin fitted out with three narrow cots and several blankets. A fire burned in the corner hearth.

"This should do just fine, boys, for a couple of nights, anyway," he said. Then he looked directly and curiously at Peter. "I heard you were coming, but I don't know what kind of man would send you out in a storm like this. We thought you'd be coming in the spring."

"Probably so Peter wouldn't make no attempts to escape," said Joe in a rush and added, "Sir."

"Probably you're right," said Williams in a surprisingly fraternal manner. "I've heard about Collins. Now, Peter, I've heard about you, too. Don't expect you know too much about your background, do you?"

"I have a mother, sir."

"Well, I expect she told you about Grandma Ruth?"

"She mentioned the name."

"Grandma is a good woman. She'll be a real friend to you, boy. And your mistress, Nora Howard, she's my sister-in-law. Ever heard of her?"

"Just the name. From your cook, sir."

"Yes, well," he muttered into his fur, "you'll be in good hands, between those two women. Don't worry."

Peter nodded, trying to figure out Williams. He had never encountered a friendly white man, outside of Walls the freighter, and certainly not in the form of a planter. His immediate reaction was suspicion, but it was hard to sustain, for the man had a round, candid face and a direct gaze.

"You're a good-looking boy, Peter, but that scar is bad," said Bart. "Now, take a rest. My wife might come and look in on you before the day is up. Don't be surprised."

Then he left. Joe and Peter threw themselves down on the cots, and wrapped themselves in blankets. It was midafternoon. Soon it would be dusk. But the two of them were exhausted, and to the sound of the crackling wood and the whistles of snow and wind, they fell asleep.

WHEN PETER WOKE UP, a cold draft blew over him and he saw, framed against the light of whistling snow and dusk, the figure of a woman warmly dressed from head to toe. He leaned up on his elbow, then jumped to his feet. The woman shut the door and glided to the fireplace where embers glowed. Leaning down she lit a tallow, and holding it up before her, moved silently toward Peter. He could see she was a fair-complexioned woman, pale and slight. Her eyes burned large.

"Peter?" she queried.

"Yes, ma'am."

"I just wanted to see you, boy. You must be hungry."

"Yes, ma'am."

"Then wake him up," she said, indicating Joe, "and come to the cookhouse for a meal. The others have eaten and gone in. But Annie kept something warm for you."

She stared intensely at Peter, so he lowered his eyes with embarrassment.

"You'll be called Peter Howard from now on, I guess," she murmured. "That's my family name. Come on, boy."

Peter roused Joe from a deep slumber and again they went to the cookhouse to be fed and treated to Annie's gossip. She was a nonstop talker with a bitter edge to her conversation that gave sharp relief to her innate goodwill. Nancy Williams only stayed a minute in the kitchen, gazing from the door at Peter as if he were some strange immortal spirit. Then she left the three alone and went back through the ever-piling drifts to the big house.

"That's the boy. No question," Nancy said to her husband Bart. "Never saw anything like it. Irish to the bone."

She shook the snowdrops out of her ash-blond hair and followed him to the settle in their parlor. Upstairs their children were already sleeping. Bart poured himself a glass of wine and they huddled together close to the hot fire.

"Gives me the willies," she said with a shudder.

"We'll just have to settle into it," said Bart. "It's going to take time. The main thing is not to let Nora know. Not ever."

"But Ruth knows."

"They might try to send Ruth away, you know. Ever thought of that?" asked Bart.

"They'd never sell Grandma," said Nancy. "She runs the place."

"They sold Ben for telling me about McCutcheon's visit. Or didn't I tell you that."

"Remind me."

"Ben was down in Carthage on business for John one day and he came on the Irishman, McCutcheon, sitting in a saloon alone. They recognized each other, and Dan, Nora's man, begged Ben to tell Nora that he was waiting for her. He wanted to marry her. Ben was kind of scared of this whole situation. He went back to the farm, and never dared to say a word to Nora. I can't blame him. I mean, because of John's temper. But for some reason he told me, came over here and told me, he was real scared."

"Now I remember," said Nancy vaguely. "I don't know why he didn't just tell Nora."

"She gets too agitated, I guess."

"Then why did you go and tell my uncle? I mean, honestly, why?"

"I was afraid for Nora. If the man came back looking for her. I didn't know about the baby then. I made a mistake."

Nancy murmured, "I would say so. You and a lot of other people, all keeping secrets from Nora. Why? Because it was un-Christian to have a baby out of wedlock? We're living in the frontier. Why wouldn't that happen once in awhile! My mother thinks she lives on the High Street."

"Your uncle sold Ben down river for speaking up, old and feeble as he was."

"Well, they didn't need him the way they still need Ruth," Nancy said. "Besides, Ruth won't say a word to Nora. They know they can trust her that way. She won't tell."

"No. But not because she loves your parents, Nancy, remember that. She won't tell for her own reasons."

"I think she does love my parents," Nancy said emphatically. A flush touched her cheekbones, a flare of self-defense. "And I know she loves Nora. You always say the slaves don't love us. I don't believe you. Annie is like my own mother."

"Think what you will, dear," said Bart, "but from where I come we see it different. Slaves are people, like any of us, but it would be a poor slave who loved his master. We see it like a contract. They work for us in exchange for food and a home. We treat them with respect. They do the same for us. Simple. Don't get it confused with love, though. It's not like a marriage. It's a business arrangement."

"But you seem to care for them, a whole lot, each one. That's why you have such a good operation here," Nancy said. "I don't understand. Never will. The family farm is a poor imitation of what you have here, and my parents believe the slaves really love them."

"Well, that's the problem right there," he replied. He filled his pipe with tobacco and assumed a thoughtful air. "Soon as you lose sight of some facts, you lose sight of them all. One day these slaves are going to get their freedom. It's just a matter of time. To prepare for that, you treat them like anyone who's working for you. An investment. Then you won't lose them in the end. They won't rise up in the night and burn you down. They'll stay on working for you, just the same as they always did. That's my opinion."

"Well, you know I support you, Bart honey, in whatever you believe," she said and stroked his knee with the palm of her hand. She smiled. "You're the finest man I ever knew."

Pleased but distant, he puffed on his pipe.

"Now, as for Peter," he mused, "he's got a lot I don't envy coming to him. Your uncle is going to have one hell of a reaction to the boy. Can't say what it'll be, but it will be strong. Why he agreed to take the boy back, I'll never understand. I suppose they were desperate for free help on the farm, now your brothers are gone."

"Yes, that," said Nancy, "and that Mr. Collins, from what I hear, acted like he knew all about where Peter came from. Maybe Betty told him. Who knows which way the wind blows next. But he threatened the folks, said a freed Peter would come back in the night and cause some kind of insurrection. No one else would buy a quadroon. You know that. Also, you know my daddy is a thoughtful man. He might not be too good with figures and accounting, but his heart is careful. He's been worrying over what they did to that baby all these years. He feels kind of responsible."

"Still. It seems like they could have arranged something different, especially with Nora the way she is about that lost baby. And what do we really know about the boy? He might rise up or figure out his origins and demand some land. We don't know, do we?"

"They're all afraid of the truth being known. In a way, they might figure it's better off hidden under their own roof than out in the world. That's how it is with people sometimes."

"True, dear, true," said Bart. "Nora's a sweet little woman, but she's got a strange side I don't understand."

"That's how she got the baby in the first place. Her strange side."

"She's too close to the slaves."

"They live by different laws than us folks. She likes that."

"Well, she may be one exception to the rule about not being loved by the slaves," said Bart. "Did you say quadroon? I think it's octoroon."

They fell silent, their fingers locked. Outside the wind continued to howl, shaving away pillows of drifts. The sky was clear. Stars glittered over the galaxies of billowing and shining snowdrops.

2

On a clear January day Peter came by sleigh to the farm where he was born. Bart Williams drove him over. Two horses, shaking silver bells, pulled them. They were wrapped in blankets in the sleigh and Peter had been given a knitted cap.

The light on the snow was nearly blinding but the horses moved with assurance across its powdery surface.

"They know where they're going," Bart said. "We make this trip at least once a month. 'Course not so frequent in weather like this. Did you know, Peter, that you and your mother Betty were born out here on the Howard farm?"

"Sir," said Peter and drew a deep, dry breath. He was startled.

"That's right. When you were just a baby, you were sent down to Collins's place. From right here."

Peter looked at Bart's rounded profile and flushed cheeks, wondering again why he was so open with him. Questions regarding his birth abounded in Peter's mind, but he didn't open his mouth. Sometimes his closed lips were the best source of information.

"So, in a sense, this is your real home, Peter," Bart said, "and me and Nancy expect to see a whole lot of you. The Howards and me exchange hands for planting and harvest times. You'll be out by our place a whole lot. I'm sure of that."

Peter said nothing. Bart glanced at him quickly.

"You look strong. I guess John will put you to work in the woods—cutting timber, working the oxen. Boy like you could do that work without too much trouble. What did you do down at the Collinses'?"

"Same as that, sir."

Bart nodded and shook the reins so the bells jangled and the horses picked up a little speed. "Now I don't come from these parts myself," Bart said. "I come from over on the coast of Virginia. Never expected to stay this long away from the cotton, but there's money in timber for now. Someday I'm going to move the whole kit and kaboodle south again. Head for the sun. Both the Howard boys left as soon as they were old enough. But this piece of property may be worth something someday."

It was only a matter of minutes before they came in view of the white frame house and barn belonging to the Howards.

"Here's your new home, boy," said Bart and patted Peter's knee reassuringly.

There was no consoling Peter. He was in turmoil, half sick with anxiety. How could he ever adjust to a new life? New faces? New chores? His system felt out of harmony with the landscape, the high hills, the gloomy evergreen groves spreading dark arms over the snow. There was no sign of life around the farm or house, but Peter could see smoke issuing from the chimneys of shanties lined up behind the barn. They passed the little hill where the gravestones stood gray and half buried in snow.

"So me and Mama were born here?" he said suddenly, his voice thick and muffled.

"That's right, boy. Right over in those quarters there. That's why we're buying you back. You belong on this ground. Here we are." Peter wanted to ask, *Who was my father?* But his mouth was parched with fear.

Bart jumped from the sleigh and walked up the shoveled path to the front door of the house. Peter sat alone in the bright gold and silver lights of snow. He looked from east to west for signs of activity. Then, up in a second-floor window, he saw a woman's face looking out at him. He stared at her, as she stared at him, until she disappeared from the window. It was a white woman, and he would not see her again for several days.

3

PETER WAS GIVEN an old cabin. It was eight feet square and sparsely furnished. A small hearth was stacked with wood. A table and chair stood at one wall, and a pallet lay folded neatly on the floor. There were no windows.

Unable to eat or talk to anyone, Peter huddled there the moment he arrived. On his journey he had caught a chill. He now had a fever and aching bones. He was glad. He hoped he would die here where he was born.

People looked in on him during those forty-eight hours. None of them was familiar, so he turned his face to the wall. He curled up with his knees up against his chest.

Almost everyone who came whispered about his color.

"Not a trace of Betty."

"Not albino neither."

Only the two women who visited him said nothing. One was Ruth; the other was Mrs. Howard, who always stood at a distance. Ruth took care of Peter. She felt his head and fixed an herb tea for him to drink. She said nothing to him, but her straight, dark, and orderly form was a source of comfort to Peter. She reminded him of his mother Betty.

On the third morning he said to her, "You Ruth?"

"That's right, honey."

"My mama said for me to look out for you."

"Well, here I am. Drink this, now. You're better today." She held out a gourd full of hot soup. He warmed his hands on it and blew through the steam. "You need to keep up your energy, boy."

"What for?"

She smiled slightly, her eyes serious. "For whatever comes along."

"I'd as soon fold up and die," he said.

"No reason to rush your last hour. It'll come soon enough anyway. You're just homesick and tired and a little out of sorts. When you're feeling better all round, you'll see things different. Now, you remember, I'm going to take care of you. Your mama was like my own little sister. So I figure you're the same. Long as I'm around, you'll be watched over." She sat closer to him in the dim light of the cabin. "Tell me a little about Betty. How's she doing?"

Peter looked thoughtfully into his soup. His eyes were cloudy.

"She's good. Works in the kitchen there. Her husband—"

"Husband?"

"Sure. Robert. They have three little children. Two girls. A boy. She's good."

Ruth sighed and smiled, "Oh, I wish I could see her again. Is she as stubborn as ever? She used to be a real fighter, that little Betty. Tough as a woodchuck."

"She's tough all right. But, you know, she's got her religion. Spends a lot of time at that, being good and all."

"Betty? That's sure hard to believe." Ruth laughed a little. "Never thought about the Lord when she was here."

"Well, Robert makes a big thing of it."

"Now isn't that something! How people turn right around and change. She was a fighter, like I say, but not a Christian believer, not Betty. Well, I'm glad to hear that."

"Why?" wondered Peter. "Does it make a difference in people?"

"Oh now, you sound like she did when she was your age. You must be sixteen, right?"

"That's what they say."

"Well, you got a lot of growing to do, and I expect you'll find your way like your mama did."

"Never going to be a believer, unless it's like a Cherokee," said Peter, "not me."

"Well, you wait and see." Ruth stood up and her face grew serious. "Miss Nora, you'll meet her soon, she's our educator in the faith. She won't let you out from under. So be prepared to listen to the Bible."

Peter shrugged, "Oh, that don't bother me, the listening. The words are fine words, I like the way they sound. But that's as far as it goes. They won't let us read anyway."

Ruth watched him swallow the soup in long, slow gulps and tried to preserve a mask of indifference. She took the gourd away and said, "You rest again today. Don't go out. I'll bring you more nourishment later on."

She left him alone again in the dark cabin. Peter was sorry to have her go. She made such a fragile connection with his past, but it was crucial. She was a link. Around him lay nothing but unfamiliar people and places.

From his pallet he could hear the distant sound of children laughing and playing inside in a nearby cabin or outside in the snow. He couldn't tell which, but he wondered how they would treat him when he came out. Would the air ring with jeers and abuses? Would his skin cause them to back away from him? He knew he wasn't white but they didn't and they would despise him.

4

RUTH WAS in the kitchen with Nora. They chopped potatoes, onions, and chunks of mutton for a stew. Outside an early winter twilight spread blue on the fields of snow. A crackling fire kept them warm.

Nora, at thirty-two, was youthful in her appearance. Her fair, slightly freckled skin was only faintly careworn because she adhered to a similar daily diet, outdoor work, and plenty of sleep. She might have been in her mid-twenties. She wore her strawberry-blond hair in a soft bun. Strands always drooped around her cheeks. Her clothes were generally wrinkled and in disarray. Her smiles were slight and quivering, though occasionally her lips spread wide, gaily, and her eyes crinkled.

Ruth now observed her quietly, unable to resist comparing her to Peter. Their coloring was similar, as was a fleeting bewildered expression on both their faces. But the boy had a striking resemblance to his father. He had his stature and his deep-set, small eyes, his square jaw, and even his dreamy expression. What, Ruth wondered, would Nora see when she looked at the boy? Would she be able to disconnect him from his functions and see him, simply, as a familiar child?

"It has all the unnatural quality of a miracle," Ruth mused, "his coming back here like this. What's the opposite of a miracle?"

She would not, herself, be instrumental in giving Nora the knowledge of Peter's identity. For several reasons, she held to this decision.

Ben had been sold away from the farm for losing his temper one day and telling Bart Williams the truth about Nora's baby and his father, Dan McCutcheon. Bart was a well-meaning fellow, but he could never resist gossip or intrigue. So he told Nancy, and Nancy told her mother what she knew. Soon, Ben was gone.

Ruth did not like to interfere with fate. "Standing still is the best way to make things go right," she often said. It would be against her nature to probe Nora's mind, but now she realized that one person might be a big problem if she didn't do something, and that was Tim. As far as he knew, Nora's baby was lying up on the hill, and Betty's baby by him was this sixteen-year-old boy or someone gone forever into the tomb of enslavement. Tim was married now to Sophie, the woman who did the laundry.

"But what if he makes the connection now?" Ruth wondered. "Why, Tim would know it was all a lie! He's not that dumb. At the same time, how could Peter possibly be his?"

She glanced at Nora dropping potato peels in a trash basket. She was humming a little tune from the hymnal she picked up on a Sunday morning in Carthage. Nora was not exactly wild, as others in her family said, but she certainly was an original. Ruth often heard her talking cheerfully to herself, and saw how little she cared for what others thought of her. She wandered around in a petticoat outdoors in the summer, no matter who was around. She wore her brother's cast-off leather boots, untied. Every Sunday her mother had to force her to dress for church. Sometimes she lounged around in the slave cabins with her feet bare, her chemise slipping off her shoulders. She would sit cross-legged on the floor, exposed to her thighs, like one of the farm children. Her parents were ashamed of her. Her uncle often slapped her hard across the face or behind, but it made no difference. Nora was incorrigible, without being either insolent or stupid.

"Daddy said the new boy really is Betty's," she said suddenly. "Minty and Betsy say he's awfully light, like a newborn calf," and she smiled.

"He's light all right," Ruth said quickly, "but those things happen."

"They do? Even when both parents are dark-skinned? I never knew that."

"Maybe both parents weren't dark-skinned," Ruth said. "You never know. Betty was forced into a lot of things."

"But still," Nora said, "if the boy is sixteen, I thought he must have been by Tim."

"Tim? Ha, I doubt it," Ruth said, confused and shaking her head. "But maybe."

"Betty hated being pregnant. But she never told me whose baby it really was. Just how Uncle John was pushing at her to have one. She couldn't stand Wash. So it must've been Tim."

"Well, honey, that was a long time ago, and best forgotten. There are always white men passing through these fields, rough men, but they get the wages because they're white. This is the truth of it. Betty has lost her boy, now, and you can bet she's suffering over that. She must miss him something terrible. I know he misses her, and needs a lot of kindness now."

"Do you think he will leave, since he can get work, with his skin so white? He won't have to stay a slave."

"He might want to stay with his friends more than be free."

"You're right, I guess," said Nora and looked lovingly at Ruth. "I'll try to be real good to him, as soon as I can, so he'll stay. Betty was my best friend. I'll feel privileged to take care of her boy for her."

Ruth squeezed her lips tight together. She couldn't help finding Nora's innocence pitiable, and she resented having to keep her that way.

"I hope, someday, she finds out the truth," she said to herself. "But let it be at the expense of her own folks, and not of ours. That's all I ask."

AT THE FIRST OPPORTUNITY, Ruth went to Mrs. Howard's room to talk about Tim. She wanted to protect him. He had Sophie and their children now, and Ruth wanted to be sure he would not, like Ben, be sold because of his unwitting part in this situation with the white slave boy.

Mrs. Howard was an arthritic. She could barely move around the house. Ruth had to spend many hours soaking her feet in salts and massaging her flaccid limbs. Mrs. Howard spent most of her time propped in an easy chair at the bedroom window, where she did handiwork with her aching fingers. She had never been comfortable with her body or her fate. She had been afflicted when young with a limp and aches. Her family lived in Rhode Island and the men were slavers, sailing from Cuba to Bristol, back and forth, and she met William only when her parents said she could have five slaves for her dowry, if she would just get married to him. They brought him home to meet her and signed her over that very night.

He was a dim but kindly person who brought her, along with Ruth, Betty, Wash, Tim, and Caleb west to Missouri, where they put down their roots and business in farming and timber. It did not suit her.

There she sat, when Ruth entered, but the light was too dim for her to do any work, even by the candle at her side.

"What now?" she said crossly.

"I want to speak with you, please," Ruth said, unperturbed by the woman's mood.

"What about?"

"Tim."

"Oh Lord, what about him?" she sighed.

"Well, you know he's going to think that's his boy who's come here. Peter."

Mrs. Howard changed her position with great difficulty and a moan.

"I hadn't thought of that," she admitted. "How stupid of me. And stupid of the men. We'll have to get rid of him."

"Of who?"

"Of Tim."

"No, ma'am, you can't do that. He's in charge of too much here. The cattle, the livestock, all—"

"Then what do you suggest?"

Ruth moved closer to her, her shoulders straight, her hands on her hips.

"I can get him to keep his mouth shut."

"I thought he was full of gossip and confab."

"No, ma'am, that's Wash. Tim is okay. And he likes it here, wants to stay."

"Well, what about Wash? What does he know?"

"Nothing. Even if he knows Peter is Betty's boy, Wash don't know nothing about time. Or care.... Years. Dates. He's not that kind. Never got help in that area."

"God in heaven!" Mrs. Howard yelped. "I wish we'd never gotten into this! Why didn't we have the boy smothered or something? I'd give anything to get rid of him for good."

"Not his fault that he's here in this world," Ruth said with a bitter smile.

"I don't care whose fault it is. The situation is intolerable. I could kill Nora. Look what trouble she's brought on this house. Having a fling with a Scots Irish itinerant on his way to nowhere."

"That was a long time ago, ma'am."

"Then how did it come back on our doorstep like a rat the cat drug home?" She slapped down the palms of her hands. "I wish we really had buried him up there on the hill. For years I almost believed we had. The shame of it. We lost Betty along with all the rest. And now—look—the bastard boy is back. What if he finds out? What if he wants money, property? Whose child is he anyway? It's Betty's one day, Nora's the next. Maybe it's none of those. Maybe Mr. Collins just gave us a boy that was due to us."

Ruth walked to the door quickly, but Mrs. Howard shouted after her.

"You take care of Tim, then, and soon. Understand? I'll tell John

Howard. What fools, not to think of that. I'll never get a rest, now, knowing this problem's back under my roof. Never. I may have to move over to Bart's house where it's civilized."

Ruth slipped away without looking back. She was not intimidated by Mrs. Howard, but was weary of the need to be both sly and firm when dealing with her. She was, like many tyrants, only able to instill in her servants the ability to be devious. It was nearly impossible to tell her the truth about anything because she was determined to have her point of view prevail. She was a woman who lacked the fortitude to endure the rigors and solitude of pioneer life. Falling in on herself, like her brother-in-law John Howard, she found nothing but anger.

"Haunts of their own making," Ruth sometimes said to herself.

5

As soon as Peter recovered, he was put to work. Wash was instructed to provide him with raw wood and tools. His cabin was turned into a carpentry shop, and he was ordered to construct a new oxen yoke and four chairs.

"Hope you know how to do it," said Wash, "'cause I sure don't know how to prentice you."

"I'll just have to figure it out then," Peter said, not unhappy to have a task that left him alone.

He examined the tools, which had belonged to Ben, and decided he should experiment on a small scale first. He had no paper to draw on, as he remembered Robert doing. But he had watched his father building boxes, tables, fiddles, and chairs, so he had a sense of how to go about it. The tools he had were the simplest, and they were all in a mess, so he organized them, by size, in the rough box in which they came. Wash hung around for a while, watching him with a kind of twisted leer, which indicated his hopes of seeing Peter fail, blunder.

"Go on, get out," Peter told him with such a cold glare that he departed at last.

Peter dreaded his first encounter with the new master and the other slaves. To prepare himself for scoffing and rebuke, he practiced sitting with his head held high, his mind focused elsewhere. If he could not be loved, he could at least be respected, and he had learned ways of coming by that.

When the bell rang Peter ventured to the kitchen. He was at least partially prepared for the teasing that followed. Wash and the children did most of it. Tim and Sophie, a tall silent woman, said nothing, but eyed Peter warily.

"How come he's so white?" asked their little boy, Minty.

"Yeah, how come?" queried his sister.

"Can I feel your hair?" asked a twelve-year-old girl.

"Go right ahead," Peter replied, leaning down to her.

"Leave him alone," Ruth snapped, ladling out thin soup with the help of another girl named Ritta. Ritta was eighteen and married to Caleb, a dark-skinned boy the same age, and as silent as Peter. He sat with his hand over his eyes, his shoulders bent. Peter felt emanations of depression from him. No wonder, he thought, the food was so tasteless and inadequate.

"Peter," said Ruth, "this little mosquito bothering you is my own girl, Charity."

The girl had her hand in Peter's hair and was examining Peter's face curiously. Peter stared back at her, trying to find traces of Ruth in her face. She was a little African but more Indian—a brown-skinned gentle girl with straight black hair, closed lips, and large brown eyes, which, like her mother's eyes, contained a mysterious mixture of flash and melancholy. Peter felt reassured by her and even by the snappy questions of the other children. At least he could deal with their candor—he sat down nearest the smallest.

"Why's he so white, Mama?" little Minty persisted.

"Don't know, son," murmured his mother. "You've seen black sheep. Same difference. Remember that gal Janie who was here, nearly white herself."

"But not all, and how did she get that way anyway?"

Charity, seating herself across from Peter, ignored the question and said, “Miss Nora lets me brush her hair. It’s just like yours, Peter, soft, a little curly. She says I can take care of her when I get to be fourteen. I won’t have to work in the fields then.”

“So ha ha to you,” sneered little Betsy, announcing to the group, “she thinks she’s so great.”

“Hush, children,” said Ruth. “Just finish your soup and hush up.” Passing her daughter’s chair to seat herself at the end of the table, Ruth brushed her hand down Charity’s back tenderly. “Don’t go bragging now about your friendship with Miss Nora. It’s not lucky. A whistling woman and a crowing hen don’t never come to no good end.”

Peter glanced at Charity with a little envy. She, at least, had her mother, and a good strong mother at that. Eating in this strange group made him more homesick than ever, and he could hardly take a sip of the mush in front of him. Cornmeal and the fat of a hog floating on watery grit.

“Sorry, Peter,” said Ruth mildly, “but the food on this farm isn’t fit for a dog—not the food they give us, anyway.”

“It’s not that,” he said, grateful for her attention and conscious of the time she had put into making the soup. He began to drink it quickly.

“Still don’t understand,” grumbled Wash, who had grown soft and sagging with the years, “why the master goes out and asks for trouble. Light-skinned boys *known* to be trouble. Never saw one lighter than this. He can’t belong to Betty. I knew her. Tim knew her too. There’s some monkey business here.”

“Happens sometimes,” said Tim with a knowing glance at Ruth. “Not his fault.”

“But how did Betty pull it off?” Wash continued. “She wasn’t all that light.”

“She might have been half white, for all we know,” said Tim. “Put another whole white in and that’s what you get.”

“But what white?” Wash persisted. “No one but the family was white here then, and that fella Nora had. He didn’t need another. Master John, now, I wonder, he’s so crazy.”

“Let’s not talk about poor Betty,” said Ruth. “I want you to tell me, Peter, if you need anything out there in your cabin.”

“Just some paper, and something to write with.”

“He writes?” asked Wash.

“No. I just need something to draw on for the chairs and the yoke.”

“I’ll see what I can muster up,” Ruth said.

At that moment John Howard entered the kitchen in stocking feet and a Stetson. He was eating a leg of mutton. His lips were greasy. “So, boy,” he snapped at Peter, “you up and around now?”

Peter said nothing.

“You got your chores cut out till the weather clears. Guess Wash did all of that.”

“I did, sir,” said Wash.

Ruth spoke up. “Peter needs something to draw with. You know how Ben always did it that way, too.”

“So give him Ben’s old tablet out from the shed,” said the boss.

He dropped his gnawed mutton leg on the table in front of Charity and looked down at her.

“Lookin’ more Injun every day,” he muttered. “Them savages attacked a wagon train few miles north of here. Beat and scalped the whole crew. One fellow murdered. Can’t feel safe even in a blizzard.”

Then he glared at Peter. “You folks think this boy is funny looking?” No one answered. “Well, forget it. He’s one of you, whether you like it or not. You can tell by the way he slops his soup around what kind of stock he comes from. Betty never had manners. Slut.”

Peter put down his spoon and gazed coolly at John Howard. The boss was a type he could spot; he had run into such men around the Collins plantation. They were usually overseers, but sometimes visitors, like mountain men who hated the human race. Peter dreaded that kind. Having one for a master would take all his attention. The little red veins on the man's nose and brow were clues and signs of his drinking to Peter.

John Howard squinted back at Peter, shifted his gaze, and grinned at Wash.

"Well, Wash, you were right. This boy has got some learning to do."

Chuckling, he left the kitchen. Peter glanced at Ruth, who tapped her temple quickly and whispered, "Master's a little tetched." Everyone smiled. Even the gloomy Caleb smiled into his lap. "Don't worry overly about him," she assured Peter. "His bark's bigger than his bite, though he's given to the whip, when he loses his voice."

"Shh," Tim said suddenly at the sound of footsteps.

It was Nora. Cautiously, curiously, she entered, clutching a red shawl around her shoulders, her hair loose and uncombed. She stared at Peter. She rested her hands on Ruth's chair, and smiled.

"I am so pleased to make your acquaintance, Peter," she said. "I hope you're feeling all well?"

"Thank you, ma'am."

"Isn't he good-looking?!" Nora exclaimed, as she leaned down to Ruth. "Betty must be real proud. I knew your mama real well, Peter. She was my best friend in the whole world. Tell me. Is she happy?"

"Mama's good, far as I know."

Ruth urged Nora to sit down, but Nora drifted around the table and cleared away the dishes. She stole looks at Peter. He could tell by the way the children relaxed in her company that they trusted her. It was as if there wasn't a white person in the room. More like a friendly dog.

"Why," said Nora to Peter, directly, "I can't believe you're sixteen years old. You look older, maybe eighteen. And nothing like Betty. Isn't that something? I remember when she was carrying you, just like it was yesterday."

Peter nodded politely, but couldn't look her in the eye.

"We were carrying at the same time," Nora went on, "but Betty always kept her secrets from me. We were like sisters, but I was the one who did all the talking about that sort of thing. She held her tongue. Or else I was so selfish I never thought to ask. Could have been that, too."

"Don't be putting yourself down, Nora," Ruth said. "Memory plays mean tricks. Betty got her piece in, don't you worry."

Peter watched Nora with a mixture of suspicion and admiration. Never had he encountered a white woman so familiar with the help. He tried to give some ulterior motive to it, but there was a quality of innocence about Nora that made malicious intent seem impossible. He realized he was judging her in much the same way others judged him, as being too strange to be trusted.

"There's a lot I don't remember," Nora said, "a whole lot. I often think what a person forgets is what belongs to God. My uncle had it out for Betty from day one. Pinching, prodding, pushing. I do remember that."

Wash, Tim, Caleb, and Peter now rose from the table and began bundling up in scarves and jackets to return to their tasks. Peter followed quickly, conscious of Nora's gaze fixed on him; it made him awkward.

She said, "I'll be out to visit you later, Peter."

Peter departed for the cold, urging Wash to supply him with Ben's writing equipment so he could get to work at once. The snow had a solid crust on top now, and was powdery under. The bare black trees pressed their branches against the skyline. Peter shuddered, letting his gaze wander across the desolate scene, when he caught sight of one flash of color over by the row of slate-gray headstones on the hill. It was red.

"What's that?" he asked Wash from behind.

"Oh, that's Miss Nora's doing. Every day, round about now, she goes out there to where her baby was buried and ties up that red ribbon. Nearly every night it gets blown apart. She don't give up. When the weather warms, she'll tend flowers up there. She's a little off like her uncle."

Peter shuddered. The story was so weird and Nora so unusual. He had never had much sympathy for someone white. Only when he was thrown into new circumstances did he remember his own complexion, and then it was like remembering that he was going to die. The rest of the time he could believe he was dark. After all, he couldn't see his own face, only glimpses of it in the river or the bucket.

There was one time he thought he saw the face of John Howard wobbling inside his own face in the water, and he jumped back and let out a shout of horror. What if that man was his father? What if he had raped his mother Betty? He wanted to be sick. He even confided the thought to Ruth who thankfully let out a hoot of laughter and shook her head violently, "No, no, no, Peter. Never that."

For some reason he could not help being drawn to Nora, especially with this story, as a pitiable woman faithful to a lost child. At the same time, there was some ice in his heart. After all, she called his own mother, Betty, "her best friend in the world," but then had allowed her to be sold. What hypocrisy!

It was easy, Peter figured, to be faithful to a grave; but to a slave not so easy.

"Don't be fooled," he told himself, "into thinking this woman is different from the others. If the lines are ever drawn, you know which side she'll be on."

6

PETER SETTLED into work as a carpenter and did the best he could. Trial by error was the normal course of his day, but fortunately no one checked regularly on his performance. Only Nora made visits to his cabin, after those she made to the others, when she gave religious instruction. Almost every day around four, she came to Peter's cabin, at first mildly reproving him for his lack of interest in religion, but then just to talk. Peter anticipated her visits and cautiously waited for her.

She would stand at the door, hugging her cloak around her, and comment on his orderliness. Although his cabin was hardly more than a carpentry shop, Peter managed to sweep away all traces of sawdust every evening and to hang the tools on pegs in an immaculate arrangement. Nora often mentioned Ben. She browsed through the drawings he had made in his tablet and, sighing, said she missed him. Peter told her he was learning from Ben's woodwork and would keep improving on it.

By mid-February the snow began to melt soon after it fell, and Peter remembered that there were such things as green and spring. Nora spoke of the ground thaw frequently, as she stood by his door. The presence of the snow was like a personal abuse for her.

"It makes me feel like I'm buried alive," she told Peter, "or at least really old, but I don't want to bother you with my talk."

Peter self-consciously continued working and listened to what she said, waiting for her to reveal some fatal flaw.

"When the snow melts," she said, "and the trout are running in the river, the boys always go fishing. So you'd better make yourself a pole. You'll need the extra nourishment, growing like you are and the food so scanty here. I can hardly believe you're only sixteen! So many muscles on you."

Peter looked down, embarrassed, at the earthen floor and breathed deeply. In her presence, he often became tongue-tied and his gestures slowed down.

"I want to be sure you get the right food in you, and enough rest," she told him. "If you get sick again, I don't know what I'll do."

"Yes, ma'am."

"Please don't ever act like you're lower than me, Peter," she pleaded. "Your mama never did. She and I were like blood sisters. Even if you haven't got the freedom I have, and that's not much, it doesn't mean you have to be scared of me."

She sighed from her place at the door. He felt embarrassed by her interest in him, no matter how hard she tried to reassure him.

She seemed to be frustrated by all that he said and did. Still she was drawn back again and again to see him.

"It's a shame," she seemed to be saying, "that you had to come work at such a poor farm, a farm without a future. My brothers care nothing for the land."

Sometimes she looked at him in a way that reminded him of Collins, and he was frightened. The part of him that Collins had damaged was still sensitive, and all it took to feel the pain was for a white person to show special interest in him. No matter what admiration and even affection glowed in her face when she looked at him, to him it was repugnant. He felt he had to be on guard.

"I can see you get along with the children," Nora said. "From my window I've watched you playing with them. I love children too. You know, Peter, you're the same age as my poor boy would be, if he had lived. Just about exactly the same."

She drifted away, leaving Peter alone and perplexed. Maybe, he reasoned, her interest in him was tied up with the baby she had lost, his being the same age. Maybe it was that innocent. He talked to Ruth about it, and Ruth said yes, it was just that, no more.

Ruth was not what she seemed to be. On the surface she was the stoic housekeeper, doing kitchen work, as well as tending to Mrs. Howard's ailments. On the surface she was, like Betty, a churchgoing woman, one who had absorbed the information about Christian teaching, which would make her more obedient than ever. But when Peter got to know her better, he discovered she was not so simple. She had not given in to enslavement; she was biding her time. Charity kept repeating this, with her solemn little face turned down, listening with her whole body.

"Me and Charity are going to be free," Ruth told Peter. "If not me, Charity anyway."

"How you going to arrange that?" Peter asked her.

"I've got schemes. Miss Nora might be our ticket to freedom."

"That so."

"She's weak-hearted, I know," Ruth said. She was sewing in her cabin by candlelight and Charity watched beside her. "But sometimes it's just those kind of people who make a path for others, stronger ones."

"Maybe. But she makes me feel like a dog sometimes, weak as she might be."

"Nothing wrong with dogs," said Charity, an animal lover. "Don't talk bad about dogs. . . . Goats, cows, pigs neither."

Peter smiled at her. She reminded him of his sister Georgia. She was silly one minute and moody the next, but she had her mother's powers of concentration and endurance. She was given various household tasks, which she performed quietly and carefully with her temper under control.

"If you want," Ruth said suddenly, out of deep thought, "I'll ask Miss Nora to leave you alone, Peter."

He looked at Ruth curiously, sensing that this suggestion came from a mysterious direction; he said nothing.

"Master John says she hangs around with us folks too much," Charity put in. "He's always at her about that."

"If it wasn't that, it'd be something else," said Ruth, "He won't be happy till that poor girl is married or buried."

"But she's his own flesh and blood," said Peter. "Can't she do what she wants? After all, she's one of them."

"Don't matter," Charity said smugly, "she shamed the family when she had that baby."

"You be quiet," Ruth said quickly. "That's enough talk about Nora." She snapped the thread in her teeth as if to emphasize the fact that the conversation was over, but Charity grinned proudly at Peter for having told him the bold truth.

7

THE SPRING was surprisingly early after the hard winter. The air filled with birdsong, and crocuses bloomed early in March. The bull was let loose on the cows in the pasture. The mares got fat. Baby lambs were the first to be born. The mill that Will Howard had constructed years before was broken down and abandoned by the riverside; it was a failure. Since John Howard had gone strange in the head, it was up to Will to take the livestock to market, and it was not in his nature to be an aggressive buyer or seller. He got cheated, again and again.

They grew tobacco and a small amount of corn. But the crops were never entirely successful, planted too soon or too late, left to grow too dry or too wet. Only Nora's small vegetable garden fared well each year. The Howards were not good farmers; they blamed their failures on the weather.

When the land grew warm, the farm turned into a battlefield. Peter was taken away from his carpentry and sent out to the fields to drive a team of oxen across the soggy fields, turning up stones. There was no overseer, only John Howard, shouting abuses and instructions from under his Stetson and waving a whip like a lion tamer. Caleb worked in the fields with Peter, as did the children who were old enough. Wash and Tim took care of the livestock. Caleb's motions were slow, weighed down with affliction. He was subject to many lashes, and his wife watched his beatings from the laundry house, her face contorted with grief. He was obviously sick, coughing and spitting blood when no white person could see.

The mysterious blindness that infected white people showed up when they thought about the people working outside. Caleb taught Peter a great deal about the rituals of planting and harvesting, about the stars too, the way they moved into each season, and which ones stayed close to the horizon.

Caleb could read the sky, the clouds, and the shadows as if they were living presences with intentions and plans. He collaborated with the natural world, and had a scientist's grasp of the holistic. No one in the Howard family, not one of them, knew this about Caleb, and they knew nothing of Tim, but left him at the level of his children, as someone to be used and laughed at. He liked to clown, but when he was alone with his family and friends he pulled out his two-stringed harp and played a complicated and melancholy set of songs. Who knew this? Not Nora or anyone else in her family. Genius was kept secret for good reason. White people could even steal that.

As the weather warmed and the pale green leaves abounded, Peter grew increasingly angry and frustrated. Shades of his earlier rage returned, as he watched Caleb beaten by the little man shaped like a mushroom, and saw the relentless poverty and failure of his master's farm work. He wanted to contribute to the Howards' ruin, undermine the whole effort, plant stones instead of seeds, piss in the milk pails, break eggs. But he kept on working with his teeth clenched. He grew familiar with the stones, ruts, tufts of green and wanted the crops to be healthy for their own sakes. He watched the trees and took care of them as if they were his own.

The only times there was camaraderie among slaves and masters on the farm was when a group of Indians moved down the hillside on horses, carrying coup sticks and arrows. They looked as alien and fearful to the people watching as would visitors from outer space. Everyone on the farm would move close, and watch and wait in terror, until the group had passed along.

The other times of camaraderie came when Bart Williams arrived for a visit. Robust and smiling as he rode on his shining piebald, he exuded the good nature that accompanies prosperity, fulfillment, and good luck. Then, too, John and Will Howard would drop their attitudes toward the slaves and move in close to them, blending with them in the consciousness of their economic failure. They would stand together in a band in the wreckage, watching Bart, wisecracking and warm, swing around them on his horse. Then it was almost as if they were one family, slaves and masters, or like a clan that could never be torn asunder.

NORA COULDN'T HELP HERSELF. She was fixated on Peter from the moment she saw him. Concealed, she watched him from her bedroom window. He plowed at a distance, hunched forward, stripped to the waist. His blond hair was stuck to his sweat. She couldn't bear the way he treated her. She couldn't stand his manners, which were those of a servant and therefore excluded her. He was colored white, yet she couldn't reach out to him on an equal basis. She would have irrational moments when she blamed the inequality on him, and in the process of realizing her mistake, she would come face to face with the evil of owning other people.

What could she do to help him? That was her single desire, to reach out and pluck him up and remake him as a free person. The first reason for this was her instant attraction to his physical type; he looked the way she liked a man to look. The second reason was her perception of his strength and intelligence. He should be able to read, write, and exert his character freely. He was young and filled with potential. But what could she do? She was forbidden to teach the slaves to read. She was trapped and powerless in a domestic structure, which, as long as she occupied it, insisted she abide by its rules.

Looking at Peter, Nora was forced to face the historical process that produced him. In their late teens, her brothers had laughed and talked freely about slave girls as sexual objects. It would only take one step beyond laughter to produce Peter. Facing these facts filled Nora with revulsion. She felt the bond of sisterhood, crossing social and racial lines, without having the words to express it.

For all her innocence, and perhaps because of its resulting in catastrophe, Nora had a mind of her own. She did not accept her mother's interpretation of her own child dying as an act of God's will. She didn't, herself, believe in such a cruel, or even personal, God, but focused her attention on the teachings. She forgave herself for having been so free with Dan, because she still thought of it as an act of love. Her intentions had been pure. She was not so sure about his. Dan had never, as far as she knew, had the will to claim her. He had been, like most of the boys and men she knew, remarkably sure of himself.

Whoever violated Betty, the results were as tragic for her as they were for Nora when she lost her baby. Betty had raised and loved Peter and he had been ripped away from her because of them both being property. *Look at him out there*, she would inwardly exclaim, *that's a boy who should be learning, who should be free!*

Often he reminded her of something or someone and she believed she must have dreamed his face before he came. His face and body seemed strangely familiar, and so easy to love that she was embarrassed. At those moments, her mind whirled in spirals around the question of his parenthood. Who was his father, whom he must resemble exactly, since he didn't look at all like Betty? Could it be one of her brothers? Could it be John Howard, her uncle? She had heard about incest, rape, and the kidnapping of young girls for sex. Her brothers told her a lot. But every time she asked this question about Peter, it curved inward, leading nowhere, and her mind became confused. She literally couldn't think about it rationally. She would end up saying, "Oh well, what does it matter," or "It'll come to me, sooner or later."

8

ONE EVENING AT DUSK Nora walked out to the field where her father walked, leading his cattle into the barn. Only a dozen spotted cows moved lazily over the soft ground, dappled with shadows. He was, as always, hatless. Over the years his body had become gnarled, his legs severely bowed, and his shoulders hunched in so his backbone stuck out under his worn shirt. His face was a myriad of lines, his eyes hidden and watery. He smiled briefly at Nora, as she fell into step beside him.

"Well, Daddy, what do you think of the new boy?" she asked. "You're gone so much these days, I never got a chance to ask you."

"Got to take off again tomorrow," he said.

"Uncle John is horrible to him."

"Who?"

"The boy, Peter."

"Oh well. You know John."

"But he specially doesn't like this one."

"Lots of people getting pesky these days, with the slaves. Lots of people. Whether we should have 'em or not, seems to be a big question these days. Hear about it in town. It's all the talk. Missouri and slaves."

"That so? But why does Uncle John have to be so mean to this one?"

"You got a special fondness for the boy?" asked her father.

"I feel sorry for him because of his pallor, I guess. People pick on him for that."

"Well, he seems tough enough to handle it."

"How do you think he got so white?" she asked.

Her father shrugged, looking back at his cattle, and narrowing his eyes. "Happens sometimes. Throwback it's called."

"But back to where? I mean Betty must've picked him up from someone around here."

"Oh, probably one of those mountain men, coming in, it's not as if you didn't know that kind," he said and quickened his pace, entering the dung-thick barn.

Nora stood behind, letting the cows lumber past her. Her bare toes squeezed at the mud. The earth felt insecure as did her own gravity on it. Clouds moving like dark hands over the blue gave the treeline the look of moving objects. The huge and aimless earth was turning with her, so small, upon it.

She had heard her father and uncle talking about Northern abolitionists, Jayhawkers, and the issue of free soil. They read the newspaper, they had opinions. But none of it seemed real or important to Nora, whose mother called those issues "men's problems."

Now that she was forming an opinion of her own, in regard to Peter, she was frightened. Knowledge and action might become inseparable someday, especially if hordes of anonymous others were forming opinions like hers, but she didn't like that idea. She strode across the muddy meadow to the hillside, where the slate stone covered the ground with a square shadow the size of a fiddle box.

HER MOTHER THOUGHT that Nora was losing her mind. She seemed to be lost in a world of her own, and, worst of all, completely obsessed with Peter.

"Why in God's name did we ever bring him back?" Mrs. Howard would wail.

Nancy would try to console her mother, telling her that Nora was getting comfort from Peter. "Besides, we needed his help over here."

"You can't change our Nora, Ma," Nancy continued. "She's not a girl anymore. Better live with it, if you can, and let her spend her time out back."

"It's God's judgment on me," Mrs. Howard moaned, "for lying, for selling the boy away in the first place."

"Well, it's too late to do anything about that," Nancy said firmly. "Peter is pulling the farm together, and that's what you wanted. My brothers let you down."

Mrs. Howard leaned forward, lowering her voice to a hiss, her hands tight on the arms of her chair. "What if she fancies she's in love with him?"

"Ma!" cried Nancy, appalled.

"Well? Someone better speak the truth now."

"How could you say such a thing?" Nancy backed away from her mother. "He's just a boy. He's a child! She's not that crazy."

"Your sister, my dear, is completely lost to us. Her behavior is a disgrace now, as it always has been. I wish she would up and disappear. Yes, I do. Disappear. And we could make that happen, if we put our minds to it."

"Ma. You already did that once!"

Nancy slammed out of her mother's bedroom, aghast. Her mother had always been able to shock her, and it wasn't easy having a mother who could do that. Nora was eccentric, but not really shocking, and not ever cruel. Her peculiarities ran in the direction of excessive shyness, kindness, and a kind of innocence that was almost stupidity. But Mrs. Howard was verbally fearless. Nancy always went back to her own home and counted her blessings.

Now she looked for her sister where she knew she would find her at this hour—out in the slave quarters with the little ones. There was a chill in the air with the autumn upon the hills. Red and yellow leaves littered the ground. Chickens ran squawking from left to right as Nancy walked toward Caleb's cabin, where the instruction was always held.

Nancy paused outside the door and listened. She could hear the querulous voices of children and Nora's responses, relating to some parable from the New Testament.

"Why did Jesus ask to get himself killed?" asked a little voice.

"He didn't exactly ask for it," Nora replied, "but he knew he must fulfill the prophecy."

"Wasn't he scared?"

"Sure, he was a little, I guess. But he didn't think of himself all the time like we folks do. Sometimes, if you can forget about yourself, you lose your fear and feel happy."

"Let's sing," someone suggested eagerly.

Nora started the singing immediately in a high wistful voice, soon lost in the louder discordant voices of the children.

Nancy opened the door and quietly stepped inside the dark cabin. The group was huddled on the floor near the fire. Nora glanced at her and went on singing, crouched near the heat, Indian fashion, with her stocking knees exposed and her hair loose.

Nancy watched her sister with an expression of pity. Although Nora was older than she, Nancy often felt the opposite. She could see why her mother was so distressed. From her vantage point of a happy marriage, reasonable affluence, and children, Nancy saw that she had done what a girl was supposed to do, and she had done it right. This gave her a sense of superiority over Nora, but it was limited superiority.

As soon as the children had run off to the kitchen to eat, Nancy stopped Nora. "Why don't you come spend a few days over on the farm with us?" she asked. "I will ask Bart if that's okay."

"Oh, I can't do that," Nora said, leaning out the cabin door and peering around, as if for someone special.

"Well, why not?"

"I have to take care of things here."

"Come on. A few days won't matter."

"No, thanks, but I just can't."

"You scared to leave home, Nora?"

"Lord, no! I've just got my duties, like you have yours. That's all. They might be different, but they're the same."

Nancy sighed and stared at her sister's face for some sign that would explain her. "You're real pretty, Nora, you know. I bet we could find you a nice man."

Nora looked at Nancy with such amazement and revulsion that Nancy started to walk away at once.

Nora did not follow her, but went instead to Peter's cabin. The dusk was thin and cold, a smell of firewood burning high in the air. Nora knocked.

"Come in, Miss Nora," said Peter.

She entered with a smile and shut the door behind her. Peter was working on his knees on the floor. A candle was beside him. He was rubbing rosin on the bow of his fiddle. He didn't look up. Nora stood over him and looked at him with tenderness in her eyes. The nape of his neck, where his hair curled, was curved and smooth, and she put her hand there. He stiffened slightly and went on working. She frequently touched him, while talking to him, but he never got used to it. Nora idly played with his curls and her skirt brushed his back.

"Did you have a good day today?" she asked him.

"Just fine."

"Did Uncle John give you any trouble?"

"Just shouts and threats, the usual."

"I keep telling him to leave you alone."

"Well, he's got a mind of his own."

"You homesick tonight?"

Nora squatted down beside him, peering into his face. She couldn't get over how familiar and lovable he seemed to her sometimes.

"Not much," he said.

"Autumn makes people sad sometimes," she said. "I keep thinking of the people I've lost this time of year."

"Well, whoever I've lost, I'll find again. You can be sure of that."

"I know, and believe me I pray every night that you'll get everything you want. Everything."

He gave her a quick and probing look. Nora in the firelight looked young and pretty. But he found her words and behavior fathomless. He couldn't trust what he didn't understand; he couldn't trust someone who didn't understand him. She never seemed to notice his reactions, which were full of anxiety and withdrawal. Instead she had abandoned the usual habits of reserve and condescension a white person develops with a slave. What replaced those habits was still not human understanding.

"I have an idea," she told him. "I'm going to write a letter to Betty and tell her all about you. You say her husband can read?"

"A little."

"Then I'll do it." She beamed and placed her hand on his. "I'll tell her how fine you are."

"Thank you," nodding, "Miss Nora."

He placed his bow neatly in the box on top of his fiddle and closed the cover. His gestures were slow and careful. Then he stood up and Nora followed. She glanced around his small tidy cabin.

"Oh, Peter, I wish you lived in a big house! A beautiful house."

He said nothing, but shoved the fire with the toe of his rough shoe.

She gazed at him, lingering over every detail of his person. Larger than she by a few inches, he was broad and muscular, but his face was still boyish in its contours. Briefly, she thought she knew his identity, his father. It was like a tune on the tip of the tongue, an intimation of something known. But then he turned with his head bowed and said, "Guess it's time to eat," in a slow low voice that scattered her memory. Drawing close to him, she placed her hands on his arms.

"Stand up straight, Peter. Don't hunch over."

Recoiling slightly, he did so. He was instantly reminded of Collins.

At that moment, his door banged open and John Howard stood framed by darkness. He was breathing so hard, it was like the rush of leaves across a hard floor.

He could hardly speak, but he managed to blurt out Nora's name and point outside at the same time. Bewildered, Nora followed his direction and he gave her a rough shove outside. Pointing at Peter, he said, "You'll feel this tomorrow, boy, you'll feel it right through."

Peter could hear Nora's questioning voice outside, as John Howard banged away into the dusk. Loose in all his limbs and trembling, he stood still inside his cabin.

He had not been whipped yet on this farm. The threats had come and gone without fruition, a normal part of the working day. This was not normal, and Peter was filled with dread. He didn't fear pain, but the rage it would draw out of him, a rage he had buried in concentrated labor or homesickness. He was scared to feel such anger again. One small burn applied to his spirit could produce an explosion beyond his control. If John Howard began to flail him, he knew he would react. He could handle the verbal abuses, but the physical were too reminiscent of his past.

Unconsciously he rubbed the thick scar on his left cheek. He could hear the voices of the other folks outside moving toward the big house for the evening meal. The voices were low, emotionless. Peter drew several deep breaths in an effort to restore his equilibrium, control his trembling. Maybe, he reasoned, it was another empty threat and he would be spared the anger he dreaded in himself.

What had happened, after all?

Nora had been caught alone with him, and this was an unthinkable situation for an inferior to be in. It was simple, and Peter understood what the overtones meant. If there was a sinister sexual plane to her friendship with him, he would be the one to blame. He had heard the saying that if there was one thing lower than a black man it was a white woman who couples with him.

Going outside to follow the others to the table, he glanced automatically at the room where he knew Nora resided. A candle flickered there. His feelings for her were more confused than ever. Suspicion and even hostility loomed large in his imagination, as he thought of her in there, and he wished she would just leave him alone. For an instant, he almost hated her.

Then there was something else, underneath all of that, which he tried to bury like a precious stone in a dark mine. That was some strange sense of recognition, which he couldn't explain to himself, which made him sometimes steal looks at her. It was in her looks, her face, her eyes that he saw reflected an impossibly familiar image. A fleeting expression would cross her features and remind him of someone else, just as a passing fragrance from the earth will whirl a person to another, forgotten time and place.

This sense of recognition prevented him from classifying her with the other Howards. He knew he could drive her from his cabin permanently if he just said the right words. She was prepared to do whatever he wanted her to do. But he kept thinking he might one night understand who she was and be satisfied. She might remind him of Collins. He might completely withdraw at last from her approaches. He might wholly hate her in the end, but until then, he had to try to understand her.

“She took a terrible beating,” Ruth whispered to him in the kitchen. “Poor Miss Nora. She took your beating for you.”

“Yeah,” Charity said loudly and angrily, “that poor Nora was punched, knocked, and swatted all around this room. It makes me sick.”

9

THAT YEAR there was no corn-shucking feast. The harvest intake was scant. Stalks hung brown and broken in the fields. The air was cold, and Nora worked in the attic, day after day, making clothes for the winter. She had sworn not to see Peter alone again, and John Howard, satisfied by this promise and the anger expelled in hitting her, did not whip Peter. It was easier for him to wound a woman than a man.

Not only his niece received his slaps. Doing housework or helping her mother, thirteen-year-old Charity often had occasion to meet John Howard in the hall or on the stairs, and he always found fault with her.

“Move along, move along,” he would snap and hit her on the behind.

Sometimes he would tell her she made his bed all wrong or folded his shirt so it was wrinkled, and then he yanked her straight black hair or whacked her cheek with the back of his hand. She was the object of his wrath only because she was more available than the others and because she was a girl.

“Come spring, I’m sending your ma over to Bart’s place,” he told her more than once, “and you’ll have charge of the kitchen. Better get ready, wench, better get yourself in shape.”

Charity was tall, slender, and serious. She received his abuses with a maddening grace. Her face was the face of a thinker, contemplative and a little sad. She was known to be intelligent and witty and was therefore forbidden to learn more than the most menial tasks. To

John Howard she looked dangerous, because she was quick but quiet. "Those Injuns always look sad about something," he told his brother.

Sometimes he caught Charity smiling to herself at some private joke, and he flew into a rage, saying he would wipe that smile off her face. When he did so with the back of his hand she never uttered a sound of protest or cried, but stared straight ahead.

Charity had been promised one thing by her mother, since she was old enough to talk: her freedom. Over and over Ruth had vowed that she would get her away from this house and these people, come hell or high water, before she herself went to her grave.

"Wait and see. I'll work it out," Ruth swore to her.

She also praised Charity for her brains and her beauty, so that the girl had a sustaining awareness of her own powers. This awareness infuriated John Howard, who hardly trusted the most self-deprecating hand on the farm.

Only Ruth, upon whom he leaned heavily, was worthy of respect. He liked Ruth for her "mannishness," as he put it. She had emptied herself, it appeared to him, of all sensuality or longing or "female stupidities." When she gave birth to Charity, and she never mentioned who the father was, the spirit of her sex departed from her, too, and John Howard was glad to see it go.

"Nothing like a man in the kitchen," he liked to say of Ruth at the oven.

His instincts were correct at some base level. Without an exertion of willpower, Ruth long ago had dispensed of any personal desire. She was happier alone than with anyone except Charity. She performed her tasks with her character bottled and corked. She amused herself with silent thoughts and observations, and lived close to the spirit of objects and weather, so that the word "loneliness" had no meaning for her.

But Charity was young, and rounding out in her body now. Despite her self-control, she felt uneven emotions, one in particular.

She loved Peter. Love, with all its appetite and hunger, made her suffer. He was the only eligible candidate for her attention on the whole farm, being the only single boy of the right age. But that was irrelevant, just one of the many facts about his presence that to her added up to the miraculous. It seemed to her that he was only here, on the farm, so that she might love him. He was a blessing vouchsafed to her.

But the blessing was immersed in pain. He didn't notice her in the right way. He didn't return her interest. He treated her as a little sister—teasing, friendly, but casual.

To Charity, he only had eyes for Nora. She was eaten up inside with jealousy and confusion. She watched them quietly, and no one, not even Ruth, knew anything about her feelings. She knew she was too young for him, but wondered if she was too dark for him, too. Wasn't his white skin the reason for his attraction to Nora?

Nora had the pale skin that Peter had. No color there, thought Charity. The age difference didn't matter. If Nora was older than Peter by many years, she was also a free woman, educated and white. Charity jealously watched him with Nora and saw that they were drawn to each other, that they sometimes stole meetings when the master was out of range.

Charity had always liked Nora and looked forward to her reading and conversation. Nora had been the only one on the farm who had recognized her intelligence and had spoken straight to her. As a young child growing up, Charity had been Nora's favorite, and they would spend time alone together, in the attic or in Nora's bedroom, talking and laughing. Nora taught the girl how to weave and sew, and often they did each other's hair. But she never taught her or Peter how to read.

There had been no change in Nora's attention to Charity since Peter's arrival. Everything went on between them as before on the surface. But Charity now gave complex interpretations to all that Nora said and did; she judged her and gave an almost supernatural significance to Nora's every move. Nora's whiteness was the worst.

Charity had no reason on earth to find white people attractive or safe company.

Soon Nora began to seem full of power and intention. It seemed to Charity that Nora talked about Peter incessantly. Charity responded to all questions about him in half-sentences, burning. Nora was becoming, in her eyes, a dangerous stranger. Her white skin and mannerisms, which before were so familiar and thus invisible to Charity, were now her most prominent features.

Charity was still in some ways very young. She liked to play marbles, jump rope, invent ring games and songs, and lie on her back and watch the clouds. She had a few hours a week of childish oblivion. But then, like a shift in the temperature with the coming of night, her whole mood would change, and she would have to assume a falsely placid mask to conceal her feelings.

Sometimes she saw Nora and Peter climbing the hillside to linger over the grave of Nora's baby. She saw Nora slip inside his cabin several times after night classes with the children, in spite of her promise not to do so. Worst of all, she had to sit in a corner when Nora came to Ruth's cabin on evenings when she knew she would find Peter there. Then Charity would sit, locked up with her own jealousy, while the three—Peter, Nora, and Ruth—talked about Betty and the old days before Charity was born. Those evenings she seethed inside and was filled with hatred for Nora.

As she saw it, Peter had come to visit her and her mother Ruth. Nora interfered and Charity was furious. This was their cabin. They were surrounded by and at the mercy of the Howards. Nora was white and free, and she had no right to force her liberty on their few minutes of peace before sleeping.

"I wish she'd just keep to the big house where she belongs," she blurted out to Ruth one night after Nora and Peter were gone.

"She has nothing to do there, child, she's lonely."

"Well, it's her own fault. Why doesn't she get married or something?"

"What's wrong with you, Charity?" Ruth said crossly. "You sound like old Mrs. Howard. Squawk, squawk."

"I'm only saying what Miss Nancy says, too. She should get married and move away from home."

Ruth gave her daughter a penetrating stare. "What's really on your mind?"

"She's going to get in trouble with Master John, the way she sneaks around Peter all the time."

"Well, you might be right about that."

"Or else she'll get Peter in a heap of trouble, and they'll sell him away."

"Peter can't say no. She's the mistress. Not his fault if she comes after him."

"Then you tell her to leave him alone."

Ruth did not reply, but blew out her candle. She couldn't see Charity through the darkness, folded up on her mattress on the floor. She assumed Charity's concern for Peter was based on his being a kind of adopted brother to her. It didn't occur to her that her daughter was in love any more than she would imagine her growing wings there in the darkness.

THE FIRST WINTER SNOW came shortly after Thanksgiving, and the pace of life on the ranch changed radically. Contact between the slaves and the Howards diminished. Swathed in snow, the row of cabins became a world of its own. For those enslaved, the bitter cold was a misery, but the drop in work time was compensation. What was left of the livestock still had to be tended and wood carried to and fro; the big house had to be cleaned, the laundry done; but even these working people had several hours, daily, in winter, closed in on themselves.

The food situation was so drastic that winter that Mrs. Howard moved to Nancy and Bart's plantation for the duration of it. John

Howard ate little and drank heavily instead. Will traveled when the weather permitted. Nora was often alone. She lost weight, as did everyone on the farm, given the modest diet that year.

Bart and Nancy arranged a family reunion at Christmas, so that everyone, slaves included, could have a feast. The Howard boys were expected to visit for a few days with their wives and children. The eldest girl, Jeannie, all the way in St. Louis, could not come. Nora only agreed to go because all of them on the farm were going.

"I wouldn't dream of going otherwise," she told Ruth.

"Well, why not? You need to take a trip once in awhile, see some new faces."

"You know how I feel about my brothers," said Nora, frowning. "I think I'll spend all my time in the cookhouse with you folks."

"Don't be like that, now," Ruth said. "Your brothers want to see you. Now I have to go out and tend to Caleb."

"What's wrong?"

"He's real sick."

"I'll come too."

"No. You just stay here."

"I want to see him. I'll read to him. Does he need more coverings?"

"Get him an extra blanket," Ruth said.

She went ahead of Nora across the icy ground. She carried a bowl of hot thin soup, containing one lump of beef, and the steam blew around in the icy air. Caleb was lying on the floor, his wife beside him. He was emaciated, ashen, his rich color drained away. He coughed in dry high hacks and spat blood into a rag. His eyes were yellow and moist.

"Where's the children?" Ruth asked Ritta.

"Charity's got them." She gave Ruth a deep melancholy look. Her hand rested on her husband's thin shoulder.

"Lift him up. I'll try to feed him."

"Why bother?" Ritta said.

"He needs food."

"He don't want it."

"Caleb," Ruth said, leaning down to him, "sit up, boy, and drink some hot soup."

The soup was boiled water with chicken fat floating on top. Right away she could see from the weight of silence in his eyes that he was dying and food was the last thing on his mind. His mouth was parched and swollen. Ruth just put her finger in the warm soup and ran it over his lips to moisten them. Blood was dried in the corners of his mouth, and she cleaned it away. Ritta had dropped aside, head bowed.

Although a fire burned in the corner, icy slats of wind entered the cabin through the wooden walls. Then Nora entered in a draft of cold air, carrying a blanket and her Bible. She went to Caleb at once and covered him. Her eyes absorbed the information on his face. She sat down by his knees and opened the book to read to him from the Psalms.

Caleb's eyes focused on Nora's downturned face. He breathed in short dry spasms. His fingers plucked and rubbed at the rough blanket, as if trying to clean it. Deep in his eyes was an accusing look, which only Ruth perceived. The accusation was directed at Nora, at her voice murmuring verse after verse of the King's English. It was a long look as if from the bottom of a well.

Then he directed his attention to his wife, and Ruth slipped aside to let them say goodbye.

Nora continued to read as the young man died. His head lay in the lap of Ritta, and though Nora infused the words with all the meaning she could muster, no one heard her. Later there would be weeping and wailing, deep grief released, when Nora left and the people were alone with the body. The sobbing continued as the moon moved over the roof of the house and into the far-off forest.

IT TOOK THREE DAYS to cut through the frozen earth and make a hole deep enough for Caleb in his coffin. Peter, Tim, and Charity did most of the digging. Side by side, under an iron-gray sky, they hacked at the ground with picks and shovels. They finally got about four feet down, as deep as they could go, and the body was laid to rest with a small service conducted by Nora. Snow began to fall. Charity shoveled in the ground again, alone with Peter at her side.

"How're your hands?" he asked her.

She held up two bleeding blistered palms to him, and he took hold of them and almost cried.

"I'll get you some rags to bind them," he said and hurried to his cabin where he ripped apart an old shirt.

When he came back, Charity was standing exactly as he had left her, with her raw hands open. Her eyes were bright, she looked as if she felt no pain, as he twisted and tied the makeshift bandages on her. Her fingertips trembled.

"You're really dumb," he muttered at her. "Why didn't you say something?"

She shrugged.

Beside them the dark hole spread open like the dark mouth on the face of the moon. Snowflakes fell inside the grave. For a moment, Peter stood with Charity's hands spread out in his. A current of heat ran between them. It seemed to be the only warmth in the world as they stared into the grave. Then he glanced at her smooth, brown face and stepped back quickly, releasing her.

Their eyes did not meet, and she ran down the whitening hill toward her cabin.

Because of Caleb's death, only a few went to the Christmas feast at the Williams plantation. Wash, Peter, and Charity traveled over in a sleigh together. Ruth had been sent ahead with the Howards to help with the preparations. Tim and his wife, and Ritta and all the little children, stayed behind.

The sky was blue and the sun bright on the fields of snow. The three of them were cheerful. It was a happy day when anyone got to leave the Howard farm and visit Bart Williams. The affluence of his life spread over onto his workers and included good food, drink, and a pleasant atmosphere.

The minute the sleigh had left the range of vision of the farm, the world seemed to open like the gates of heaven and spread into an airless infinity. As a bird must feel when freed from a cage, the trio in the sleigh felt then. The air seemed cleaner, the shadows shorter, the snow brighter than on the farm. Even Wash, still mourning, dropped his usual hostile air, and seemed to trust his place in the world. He took on a nostalgic expression and sang at the top of his lungs.

Peter and Charity smiled and listened to him as their eyes squinted at the brightness of the sun on the snow. Peter was remembering his arrival in this part of the world on a day like this one. It was stunning to realize how short a period of time it had been and how quickly he had adjusted—stunning, and awful. Days passed days without any marker except the sky. Full moon, half moon, Venus, snow.

And here was Wash singing a song he remembered from his Collins years. He never sang it on the farm, but the experience of leaving there seemed to produce the memory. Peter was flooded with thoughts of his sisters and brother, and Betty. His heart yearned for them but the memory of the landscape, the shapes of the fields and rocks, turned into one dark shadow in his mind. He glanced at Charity's girlish profile beside him. She gazed intently into the blaze of white. And she seemed to be hiding something in her hands on her lap.

"Now Miss Nora," Charity, ignoring him, said, "she thinks she's the prettiest woman in the world, just 'cause she sees no one else. That way she can believe it."

"She sees other people—you, your ma, her sister."

"Ha. Her sister's the only one she compares herself to, being white like her."

"Now don't say that about her," said Peter. "She never did anything to hurt you."

"You just think she's pretty, too, because she looks like she could be your own sister."

Peter moved away from her on the seat. "She's too old to be my sister," he told Charity. "Why, she could be my mother."

"Someday you'll be somebody's master, too," she said to him, "pale as you are and able to pass. You'll leave us. I just pray I'm not on your plantation, Master Peter."

"And how will I get to be master?" he asked.

"Why, Miss Nora will take care of that."

"Why're you being so mean about her?"

"I just wish she'd get married and move along, that's all."

"But she's the only friend you've got in that family."

"I can get along just fine without a friend on the Howard side."

"Okay, do it," Peter shrugged.

He was going to leave it at that, but the day was so exceptional, he couldn't leave the air between them charged with pain. He reached out and pulled Charity's hand out of her lap, and pried it open. She pulled back then let her fingers drop. Out fell a sliver of mirror glass about the width of her hand. Peter grabbed the glitter off the floor and held it up just so he could see his own reflection there. He had never seen his face this close, only once or twice in a dirty puddle near the barn. Now he saw his lips and nose and cheeks, but not his eyes, and studied them briefly before smashing the glass under his boot.

He jumped up and told Charity never to carry such a sharp thing in her hands ever again. He was near to tears and strode away from her as fast as he could go.

10

THE HOWARD AND WILLIAMS CLANS did not mix well. Bart did his best, in an effort to please his wife, not to raise certain subjects. He didn't like her brothers, who were thick, bearded, heavy-drinking vulgarians in his eyes, and he couldn't stand her uncle. The brothers' children combined the brawling of their fathers with the whining of their mothers. He could never understand why the girls, Nora and Nancy, came out so well—gentle and thoughtful. Bart spent most of the time with the children in order to avoid the Howard boys. He was a proud and adoring father and observed happily the superiority of his and Nancy's children to their cousins.

When Christmas was over, and to Bart's relief, everyone was making plans about going home, he settled the children at the long dining-room table and took out a deck of cards and a game board. He organized games like this each evening in an effort to keep the peace before the children went to bed.

When everyone was settled into one game or another, he leaned back and observed the ring of smooth faces around him. He realized all children could be pretty when muted and concentrated, and there were physical likenesses between them. Blue eyes and reddish hair showed up in a couple. Nancy's full lips were copied on the mouth of one of her nieces, he noted, and his daughter had a strong resemblance to Nora.

He could hear, through the darkness outside, the loud talking and laughing of the folks gathered in the cookhouse. He liked to feel they were as happy as everyone in his house, and that he was responsible for their happiness. He had a fantasy of owning the Howard farm someday and imagined it might not be a far-off day, considering the condition of their crops.

He was enjoying these thoughts when Nora restlessly entered the dining room. She never stayed long in a room with her brothers, and she, like Bart, spent most of her time with the children.

"How you doing, Nora?" Bart inquired. "Sit down."

She took a chair beside him, while the children said *sshh* so they could concentrate.

"Just fine," she murmured.

"Now why don't you stay with us a few days after everyone's gone?"

"Got to get back to my duties, Bart."

Almost every time he looked at Nora, Bart thought of her history. Now, seeing her in the same room with his daughter, noting their facial likeness, he thought of Peter across the snow, out back. Bart realized with a jolt that Peter rightfully should be sitting in here with his cousins. How could he be a slave to his own family? He moved his body around in his chair and cleared his throat. It was almost irresistible to him, breaking the silence with Nora on that subject, now more than ever. He quickly conjured up a new topic.

"You need to find yourself a good man, Nora, before you wither right away. No need for you to be a spinster—not with your learning and looks."

"Thank you, Bart," she said firmly, "but I'm fine as I am."

"Really?"

"Really."

She stood up, facing the window. "I think I'll go on out and see what's happening in back. Sounds like they're having a good time."

"Leave them alone, Nora," Bart said, standing beside her. "They don't want you out there." He noted her hurt look when he said this, and added, "I mean, you know how they are on a holiday. They like being on their own. Never get much of a chance for that."

"I suppose you're right."

"Just leave them alone." Then he couldn't resist saying, "The boy, Peter, he's doing real well, isn't he?"

Her face brightened. "Peter's just wonderful. Works day and night. And so talented and inventive! Hard to believe he's just seventeen. Betty sure knew how to raise him right."

"I never knew Betty." He cleared his throat. "Does he look like her?"

"Not a whit. Must be his father's son, the spitting image, whoever the man might have been. Believe me, if I could get my hands on him, I'd give him a piece of my mind. That boy should be free and educated."

"I suppose that's true of all of them, Nora. To me he's got the build of an outdoor man, not a scholar, that boy. I wouldn't mind owning him myself."

"He only looks that way because of the life he's had to lead. If he had been raised like these children here," she said, with a wave at her nieces and nephews, "he would look different, more graceful."

"Nothing wrong with being a farmer, Nora. Wouldn't mind my own boy doing that."

"But Peter's not a farmer, he's a slave, and there's a difference," she said.

"True."

He eyed her with pity. It seemed cruel beyond words that she should be ignorant of Peter's identity! If he was her son, she should know it. He told himself that someday the cat would come out of the bag.

"You turning into some kind of abolitionist, Nora?" he asked with a smile.

"Don't exactly know, yet. What about you?"

"I'm a man who swings with the punches. If it goes that way, it's okay with me. If it don't, I'll stick by what I've got and make the best of it."

"Well, at least you're a good master, Bart."

"Thank you, Nora. From your lips, I know that's a big compliment."

Nora drifted away to the sitting-room door, and hung there, looking in through the cigar smoke for someone she could feel comfortable beside. But she realized there was really no one. Her real friends were across the blue snow.

11

Nora was sick for several weeks after the Christmas holiday. A chill went deep into her chest and lodged there, and she coughed night and day, a fever coming and going. She could not leave her bed. Ruth urged her to move around or sit in a chair by the window, but Nora was inwardly immobilized.

Her physical illness seemed bound to an emotional malaise; her will to live was low. She knew this herself. She knew she was making herself sicker than she needed to be, but nothing could entice her to fight it.

This year's winter seemed more severe than any before. She didn't even wish to visit Peter or the children in the slave quarters; she didn't read her Bible at all, but lay in the warm nest of her own limbs, aching and mourning some nameless loss.

Her mother came home to check on her, fearing she might have caught Caleb's illness. But when she visited Nora, all she could manage to say were things like, "Look what I've suffered, and I'm still walking around doing what has to be done. You are letting self-pity drag you down. Women suffer. That's what you're here to do." Mrs. Howard did not believe that these were negative statements and imagined they might drag Nora from her bed.

"You expect too much of life. This is what results. Complete disappointment and selfishness," she said crossly, her arms folded over her bosom. Moral imperatives often made Nora act. In this case, they fell on deaf ears.

Her father looked in on Nora daily when he was home. He stood in the doorway and asked if she had everything she needed. She responded in a weak voice, yes, and usually buried herself deeper in the bed.

Her uncle, for fear of catching her sickness, would not come near her. He was afraid of her dying, since then there would only be three people living in the house. This was known to be bad luck. If Nora died, he planned to move Charity into the house so there would be four.

Nora heard everything everyone said to and about her, and she tried as hard as she could to make meaning out of the phrases as they passed. "Idleness breeds evil," said her mother, and Nora tried to put the moral force behind the words to good use, but they had lost their meaning. *So what?* is all she really felt.

"I've lost my mind or fallen from grace. They come to the same thing," she told herself.

She felt threatened by the outside physical world—especially by the tread of her uncle's feet. She felt disposable, mortal, at anyone's mercy. It was as if her watery nature had frozen into character. Where before she had been an ashamed person—ashamed to get up, ashamed to sit down, ashamed to occupy space, be seen, heard, or believed—now those characteristics had physically resolved themselves. She had been bullied by her brothers and her uncle all her life; she was, as a result, a person who felt closest to weak people, not to the strong.

When alone she was happy and relaxed her coughing. Half-seated in bed, she watched the snow dissolving outside. These hours were full of thought. How could she make herself live again? What was the point? She was smitten with despair. If she looked at her body, she saw it was still youthful, though womanly.

When March came, the snow was gone. Knowing one day that she was alone and would not be disturbed, Nora went weakly to the window to look out. She knew her father had gone to purchase cattle. She could see Tim and Wash pushing dirt around out in the field. Sophie was hanging up clothes to dry. Ritta must have been tending the children somewhere out of sight. It was a windy, cool day, the clouds scudding fast over the dark earth. The land looked fresh. She peered around at the hillside, craning to see the bare, undecorated gravestone.

Her heart tightened at the sight of it, and she realized she could never explain to anyone why a little stone on a pile of dirt should have so much meaning to her. She knew it made no sense to anyone else, but to her the stone was a sacred object, conjuring up an intense memory of love and childbirth. It was to her what a piece of jewelry, a special picture, or a lock of hair was to someone else.

It was a reference point, a physical mark of a time when she knew what she wanted.

BUT NOW SHE CAUGHT the sound of her uncle's angry voice and saw Peter stripped to the waist, being tied up by Uncle John at the end of the slave quarters. She could not see Peter's face, but saw him struggling. Wash was coming running to help tie him to the birch tree. They bound him, and then he was lashed. Nora momentarily covered her eyes and then rushed for her clothes. By the time she was dressed and out, Peter was nowhere in sight. Nora looked here and there, but stealthily, not wanting to be seen. Thinner than when she had gone to bed sick, her stark appearance was heightened by the colors she wore—dark, almost black blues. Her hair was pinned tight away from her face.

She noted that purple and white crocuses were pointing out of the dark soil around the stone. The sight of them filled her with relief. She turned her face to the wind, closing her eyes, and let the soft cold air blow through her half-open mouth. Taking a deep breath, she strode down the hill toward Peter's cabin.

She knocked on the door, waiting anxiously for a quick response, before she would be seen and discovered.

"Miss Nora! You're well again."

"I hope so. Please God. The winter's over, anyway, and you know that makes me feel better. Can I come in?"

"Come in," he said and stood aside.

She gazed at his face, noting he had begun to grow the slightest tracing of a beard, circling his full lips and the scar. He looked outside toward the big house with some trepidation and shut the door behind them. The cabin was dark, damp, but neat. With the door shut, Nora could hardly see him.

"You sure you're all well now?" Peter said.

She smiled, "Pretty sure."

"I'll light a fire," he said and moved by her. The air he moved in passing filled her with the first rush of happiness she had felt in weeks. She watched him kneel down before a pile of logs and went to stand behind him.

"May I see your back, Peter?" she asked.

Startled, he looked up.

"I saw them whip you. I want to know you're healing right."

"I am."

"Seeing is believing."

"It's all right," he insisted, putting fire to the wood. He didn't rise.

"I hate him for hurting you!"

She reached down and drew up his shirt, while he sat immobile on his knees. Welts ran in straight bloody streaks across his skin.

"I hate him!" she cried again.

"It'll heal."

"Has he done it before?"

"This winter? Maybe two, three times."

Nora dropped his shirt and sat on her knees beside him.

"Your uncle will get mad at you, Miss Nora," he said, "coming out here."

"I don't care."

Peter stood up and leaned his hands against the chimney stones, looking down. He said, "I have been beaten by a few men in my life and I've had time to think about it. What was driving them. What was wrong with them."

"What, Peter? What was it?"

"It was my eyes looking at them. You see men do this with their own children, turn on them with hate, because of their being so needy, needing them. It sickens them. They go crazy looking at weakness and need so close up."

"But you don't have those qualities. You don't. You aren't weak. You aren't needy."

"Being a tool makes you look like both those things, no matter what."

"Uncle John was hit on the head with a steel rod when he was here in this country only five years. Two more years indentured to go. Someone went after him. He went on working but with a vengeance. He hated this country as much as my mother hates this farm. They didn't want to be here, either of them. This is what my father told me once."

"All this bad feeling is going to hurt the land itself, I tell you."

"I want to take you away with me from here," said Nora.

"I don't belong to you," Peter said, and his voice was hard.

"Then who do you belong to?"

"Me," he replied, "and the other folks, Betty."

"Don't you want to get away and be free? I could do it, I know I could!"

She sounded so distressed he softened his voice slightly, speaking to her behind him.

"What about the others, Miss Nora? The only reason you have this wish for me is because I look white and I'm not. But what about the others?"

She stared uncomprehending at the back of his head.

"What others?"

"Ruth, Charity, Tim, Sophie—the others who can't even call this home. What about them?"

"Peter," she said sadly, "I can't do the impossible."

"Then what you are offering me has no meaning."

"Peter, don't treat me this way. So cold!"

"I don't know what you want with me, Miss Nora."

She realized he must be in physical pain and said gently, "I want you to be free. To be educated. To wear fine clothes. To be a man."

"I saw myself in glass. I know what I am," he said. "And it's not what you think. Fine clothes? For what? I wouldn't want them. I've seen too much."

She nodded to herself alone and turned away. Peter's face softened and he moved around to talk to her directly.

"Thank you for wanting to help me, Miss Nora," he said, "but if it's just me, I want no part of it."

"Why not?"

"Where I lived before, with my mama and papa and sisters and brother, that was home to me, but I was sold away like I was just a passing guest. Now I try to call this home, but I know, any minute, I could be sent away from here, too. So now I call my own self home, and if I'm ever forced to leave, this place will come with me, up here, in my mind. You can only say goodbye so many times, Miss Nora. For me, once was enough."

What he was saying, and he had never been so outspoken with her, went through her mind like a vapor. She hardly heard him. In the dim light, he looked incredibly familiar. She moved to the door and threw it open to let the light flood over him. Then she stepped backward, nearly staggering. Her face was dead white. As vivid as her dreams of his father was the figure of his father, Dan McCutcheon, now in Peter, right before her eyes.

She ran.

Peter thought he had hurt her feelings and driven her away for good. He had never talked so freely or so much with anyone. But he had only spoken the truth, and if his anger at her uncle had spilled onto her, he couldn't take it back. The truth was too much for white people to bear, no matter who they were, or how well meaning, he thought. She was better off leaving him alone, anyway. Still, he felt some remorse, and tried to reason that his driving her off like that was for her own good. She would not have to suffer more whacks from her uncle; she would be safer this way. And at least it was truth and not some ingratiating lie that made her run away.

He talked to Ruth at dinner while Charity set the table for the Howards in the other room.

"Miss Nora's all better, it seems," he said.

"Why do you say that?"

"She was out to see me today."

Ruth turned. "But she's up in her bed right now."

"Well, she stopped in on me for a while, after the boss was finished whipping me."

"Master John says I'll have to move to Master Bart's when Nora's better," Ruth murmured.

"She didn't look all well yet. She acting strange tonight?"

"Just wants to be alone."

"Don't blame her," he said, "with that mule of a man hanging around."

"Peter, you'll get yourself in trouble."

"I tell you, if he whips me again, he's a dead man."

Ruth looked at him closely, reading in his face and posture such an intense collection of emotions, she was afraid.

"Go on back to your cabin and cool off," she told him.

He saw that she meant it, that she wanted him out of her way, and probably out of Charity's path, with this mood on him now, and he didn't blame her. He stood up and took the piece of bread she handed him.

"I can't take back what I said," he told her, "but I'll do my best to quiet down."

"You do that."

With great anxiety Ruth watched him go. She wondered if Nora was giving him ideas about himself that could never be fulfilled, ideas of power that could only backfire. She sometimes thought that Nora was a little crazy and decided she'd better try to reason with her about Peter right away. Nora would have to understand that Peter was just like the rest of them, and it was kinder to leave him alone than to fill him up with false hopes.

"It's one thing for me to tell Charity, my own daughter, that she will get her freedom one day. But it's another thing for Nora to tell Peter that."

But it was impossible for Ruth to ignore the irony in her thought.

She halfheartedly went to Nora's room after dinner. Nora was curled up in bed. The tallow burned low beside her. Ruth sank down next to her, placing her hand on her knee.

"Still feeling bad?"

"No."

"Then why didn't you come down to eat?"

"Not hungry."

"You've got to eat, honey. Food's improving."

Nora said nothing.

"Peter said you were out to see him." Ruth paused, waiting for a response which never came. "You know, he got a bad whipping from the master today."

"Ruth?"

"What."

"Tell me who his father was."

"We've been through this before. I don't know."

"You do know."

"Who?" said Ruth, stiffening.

"His name begins with a D. His initials are D. M."

Ruth twisted her hands together, staring into the flickering candlepoint. "Can't figure it out," she said.

"It's as plain as the nose on your face." Nora's voice was high and hard, and she moved deeper under her covers. "He did it to Betty while he was doing it to me."

"No," said Ruth, "it's not true."

"No other explanation."

"For what?"

"For why Peter looks just like Dan McCutcheon."

"Memory. Playing tricks."

"No. Not this time."

Ruth stood up and walked around her own dishonesty restlessly.

"This time I'm right," Nora said. "He did it to Betty, while he was doing it to me."

"If that's so, I don't know anything about it. He wasn't that kind, as I recall. Can't say any more than that."

"Would Betty tell?"

"Never," said Ruth.

"Then I have to believe what I see, and that's all."

"You're going to make yourself sick again."

"No. I'll be okay."

"I came here to ask you a favor—about Peter."

"What about him?"

"Do you care for the boy?"

"I did. Just as if he was my own baby, had he lived. But he doesn't want any part of my affection."

"Peter's a good boy, but he's just a poor slave child, Nora. You mustn't be putting ideas in his head about him being more than that. He doesn't usually say much. He's getting troubled and troublesome. Why, just tonight he said he would kill your uncle if he whips him again."

"Don't blame him," Nora said.

"Don't you understand, honey? Your uncle would get him first. He'd kill Peter. He's the one holding the gun and the whip. Not Peter."

"Peter doesn't want my help," Nora said.

"All you have to do is talk to your father. Tell him to get Master John to lay off Peter. That's all."

"They probably know."

"Know what?"

"Whose son Peter is. I bet they know."

"Nora, stop it. Let that idea go. What does it matter anyhow? Peter is who he is, father or no father. And I thought you cared for him."

"I can't even look at him now."

"I thought you were a Christian woman."

"Poor Betty," Nora went on. "What she had to go through, and couldn't even tell me. So evil. He must have forced himself on her. Poor, poor Betty!"

Ruth walked to the door, impatiently sighing.

"You're making me real sad, Nora."

Nora sat up, abruptly, reaching out her hand.

"I'll do it, Ruth, don't worry, I'll talk to Daddy about Peter. I'm not that bad."

"It's okay, honey. I knew you'd do your best."

She went slowly, heavily down the stairs as if each step was a lie she had told.

12

THE NEXT DAY her father was still away, but Nora dressed and ate a little and went to find her uncle early in the day. She wanted to talk to him directly. He stood at the edge of the timberline where hogs were running loose. Snorting and rolling in the mud, the bristly young creatures were enjoying the spring mud's warmth.

"Look at them," John said. "Just about ready to kill and cure."

"Not yet," she said.

"You feeling better?"

"Little better," she said. "Where's Peter?"

"Chopping. Why?"

He gave Nora a suspicious glare from under his hat's rim.

"No reason."

"You better not be hanging around him no more."

"Don't worry," she said coolly, "but I want to make sure you're not whipping him just for fun either. Daddy doesn't like that."

"Too bad. When Daddy's not home, what Daddy don't like don't matter."

"Uncle John, he's not bad. He works hard."

"He's uppity. Dangerous."

"Then leave him alone."

"Who are you, telling me what to do with my hands?" he shouted, reddening, and he grasped her arm. "You come with me."

He pulled her along after him to where Peter was rolling and chopping wood. His face dripped sweat. He raised himself up straight as he saw them approaching. Nora stood at a distance with her head bowed.

"Go kill a hog, Peter," said John.

"They aren't ready yet."

"What do you mean not ready? They're fat as the kitchen stove."

"Need another month. Master Will said so."

"I'm your master now. You do what I say."

"He told me that before he left."

The two men stared angrily at each other while a crow made squawking noises from a nearby tree. Nora's knees trembled. She didn't even look directly at Peter. She feared seeing who he was again. The atmosphere seemed stretched and creaking like black ice on a pond about to break. Her mouth was dry and she had no words to say, but she saw her uncle pull his whip out from his belt. One screeching crow flew over them, then another.

"Two crows mean bad luck for someone," rasped John, "and that someone's you, boy. Take off your shirt."

"If you want this shirt off, Master John, walk over and pull it off," Peter said.

Nora turned. Across the mud and broken timber and moving figures of chickens and hogs, she saw Ruth walking into the big house. She started to slip in that direction, hearing her uncle say, "I won't try to whip you because you ain't worth it. From the day of your birth, you've been bad luck, nothing but a curse on our house. Better off dead. Better for everyone. A whip?" He flashed it in front of himself. "That's chicken shit, boy. I'm going to get my gun."

Nora, moving backward and stumbling, saw Peter, as swift as a fox, lean out to his ax, hoist and hurl it, whistling blade first, through the air. Her uncle ducked, and it fell with a thud, blade down, behind the little man.

Dizzy and airless, Nora ran to the house as fast as she could in her loose skirts and muddy slippers. She ran straight into the kitchen. Her eyes whirled stars.

"Hide his gun! He's coming!" she breathed at Ruth, and sank gasping down on a chair.

Ruth knew what she meant at once, and went straight to the cupboard in the hall where John Howard kept his one gun, a musket.

She grabbed it and carried it down to the root cellar, dropping it into dark earth there. Then she tore up the stairs again to join Nora at the kitchen table. They were sitting in silence, gaping at each other, when John Howard entered.

He roared around the house, throwing things, in search of his gun. "Where the hell is it? Where's my gun? I'm going to blow that boy off the face of the earth at last."

Stunned and terrified, the two women sat listening in the kitchen. Soon he would come after them. They dared not utter a word to each other, but tried to occupy themselves with the cutting of chicken. He crashed up and down the stairs three times, hurling around chairs, throwing clothes out of trunks and drawers. Finally, he appeared panting at the kitchen door.

"My gun, where's my gun?" he nearly sobbed.

"Don't know," they both murmured.

"But he's going to kill me! Judas Priest, he's going to kill me!"

"I'll take care of him, Master John," said Ruth in a steady voice.

"Lock him away somewhere," he begged her. "Get him away from me." And he wandered out of the room, moaning, "My gun, my gun..."

Ruth moved outside and Nora, at the door, watched her approach Peter and lead him to the laundry house, which had a door lock, and put him in there. Nora's heart was racing. Still weak from her illness, her breath seemed insufficient, and she gasped on the air. She felt she could die from misery and fear; the violence she saw was like a hatchet cutting her in two. Where were her loyalties? What could she do?

She heard the deadly clank of the liquor bottle in her uncle's hand in the living room. She and the help were now alone with him. If only someone, in the form of her father, would come! With her uncle drunk and enraged, who would take charge? Authority did not come easy to her, and now she felt she was on the other side of the line, facing her own kin and at his mercy. She began to quake.

By dusk John Howard was raving drunk. Nora, hiding in her bedroom, heard him shouting about Peter and how he would kill him as soon as he got hold of his gun. Without it, he was impotent, for his fear of the avenging slave was coming true in his mind and his whip was like a blade of grass in his hand. He wanted blood even if the blood was his own family's.

Downstairs, all the slaves but Ruth and Charity ate and ran back to their quarters. They stayed behind in the kitchen, cleaning as fast as they could, half desperate to escape the house.

"You go, I'll do it," they kept whispering to each other nervously, but neither would leave the other alone.

"What about Miss Nora?" Charity whispered.

"If she just lays low, she might be okay."

But then the inevitable, as it seemed, happened, for John's form appeared, swaying darkly in the door. His whip, a cat o' nine tails, switched at his side. He glared at Charity.

"That bitch took my gun, I know it," he slurred. "She's got her eye on that boy out there. Don't think I didn't notice the way you watch his ass, Miss," he said. "I know what you want from him."

Charity's eyes burned and filled. She couldn't believe her ears, how strange and awful that this man, crazy as he was, had perceived her longings, when no one else had. How ugly they sounded on his tongue.

"Get out back," he said, waving his whip at her.

Ruth was paralyzed, for if she said she had the gun, he might go on a rampage with it. She couldn't speak or intervene. She had to hold her tongue and watch her daughter being led from the house to the porch and hear the rip of Charity's dress coming down, the crack of the whip on her young flesh, over and over. Her stomach heaving, Ruth sobbed into her hand, and moved toward the door, thinking of Peter, of letting him out, of getting to him, so he could stop the master.

But it was Nora, suddenly, who rushed down the stairs in her nightgown. One of her mother's canes was raised over her head. She ran by Ruth onto the porch, screaming "*stop, stop*" at her uncle, and pounding him hard on the back till, clutching his head, he staggered into the gloom and fell on the ground.

The three women watching on the porch didn't move until he had fallen. Then Nora helped Ruth draw Charity inside.

13

WHEN JOHN HOWARD was not in a trance induced by alcohol, he wore a strange, moist, and distant expression, which was almost more frightening than his drunken rages. Even if he was a small and cowardly man, the mental torment he suffered could only be spread around, and his one aim in life seemed to be the sight of it spreading.

His brother was hardly able to control him better than anyone else. Will almost wished that Peter had thrown that ax with greater dexterity, thereby ending the life of terror his brother had brought upon the farm. Instead, the one good result of that incident was that John was truly afraid of Peter, and Will felt that in an extreme situation he could run to Peter to control his brother.

John's superstitions prevented him from killing Peter, for surely his ghost would return from the grave to haunt him. If Peter was not already a ghost, John figured he was close enough to it to have supernatural powers. The throwing of the ax was only a warning. Peter was a blood relative. He had to be kept at bay. John had wanted to murder Peter's father, the Scots-Irish surveyor, Dan McCutcheon, as soon as he realized he was fooling around with Nora, rolling around in the meadows, pinching and squeezing her and lifting her skirts. John drove him away, but it was too late. This birth monster was already in the making. Peter, a fiddler like his father, skilled with his hands, and now an abject slave, a humiliating mirror image of the free white man. A throwback to show they were all just play-acting at being human.

What was a human being anyway? It was something John brooded on whenever he contemplated Peter working. Here was a slave with all the mannerisms and bad attitudes of slaves who looked like him. He was sloppy, he slumped, he laughed too loudly, he was uppity. White and English. Why did the figure of Peter conjure up such turmoil in John just as it had in Collins? He wanted to hurt him, his fingers itched with the desire to humiliate him, to rip off his skin like a mask. He didn't want Peter to exist.

MRS. HOWARD spent most of her time on the Williams farm and Ruth was sent there to help. Charity was left behind to cope with the cooking and cleaning. Nora helped her as much as she could. Both of them missed Ruth and both of them lived in a state of perpetual fear that John Howard would go berserk again.

When Will was home, the two brothers ate in silence. One hung over a newspaper, the other drank straight whisky and stared into space. Self-conscious, Nora ate all her meals with the help, and no one protested. The order of the farm rapidly deteriorated.

There were frequent outbursts between the brothers—over the one white shirt between them, over the handling of the slaves, and over the buying and selling of cattle. Will blamed John, and John blamed the slaves. With Ruth and Mrs. Howard gone, the two men were constantly aware of their failures and disorder.

"Why don't we sell Peter?" John suggested again and again.

"Because he's pulling more than his weight," his brother Will said. "Besides, so long as I'm alive, we'll never sell that boy. Not again like that. It was a bitter feeling when we packed him off with Betty. He is ours. There's such a thing as responsibility. Christian responsibility. What civilization hangs on."

John snorted sarcasm. His only ally against Peter was Wash, who had never stopped mistrusting Peter and reported every mistake he made to the master.

Will depended on Nora for common sense and company. They began to talk in the evenings or outside on the farm about more than the usual mundane details of the day's work. Will tried to explain his brother to Nora.

"You can't deal with him like an ordinary man," he would say. "Something went wrong. Used to be, he could be funny, show a little wit, you know, even be generous. Remember the things he used to bring home? That little horse?

"Well, I don't know what happened. Drink, I suppose. My father had a problem in that area, too. Used to go on long binges, then repent and be sober for weeks. But when he was bad, he beat our mother and us boys, and forgot it all, as if it never happened. Guess it just runs in the family."

"Sometimes I used to feel sorry for him," Nora said.

They watched John slogging through the mud carrying buckets of slops to the pigs. His head was hidden in his huge Stetson. At a distance, Nora pitied his mental prison.

"And sometimes I really hate him," she added.

Something had snapped in her the night Charity was whipped. It was the link that bound her to her family as an obedient handmaiden. She had discovered the link was loose—even self-made—and with a shake of her wrist, she was free.

Her father went away from the farm as often as he could, either to Carthage, which he called "the marketplace," or to the Williams farm to visit his wife. He often brought his few slaves to nearby plantations and hired out both men and women to get money for his own pocket. As a result, Nora was often alone with Charity and the children, who worked in the fields and stables.

She and her uncle avoided each other by mutual, unspoken agreement, but she had to intervene more than once when he took the whip to a child. The figure of Peter often appeared at such moments to cast a vengeful shadow over the boss. Will always left Peter at home on the farm, just in case. And Peter only had to stand close by to make John Howard shift the direction of his fury and back off.

NORA HANDLED her new responsibility well. Each day seemed like an arena in which she played out a personal drama around the subject of justice. She wanted to see justice done, to the children, Charity, Peter, and herself. It was her duty to see that each person got what was their due. But she still didn't allow herself to see that the entire structure of farm life, as they lived it, was skewed at the roots. No wages paid for work done—this was the first sin on her family's side. How could this be just? It was only their privilege at being born white that set the standard. This much she observed through her ethical instincts, but Nora also had an inability to see more shocking realities.

Now, feeling sure that Peter was Betty's son by Dan McCutcheon, she cared for him more than ever, and was increasingly obsessed with the desire to set him and the other slaves free. But she was silent and never spoke of this to anyone. She listened with acute interest to any mention of Northerners and abolition, but held her tongue. Her new view of Dan, as a man who had assaulted a slave girl, obliterated all her romantic fantasies and memories of him. She never mentioned his name to Peter who had been her friend again since that one awful night when she had intervened for Charity.

Peter trusted her now, and often they stole away to a grove of trees to talk, or, when her uncle was snoring, Nora would call Peter up to the little grave on the hillside where she felt most at home. He found his tongue loosened when he was with her; he could speak like anyone else.

"In fact, this is the only place I can really call my own," she told Peter by the small stone. "Peculiar as it sounds."

"I get it," he said.

"Do you? You are so good at caring for this place, look at the gardens bursting now, and the health of the animals. All thanks to you. It's as if you have a special understanding with this little acre of land in the middle of nowhere. Truly, Peter."

Now he had a thick reddish beard, and his hair was heavy and long. He was big-shouldered and manly. Whenever he was alone with Nora, he dropped his tense, attentive posture, which carried him through his fieldwork all day, and relaxed in spite of the danger of their meeting.

Nora asked Charity to watch out for her when she visited Peter, and to ring a bell if she saw her uncle coming out. With mixed feelings, Charity would do as she was told. She was always jealous of Nora's relationship to Peter, but without her mother at home, she had come to depend heavily on Nora's affection and confidence and on some basic trust she felt for her. Sometimes she could almost believe that Nora's love for Peter was even more innocent than her own.

John Howard never believed it was innocent. As he saw it, the possibility of incest was rampant, and something deserved. A lurking germ was lodged in the atmosphere around the farm. He had a neurotic fear of the sexuality of black men, and Peter, though his own flesh and blood, had all their mannerisms. To John, Peter was filled with an ancient potency. John kept his eyes glued on Nora and Peter with an almost lascivious desire to see his prophecy of incest fulfilled.

14

One sunny summer day, Nora drew Peter up to the grave, away from his work catching hogs in the timber. Charity kept watch at the big house. The snorting pigs ran all over the hills and the job of catching them was exhausting and funny.

"Peter, I've got something to show you," Nora said excitedly. In her hand was a piece of paper. "I've got a letter here from Betty! From

Betty, yes. At last, after all this time. I wrote to her, as I said I would, months ago. At last—here—look—"

They stood in mottled shadows near the gravestones. She held out the paper and Peter smiled, thrilled.

"Read it—please—" he begged Nora.

She read slowly so he could savor every word:

DEAR MISS NORA ROBERT WRITES YOU A LETTER FOR ME I WANT YOU TO TELL PETER I AM HEARTSICK WITH MISSING HIM SO ARE HIS SISTERS AND BROTHER SO IS HIS PAPA OUR MASTER COLLINS GOES ON ABOUT THE SAME I WANT TO SEND PETER SOME THINGS BUT DON'T KNOW IF HE IS STILL THERE TELL ME PLEASE MISS NORA HOW IS OUR BOY AND IF WE SHALL NOT MEET AGAIN ON THIS EARTH I HOPE TO MEET HIM IN HEAVEN EXPRESS TO HIM THE GRIEF WE FEEL TO HAVE HIM AWAY FROM US ALL BUT ISN'T THE LORD STRANGE HE IS THERE WITH YOU WHAT DOES HE LOOK LIKE NOW TELL HIM I LOVE HIM FOREVER I REMAIN YOUR TRUE FRIEND BETTY COLLINS

Tears ringed the edges of Peter's eyes. Listening, he squatted down to conceal his emotion and prodded at the grass with his hands.

"Keep the letter, Peter," Nora said gently. "I'll read it to you whenever you want."

He took the paper from her and studied it for several minutes. His head was bent.

"So many times," he said, "I thought she was not my real mother. I'm ashamed."

"Of course she's your mother," said Nora quietly, "but no one could blame you for wondering. I'll write her again, I promise, and tell her you are still here and well."

Peter nodded, and Nora turned away and walked close to her favorite stone, looking down at the little marks and details. Every ridge and bump in it she knew by heart. She had a longing to tell him who his father was and to explain to him why he looked the way he did, but then somehow she felt it would be too intimate a confession and would confuse him. Would she say he was a "throwback" to Scotland and Ireland? Would she offer to find his father and return him to him even across the sea? What kind of man could Dan McCutcheon be, if he got both her and Betty pregnant?

Instead, she said in a loud voice back to him, "Peter, I tell you someday I'll get your freedom for you. For all of you together. Just the way you want it."

He stood up and gazed at her, and she was almost blinded by his resemblance to Dan McCutcheon, the only man she had ever loved, and now known to her imagination as a betrayer and seducer.

"There will be a way, and I'll find it," she said angrily, "because I can see how wrong it all is. My father and mother were bad, and sometimes I hate them for it. I hate them for selling you and Betty away. It was the same time they buried my baby here and all without letting me be part of it, or even *see* him. I had only one glimpse of my own child! I hated them then, and I'll make up for it, somehow, through you, Charity, and the others. I promise. I won't rest till this is done."

He silently listened to her and believed her, so that he was filled with a kind of excitement and promise. And as he penetrated her with his gaze, he felt again that he recognized her by some swift expression on her face. He realized that the familiar look was there when she was blazing with a feeling of anger or hope. For a flash, he thought maybe it was his own expression he recognized on her, mirrored on her.

Impulsively, she walked over and threw her arms around his waist and hugged him. Her cheek was pressed to his warm chest, small as she was.

John Howard stood in the dark green trees with his whip. He was grinning, his eyes moist and otherworldly. "Gotcha," was all he said.

Crickets chirped dryly in the brown summer grass. Then there was the switch of the cat o' nine tails as dry as the crickets' breath. Peter and Nora drew back and stared.

"Go home, Master," said Peter, "and get your gun. The whip won't do no good, and you know it."

"No!" cried Nora, rushing to her uncle. "It was all my fault."

"You think I care?" asked John. "I don't care. But your daddy will when I tell him. You wait."

He took Nora by the arm and pulled her along beside him down the hill to the house, saying, "The fruit doesn't fall far," over and over.

Peter stood and gazed down the hill. He was not afraid of the boss. He understood for the first time that John was really afraid of him for some reason other than the throwing of the ax.

Nora had extracted Peter from the usual social rules and done the unthinkable: she embraced him, a slave. He was uneasy. He was not a boy anymore. He was a young man. He often woke up filled with desire when his solitude felt like loneliness. The wish to make himself felt by another was growing in him as an almost aggressive sensation. He wanted to fall onto someone and win a response.

He had no such emotion regarding Nora, but he was old enough to know the implications of John's rage. He should not have to defend himself against an action or intention he didn't even possess. And he did not, for a minute, imagine Nora had such an intention when she embraced him. She was not a female Collins, but he felt embarrassed since sex crossed all social lines.

It was embarrassing to have to think about it at all, especially in regard to a woman old enough to be his mother, but he had to think about it in order to convince himself that he would be punished for the wrong reason and would therefore be free of pain.

"This time you're going to get it," John shouted at Nora. "You promised you'd never see him alone again! That's what you said and you lied. Wait till your mother finds out, and your daddy. You were holding him, stroking him!"

He paced the parlor with his whip while Nora sat stonily on the settle.

In the kitchen Wash and Charity listened, waiting to hear if he would whip or slap Nora for what she had done.

"She's really done it this time," Wash hissed. "She's in bad trouble."

Charity's face was contorted with guilt. "It's all my fault. I didn't pay attention! What'll they do to her?"

"To her? Not much. This time Peter's had it. Imagine fooling around with Miss Nora. Boy must be crazy," Wash hissed. "Too proud of himself. All he wants to do is pass and get his white ass out of this place. He'll do anything to get there, including courting his own mistress!"

"Shut up, Wash," said Charity. "You just hate him whatever he does, and I bet he didn't do nothing."

"Ha."

They heard a couple of slaps and then heard Nora running up the stairs to her room.

"Go up there and stay there!" John shouted. "Don't you come down till your daddy gets home! Crazy wench."

They heard her footsteps overhead, but John went on yelling, "I tell you, if you knew the half of it, you'd throw yourself in the river. Right in the river. That's right. If you knew the half of it!"

Nora's footsteps stopped and John stomped away outside. Charity ran to the window to see which way he was going.

"Wash, you better get out there. He's getting a horse, must be taking off."

Grinning, Wash ran outside with his hat in his hand. John Howard rarely left the farm and Charity almost jumped up and down with joy at the thought of a few hours' freedom from him. She thought of running up to Nora, but ashamed, stayed put. Not until John Howard was saddled and riding away did she run out to the timber to join Peter in catching hogs.

On his hands and knees, he was sneaking up on a big one, when she pounced on him from behind. Startled, he threw her aside and away from him, and she furiously whacked him on the arm with her fist.

"You watch it," she snarled.

"*You* watch it," he snapped back. "Now look, the hog got away. What are you doing, sneaking up on me like that?"

"I wanted to know what happened with you and Miss Nora," she said. Her face was moist from the heat and streaked with dirt. She frowned at him.

"None of your business," he said, leaning back on a log. But then he lurched forward, drawing Betty's letter from inside the back of his pants. "Keep this for me, okay?"

"What is it?"

"I'll tell you later. Just a letter," and he stuck the paper down inside Charity's dress. "Keep that till tonight."

She melted at contact with him. "I feel bad, Peter, I didn't ring the bell. I had my head in the oven."

"Not your problem."

"It is. I should've been watching."

"Then you would've gotten in trouble. What did he do to Miss Nora?"

"Slapped her. He's gone to get Master Will. I'm scared they're going to do you harm."

"If they're going to do me harm, why are you scared? It's my hide."

She gave him one of her silent, luminous looks that softened his tongue.

"Nothing bad happened up there," he said to her. "Miss Nora just read me that letter. From my mama. That's about it."

With a deep sigh, she suddenly jumped up and ran back to the big house.

"You take care of that letter!" Peter shouted after her.

Then he turned at the sound of a nearby snorting hog and went on his hands and knees again to stalk it. He was filled with a pent-up energy, a mixture of tension and emotional hunger, which he now poured into the catching of a hog.

THAT NIGHT John Howard returned, but he was not alone. Mrs. Howard and Will came, too. They went to Nora's bedroom at once.

Nora, seated in bed with her Bible, stared in alarm at the figures of her parents, who stood so serious and dour by the door. All the childhood awe that such a picture can create came into her then, and she felt her stomach sink.

"What is it?" she said.

"You're coming with us. Tomorrow. To your sister's house. And that's where you'll stay."

"Daddy!"

"That's right," he said, quietly and firmly.

"But why?"

"You know why," said her mother. "You're getting too close to the slaves, one in particular. It's time we took you to a more civilized environment."

Nora stared down at the black words before her. They wobbled like rows of insects.

"What about this house?" she asked, "and what about me? Can't I speak for myself?"

"Not in this case," said her father.

"And this house is a shambles since I left," said her mother. "I'm ashamed!"

"But I'm a grown woman! This is my home," Nora said.

"I'm afraid to say, it's more my home than yours. Yes it is," Mrs. Howard replied, "and I can say who does what when they stay here."

She swept away, followed by her husband. Nora felt as if she were falling down a tunnel. Infantile, destroyed, and homeless.

Charity was sent to help her pack. Soundlessly she gathered Nora's clothes together. Nora sat immobilized before the inevitable.

Charity said, "Don't stay away too long, Miss Nora. Don't know how we'll get along without you. At least you'll have my ma there."

They looked at each other quietly for several seconds, and then Nora hauled herself out of bed to help the girl pack.

"Yes," she said.

"And you'll come back soon?"

"Don't know, really."

"Give my mama my love, please. I'll watch out for Peter for you," Charity said, then covered her mouth as if she had said too much and was ashamed.

By the heartless nature of her mother's words, Nora had been hurled back to youth and early weakness. When she heard Peter's name, she sank down, crying. Now she heard his words, which had seemed strange before: "I try to call this home, but I know, any minute, I could be sent away from here. So now I call my memory home, not the place I'm in."

15

AT DAWN the next morning John Howard told Wash to hitch up some horses. "Mrs. Howard and Nora will be going over to Mr. Williams's farm," he told Wash."Who's going to drive them, Master?" Wash asked eagerly, wanting, as all the slaves did, a chance to stop over at the other farm. "Don't look so wide-eyed, boy, that's right," said John crossly. "If you're wondering why, it's because Master Will said so. That's why. He wants Peter to start moving around more. Be the driver for a time. Not you, no more."

Wash was furious, hurt. His skin prickled, and he stamped into the barn, cursing Peter under his breath. The smell of horse manure was heavy in the morning heat. Flies buzzed all over the stamping, tail-switching horses.

"Sick white bastard," Wash muttered, "uppity son of a bitch… sucking up to Miss Nora… paleface."

He was sweating profusely as he dragged out Bill, the usual carriage horse. Blaze, the other, followed. Suddenly Wash paused; he had an idea. He would put Blaze out to field and hitch up Cottoneye in his place, the meanest nag on the farm. He would let what happened, happen. None of the horses were in good condition, but no one but he knew how short-tempered old Cottoneye could be.

Smiling excitedly at his own plot, he shoved Blaze out into the pasture, and led the two other horses out front. Will and Peter waited for him.

"What's wrong with Blaze?" Will asked.

Wash gulped. "After last night's ride, he's a mite lame. Hard on him, dragging that carriage alone."

"Okay, hitch 'em up," Will said and glanced at Peter. "Shouldn't be no problems, boy. Just take them straight down the road. Stop in, get a bite to eat, then come on back. Gotta keep you and Master John out of each other's hair for a few hours."

Peter nodded and watched Wash hitch up the two horses. He saw Cottoneye roll his eyes and snort, but he was not familiar enough with the horses to say anything. Mrs. Howard and Nora came out on the porch. Charity followed with their bags. Nora was pale, her eyes ringed with shadows. She gazed intensely at Peter before climbing up into the wagon with her mother.

"Okay, Peter. Come back later on, you hear?" said Will. "Tell Bart I'll be down there myself in a couple of weeks, dear," he told his wife.

Mrs. Howard sat on the rear seat with the bags and Nora sat in front, a foot away from Peter, who jogged the reins, ready to start right off. The carriage jolted forward, but then Cottoneye put back both his ears, reared, and tossed. The wagon swayed. Bill bucked nervously, and Peter felt Cottoneye drag—about to bolt.

"Get out!" Peter shouted to the women. "Quick!"

Mrs. Howard hauled herself out of the swaying carriage. Her husband ran forward to help, but Nora didn't move. The carriage rocked from side to side, the horses banging against each other.

"Miss Nora, get out!" Peter shouted.

Nora didn't budge, and the horses broke into full canter, crashing eastward down the path toward the hills of timber. Nora, grasping Peter's arm, didn't speak but stared wild-eyed at what lay ahead.

The wagon slammed into a tree.

Nora was thrown. The back of her head struck a large branch of timber. She lay there, still. Peter leaped from the turned-over cart, still holding the reins on the bucking and frothing horses. He rushed to Nora. He fell on his knees beside her and raised her head in his hands. Before his eyes swam the vision of the ox he had downed. He saw the blood coming from her nose.

Peter heard the cries of the others as they ran toward him, and he was overcome with a rush of tenderness and fear for Nora. He didn't want the others to touch her—those people for whom he felt nothing at all. She might have been his sister, the way he leaned over and lifted her up, as if she were merely sleeping and he was carrying her to bed. He carried her toward the big house, oblivious to the shouts and queries of the others, who stood back to let him pass.

John Howard shouted abuse at Peter. "Why didn't you get thrown? Why her? It's all your fault!"

His brother held him fast, and glaring at him, said, "Shut up, John, shut up. You don't know nothing."

John, who always blamed someone, screwed himself loose from his brother's grasp and strode to the scene of the accident, where the horses now stood quietly. He knew enough to see that Cotton-eye was not the carriage horse and that what had happened was not Peter's fault.

He stood back, baffled and forlorn, and watched the others trailing Peter into the house. Only Wash stayed behind, outside. He was slipping quickly into the stables. John went to get his whip where it hung on a peg on the porch, and went after Wash, his usual ally. His whole body tensed with excitement as he reached for the whip. This is what happened every time: a seizure of pleasure at the slap of the whip on skin. It was his secret reward.

Inside the house, Peter carried Nora upstairs to her bedroom, which he had never seen. Her parents called instructions behind. He gently laid her down, and pulled a quilt over her legs. Then he pushed aside her hair and saw a large red scrape buried near the base of her skull. He winced, glancing at Will Howard.

"At least she's alive," he said.

"Thank you, Peter," said Will.

"You may leave now," added Mrs. Howard. Her arms were folded, her body slack from the shock.

Peter turned and looked at her coldly. His head was held high, his eyes filled with a reflection of Nora's suffering. Mrs. Howard looked back at him and for the first time that their eyes had ever met she looked away as if ashamed.

Nora uttered a soft groan, and Peter, moving to the door, paused to look back at her. He saw her eyes roll and her lips move.

"Peter," she whispered. "Is Peter all right?"

He left the room and hurried downstairs. Charity met him there.

"Is she all right?"

"She's awake at least," he said, and didn't stop moving toward the door.

Charity ran along beside him.

"Are you all right, Peter?"

"Just fine." They both stepped outside, and he paused to look at Charity. "Guess I'll get a whipping this time for sure."

"No," she said with triumph, "Wash got it. He was the one who hitched up Cottoneye."

Peter saw John Howard step out of the barn. Quickly he moved away from Charity toward the slave quarters. She wanted to follow him, but Mrs. Howard was calling her name; so, confused between her own desires and those demands, Charity stamped her foot, cursed, and went nowhere.

Peter lay face down in his cabin. He breathed slowly and deeply, trying to absorb what had happened and lay it to rest inside himself. He was sad. Nora's grasp on his arm as they raced toward the tree was something he still felt. It was a desperate hold, deliberate in its self-destructive goal, and it lingered on him like a sting. The space between them was an impassable abyss, a social accident protected by law. He could do nothing. If she died, he would feel guilty and bereft.

He realized that in spite of her frailty, she gave him hope. She was like a bridge made of reeds, leading to more than freedom. She led him to believe that the barriers between slaves and their owners could be dissolved by an act of faith and goodwill. Her presence seemed to say it was really possible to cross those lines and switch destinies. If she died, he feared the return of his own bitterness.

Then he heard a tap on his door and lurched up.

"Who is it?"

"Charity."

"Come on in," he said.

She entered the pungent, damp cabin, closing the door behind her.

"Are you all right?" she asked.

"I told you, I'm just fine."

"Then what are you doing? She's going to be all right. If she's talking, like you say."

Peter gave a quick laugh.

"And you'll get a whipping if you don't go back to the big house," he said, and lay down on his back, his hands clasped under his head.

"What about you?" she asked as she stood looking down over him.

"I'll get a whipping, too," he said.

"You said you'd never let him do that again."

"At this moment, I don't give a damn."

"Why? What's wrong?" she asked, kneeling. Her dark face in the gloom shone slightly. Moist, her pink lips parted.

He smiled and looked at her carefully. She was, he realized, beautiful to him. With serious lips and melancholy eyes, she was not as funny and childish as he had thought her. Her presence was suddenly very forceful, hovering there beside him, and he cautiously looked into her brown eyes to see what she was feeling.

She was breathing high and hard but he caught the rhythm of it. He held his breath and felt heat spreading from his navel, inside, to the surface of his skin. He heaved an involuntary sigh, and tentatively held his hand up to press it against her curved neck.

She covered his hand with her palm and sighed, too. They both felt hot like melting objects.

"You'd better go," he whispered.

She nodded, and rose to her feet slowly, slipping out of the cabin.

Peter rolled back onto his stomach, letting the heat drain out of him slowly. A wake of grief was left behind.

16

IT TOOK MANY WEEKS for Nora to recover, but her accident produced various changes on the farm. Her fall seemed almost symbolic of the desolation of the land and household. There was a flurry of activity to rectify the situation. The two Howard boys, Nora's brothers, returned and took over some of Bart Williams's property to build houses on. Bart Williams took more and more charge of the Howard affairs, buying and selling their cattle for them. Mrs. Howard moved home again, on condition that John Howard let her rule the roost and that her husband stay at home more. Peter was sent back and forth, weekly, between the two plantations.

Through the fall, Nora remained prone or seated at her bedroom window and took note of all these changes. She felt gratitude that she was still at home. She suffered bad headaches, but felt she could suffer anything as long as she was on the farm. She watched the leaves turn from green to gold to red and brown, and the trees grow bare before winter. She vowed she would not be depressed this winter, since she was tucked away safe in her own room.

She vowed, too, that she wouldn't follow Peter so closely when she was well. Whatever wild streak that drove her nearly to kill herself rather than leave home or him, could be put to better use. She had many hours to listen and to think. She heard her family talking in high-pitched and anxious tones with increasing frequency about the issues of slavery and free soil. She heard the slaves talking about other homesteads and other places where they all could meet for religion and for dancing.

She went over the facts. Peter was the half-brother of her infant lying in the grave. Peter was Betty's baby by the same man she had loved. In one farm after another, from Missouri to Louisiana, there were children like this, born of one man by varieties of women, most of whom hated the men wrestling with their bodies and planting their seed in them. A new nation was arising out of this violent shame and division.

Missouri was a slave state, but nearby in Kansas, slavery was abolished. It was all happening so fast, and out of random and conflicting desires for land, so that the Bible stories were really the only moral maps available. Nora listened and pondered. Her own body was like a fragment of a land in turmoil. Her baby, buried; the slave baby survived but had no real home. Peter did not share her blood, but his father's seed had traveled through her body and been turned into the boy who lay underground. Peter should inherit the farm that she loved. He worked the gardens, the animals, the trees with skill and attention. He was almost hers. She cried every time she thought this way, which was often. She grew up around livestock and reproduction. Peter was close enough to being hers that she thought it was not crazy to imagine him running the farm in years to come.

SOMETIMES ALONE UP THERE, curled around her pillow, Nora remembered Dan's smell that was unlike her father and brothers. It was sweet, as if the hairs on his chest were nurtured in wet foreign grass. His mouth had the taste of his smell. Their ritual was that he would remove her boots, and then she would remove his and they would lie in dark shadows under an elm and play with each other. It would conclude with his seed deposited inside or outside of her, the sad and happy voices they made together.

He would talk, then, for a long time in colorful monologues about his home and family, and about politics—the French and American Revolutions, the Bill of Rights, the dream of a perfect union, equality, freedom—about the British and their oppression of Ireland. The Louisiana Purchase. The French and Indian Wars. He gave her the most perfect lessons in Western history anyone could have. He liked adventure and experiment and seeing how things worked.

This she finally decided was what he did with Betty—tested her, to see what a dark girl felt like—just once or twice. And then he was gone. But first he told Nora that he would return, on his way east again and bring her with him to the mountains of heather and gorse where she belonged.

She thought with sudden clarity that her mother had sent Betty away with Dan's baby by her so Nora would not know what he had done while he was getting her pregnant. Her mother wanted to protect her from the shame of being used like that. Her baby had died, but Betty kept hers, Peter, and he came out looking just like Dan McCutcheon. That's what Nora came to believe in order to explain Betty being sent away, and in order to think no ill of her mother.

SHE WATCHED HIM out in the fields and her eyes burned with pity for him. She wondered why one person has more value than another. When her mind was on fire, her questions streamed out of her, and she had the urge to pick up a fist and break the window glass. What gives one person a price and another none? Is it all about the work each one does? What would Dan say? Abolish slavery is what he would say. It had already been abolished in England. Give everyone a piece of land, some shelter, and the freedom to come and go, is what Dan would say.

NORA KNEW that there were different ways of running farms and plantations. Bart Williams went out into the fields and worked beside his laborers; so he knew them all well and personally. They discovered and watched together. She knew that they had shelter and food. But they were not paid. They were not free to come and go. It was wrong!

The fruits of their labor did not belong to them. Any payback would go to the landowners. And what about the Collinses' place where Betty was? Peter told her there was an overseer and the master never came out to work, or bothered to know any, but one, of his slaves well. When Nora got new information, she worked it over. But it took a long time. She had to go through many contradictions in what she imagined before she could see what the reality was. Now she had boiled the matter down to anger at her mother who confused society with religion, church with God, and God with magic. She even prayed to a God who would manipulate people's feelings and bankrolls. Her mother was proud and had never gained respectability or power over her situation. Depression plagued her. She prayed that her daughter would lose the illegitimate child she carried so that no one would condemn her.

Nora would never know that Dan came back a year later looking for her, that he was hurried out of town and lied to. There was a lot Nora would never know because her thinking was slow but not stupid; it was slow and it was careful. She knew how to love and to understand the political realities that were personal too. But it took her a little too long to put two and two together.

The Object He Became
1854

1

ON A WARM AUGUST SUNDAY, a surprise visitor arrived. The sky was hazy and the grass wet. Sunflowers bowed their clocklike heads and foxgloves dripped water. In her garden, Nora lifted her head at the sound of strange hoofbeats approaching. A man sat on a strawberry roan, his face shadowed by the brim of his hat. His posture was straight.

Nora thought it was Dan McCutcheon, and felt dizzy. She hung onto the stalk of a pink hollyhock for support and watched the stranger approach.

He saw she was the only one about and reined in beside her garden.

Releasing the flower from her grip and shading her eyes with her hand, Nora looked up at the man and asked, "Can I help you?"

He took off his hat. "Well, I don't know," he said. A smile crossed his face. He was honey-skinned, blond, blue-eyed, slim. His expression was intelligent and reserved. "Is there a man about the place?"

"My father," said Nora, "is inside the house."

"I was told by some people called Williams that I might find a room to stay here for a few days."

"Oh yes," said Nora, approaching the man and resting her hand on his horse's flank. "I guess you're a Northerner from your manner of speech."

"From Boston," he said. "My name is Nolland, Nick Nolland. Just doing a little research on wildlife in these parts. Mushrooms, herbs—that sort of thing."

"Really!" she cried with honest interest.

"Do you think your father will let me stay?"

"I don't know why not," she said. "You wait right here, and I'll go get him."

She smiled excitedly into his eyes and ran toward the house. The man dismounted and left his horse standing while, flower by flower, he examined Nora's garden with more than idle curiosity. He held the head of a flower in the palm of his hand and cupped it gently sunward in order to see the interior design.

Nora and Will returned almost immediately. Will looked fierce and suspicious. Nora was all leaps and hopes. Nick Nolland was clearly a man who couldn't hurt a fly, but Will asked sharply, "What you doing in these parts?"

"Well, as I told your daughter, I'm a naturalist. Doing a study on plants that grow in dark places."

"Well, you can't stay here," Will snapped with a sharp glance at his daughter. "No question of it."

Nora's face fell into despondency.

"Why not, Daddy?" she asked. "We have the room."

"I'd be paying, of course," Nick said quickly.

"Nope."

Nora examined her father's strong profile and realized what he was thinking. Her cheeks burned, and angrily she dropped her eyes to the ground.

"No, you go on to the next farm," Will said, "or back where you came from. Don't be hanging around here." Nick was confused. Will continued, "These parts are full of trouble. My wife isn't well. Nora, here, and I are pretty much in charge. We only have a couple of field hands on the place. The rest work over on the south farm, the Williamses' place, and we've got our hands full."

Nick, shrugging slightly, gazed at Nora's downturned profile.

"That's too bad," he said softly. "But I want to congratulate you on your beautiful garden—Miss—?"

"Nora," she said firmly.

He turned at the sound of footsteps. Peter was crossing from the barn, his eyes fixed on the trio by the garden. He was carrying a basket of potatoes.

"Is that your son, sir?" Nick asked of Will.

Will turned scarlet. "No, that's Peter. He's a hand." And he strode away to meet Peter halfway and block his presence from the stranger.

"I guess I'll head back to Mr. Williams then," Nick said quickly to Nora. "I think he just sent me over here as a favor to your father. I'm sorry I embarrassed him, about the boy there. Is he a foreigner?"

"No, no. That's all right. Peter is unusual. We're all used to questions like that." She smiled warmly at Peter, then turned back to watch Nick mount his horse. "I hope you have good luck."

"Thank you. I hope maybe we'll meet again during my stay out here."

"Maybe," she conceded, smiling.

She watched him turn and ride back in the direction he had come. She felt both glad and sorry. She was immediately attracted to him and his Northern manner, which seemed kinder and more sensitive than others. It was a mental attraction, drawn from words she had read about and by Northerners.

Her father went to her and said sternly, "Why did you encourage that fellow? You know where he comes from, and you know what that means. Besides, don't you remember what happened the last time someone from out there stopped here?"

"He's nothing like Dan McCutcheon," Nora said coldly. "Not a man's man. He's American. And whatever his views are, I'd be interested to hear them."

"Ever since you banged your head," her father said, "you've been too free with your tongue. Don't understand it, don't like it."

"The bang on my head just loosened my tongue," Nora said. "It's real simple."

She brushed by him to return to work in her garden. Will watched her disappear into the tall rows of foxglove and lavender. He returned to the house, where Peter had left the potatoes.

Either he had to go to market or he could send Peter. His two sons and Bart Williams had taken over his life. John lived over on the south farm, too, in his own sordid cabin. The less Will had to worry about, the more indecisive he became about the little things left in his charge.

Nora's garden now was a very prolific space on the farm. She did all the work there. She grew not only flowers, but green vegetables.

The rest of the land was ably tended by Peter, who grew the root vegetables and the corn. No more cattle grazed on Will's land. Bart had taken over the livestock. A few chickens, mangy dogs, and horses remained.

Will realized he had failed at the farm. His earlier stoicism had been broken down into a kind of self-pity, and he was often irritable. His head was filled with reactionary ideas and opinions on politics and human behavior. He believed that England was right to keep her monarchy and class system in place; to leave property to the eldest son and to continue to use slave labor on the Caribbean islands.

For him slavery was about caste, not color. This was not unusual, for white people to have a class attitude that infiltrated all their opinions. He needed free labor the way other people needed domestics, free guns, and animals. Trafficking in slaves was not too far from indenturing servants from Ireland, or buying ammunition from the French. It was all about money. Nobody thought much about differences between people from unexplored countries, except that they were low, born to work.

He loved Nora more than his other daughters, and his protective feeling for her, which was so strong, had not been very useful.

The thought of a new man coming along and playing with her again—especially a Northerner!—was ugly to him. From the inside window he watched Peter entering her garden. The two of them were examining some sprouts together. This ironic image struck William Howard hard in the head and chest. He was filled with a blast of memories like a forge going into full blaze for he had been told, firsthand, by his brother John, what had happened one night almost twenty years before. He had never let it sink in.

2

ON THE SOUTH FARM Nick Nolland sat out on the veranda with Bart. They had just finished a good dinner and were smoking pipes. Through the warm summer darkness came the sounds of children.

Nora's two brothers lived a few yards from Bart's house in two separate farmhouses. Their children roamed the property freely. John Howard's cabin lay farther away, closer to the slave quarters, where he spent his nights drinking alone.

"That man's my one complaint in life," Bart told Nick. "Can't stand his guts. But I'm stuck with him."

"Why doesn't he live on the other farm?"

"Oh, too much trouble there, too much trouble. Got to keep him away from the white boy as much as possible." Bart sighed and blew smoke rings slowly. "Slaves have no legal protection against a man like that. On the contrary, they're at the mercy of the law. People like myself have to take measures and keep our own folks in good shape. It's up to us."

Nick listened acutely and remarked, "Sounds like you don't support the slave system wholeheartedly."

"I'll tell you. I don't like it, never did. But I live in a nest of it. What can a man do? I do the best I can. Feed them good. Give them time off."

"I know this part of the country is torn over the issue," said Nick, "ever since the Compromise. Some go with the Union, others don't. Must be hard holding on to your own opinion."

"Well, my wife and my sister-in-law, Nora, they share my point of view. But what can a woman do in a case like this?"

"Not much," Nick agreed, "but tell me something about Nora Howard. Will you?"

Bart smiled. "She's a pretty little thing, isn't she, despite her age."

"How old is she?"

"'Bout the same as you and me."

"She looks younger."

"Surprising, too. She's a woman who's suffered."

"Yes, I could sense that."

"Quite a story there," said Bart.

Nick said nothing, realizing he didn't have to urge this man to talk. He liked Bart, who combined intelligence with heart. He felt he could trust him.

"Happened over twenty years ago," Bart said slowly. "Long time, really, before my time here with the Howards. I guess Nora was about sixteen. An Irish man came to the farm to stay, a surveyor for the railroads. Well, Nora fell for him and he for her, and they did the natural thing, if you know what I mean."

Bart chuckled, puffed, and continued.

"He went north, promising to marry her, before either one of them knew she was carrying his child. He was gone for the duration of her confinement. Her parents—well, they near hit the roof. And the night the baby was born, they did a terrible thing."

Leaning to the side, he cupped his hand over his mouth and whispered the secret of Peter's history into Nick's ear. Then he paused to check on Nick's reaction. Nick was openly astounded.

"McCutcheon did come back in fact," Bart said, "but an old slave—a great old fellow, Ben—was sent to shoo him away. McCutcheon left. So we have a situation, now, where Peter and Nora don't know anything. Terrible story. And some of them there know the whole of it. Terrible."

"It certainly is," Nick said.

"The sad thing is, Nora has a real mother's love for that boy, Peter, and all without a whit of knowledge."

"God!"

They fell silent and leaned back in the darkness. Crickets chirped from the trees and grasses. A soft evening wind blew down on their faces.

"So what's your situation, Nick?" Bart suddenly asked.

"Oh, I'm just doing a study—won't be around for long."

"Married?"

"Widower, now," he said. "Lost her in childbirth seven years ago."

"Sorry," Bart said kindly, "real sorry. Got any children?"

"None."

"Then stay awhile. Enjoy yourself. I like the company."

Nick quietly thanked him and stared with wondering eyes into the darkness.

Two days later Nick ran into Peter. Nick was beside the trail that ran between the farms. His horse grazed nearby while he prodded through pine needles and examined specimens of moss. He heard the sound of wagon wheels and saw Peter, alone, in the cart on the way to market.

Nick smiled, stood, and approached the wagon as Peter drew in the reins.

"Hello there, Peter."

Peter nodded.

"Fine day, isn't it?"

"Just fine."

Nick appraised Peter. He was a full-bodied man, bearded and muscular. Nick could not understand how he could be called a boy.

"I'm glad I ran into you this way," Nick said slowly as he looked down the road, "because I wanted to ask your help with something."

Peter waited.

"I'd like to see Miss Howard, Nora, again, some time," he said haltingly. "I know her father doesn't like me. But I thought, if you would, you could find a way I could see her again."

Peter smiled slightly. He gazed into the blue between branches and thought of Nora's reaction. Nora had liked this Northerner. He knew it. She had said she wanted to talk to him more and get some information about things in that part of the world. She said she was sure his attitudes were different from the men they knew, and she'd like to hear them. Peter knew that she was referring to Nick's attitudes on slavery. So he was filled with delight at this encounter.

"Well, sir," he said slowly, "I know where you can find her on Sundays around six o'clock. She's down where you are on the south farm, visiting the slave quarters. She often stays at Ruth's cabin."

"Ruth?"

"Works in Frank Howard's house."

"Ah, I see!" smiled Nick happily. "Thank you."

"Nothing to it," said Peter with a flash of a smile as he jogged the reins and started moving forward again.

Riding away from Nick, Peter still smiled to himself. He had already felt good, but now he felt better. The Northern man might be a promise or sign of some kind. Maybe he would sweep Nora off her feet and make a way for her and the others to escape. Maybe there was hope after all.

He shook his shoulders a little and tried to check his longing. He loved Charity openly now. Sometimes this love gave him a sense of expectation disproportionate to his situation. He wanted to see the happiness he had in himself impressed visibly on the landscape and faces around him. In flashes he felt he could see it.

He knew he shouldn't ask for too much. Things hadn't been too bad on the farm lately, with John Howard gone. That was probably enough to ask for a while. Most of the other slaves were rarely around, so he had his solitude and the right to work the land as he saw best. He was all but free.

He could move between town and farm. He could play his fiddle over on the south ranch on Saturday nights while everyone danced and he could have Charity to himself when their day's work was done.

Then they could sit together alone for a couple of hours and watch the sun set on the plowed land that felt like Peter's own.

3

NOW THE DAYS of midsummer were long and warm and hazy. The following Sunday, at six, the shadows were long but mellow, and people lounged around outside and listened to the birds riot in the dusky trees. Nora came to see Ruth and stayed an hour before returning home. They often sat on the grass or stoop outside the little cabin, their faces turned to the sun. Slapping at mosquitoes and flies, they idly exchanged details of their weeks.

That night when Nick Nolland approached, everyone was prepared. Peter had warned Ruth and had told Nora about his conversation with Nick. She fidgeted nervously, watching Nick walk down the dusty trail past the slave cabins in their direction. It was not romance, but information, she was after. She was afraid of being misunderstood.

"I'll tell you," Ruth whispered, "he's a gentleman. Always says please and thank you to the girls."

He stood before them in a minute.

"Just taking an after-dinner stroll," he explained quickly. "Glad to see you again, Nora."

"Are you looking for specimens, too?" Nora asked, rising anxiously and brushing grass off her skirt.

"Well, I always keep my eyes open for some interesting plant," he smiled. "Would you like to walk along with me? Just up the path a way?"

Nora looked at Ruth for an answer and got a quick nod back. She went with him. Her heart pulsed hard. Her breathing was uneven as if she had walked five miles. Her mind was a complete blank, and her tongue like wood.

He seemed as shy as she, but then good fortune appeared in the form of a grotesque pink-tinged mushroom.

"Look at that!" Nick exclaimed and left the path for the dark underbrush. Nora followed and kneeled beside him.

"Are you going to pick it?" she asked. "Is it edible?"

"Yes, I think it is edible. But I'm not sure."

"Then leave it."

He delicately lifted the cap and turned its fringe upward. She saw it was made up of strangely beautiful velvet pastels and folds. He told her its name and its origin and gave her a brief history of mushrooms. Nora was enthralled.

Briefly she forgot he was a man, and a stranger, because he was so interesting. As they moved on down the path and talked, she had to think of Dan. His form, as it appeared beside her sometimes, produced such a conflict of emotions, she would bite her lip in pain. She glanced at Nick beside her and felt his attraction.

He smiled reassuringly and asked her about herself. She told him she was a very uninteresting person who had lived all her life in the same place.

"I'm a quiet person myself," he replied. "I'm a scholar really, not a traveler. If it wasn't for my interest in mushrooms and such, I wouldn't be here. I have no family, but live alone in four rooms on a road facing the Charles River. I go to the library. Sometimes I present a paper to other naturalists."

"Weren't you afraid to cross this huge country all alone?"

"Well, I'm enough of a coward to avoid certain unpopulated areas. I would like to see some buffalo, though."

"You'll have to go a little farther west for that," Nora said. She wracked her brains for a way to raise the topic of slavery with him.

But then the path ended in a thicket and the two turned and walked slowly homeward. Nick frequently looked at Nora, but she kept her head bent down and glanced into the woods from time to time.

"Well, I think I'll do that tomorrow," he said. "I'll set off west."

"So soon?" She looked wounded and surprised.

"Oh, just to see the buffalo. Then I'll stop back here on my way home." With a nervous cough, he added, "I'd like to see you again."

Nora paused in her pace, suddenly feeling dizzy.

"Are you all right?" Nick asked anxiously.

"Yes, yes, I just must be overtired or something. From gardening, all week, you know."

"Yes, but it's worth it. You've done a beautiful job."

She nodded, but started forward at a stride now. Her face eagerly strained for the end of the path. She saw the first cabin, then the second ahead. Her heart reached for the familiar harbor of Ruth's cabin, at the least, but more so, Peter.

Almost in answer to an inward plea, Peter appeared at a bend in the path. A fishing pole lay against his shoulder. His catch was strung on a stick in his hand. He heard them behind him and turned.

"Peter!" Nora called.

He waited, hearing the urgent tone in her voice. She looked at Nick briefly, saying, "I'll see you then, when you come back," and rushed forward to walk beside Peter.

Nick, standing behind them on the path, knew what they could not know. It was the most touching sight he had ever seen—the two of them walking innocently through the shadows together—and one he would never forget.

4

THE WEEK NORA WAITED for Nick's return, his name came up again and again. To the Howards, Nick symbolized all that was effete, decadent, and potentially dangerous about the North. Will and his wife discussed him over dinner and with Bart over drinks. In a sense, they were fascinated by what they most feared and their talk filled Nora's mind with a sense of Nick's importance.

Bart said: "I like the fellow. He doesn't interfere, does his work. Keeps to himself. What's the problem?"

"I think he's studying us, not toadstools and whatnot—that's the problem," Will said.

"Northerners are like that," Mrs. Howard said. "Believe me, I know. I come from those parts. Never could stand the way they think."

"You didn't spend all that much time in Bristol, Mother," said Nora. "At least you always used to say that England was your real home."

"Listen to her," snapped her father, "defending a man she knows nothing about. Last time that happened, it led to—well, we all know what."

Bart spoke in Nora's defense. "She was young then, Will. If she likes this man, I don't see how the same thing will happen."

"I don't much like him," Nora said, "because it's true I know almost nothing about him. But I think you are being mighty hard on a stranger, Daddy."

"He's coming back, and he's going to stay with me," Bart said firmly. "I expect him Sunday."

"Well, Bart, it's your home. I wouldn't let him stay in mine for all the gold in the West," Will said. "His opinions on Franklin Pierce, on the Compromise, on slavery—rubbish. Didn't you hear him talking?"

"He says what I say," Bart stood up angrily, "and you can call it rubbish if you want."

"Must we talk politics?" Mrs. Howard cried.

"We'd better talk it," said Bart, "because the whole setup we've got here is going to be affected by what we think. If the family is split on these issues we'll be in real trouble."

"Well, you men discuss it alone."

"I'm curious, too, Mother," Nora said, standing beside Bart, "and I don't wish to be kept ignorant just because I wear a skirt."

"Well, one thing I know is you're not going to Bart and Nancy's this Sunday. You're not going to talk to that man and get full of ideas," her father said, adding, "and that's an order."

"She can come to our place any time she wants, Will, and she's entitled to her opinions." Bart gave Nora a sharp nod. Turning on his heels, he swiftly left.

Nora stared at her parents, who looked, beneath the angry surface, deflated and frightened. She felt a moment's compassion for them.

"Bart won't stay mad long," she said. "Don't worry."

"Now, you listen here, miss," her father returned, "I meant what I said. You're not going to consort with that fellow—not over my dead body."

"Yes. Speaking of dead bodies," added her mother, "we don't need any more of those following on your wild sprees."

Nora strode from the room and into the kitchen where Charity was idly stirring batter and staring off into space.

"Charity, I need your help."

Charity's eyes lit up and she moved over to let Nora sit beside her.

"You know that Northern fellow?" said Nora. "I want to see him again. It's important. But my parents are being nasty about it. You and me have got to figure out a way."

Charity studied Nora's flushed and freckled face.

"What's so important about it?" she asked.

"Well, it's kind of hard to explain. But I feel that he might've been sent here, somehow, you know, by the Lord, and can give me some knowledge and directions. I just feel he's got things to tell me. Nothing romantic."

Charity moved the wooden spoon slowly around the edges of the bowl and mused. "You think he's special because he comes from the North. Isn't that right, Miss Nora?"

"That's part of it. Why do you look so worried?"

"Well, I'm thinking if you married him, you might take Peter with you. That's all."

"Charity, I would love to get Peter away from here, and you know that. But I'm not thinking about marriage. I don't even know this man. I'm thinking more about his ideas—that's really all."

Charity was not yet comforted. No matter what affection she felt for Nora, a complete leap of trust was out of the question. Her destiny was not her own as long as she was a slave. Those who could pick and choose like Nora were capable of unconscious cruelty. In some subtle way unknown even to themselves, white people undermined the ties Charity's people had with each other. Charity knew that Peter could be torn away from her, even under the guise of an act of love.

"Well, he seems to have his eye on you, anyway," said Charity coolly.

"I'm too old."

"You don't look more than twenty-five."

"Whatever I look, I'm too old to feel romantic. It's just not in me."

"Well, then, what do you want me to do?"

"You and Peter figure something out. I know you can. A way for us to meet. Peter will be traveling over to Bart's tomorrow. I know that. So maybe the grapevine telegraph can get to work. Okay? Please?"

"Sure, Miss Nora."

Charity grimly poured the hominy in a pan. Nora, engrossed in her own situation, was not sensitive to the girl's emotions.

5

AT SEVENTEEN Charity was her mother's daughter in ways of work and conscience. She might stir the batter half-heartedly, but she did it. Her sanity came from her constant activity. A pause from labor made her imagination snap loose like a kite string and take off into the sky. This was a feeling she didn't enjoy.

Now she was slender and round. Her complexion was mocha, but dipped into a deeper darkness in her curves. She was always starchy clean to her ankles in her white chemise, and held herself straight. Her head of hair, a thick black mane, was a great source of pride.

Like Peter, this year she was happy, although happiness was no more than release from pain. John Howard was over the hill and out of their way. What more could a person ask? His distance meant blissful softenings to the edges of each day, possibilities of truly individual actions. Only one who has suffered from the effects of a tyrannical personality could know what joy its removal brought. Just as hair tied up could, when suddenly unpinned, transform the image of its owner, the slightest release in tension in the atmosphere made the world's beauty visible.

Charity and Peter took it slowly and carefully as a luxury. The threat of permanent, or long-term, separation was always present. This threat produced in both Peter and Charity a set of reactions neither dared mention. It made them afraid of getting too close and it made them crave a complete fusion right away.

When together in the evenings they sat and Peter practiced his fiddle, or whittled, while Charity hummed songs, or sewed. They luxuriated in each other simply and said little.

Ruth had advised them to go slowly and enjoy their youth and freedom from caring for anyone but each other.

"A baby would only bring you worry now," Ruth said, "and I want you to wait and be married first."

They couldn't help stealing an occasional long and devouring kiss or desperate hug in darkness before saying good night.

One night after talking to Nora, Charity found herself happily alone with Peter. They met on the stoop outside his cabin.

The nights already were getting shorter, so by eight the air was dim and gray. A harvest moon winked behind the slow veils of cloud. A few mosquitoes buzzed in the air. The frogs in the woods and the crickets made a loud cacophony. Peter watched his view of the corn grow dim. He was proud of the work he had done that year in the fields. It had been a better crop than when he was under the yoke of John Howard.

"Soon it'll be time for harvesting," he told Charity, "and the boss will see what a sweet crop we've got this year."

"All thanks to you."

"How all this corn came to be still surprises me, even though I planted it myself." He smiled to himself. He began to sand a long wooden ladle.

She looked at him lovingly and then drew a deep breath. "Nora came asking us for help today."

"What kind?"

"That man from up north. Seems like she wants to get close to him, but the boss won't let her over to Bart's farm to see him."

"That so. From what I hear old Master John is just dying to get the two of them together."

"What for?"

"I figure he wants Nora out of his way, so he can move back over here again."

Charity fell silent. The notion sounded reasonable and awful.

"Then we better just leave it alone," she concluded. "Better not get involved. I don't want Master John back here—not ever!"

"No," he said softly and laid down his work to look at her. "But there's another side to this, too. If Nora was to marry a Northern man, no telling what good it might do for us."

Charity's eyes narrowed. "That's what I'm saying, Peter. She'll take you away. Let's just leave it all alone."

Peter rubbed her back, up and down the spine, saying, "No, that won't happen. She made a promise to me once. Said she'd get us our freedom—not me alone, but all of us together."

"Do you believe her?"

"Don't know why, but I do."

Charity relaxed and leaned closer to Peter.

"I don't know why neither," she smiled, "but you might know something about white folks I don't know. Besides, Mama says sometimes weak people like Miss Nora make paths for others stronger. If she goes north, who knows? We might could all follow."

"Don't hope for nothing too clear," he said. "It's dangerous. Just put it out before you and don't look at it."

"I guess I know what you're saying."

"Well, what will we do for Miss Nora?"

"She said maybe you could figure something out over at Bart's tomorrow. Mama will help."

"Might be some way the Northern man can steal over this way Sunday when the boss and missus is gone to Carthage," he suggested with a smile. "I hope so."

"You'd do anything for Nora, wouldn't you?"

"Just about... But I'd never leave you behind. Understand?"

Charity nodded and was comforted.

"Only a fool can't be consoled," her mother would say.

6

WHEN NICK RETURNED on Sunday, he first went to the cabin, where the field hands had convened after the midday meal. Charity and the others were shelling peas. When she saw him coming, she dropped everything and ran up to meet him.

"Looking for Miss Nora?"

A little abashed, Nick glanced at the ground and asked, "Where is she?"

"Back on her home farm, Master Nolland. Her folks wouldn't even let her go to church today. She's up there alone."

"Why? I don't understand."

Charity wasted no words in explaining the situation to him. "They don't want her seeing you. You might give her ideas."

Nick scanned the faces of the slaves watching him from the cabin steps. A bright midday sun dappled their faces and shadows danced in the dust.

"I'm glad you told me this," he said, "but now I guess there's nothing I can do to see her."

"Oh yes there is," she said. "How about sneaking over there, now, while her family's here? We can tell the people you've gone fishing with Peter. She's up there all alone. Won't take you but an hour to ride over. Her folks won't get home till near dark."

"Are you sure?" he asked anxiously.

"I'm sure."

"Then I'll do it."

"We've got a horse ready for you round the bend in the road outside. Peter's there. Your own horse will be right here, so no one will guess where you've gone. Don't be uneasy now. We got it all planned out."

Nick smiled happily into Charity's eyes and absorbed all the meaning of her words. Thanking her warmly, he set off toward the road outside the farm. Charity almost jumped up and down with excitement. Returning to the others, she said, "I just wish I was a little bird and could follow along after him. I'd sure like to see what's going to happen."

"It's none of your business," Wash snapped, "what white folks do alone together."

"Seems to be a lot of our business," she said.

NICK AND NORA spent five hours together. They passed some of the time in her garden among the big yellow blossoms on the gourd vines, some under the row of sugar maples, and some on the porch when the sun arced downward.

This time they talked eagerly and fluently, as lonely people will. They only mentioned the issue of slavery briefly, so intent were they on reaching a clear sense of each other's character. By the time Nick left, they had achieved what each wanted. They had discovered themselves to be kindred spirits in the vast Missouri landscape.

"I feel as if I've known you since childhood," Nick said, moving toward the horse Peter had loaned him.

"Well, the Northeast seems a long way away," Nora said ruefully. "Time and distance come to the same thing."

He turned and looked at her intensely. "I'm a determined man,

Nora. I raised myself out of poverty and illiteracy, and I think it's all because I was able to be patient. I think we understand each other. But patience is what we'll both need now. We must write letters."

Nora looked at him inquiringly and openly.

"What I'm saying, Nora," said Nick, "is that I've chosen you to be mine." He smiled, "Whether you like it or not."

Her cheeks turned red and she smiled down at the ground.

"Well, we'll have to see about that, Mr. Nolland," she murmured.

Without a kiss or a farewell, Nick got on the horse and rode back the way he had come. Nora watched him till he was caught in the arms of the bending roads and trees.

Near the south farm, Nick came upon Peter where he had met him. He was waiting with his hands full of a day's catch of river trout, which he silently passed on to Nick, in the dusk.

Nick watched Peter's graceful transaction and sought out in the youth's face any traces of his mother's. He noted a similarity of expression rather than of feature.

"Peter," he said, "thank you for the day you have given me and Nora. I won't forget it. Someday I'll repay you for your kindness. I won't forget. I promise."

With the string of fish in his hand, he walked back down the road. He was gone.

7

NORA WAS CHOSEN, but did this mean she had no choice? After Nick left, she was confused. His letters arrived weekly, were picked up in town along with the newspaper by Peter, and secretively handed on to Nora. She read them hungrily and replied. She was flattered and excited by his attention. He seemed sent to her by the grace of God. He was a Northerner who might help her in her mission to see her father's slaves freed.

But she was troubled by his determination to marry her and take her away from Missouri. This had not been in her mind when she wanted so much to see him. The dimmest flicker of romantic desire remained in her. She viewed Nick only as an ally in her moral goals, rather than as a husband. He was sympathetic, even if he was a man. She could speak from her heart and mind in her letters to him and in person.

Her conviction that her first and only lover had violated her and Betty damaged her notion of romantic love. The idea that she was chosen scared her by its implication of her own absence of will. If he believed he could have her just because he wanted her he must be like the one other man she had known. She told him this in her letters and refused to hide from him what she felt.

The idea of leaving home was awful to her. To be separated from her little world was more than she could bear. She expected Nick to take her seriously. Instead, he replied that he was returning to Missouri soon and that he would not give up on her easily.

The following spring, he returned by stagecoach, and stayed at a hotel in Carthage. Nora could not tell her family he was there. Again she turned to Peter and Charity for help. Peter said he would take her to Carthage on the pretext of buying some seedlings for her garden. She told her mother and father she also wanted to purchase some bolts of cloth. They considered this a surprisingly venturous gesture. Nora never liked to leave home, unless it was for church.

"What's got into her?" Mrs. Howard asked Will.

"Beats me, but John's going to be in town today, too, if I know him, picking up his regular stock of whisky. He'll probably run into Nora down there."

"Well, that should keep her in line all right. She's been strange enough lately. She's so kind of pleased with herself, it makes me nervous."

"She made it right through the winter without one bit of complaint or fever. Mighty strange."

They sat side by side on the veranda and watched Peter hitch up the wagon to take Nora into town. It was a cool April day. Nora wore a dark blue cloak over her dark blue dress. The trees were hazy green. Soon the cottonwoods would float white pollen down like snow from above. Nora was full of praise for the day, chattering as if it was her first spring and she couldn't say enough about it.

"She's full of spirit all right," Will said.

"You don't think she's planning to run off with Peter, or something like that, do you?"

"Not likely. She spent the last few days digging up her garden and getting it ready for seed. Only has one gold piece in her purse."

"Then I guess spring's just gone to her head." Mrs. Howard sighed disapprovingly. "She still gets so excited by things."

They waved goodbye and watched the cart jog down the trail. Peter and Nora sat side by side.

"Sometimes I just plain forget," Mrs. Howard said, "and then, when I see them together like that, I get scared. How can I have my own flesh and blood—a slave?"

"It's damn strange. I know what you mean," Will said with a heavy groan, "but better not to think about it. Better let sleeping dogs lie."

PETER WAITED OUTSIDE the hotel while Nora went in. He wished her good luck, but could see that she was full of conflict. Luck was not the issue. Never having entered a hotel, she shyly went inside and asked the man at the desk to please tell Mr. Nolland she was waiting downstairs.

The lobby was fitted with red carpets and chandeliers. An elegant dining room adjoined it. She observed the white-clothed tables and sparkling glasses and silverware, though no one ate there at this hour of day. It was eleven in the morning; they had ridden for two hours to get there.

Nora sat down in a high-backed armchair in a corner, while the clerk went upstairs to find Nick. The hotel was worldly and unfamiliar and filled her with a sense of her own helplessness and ignorance. It was like a small taste of the outside world. Her sole comfort, she realized, was the knowledge that Peter was outside and would take her home again when she wanted to leave.

Nick finally appeared on the stairs. Smiling, he rushed to her and took her hands in his. His eyes were bright and bold.

"Come upstairs, where we can be alone," he urged her. "We can't talk here."

She assented, feeling she had no choice, and walked at his side up the winding staircase.

In his room two red velvet armchairs sat at the bow window. His bed, also crimson, was immaculate. Nora quickly chose to sit in a chair by the window, where she could look down and see the beloved figure of Peter. First she looked at Nick to see if he was the man she remembered. He was. The many letters they had written gave a new depth to his appearance. She was moved by his presence and recalled his script.

"I'm so glad I came all this way," he said. "You're as beautiful as ever."

"I don't know what to say!" she confessed.

"Don't say anything. I just want to look at you."

He stood over her. She gazed anxiously sideways out the window. The aura of the room and the adventure of her arrival increased the pressure of her conflict.

Nick put out his hands and gestured to her to stand before him. "Nora, I'm more sure than ever that I want you," he said, placing his hands on her waist. "Won't you say you feel the same?"

Many years had passed without physical contact of this nature. His hands on her body felt heavy and ominous, and made her breath come short. She resisted a moment's relaxation, but he did nothing rough or hurtful, only lifting his hands to stroke her hair back from her face and touching her neck gently.

"Come back east with me," he said. "Please marry me."

The motion of his hand on her neck eased her slightly. Being neither tall nor broad he did not seem physically threatening.

"So you are the man who wrote me those letters," she said with a smile.

"I'm the same one... I know it's strange."

"Well," she said softly, resting her head sideways on his hand, "I'm the same woman. And you know I can't make up my mind."

"I'll make it up for you."

"I've never left home."

"I'll take care of you, good care."

"I don't know if I can do it."

She faced him frankly with her doubt, and he drew her against him, not kissing her mouth, but her temple and hair. Her resistance was slow in breaking. For several moments she was like wood, but the heat and pressure of his body began to seem more emotional than physical as he persisted in moving his lips and hands around her. She closed her eyes and felt that young girl, the wild one, she had once known. Overcome with memory and emotion, she sought his mouth with her own.

For several minutes they hung onto each other, and then, both trembling, they withdrew and moved to the window. Holding each others' waists, they leaned there and looked out. Nick saw Peter below in the wagon.

"You can bring Peter with you, north," he said, "and give him his freedom if that will make you happy."

Nora pressed a kiss on his cheek, but her eyes darkened.

"I promised him I would never take him and leave the others behind in slavery. I can't break my promise."

"You care for him very much, don't you?"

"Very much," she said.

"Is it because he helps you?"

"No. It's something else in him." She stiffened slightly. "I love him for his character."

"Ah."

He watched her lovingly as he saw her expression change from mild introspection to something like shock. He followed her glance outside and saw her uncle talking to Peter below, but looking directly and curiously toward the hotel.

PETER HELD the horses' switch across his knees and gazed impassively into the crumpled face opposite him. No one would know he felt any alarm. Least of all, John Howard.

"So what are you doing in this part of town, Peter?" the man asked.

"Just waiting for Miss Nora, Master John."

"Why here?"

"Giving the horses some shade," Peter said with a glance up into maple leaves.

"So where's your mistress, boy?"

"Down a ways, buying seeds for her garden."

John guffawed. "Nora—out shopping?! Never heard of such a thing. Thought she was too delicate to leave the farm."

Peter said nothing. His hands toyed idly with the whip on his knees. John Howard squinted up and around. He was curious and unconvinced. His suspicions would never rest, under any circumstance. He could convert even the mildest remark into a plot. This was his nature. Unfortunately for others, it often led him to the truth.

"I'm going to check you out on this one, boy," he said.

He marched directly into the hotel, and only when he was gone did Peter's expression mirror his feelings. He was afraid for Nora. He didn't know what to do and glanced from window to window, praying he could warn her. No face shone back at him, and he sat helplessly in the shade.

John Howard went to the desk clerk, a young, long-jawed boy, who stared at him wonderingly. Dirty and disheveled, the little man looked thoroughly out of place in the hotel. The clerk sniffed.

"What can I do for you?" he asked in a high voice.

"I'm looking for a young lady, kind of middle-aged, red haired—that's her driver out there," John said, waving toward Peter outside in the wagon. "Got a message for her."

"She's upstairs, mister, visiting one of our guests."

John smiled, revealing a row of blackened teeth, "I know that. But how do I get to her?"

"I'll go tell Mr. Nolland you're here," said the boy. "What's your name?"

John's eyes burned. He turned around full circle, devouring the glitter of the environment with his eyes. Facing the boy, he pulled down the brim of his hat and said, "Never mind. I'll wait outside."

Grinning, he bounced out of the hotel and went down the street directly to the swinging doors of a saloon. But first he shouted: "That justifies anything I do! And I'm gonna do it."

PETER SAT STILL and waited, watching horses and people drift by in the activity of a market town. Shortly, Nora came out of the hotel. Her cloak was wrapped close around her and her face was turned down.

"We better get what we came for, Peter," she said as she climbed up beside him. "I can't go in, Peter," she said. "Take my money, please, and get me what I need."

He took her purse and did what she asked him, as swiftly as he could. He sensed her anxiety, knowing she would only want to go home quickly. The people in Carthage knew who Peter was and whom he belonged to. They were used to having him handle money. He was the subject of some gossip, the only presence who lent any interest to the Howard family. The Howards were considered small-time farmers, plain churchgoers without zeal. Their ownership of a white slave was their only claim to local fame.

"How you doing, boy?"

"Hello there, Peter."

"What you going to buy today?"

Offhand, friendly remarks accompanied Peter around the general store. Often he felt awkward, handling these transactions and dealing with these plump white merchants who eyed him with open curiosity and whispered remarks. Like Nora, he wanted to get out as fast as he could and go home.

Nora smiled wistfully and gratefully at him, when he returned to the wagon.

"You're real good to me, Peter. Thank you."

He jogged the reins and off they went. Without speaking, they traveled down the silent, forest-trimmed road away from Carthage. Only the clop of the horses' hooves and the chirp of a bird could be heard. They both relaxed in the wagon.

"I guess Uncle John found out about me being there," Nora said at last.

"Don't really know."

"He did. The desk clerk said so."

"You feeling all right?" asked Peter.

"Just kind of sad."

"Might turn out Master John is happy for you."

"Might."

He glanced at her inquiringly and saw in her troubled face that swift expression which always seemed familiar to him, but one he could never place.

"I can't make up my mind what to do," she said, "and now he's going back east to wait for me."

"He seems like a gentleman," Peter said.

"He's just that," she agreed.

She looked at Peter intensely and tenderly. "I can't just up and leave you, Peter, not after what I promised you," she said, "and not with the way I feel about all of you. I don't know a thing about the world out there, not one thing. I think I might just, well, fall away."

Peter could not contradict her, knowing how emotionally fragile she could be, and how confined her life had been. But he hated to see her lose a chance to be loved by a kind person.

"You aren't getting the kind of treatment you deserve out here, Miss Nora," he said. "It's not much of a life for someone as thoughtful as you."

"I'm happy enough," she said. Gazing into the passing thicket where sunspots danced on leaves, she shivered, remembering Nick's touch and his departure. "I just don't know," she said.

"Well, maybe if you follow the man, you might be able to bring us on after you. That might happen, you know."

Nora beamed at this prospect and allowed her head to swim with images of a moment where she, like Moses, could lead the slaves to freedom, where she could have both Nick and the people she loved, and live as a strong independent woman in a strange land.

"Oh, Peter, that would be the best thing in the world!" she said.

He smiled, pleased by the vision himself, but not daring to let it go further than that, not daring to hope. He could not forget her uncle, who, if he did not stop Nora from leaving, would surely return to the farm and make life hell for everyone again. There seemed to be no way to win. The only happiness came from giving this woman a moment's hope, which he couldn't share.

8

THROUGHOUT THE SUMMER, Nora was fraught with indecision. This was such a familiar condition for her to be in, she was disgusted with herself, and wrote furious self-deprecating letters to Nick. He responded regularly to build up her confidence in him, insisting they were meant for each other and would be happy. He praised her and begged her to return, if only to help him make a beautiful garden behind his house.

Nights she tossed, caught between an infantile terror of change and a great longing to become the woman and lover he wanted her to be. She read romantic novels, passed on to her from her sister Nancy, and the newspapers, which, with their increasing tales of bloodshed in Kansas and conflicts over territory and slavery, made the novels look foolish and her longing a dream.

Her uncle, when she saw him on Sundays at the south farm, made cracks to her about hotels, about the North, and once directly about Nick.

"That Mr. Nolland, wonder what happened to him," he said, winking at her. "Guess he's like that McCutcheon fellow, Nora. Takes what he can get and runs."

Heating up, Nora rushed in horror from his side to the slave quarters.

One night, when it was pouring rain and the sky was bolting lightning, she had to sleep at the south farm in a small room downstairs. In a narrow bed, she lay alone in a nightgown loaned to her by Nancy and listened to the violent cracks of thunder and the rain pouring onto the wooden walls, while everyone else slept overhead.

She heard knocking sounds in the dining room. They were clearly human. She sat up in bed to light the tallow beside her. The sounds were shuffling and awkward and filled her with a strange dread.

Then her bedroom door was opened with a bang, and her uncle stood swaying there, soaking wet from head to foot. A heavy smell of tobacco and liquor pervaded the room. He fixed Nora with a long, moist look, and she recoiled automatically, covering her chest with her blanket.

"What do you want?"

Slurring, he moaned, "Why don't you just go away? If you go, I can come home."

Her mouth seemed to dry into parchment. Her lips sealed, she couldn't speak.

"Just go," he went on. "Go east, north, south, wherever. Just get a man on you and go."

Now he moved into the room, swaying close by her bed. His eyes were red and tearful.

"I'm sick and miserable. I don't know why I'm on the other farm. Listen to that storm. That's me, inside. I'm miserable. Treated like a criminal."

He looked down at her, but not as if he saw her, barely able to keep his balance, rocking. His hand went down to his crotch and he made a smile. "Look at me, I'm a man! I know what it's all about, what you did, what you like to do. In that hotel. Why don't you follow him, get some more? You like it, you do it."

Swaying, he seemed to lurch toward the bed. Nora, in a leap, banged her fists on him and ran from the room. She rushed through the dining room and out into the rain, her hair flying, her mouth parted in an effort to make some sound. She ran through the darkness and trees, which floated and flapped in the thunder around her, until she came to Ruth's cabin, and she threw herself in the door.

NOW NORA'S MIND was made up. She would go, she knew that night, stretched on the floor beside Ruth, go north and take her chance. She could never look at her uncle again, whether he remembered or not what he had said and done.

At once she announced her plans to marry Nick Nolland, and her parents, though stunned, did not protest. She went about her packing with such intensity of purpose, they knew they could not stop her; and she revealed to them, finally, the packet of letters she had from the man. Her mother said she would travel east with her, stopping off to visit long-unseen relatives in Philadelphia, and would help arrange the wedding.

Within two weeks, the two women were ready to go, and Nick was informed, though he had no time to respond. Only Ruth, Peter, and Charity knew what had thrown her into her decision, what had happened that night on the south farm.

On a bright August morning, Will Howard himself hitched up the wagon to drive the two women to town to meet the stagecoach, and Peter and Charity came out to say goodbye. But Nora was nowhere around, though the wagon was loaded, the horses ready, and Mrs. Howard seated at her husband's side.

"Bet she's up at the graveside, Peter," said Will. "Go get her and tell her to move along now. We don't want to miss the coach."

Peter walked around the barn and up the hillside, where he could see Nora standing by the grave. He hated to disturb her, and moved slowly up the hill to get her. But she felt his presence before she saw him and turned to meet him, walking with her face pale and drawn down the slope and grass.

"I know," she said to him. "They're waiting."

Although she stood at a higher incline than Peter, he was taller than she, and he looked down at her face with a rush of emotion. Over the years, he had become a kind of protector; it was hard to let her go off alone into the unknown. He felt this anxiety even more than a sense of his personal loss at her going.

"Now you take care of yourself, Miss Nora," he said.

"I will not say the word 'goodbye' to you, Peter. Not as long as I live."

Nora breathed deeply and walked by him with all the strength she could muster. From afar, he watched her go.

9

THE QUALITY OF LIFE on the farm underwent a transformation with Nora gone. What little thread she tied between indoors and outdoors was cut now. Relations between them were harsh and formal at best. Tim, Wash, and Peter were all that was left of field help. Charity continued to work in the house. Nora's garden became a mass of vines, weeds, and tangles within a year of her departure. The productive energy came increasingly from the south farm where

Peter attempted to sustain the high level of produce from the fields, but saw it was almost beyond his control.

He missed Nora. Her absence seemed to fill the world with negatives. Reports of disorder and slaughter in nearby Kansas, of fights between slaveholders and freemen, and political struggle—all these issues grew more personal daily. It was not possible to feel safely insulated from the rest of the country. The railroad was expanding through Kansas and Nebraska, bringing with it a whole new breed of men with foreign ideas and hungers.

Strangers appeared frequently to water their horses and rest. Some were displaced Indians. Most of them were white men with big bellies and brown teeth. Loud and crude, they leered at Charity or grabbed at her, till she ran to Peter for protection.

He would easily kill one of those men. They never suspected he was a slave, however, and usually backed off when he approached, believing him to be an armed overseer. Often they talked to him freely about their ideas and their appetites, about whores they had known, and where they stood on the slavery issue. Some believed in the system, and others did not, but whatever a man believed appeared to have no effect on his manners. He had come west for one reason: to get something for nothing.

After one of these strangers had left after making a lunge at Charity's body, Peter decided he would marry her now before someone could hurt her. She was eighteen and ready. He was constantly worried for her, and for himself. He feared she would be stolen away one night and that he would lose her forever.

Their relationship was filling with frustration. They had restrained themselves over an extended period of time for reasons both complex and simple. Now, with the ominous figures of other men appearing on the farm, it was impossible for Peter to sit out with her on a summer evening without wanting to possess her completely. It was emasculating. Those men carried guns. He had nothing but his body.

"Let's jump over the broomstick," he said with a smile that summer night.

She beamed happily, then became pensive. "If Miss Nora was here, we'd have a real wedding. I bet she'd make me a white dress and I'd have flowers."

"No flowers around here since she left," he said. "You think your Ma will say it's okay?"

"She said it already. There's safety in numbers. We're going to have lots of babies, Peter, lots and lots."

"You really want to make a bunch of little half-breeds?"

"The day you forget about your color, Peter, I'll be happy. I don't see it anymore myself, and I'm the one who has to look at you. You can't see yourself. Look, your freckles are just Betty trying to come through."

"We will have lots of children, okay," he said. "They will do better than us, much better."

She smiled. "Let's jump over the broomstick at the south farm on Sunday. I don't want to wait."

"All right, Charity," he said, holding her against him, "I just know when we can really live together, I'll be a man."

She shuddered, intensely moved by his touch.

"I know it, too, Peter," she said.

The following Sunday, they were given a little party with cakes and sweet tea in the cookhouse and out on the lawn. Nancy let Charity wear one of her dresses, and the whole Howard and Williams clan gathered to watch her make her successful leap with her skirts raised over the broom that Tim and Wash held. Peter followed with a laugh and a hoot. The day was mild and sunny; there was music and dancing, but everyone was restrained under the cool gaze of the white people

10

A YEAR OF MARRIED LIFE in the Northeast had not been happy for Nora. She was literally pining away for home, and Nick could do nothing to comfort her. City life frightened her, and she passed most of her time in the little plot of land behind their townhouse, where she tried to make a garden. She had no interest or ability for socializing. She fed herself on books—fiction, poetry, and the works of naturalism that Nick brought home. She did love him, especially when they were alone in bed together, at night, reading or making love. She was one person at night—passionate and affectionate—and another by day—tense and self-contained. She lived for letters from her mother.

When she heard Peter and Charity had married, she found herself in tears, miserable to have missed the occasion; and she promptly set to work making a dress to send to Charity as a present. She felt like a bird that has been lost in some migratory move and finds itself in a foreign and hostile environment. Her husband's arms were her one shelter, and fortunately he was a quiet man who asked only that she be there for him, not for others.

Her one year of marriage stretched into two. She longed to have a baby, but none came. She heard that Charity was pregnant again after having a daughter. Time and distance did nothing to dissolve her involvement with home, and the reports of bloodshed, of John Brown's massacre, and of the Wild West only increased her involvement.

Feeling mean and ungrateful, Nora spoke little of her homesickness to Nick. She held it inside and only raised the issue in abstract discussions of slavery.

"How could I free those people and bring them here?" she asked him. "I can't forget them! What could I do to help?"

"They know where to find you, Nora," he said. "When the time comes, you can reach out to them."

"When what time comes?"

"Emancipation."

"It will take a war, an awful war."

"I think you are too morbid at times," he told her. "It may be accomplished without bloodshed, using law and language instead of weapons."

"No. I wager I know those men better than you, Nick," she said with thoughts of her father, brothers, uncle. "They are rough, and raised to think little of a human life."

"But they have no power, dear," he countered. "The ones who have power are our legislators and senators."

"The people with power are those who hold the guns," she said.

"Well, we'll see," he said mildly.

Too nervous to attend political rallies, Nora nonetheless read the newspapers and kept track of the abolitionist cause. Nick did not know, and never would, as well as she did, what the meaning of slavery was, to those both owned and owning. His views were academic, but Nora suffered at the reality of the lives of those she had left behind.

One night, after she received a letter from her mother mentioning that Charity had given birth to a son, Nora dreamed of home and of Peter. She dreamed he had turned into a boy, a small boy, her son, and was playing around her in her garden at home in Missouri. He came to her, trying to tell her something, looking up into her face, his eyes expressing desperation; but she couldn't understand his meaning. She woke up in tears. The house was dark, and Nick was fast asleep, but she woke him up to tell him the dream.

"I want a child!" she cried to him.

He held her close, and was unable to fall asleep himself.

"If there is a war," he told himself, "I will take her home, and I will tell her who Peter is."

11

PETER AND CHARITY liked to go dancing. Saturday nights they would leave the children with "Grandma" Ruth, at Bart's place, join up with several others, and head off for a meadow in the woods, where they could have a campfire and do as they pleased. Peter played the fiddle. Out in the meadow, under the moon, those good times were harmless. But sometimes bands of bored white men patrolled the areas where slaves met, breaking them up with gunshots and threats, with lynching, with assault and sometimes rape, and sometimes with the theft of a slave or two to bring south for money.

To counter the dread of danger, they began to prepare themselves, mentally and tactically, and to become stronger for it. They knew where their own masters stood, for there was open division of opinion growing between the families. Bart Williams went so far with his sense of responsibility for his slaves, and his own pro-Union ideas, that he let Peter carry a gun to the Saturday night meetings.

Will Howard, and his son, Frank, supported the Confederacy, and Frank soon moved his family to the other farm. Worst of all was John Howard, who was never permitted to return home because of his drinking and erratic behavior. He lived in his hovel on Bart's land, close to the slave quarters, and became increasingly dependent on their cooperation to keep himself alive. He whipped whoever failed to bring him what he needed, whether it was wood for his fire, liquor from the store, or bread for his table.

Wash remained his main cohort and was ordered to steal gold pieces from Bart's saddlebags. John was acquainted with a couple of men who made their living stealing and selling slaves, and he paid them in gold to bring him his regular supply of whisky. These two had been mountain men, coarse but clever as foxes. Like John, they were heavy drinkers and misogynists. Unlike John, they were strong, and survivors. They didn't like him, but wanted his gold.

Bart knew that this man, his wife's uncle, was terrorizing the slaves, and he hated him, and berated him. John, though, was something he was stuck with, as the last contract between the two families. They were in opposition politically, yet remained, through the marriage and the land, economically bound. Bart agreed to keep John on his place as an expression of his trust in the families' relations. Bart was making plans, as yet unknown to anyone, to move his family to Texas, where he could free his slaves and start a cattle run up through the Midwest. He could afford to be patient.

PETER, watching his children being born where he and Charity were also born, had to swallow surges of rage and resentment. He stayed out a lot, because he had a good relationship with the ground under his feet and the trees; the views and the sound of the wind ever blowing. These could keep him calm, able to work with rhythmic gestures, to learn.

He worked hard on improving the land. It was he who was responsible for the crops, good or bad, and therefore was responsible for the success or failure of the farm itself. Yet after a day's work, he watched the rewards of his labor slide from his own hands into the big house and into the mouths of the Howard children, Frank's boys and girls who grew plump and strong.

His own children, a fine little brown-skinned boy and girl, couldn't eat an extra peach without being called thieves. Without Nora around, and with the Howard views on slavery becoming more ideological and self-justifying daily, there was no emissary of kindness coming from the big house to the slave quarters. There was no instruction; there were no treats. He couldn't bear to see them suffer. Their grandmother was of the same mind as Peter. Having raised Charity with the promise of a freedom that never came, she couldn't bear to see her grandchildren growing powerless, too. She and Peter talked about it often when they were alone.

"But don't go showing these feelings to Charity," Ruth said. "She doesn't need to hear what she already knows. And she frets over your temper, Peter, fears if you get too mad at the boss one day, you'll be sold. So don't talk to her about it."

"I still have my hopes," he confided in her, "that Miss Nora will find a way."

"Peter, we all know that Miss Nora would come and get you any day she could. And why?" Ruth's face, though faintly lined, was still impassive most of the time, and she looked at Peter as if from afar. "Because you're white. You're still the only one of us with any hope, boy, because of your color."

SHORTLY AFTER this conversation, when rumors of war were increasing daily, Peter learned that Nora was coming home. Her mother was not well, and this gave her an excuse to make a trip to Missouri. Peter wanted her to see his children, and still hoped she would find a way to free them all.

Almost immediately, he went up to the graves and gave some attention to the long-neglected mound where the bones of her baby were said to lie. It was early autumn and the grass was long, brown, and dry against the stone. Old flower stalks from perennials hung broken. He tidied and clipped the overgrown area, promising himself to have it in shape by the time she got home.

That night Charity and he lay fondling each other in the dark. Their children breathed asleep beside them. Peter whispered, "Maybe our chance is coming, maybe Miss Nora will find us a way out of this."

"Oh, Peter, you forget what kind of woman she is, and how much older she'll be. Weaker, even, than before."

"But she's been a long time in the North. She'll know things she didn't know before."

"Lord, I hope so, but you're the one who always tells me to go slow."

"That's because I love you," he said, kissing her, "and I don't want your feelings getting hurt."

"They're bound to get hurt sometimes, and so are yours."

She sighed against him, and with his hands he marveled at her firm smooth muscles, so pliant and familiar to him now. Time had only softened the rough edges between them, fitting each to the other's shape in increasing depths. Their nights with the children, and alone together, were what they lived for, and Peter imagined himself and Charity and lots of children, the other folks like a tribe in their own right, setting forth to Kansas.

"If I could just have my own piece of land," he often sighed inwardly before sleep, "with all our friends on it, I would feel all these days were worth it. The anger would finally go." This night he added, "Please Miss Nora, come and help us out. Please make your promise come true!"

12

IN LATE OCTOBER Nora returned with Nick. She was thinner and paler and older, though her hair was still red-gold. She was dressed in fine style, sky-blue satins, and in her trunk she brought clothes for everyone in her family and for Charity, Ruth, and the children.

Peter watched her arrival from his place at the plow in the field, saw the figures of her family swarming around her, and Nick watching, at a slight distance. At the sight of her, Peter felt a trace of anxiety. Would she still be the same good woman? What if she had changed, become worldly and cold?

She entered the house, and Peter returned to his work with his head bent against the bright fall sun. He imagined she would come and see him at the end of the day. Or maybe not at all? He quivered with a hard shove against the plow.

He didn't see Nora come out on the veranda and shade her eyes, looking across the fields at him, or hear her quick and quiet approach. His nerves jerked when he heard his name.

"Peter!" she cried, a few feet away from him.

He dropped the plow and smiled happily. She rushed up and took his hands.

"You look wonderful!" she said.

"It's good to see you, Miss Nora," he replied, seeing how she had aged and did not look well.

"You must come now and show me your children. Come on." She pulled him away from the plow. "No one will mind. Are they being good to you, Peter?"

"Same as ever."

"Well, Uncle John's not back, and that's something."

She walked swiftly, but gave an impression of false happiness. She veered around behind the barn. Peter followed her up the hill where they had said goodbye.

"I just want to stop here first," she said over her shoulder.

He was glad he had fixed up the little grave in advance for there she stopped, seating herself on the headstone. She looked up at Peter with a deep sadness in her eyes.

"Is your man being good to you?" he asked her.

"He's never been mean."

"Are you glad, coming home?"

"Nothing looks quite the same as I remembered," she said slowly. "Things are smaller, people older. Everything has changed. It's about a thousand miles from here to there, and all the way I was thinking how good it would be to come home. And it is good. But I'm scared. A war is coming, and my Nick will go and fight for the Union. I'll stay here at home. Who will I talk to? My family and I don't agree."

Her voice trembled and her eyes filled.

"You can talk to me," said Peter.

"I haven't kept my promise, Peter, but there might be freedom coming for you anyway. Can you forgive me?"

He burned, internally, stirred by some bitterness.

"You can't," she said, "can you?"

"Why have you given up?" was Peter's response.

"I don't know," she said off into space. "It's a man's world, a man's war. Nick is on the other side, I don't have a chance."

His disappointment was so great, his temples pulsed, his mouth dried.

SHE LOOKED AT HER HANDS, folded on her lap. They were silent, as a few leaves drifted off surrounding trees. Peter saw her lurch and cough suddenly, the same kind of cough that Caleb used to give. His old anxiety for her returned in a rush.

"Better get a cloak on you, Miss Nora," he said, "before that cough gets any worse."

"First I want to meet your children."

Rising, she coughed dryly again, and this time it was she who followed him as they moved down the hill. His fists were clenched, his eyes on fire with the hurt of her words.

13

SHORTLY BEFORE Nick left Missouri to return home, Nora's disease went into a remission, and her youth and health appeared to return. Her cheeks were flushed, and she became fired with all sorts of ideas. She believed, once again, that she would free her father's slaves. She talked incessantly to Nick about her schemes, all of them wild and impossible, and if he had not known the nature of her illness, he would have believed her mad.

Instead, he patiently listened to her, even encouraged her in her plans to steal Peter, Charity, and the children away at night, stop off at Bart's to collect Ruth, and keep going, on foot, a thousand miles to Boston. She was not so deluded that she spoke to her parents about any of her social attitudes. Her mother was sick with an intestinal disorder, and Nora took care of her.

At night she lay beside Nick in her childhood bed. In the candlelight, she looked like a young girl.

"If something goes wrong in our escape," she told him, "I want you to promise me one thing."

"Anything, dearest," he said.

"You won't let anyone hurt Peter or the others, and you'll make sure they get their freedom and all they deserve. They want to stay together."

"I promise."

"I know you'll always do what you say. You're such a good man."

"I hate to leave you."

"Oh, Lord, come back soon!"

They looked at each other passionately, and Nick, drawing her head into the bend of his arm, remembered the vow he had made to himself that night in Boston. Now that the moment had come, he found he couldn't utter a sound. The revelation of Peter as her own son might throw her over the deep end. Her reaction might be so intense and erratic, she would get even sicker before he could return to her. If he were not about to leave her, and if she were not sick, he reasoned that he would tell her. But how could he do it now? *And how can I not do it?*

Now he wished to God that he didn't even know the secret, wished that Bart Williams had kept his mouth shut. A secret and a lie came to the same thing. What would Nora think of him, telling her only now what he had known all along? Her whole life had been played out in the shade of the unknown. When they were far away, he had learned to forget it. Now the presence of Peter made him conscious every minute of his sin.

"I am as bad as the rest of them," he thought. "How will I ever make up for it?"

One part of him said *Tell her*; the other part said *Don't*.

He thought he might lie further, tell her he had just discovered the truth, and thereby be free of her anger.

What should he do?

She slumbered on his arm, and he leaned out, gently, to blow out the candle. He gave her at least a year more of life, for he had known other victims of tuberculosis who lived many months between depressions and remissions. He planned to be away for only a few months. The war would be resolved efficiently, quickly, and he could return to bring her home.

"And then her slaves will be free anyway," he thought, "and we can move Peter and his family north. I'll tell her then."

After Nick left, Nora began to fail again. She could barely move from room to room, and the household was reorganized around her illness. Frank and his family moved back to the south farm, so the children wouldn't catch it; and Ruth came to take care of Nora.

The snow began to fall after Thanksgiving, affording a respite from the talk of war, of marauders, of endless danger. The snow seemed to serve a positive function, shielding the farm from invasions from outside. Nora lay coughing in her room. She wanted Nick. She asked for Peter. But one was too far away, the other forbidden to see her.

Her uncle, instead, came to visit her on an unseasonably warm and slushy day, when the world outside was dripping and gray. Nora was sitting alone at the window in her room when he arrived. She saw him ride up, and her heart instantly began to pound wildly. She wanted to call for Ruth, but was too weak to make a move or a sound; so she listened to him, his voice rising up through the floorboards.

The sound of her own coughing blotted out what he said, but she heard him, unmistakably, outside her door.

"You dressed and decent in there?" he shouted.

She didn't reply. He entered and squinted at her from the door. He was too fearful of illness to come any further.

"So you've come home to die?"

The blood in her ears thumped.

"You sure look fit for a shroud." He glanced suspiciously around her bedroom, then back at her. "Guess your old man couldn't take it. Split for the War? Well, it'll be a long time. I come over here to get myself a blanket. Still stuck over on Bart's place. Living like a dog. Cold, cold to the bone."

He turned and closed the door behind him, but still hovered there, feet away from her silent figure.

Lowering his voice, he said, "Now's my chance to tell you something you should've known a long time ago. I come over here to get myself a blanket and to tell you something. You listen real careful," he hissed.

"I warned you outside the hotel that day. Some day I would get into you. It will get your blood going."

Nora listened as he talked and watched his mouth move. The shadows in his face darted and reshaped themselves. He told her about Peter, what her parents had done, and how Peter was her natural son. As he spoke, Nora saw him as something stranger than a mere messenger. His dwarfish figure swam around before her eyes and was transformed into a demon that fell from the sky with a crash before her feet.

"Peter?" she said, and felt her heart break.

THE RIGHT SIDE of Nora's face was slack, her right arm paralyzed; she had lost the power of speech, but was still filled with understanding. Everyone blamed her stroke on John, though no one knew what he had done or said to induce it. She alone knew and found it appropriate, somehow, that it was he, that wild and diabolic figure from her youth, who should be the bearer of the truth. Or was it the truth? He was a sadist; he could be lying up to the very end.

With this doubt, she knew she was finished, not so much by her symptoms or physical pain, as by the sense that her illness was familiar, a summary of her whole life. She must talk to Peter; yet she could not. If she uttered a sentence, it came out as a mad babble. Even if she could write a message, the one to whom it was written would be unable to read it.

Her left side responded to all stimuli, while her right side lay still as wood.

The doctor came and said "apoplexy" and her mother went to her own room to hide with her grief. Her father came in the evening and asked if there was anything she wanted. She tried to say Peter, but the sound she made was not his name. Her eyes were luminous and desperate. He couldn't bear to look at her twisted expression, and went to find Ruth, who would sit by her bed for the night.

NORA LAY AWAKE in the darkness, rehearsing a gesture with her left hand. She would wave up from her belly, in a swoop to show pregnancy, then point to her heart and out to the air, where she wrote a question mark, where she imagined Peter standing, watching, and understanding her.

Ruth saw by the light of the moon the hand moving up and around in a meaningless way. She had seen others dying, doing the same, plucking at imaginary bits of lint on a blanket, the hand darting out toward invisible shapes. These motions were a sign of the approaching end, and she slipped to the bedside and asked Nora if she wanted her mother or father to come in the room.

Nora closed her eyes. The left side of her face was in a frown. Her hand continued to move up and down. Ruth sat beside her, took the hand, and leaned down close.

"Do you want to see Peter?" she asked.

Nora opened her eyes and looked imploringly at Ruth.

"I'll get him then and sneak him in."

It was both very late and very early. Nora saw the sky turning violet, and she heard one bird sing. It must be around four, she realized, and imagined it was spring. Her hand, circling, rehearsing, was growing tired. The wheels grew smaller and smaller. Solitude engulfed her. She began to cough in quick, violent jerks.

The final stroke came as a relief from the coughing that racked her chest. She was engulfed by her own blood, her left eye fixed on the blue of the sky. *The wind is so quiet*, she thought, *escaping*, and saw the figure of Peter looking down beside her.

Her hand swooped up in a final energetic gesture, and she pointed to her heart and to his, and then she died.

Peter fell to his knees beside the bed. He had only understood the gesture to affirm that there was love between them.

Open Doors of Time
1860–1865

1

PETER CONCEALED his own grief even from Charity whose face had become half-sorrow and half-spirited like the moon's phases. Why should he care so much, he wondered. Nora had been gone for years, had failed to keep her promise to him, and was just another white woman bound up in the slave system. Why should he feel so broken? He was embarrassed by himself, and it took all his self-control not to shed one tear at the funeral service beside her baby's grave. Only Ruth, carefully observing him, seemed to perceive and understand his mourning.

Ruth never imagined that John Howard had told Nora the truth about Peter, but after that stormy night on the south farm, when Nora tore into her cabin, she could easily imagine him scaring her to death.

"I would like to see that man laid down in the cold ground, too. Seems like the better you are, the harder you have to hurt to get to the other side," she said, "and that being so, John Howard won't have a minute's pain."

Peter, clenching his teeth and looking out across fields of snow, murmured, "He won't get off easy, if I have anything to do with it."

He remembered Nora seated on the headstone and could not come to terms with her death. He longed to give it some meaning, but all he could think of was some violent act against her uncle. Revenge: the word had meaning for him now. An eye for an eye, a tooth for a tooth. He felt he had been careful, even too patient, for too long. John Howard had terrified others for years, but now his turn was coming.

Peter did not worry others with these feelings. He saw the old master and mistress sink into sudden age after Nora's death. Their sons enlisted in the Confederate Army, and left Missouri. Peter was given increasing responsibility for the farm work. At least three times a week he went to Bart's place or Carthage, on one job or another. By spring, he was overseeing the fieldwork. He was not, however, allowed to carry a gun again, or exchange money.

"No slave will ever carry a weapon on my place," Will said. "Not even Peter."

Unarmed, Peter had to watch out for marauders and horse thieves. He carried no traveling "pass," because he was well known in the neighborhood, and anyone who didn't know him would never believe he was property. So he moved freely back and forth, as the old master sat ever watchful on the veranda with a rifle on his knees.

Every time Peter realized Nora was gone he felt a shot of grief with an angry spasm aimed for her uncle. She would never see the slaves get their freedom, if they ever got it at all. Sometimes Peter thought it might be a kind of blessing that she died at the edge of the War and never had to see the inevitable violence. The values of a whole society were thrown away like chaff, and nobility of intention was almost invisible. Even the Union soldiers were crude and dissolute. The slaughter in nearby Kansas was not limited to pro-slavery forces.

And where would it end? Peter couldn't guess, and only fretted over the fate of his children and Charity. Between them and any number of atrocities was the aged figure of Will Howard, rifle on knee, when Peter was gone.

One spring day, Bart Williams set off for Texas to investigate the cattle-train prospects. Left in charge of his farm were the two friends of John Howard's, the strong ex-mountain men, and John Howard himself. Will was supposed to keep an eye on things, too. Bart had no choice but to leave the farm like this, given the absence of any other family men around, and he did it uneasily.

"Just stay out of John's way," he told Peter, "and those two big fellows—Bobby Allen and Tip Crotched—will keep an eye on him."

For a couple of days, all went smoothly. But on the third day, Peter found himself face to face with John. Peter had just put four horses in the paddock behind the barn and was setting off to the cookhouse to get a meal. It was dusk, and he planned to sleep at the south farm, so he'd be up at dawn to help with the planting. The horses had come with him to help draw the plows.

"Where you going, boy?" asked John, emerging from the barn. Peter looked at him coldly without a pause in his stride. "Stop!" the boss shouted. Peter stopped and turned. "Get those horses out of my paddock," John said, "go on."

"What do you want me to do with them?"

"Just put them out to field."

"What for?"

"What do you mean 'what for,' boy? Jesus Christ, I never heard such an uppity question."

Peter moved a foot away from John. "What for?" he said again.

John warily looked up at him. "You do like I say, boy, or I get the nigger beaters on your back."

"If I let the horses out, they'll head back for the home place, so what's the advantage in that?"

"Just do like I say."

"Okay. Boss."

It took every ounce of self-control for Peter not to throw the man against the barn wall and pound on him. He went instead to the paddock. He slapped the backsides of each horse passing out the gate, and said, "Go down, then, go on, go down." His eyes blazed at John Howard.

The horses moved at a fast walk up into the free grassy pasture, then stood in a confused group.

John went back inside the barn.

Peter quietly moved back in that direction and sensed that the man had something on his mind. He could hear, inside, the rough voices of John and the other two white men, Bobby and Tip, but not enough to catch the words. Just a soft laughing and a murmur. Boldly Peter went to the entrance and looked in.

"Anything else you want me to do, boss?" he called.

The three men laughed in response from the shadows. Shrugging, Peter went on his way.

Before dawn, Peter was called from the cabin where he slept with Tim and Wash, and was confronted with the burly figure of Bobby Allen. The moon was sliding away through a dense, damp fog.

"Them horses is gone," he said. "Better wake the boys and go after them."

Peter scrutinized the man through the deep gray air, trying to read his intentions. The big ruddy face held some kind of information, which Peter was at a loss to interpret. He knew something was up, but he went to do as he was told, waking Tim and Wash.

The three drifted sleepily up through the wet morning grass, bathed in waves of slow-moving fog. The air was silent. No birds sang. Large drops hung and blinked like eyes from the branches. There was no trace of the horses.

"They've gone home like I said they would," Peter murmured.

Tim and Wash drew near. "If we don't bring them back, we'll get a whipping."

Peter gazed into their anxious faces. "I know."

He felt tremendously sad, dumb, and blind, gazing through the whirling fog. He stooped and picked up a rock.

"Boss wants to beat us. No way to win," he said.

"Think those big white hunks are hanging around in this field?" whispered Wash, clutching Peter's arm.

"Your guess is as good as mine."

"What'll we do?" said Tim. "Paddy rollers might be out and about."

"Let's go home," Peter said. Holding the rock, he moved along in the direction of the farm, almost invisible to himself, and only able to see the grass at his feet. "Might as well get beat on a full stomach."

The trick and the fog combined to make him feel defeated. He felt he had unwittingly dragged Tim and Wash into regions intended for him alone. John Howard was out to get him. In this country and in these times a man without a gun in his hand was no better than a rabbit without ears. He could only defend himself by his wits, and his wits had failed him.

"And if I was smarter, what could I have done?" he wondered. "Nothing" was the only answer.

The sight of the boss, whip in hand, waiting for him was enough to arouse his old angers again and blot his feeling of depression. The man he connected with Nora's death stood wrinkled and waiting. Peter walked by him without a glance and picked up a wash-pan full of rainwater off the steps of the icehouse. He squatted down, dashing the cold water on his face. Tim and Wash stood before the boss. They were grinding their teeth.

"Tim," said John, "go put some food in your belly, and you too, Wash. Got something for you to do when you're fed."

They hesitated before heading to the cookhouse, and John approached Peter, looking down at his bent back. He never came too close.

"Want to eat first and get beat later?"

Peter stood. "No. Let's just do it on an empty stomach. That sounds just fine to me, boss."

He started to unbutton his shirt, his eyes fixed on the smaller man's face.

Peter said, "Maybe you'll do it, and maybe you won't. Never can tell with you, boss. If you do it this time, why, I'll be mighty surprised. You know I'm going to get you. You know it like you always did. Just a matter of time. I don't know what you had against Miss Nora, but I know how bad you hurt her and that's enough."

Peter did not lower his eyes as he spoke and watched the man's face turn a pale gray. Peter knew that he had the power to terrify the man, through words. Lacking other power, he used them fully.

"You don't know what I know," he said, "but I know everything you know. You want to beat me? Go ahead. You want to kill me? Well, that's too bad, because I won't die. No, I won't die. My skin? It feels nothing. Like a ghost feels nothing. Want to touch it and see?"

He moved forward, his arm raised, toward John who, grasping his whip and his gun, backed off, shouting out the names of Bobby Allen, Tip Crotched, Tim, and Wash. Peter, shirtless, was bathed in the wreaths of gray fog, his skin pale and his hair damp and golden.

"Here. Shoot—whip—whatever," he murmured. "Go on, boss, do it. I won't die."

John turned and scurried toward the barn as the two bigger men were coming out. Every form was swallowed in the dense fog. Peter climbed over a woodpile and up onto a pile of small boulders, and stood there, half smiling. It was wonderful to discover the power of words. He waited, and watched, and saw Tim and Wash, veiled and murmuring with the white men. It was a question of who would do the beating.

"Tim, you tie him," said John Howard, "and Crotched here will apply the lash."

Tim backed off, saying, "Master John, I can't tie him, no, enough, I can't." A brutal shove knocked him backward.

Peter climbed down with his wrists extended before him and emerged from the fog. He held his arms out close before John Howard, saying, "Go on, boss, do it yourself. Don't you want to touch me? Don't you dare? Go on. Here I am."

"Crotched," John said and jumped behind Wash.

Crotched slowly removed the rope from his belt, belched, and approached Peter to tie him hard. He gave him two big shoves backward with a sharp-eyed look. "Lean down, pale face, and let's get it over with." He turned back to John and shouted. "You want to beat him? Here he is. Beat him."

Then he stood, paring his nails with a knife. His heavy body was easy in all its parts. Peter drew a deep breath and leaned over, prepared to withdraw through numb walls of flesh and enter his hidden cave.

He heard the big white man say, “It’s a coward’s game, Howard, beating a man on the back when he’s tied.”

“That’s not a man, that’s a slave,” said John.

But the whip hung limply by his side.

Crotched belched again. “Well, let’s get on with it. Looks like you enjoy it a little too much. Give you pleasure, huh?”

John reddened and gave Peter three brushes on the back, no more than the brush of forest branches, then dropped his arm and stared, as if transfixed, at Peter’s bare bent back so marked with raised scars.

“What’s wrong, Johnnie? Got the fear of God in you?” asked Crotched, grinning.

“Can’t do nothing with the pack of you watching,” said John in a low voice. “Can’t do nothing.”

So Crotched slowly and impassively moved away and was swallowed by the gray fog. Hearing silence, Peter rose, turned, and saw the boss right by him, the whip hanging loose. He was rubbing his eye and temple hard, as if in pain. Peter observed him closely, coldly, and saw that he was a sick man. His face was ashen, his eyes lined dark and blue. Cruel and violent words crowded in Peter’s mouth, but he clenched his teeth and held his tongue.

“Start walking,” John said to the ground. “Go home and get those horses back here by noon.”

Peter looked down and saw the point of John’s boot digging into the dirt. An ant crawled into the niche he made there, and he covered it with a kick of dust.

2

PETER WALKED to get the horses home that day, and while he was gone John Howard went on his last rampage. No one could stop him, not Bobby Allen or Tip Crotched or poor Nancy who, after untying Peter, had hidden. He lashed one slave after another, children included, roughly throwing their small bodies around. He tied Tim up in a tree by his thumbs, and left him there, swinging.

Even Ruth, whom he always left alone, was struck across the face. When Peter came home she said, near tears, "It was a real bad thing, oh terrible, like the devil had gotten right under his skin. No one could stop him. He went here and there, cursing and abusing the first person he saw. He was like a man filled with lust, like one of them soldiers you hear tell about, when his captain is sleeping and he's in a strange town they've taken that day. He didn't know us. That was the fearsome part. He didn't even know us."

"I'll go now while he's sleeping. I'll kill him at last," said Peter, breathing as if his chest would break open.

She held his arm, saying, "Don't worry about that. He's as good as killed himself."

"Why didn't he whip me? Why? If he had whipped me, it would've been all right down here while I was gone." Peter covered his face with his hands and felt, as never before, a hatred for his whiteness. It was all he could see. What he had imagined as power, his power of speech, was nothing; the only reason the man left him alone was the color of his skin. Nausea filled him, and he took Ruth's hands, asking, "Will he die? Tell me he'll die."

"He will, all right. I see it coming now."

Peter went outside in the dusk and visited several of the injured people, including Tim, who lay in darkness, his misshapen hands bandaged with rags. The slave quarters, foul and falling already, were shambles. The more effects of John Howard that Peter saw, the more enraged he became. He stood in the damp and listened to the sounds of people murmuring, children whimpering. Then he heard his name.

"Peter!"

He thought it was Nora. His heart leaped, and he whirled around. Hugging herself tight, Nancy stood in the gloom. Her face was pale and tense.

"Peter," she said again, "you must go to the doctor. The master—John—has taken real sick. Wash is driving him up to the home farm. Go get the doctor and bring him there."

She stepped closer, searching his face with her eyes.

"Let's pray," she whispered. "Let's pray it's the end."

He responded silently, and went to get his horse. He was bone tired, having walked all that way during the day, but exhaustion seemed to drain from him in a flash at the thought of that man's passing.

NEAR MIDNIGHT, Peter arrived at the doctor's neat white frame house on the outskirts of Carthage. It was the man who had come to see Nora. A burly man with a curling gray beard, he knew the Howard family slightly, and Bart Williams better. He let Peter into his hall by candlelight.

"Which Howard brother is it?" he asked.

"John, sir, the one on the south farm."

The doctor snorted slightly, indicating both contempt and knowledge, and cleared his throat.

"Is he real sick, Peter?"

Peter looked him in the eye and smiled. "No, sir, I wouldn't say so."

"Well, then, put up your horse. We can hold off till morning," said the doctor with a bright smile. "A little time won't hurt him. Or anyone else," he added.

Peter went to the barn and lay down on some straw for the night. He could see a sprinkling of white stars from where he lay, and for an hour he believed he would be a free man one day.

After breakfast the next morning he and the doctor took a leisurely ride to the home farm twenty miles away. The sun was bright, the leaves a luscious green. He and the doctor conversed quietly, as equals, giving Peter another taste of liberty. They talked about the Howard clan, Bart, farming, and about the War. "It's going to go on a long time," the doctor said, "for civil war is always the most violent and long-lived. But at the end we'll all be better for it, I hope."

When they arrived at the farm, old Will was out on the veranda in his usual position, but leaped up when he saw them coming.

"What did you take so long for?" he shouted. "What were you doing, Peter?"

The doctor reined in beside him and looked down.

"Peter came," he explained, "shortly after I came home from another call. I told him I needed some rest."

"Well, get yourself in the house, doc, and see what's wrong with my brother."

Will gave Peter an angry, suspicious glance, and hurried back to the house. The doctor, shrugging and smiling at Peter, remarked, "Don't envy you, my friend," and he went inside the house.

John lay dying in his windowless old bedroom. His face, under prickly white hairs, was bright yellow. His lips were cracked and dry.

"Nothing I can do for him," said the doctor to Will and his wife. "It's the drink, finally got to his liver. He'll just want some water, which you may give him."

"How long does he have?" asked Mrs. Howard with open distaste.

"Couple of days at the most."

Jubilantly, the news was carried by Wash to the south farm. Tim and Ruth were instructed to return to say goodbye to their old master. Cheerfully, they did as they were told and returned the following day in a wagon. The only person who felt any remorse for the dying man was his brother.

"I can see how it happened, where all his bad habits came from," said Will. "Not all his fault either. We didn't have much of a chance, neither of us."

He lined the slaves up in a row outside John's door. The gesture was symbolic for him of the order he was trying to sustain. The slaves should be respectful up to the end. Will believed they admired and even loved John. Tim, clenching his twisted and still hurting hands, was the only one who balked.

"Don't make me do it, Master Will," he begged in a whisper.

"Do as I say, and don't be ashamed to show your grief," said Will, giving him a shove.

Tim entered the dim and odorous room, and hung by the bed. He stuck out one of his hands, and John, from his nest of pillows, his face as lifeless as a ball of parchment paper, blinked and grimaced.

"Get away," he whispered through his thin dry lips.

Tim left, fast, and the others entered one by one, squeezing the limp and bony hand of the dying man with a murmured goodbye and disgust. Peter was last. He folded his arms and stood staring, immobile, beside the bed.

He heard the far voice whisper, "I'm going home."

Peter said nothing. But he watched John's hand rise slowly from the bed. The fingers drooped. Peter couldn't bring himself to shake or touch it.

"Do it, boy," the far voice whispered again.

John's eyes filled with a look of terror, his cheeks sunk in, and his lips quivered on soundless words.

Peter turned and left the room. He felt nothing—not relief, pity, or anger. Only his shoulders felt lighter.

As he had requested, John Howard was buried above the usual burial ground, on a rocky incline facing east. Peter, Charity, and Wash dug the hole to lay his body in. It was hard work breaking through lumps of granite, and two days passed before they could bury the body. Along with the slaves from the south farm and Nancy, they attended the brief service.

When it was finished and the Howards had returned to the big house for a meal, one of the slave women, a very deep-lined elderly woman who had done laundry for years and whose hated husband had died before her, slipped over to Peter's side.

"Before you cover the wicked man over," she whispered in a toothless lisp, "drop this letter in." She pulled a scrawled note from inside her dress. “It’s going to my old man down below. I got one more thing to tell him and that body there is going to the same place.”

Peter cheerfully took the letter and when he was alone with Wash, Tim, and Charity, dropped it down into the hole. Then Peter and Tim, in spite of his aching hands, rolled a big rock over and into the hole, where it landed with a thud on the wooden coffin.

“There,” said Peter, smiling, “That should hold him in.”

3

WITH NORA AND JOHN both dead and gone, with Nancy following Bart in all his designs and opinions, and with Jeannie silent and far away with two sons in the Army, old Will and Mrs. Howard didn’t know what to do with the rest of their lives. They were frightened. This world was not the one they had known.

They sat together for many hours on the veranda and looked at the patches of waste spread out between small sections of arable and working land. Peter was trying to keep it all under control. Without more help, he was nearly useless. But more important, without more control over the help he had, he was immobilized. Will would not hand over the reins of power to Peter.

“We don’t even know for sure who Peter is, where he came from,” he would say.

“I never did believe he was Nora’s,” his wife replied vaguely.

“Nope. We took him in. That’s all.”

“Maybe a mistake. No proof.”

“I’m going over to see Bart today,” Will finally said to his wife. “Can’t just sit here another hour watching the troubles accumulate.”

“You’re not leaving me here alone,” she said firmly.

“No. You come along. That’s right.”

“Then who’s going to watch out for thieves?” she asked. “Think we should give Peter the gun?”

"Never," he said. "We'll just take our chances."

She sighed deeply, but didn't quarrel. Since Nora's death, she had lain to rest her fighting part and was close to living a vegetative life. Sometimes her mind became alert for a short span and her critical powers would return but then they would be engulfed by a kind of fatigue and boredom.

Will told her, "I don't trust Peter as far as I can throw him. Not with all this fighting going on. He's smart, but he's still a slave, mine, just about the last piece of useful property I got. Give him a gun, and you'll see what happens."

So they rode away together in the cart and left the farm in Peter's hands.

He knew they were fools to leave him unarmed. He knew why they did it and wondered why he shouldn't just pack up his things and go that night, taking Charity and the children. They could head west for Kansas on foot and travel by night. Why not?

He went up to Nora's grave, which he always kept in good order and prodded around in the soil. He thought about escape. *If we head east, we'll be recognized at once. If we head north, we'll get into towns and cities, fast. If we head south, we'll be done for. If we head west, we'll be in Kansas. Kansas.*

He always thought of Kansas when he thought of freedom, though he couldn't exactly say why. The border was an open bleeding wound. Residents were pushed this way and that by the government forces to accommodate the madmen like Quantrill, pro-slavery butchers. But somehow he imagined that if he could cross that wound, he would be at home, which, for him, meant anonymous.

To be anonymous would be a blessing beyond all others. To be absorbed by a tremendous sky and landscape. Kansas was nowhere, and nowhere was where he wanted to be.

"Well, Miss Nora, what'll I do?" he murmured.

The silence engulfed him, and he swung around on his knees to look at the farmland he knew so well. He had strong feelings about what could be done to improve the farm. In Will's hands, nothing ever got done. Consequently, Peter felt increasing indifference to his work, a kind of anger. He was getting careless, and he knew it.

The thought of escape returned to him. Nora would probably urge him on. Certainly Ruth would. And Charity?

He went down to the big house to talk to her and found her in the kitchen with the children.

He immediately said, "Why don't we just pack up and hit the road?"

Charity gave him a long dark gaze.

"Just one reason," she replied and nodded at the two children. "We wouldn't make it."

"You can't be sure of that."

"Honey, this war is everywhere you put your foot. We'd be caught up in it in a minute. The woods are crawling with men and their guns. You know that."

"I could pretend I'm your boss," he suggested.

"Without a gun? Some of them wouldn't care if you were boss or not, long as you didn't have a gun. They'd take me and the children."

She was right. He sat down, pulling the children onto his knees, his large hands in their hair.

"Well then, let's just enjoy a day alone here," he said. "We can pretend we own the place."

"Yes, we can pretend," she sighed, casting an anxious look out the door. "Long as no strangers come around, we can pretend all right."

They spent the afternoon seated on the veranda, like the boss and his missus, watching the children play. The air was cool, and the sun warm until late afternoon, when it reddened into a hard ball and dipped down. Those were hours of sheer pleasure, when no one threatened or called and they could luxuriate in them.

When night came at last, they drifted to their cabin. They were full of ideas of what it would be like when they finally got their freedom. They imagined it might come soon, if the old folks died, or if the war was settled as it should be. Then they agreed they would head west for Kansas and put a claim on some land there. They murmured these thoughts in the dark, as the children drifted off to sleep. Around nine, they were interrupted.

Peter rose from the mattress to see what the noise was out in the dark. The dogs were yapping. Beside his door he kept a rock and a heavy stick, but they would be of little use against bullets. He opened the door slowly to look out.

Three men on horses were riding around the barn.

He heard one shout, "Place is abandoned. Let's snatch them horses." There were hoofbeats, whinnies, confusion under the moon. Peter's heart pounded high in his throat. He glanced at Charity, who lay on her side and watched him with wide eyes.

"If they just keep going," he whispered, "we'll be okay."

The men seemed to take an endless amount of time, organizing the Howard horses, conversing, and laughing. All of it was worth it when Peter heard one say, "Okay, boys, let's get the hell out of here."

He watched and heard them thunder away into the darkness. Peter returned to Charity, folding her up in his arms, and both were smiling.

4

THE HOWARDS RETURNED. The loss of their horses was the final loss they could endure. Their son, Frank, came home soon after, having suffered an injury in his hip during the war. He decided to remove his parents to Kansas.

"I'll take care of the home place, Pa, till this war is all over," he said.

He was not a generous or kindly man and this announcement made Peter and Charity shudder. They learned, soon after, that Bart was moving his family and slaves to Texas. The structures were remodeling themselves.

"I'm just so frightened," said old Mrs. Howard, "I don't know what to do. I want Grandma. Send Ruth home."

She knew she couldn't make the long trek to Kansas and involve herself in a search for a new homestead, but there was no other hope for survival than to let her son and her husband go ahead and look for a home for them.

"Grandma is still our property, and I want her back," she kept insisting.

Bart reluctantly agreed to return Ruth to the Howards. He had hoped to bring her south with him, and give her, along with his other slaves, their freedom and jobs at the same time. It was a confusing issue and transaction, sending her back, for in his heart he believed her to be a free person. Yet he was sufficiently locked into the system to agree with the Howardses' claim that she was their property.

"You take her, Frank," he said, "but I want you to promise me one thing. When this war is over, you let Ruth and Peter know where I am. Understand?"

Frank smiled, "Why, sure, Bart, though I don't know what good it'll do them. The South is going to win and nothing's going to change for them folks."

"That may be," Bart said firmly, "but I want you to hold to this promise."

Frank agreed. He was a heavy, pudding-faced man with long taffy-colored hair, and no beard. His anxiety for his parents was not selfless. It would be in his best interest to remove them to Kansas and take over the running of the farm. He was no genius, but had enough self-confidence to organize labor. His goal was simply to get control of that acreage and make a small fortune off it. The handful of slaves he had would be of some help, especially given their familiarity with the soil.

So he and his father headed for Kansas in early spring after an easy winter. Mrs. Howard was left behind with Ruth, Peter, Charity, Tim, Wash, and the children. Tim's wife and children went south with

Bart, since Frank decided they would be too many mouths to feed. Tim did not grieve because it meant that at least his children would be free. The confusion over the meaning of ownership was seeping into the Howard household. The old woman, alone with the slaves, was not long in abandoning her sense of power.

"I'm scared," she told Ruth, "those marauders are all over the place. I got to give the boys the guns. Put Peter in charge."

Ruth carried the two heavy guns out to Peter's cabin that night. Smiling she carried them across her arms like a tray in front of her. A box of bullets was clenched in her fist.

"Look what I brought you, boy," she said from the door.

"My Lord!" cried Charity.

"That's right, Peter, the old missus said you got to be in charge of the guns now. You know how to shoot?"

Peter, smiling, took the guns. "I guess I can learn. Must be something like using a bow and arrow."

He held one of the heavy weapons in his hands and ran his fingers along it with a feeling of intense excitement. His mind ran back to those days, many years before, when his young Indian friend instructed him in the arts of fishing and hunting. How whole and equal to all he felt at that time! It was the same feeling again, though he was now a man.

When he slept that night, the gun on the wall beside him, he dreamed of that Indian boy and hunting.

FOR A WEEK, Peter practiced shooting and Tim and Wash took turns with the gun. They stood in a small meadow beyond the barn. Various rocks and logs were their targets. Mrs. Howard sat out on the veranda and watched from afar. She was not being unreasonable in her fear. The area was under siege from Army deserters, marauders, patrollers, and thieves of all kinds. Her mind now slipped into long moments of complete senility.

Once she remarked to Ruth and pointed a swollen finger toward Peter, "I feel so much better having a member of the family on the farm. Tell Peter I'm real glad to have him at home."

Ruth reacted with an ironic and bitter glance at the back of the woman's head. She did not tell Peter. She proudly watched him with the gun and molded more bullets over the fire at night. He would, she was sure, get what he deserved in the end. Sometimes she dared to imagine that he would inherit this land, that fate would turn full circle and hand to him, as Nora's son, the land he had worked for so long.

"But the only time I see justice is when two children get together over something," she told herself.

That night, the outside world with all its broken codes and values made its move on the old Howard farm. While everyone slept, five armed men rode in. They were looking for slaves to sell down south, and they rode in brazenly, but silent as foxes.

Charity woke up first, feeling a weight across her chest. It was a rifle, its butt end pressed to the sleeping Peter's heart. A white man with a bristled face hung, heavy smelling, at the end of it. Not even the children awoke, though his breathing was raw and harsh.

"What's a white man doing in your bed, wench?" he whispered, close to her ear. "Can I have a little piece, too?"

Her mouth was parched and dry, but she responded in a whisper, "Don't kill him, that's all."

Suddenly she caught sight of another figure in the shadows, a darker man with his hat pulled down, standing at a slouch. Her whole body twitched and quivered.

"My children," she whispered.

Their little dark curly heads were still, their breathing soft, only a few feet away.

The rifle slid slowly back from her chest, and the man moved close against her. Stinking of sweat, he moved his hand under the blanket. She couldn't stand it, and her hand knocked Peter awake.

He awoke gently without imagining danger, then saw the alien face close by, and his throat caught, he lurched up, putting his hand hard on the man's face.

"Shoot him, Red, shoot," the man shouted.

The other stepped from the shadows, long rifle in hand, and leaned over to pick up the gun. Rising, his eyes observed Peter with interest, mild surprise, and he said, "No fights. We got work to do."

Peter dropped his hands from the man's face he wanted to claw apart, and he covered his eyes. He heard them take his guns from the wall. The sound of their boots roused the children. Charity moved around quietly, hurriedly.

"Just don't shoot," she kept saying. "We won't fight. Don't shoot. Leave him alone, don't shoot…"

The men were by the door and the cool outside air wafted in. Peter heard them saying, "The guys have got the other niggers rounded up outside. Get a move on, come on, let's go." He looked through his hands, ashamed of the tears that poured from his burning eyes, of the pain in his temples, the sense of complete exhaustion and despair.

From the doorstep, Charity looked in on him, her eyes huge and questioning.

"Get a move on, wench," the bristled man said and he poked at her back. "Last thing we need is a white man. Specially a mean one all mixed up with blacks. Go on!"

"Papa!" his son cried.

Peter got up slowly, wiping his face, and moved to the extended rifle, without fear, but filled with grief. Having to beg was worse than almost anything.

"Let me come along," he said. His voice was dull and weak, and he made another, stronger effort. "That's my family you got. I want to come."

The white man looked around himself grinning, but the darker man had disappeared outside, where the figures of the other slaves were grouped.

"Not a chance," the man said. "We'd be a laughingstock along the road. You a free man, or not?"

"Not," said Peter, unwilling to call himself a slave. "You can't take them away from me. They're my family!"

The man shoved Charity and the weeping children forward, and he walked half-turned, the rifle pointed at Peter. Charity kept turning circles, looking back at him. He slumped, stooped down, and picked up his old rock, squeezing it in the palm of his hand. It might as well have been dust for all the good it did him now, and he hurled it to the ground. The spontaneous action suddenly freed him. His anger returned in a rush, and he strode after the man with Charity and the children.

"I'm going with you!" he shouted. "You're not taking them away without me."

Ruth cried out, "Peter, no, stay!"

But he wouldn't listen, and he cared nothing for the guns. His instinct directed him to the dark-skinned man in the low-brimmed hat, and he pushed by the other to get there.

"You can sell me, too. For good money," he said. "I been a slave all my life, and I work long hours. I'm young and strong, you can see that." He lifted his arms and bared them to the man. "You can sell me along with the rest of them."

The man smiled, removed his hat, and scratched his head. His straight hair was coal black. Hatless, he revealed himself to be Indian.

"You that boy, Peter Collins?" he asked.

Peter looked back at him, some recognition beginning to rise in him. "I was Peter Collins," he said.

"And I was your friend in those days. Now, ain't that something." The Indian turned to his elderly friend, "I got a story to tell you, Riggs, and you'll get a kick out of it. Hop on board, Peter. I like the way things turn out, sometimes."

So Peter climbed in the wagon with all his friends and family. There were four on horses, three men and a boy, and a young white driver. Tim, Wash, Ruth, Charity, Peter, and the children huddled close together for the southerly journey through night.

When Mrs. Howard found herself alone, she also discovered that she had lost the ability to care for herself. She was helpless without her servants running between herself and the world. Nature was a blank, or hostile, witness to her demise.

At first she shuffled from room to room, crying; then she lay down on her bed and gave up. Her pain and her willpower departed, and she lay staring at the ceiling, waiting without fear for the face of the world to flip into the other.

Her body was discovered by Union soldiers on their way to Kansas. They stopped at the farm for refreshment and found starving dogs, remains of chickens, and the carcasses of two cows. Flies were everywhere. Turkey buzzards swooped in the air overhead.

The soldiers helped themselves to water from the well, and commented only on the dreadful familiarity of the scene.

5

TRAVELING, Ruth and Charity held the children close. Charity, pregnant again, had not yet told Peter that she was carrying. Seeing his intense despair, she dared not tell him now. He silently sat in the wagon, still as a rock, as if in chains.

At daylight Charity looked at the men who had stolen them. The head man, the one who had come after her, was named Riggs; he was elderly, tough, with a twisted, unbalanced face. The other two men, aside from the Indian, were younger but softer, probably brothers. Their faces were similar, reddish and ignorant.

Then there was a boy, about sixteen years old or less, called Johnnie. He was, she realized, about the same age as Peter when she had first seen him, and he had the same anxious air. He rode with lowered eyes, and responded to questions with the slightest gesture.

All of them carried six-shooters. Riggs carried a couple of rifles in his pack.

They stopped and made camp in a clearing beside the well-used trail, the most frequent passage for southern travelers. Remains of old campsites lay about the clearing. Tim and Wash lay out a fire, and Charity was given utensils and bits of food to fry. The two brothers, Roy and Steve, lounged in the grass.

"Ain't it great being waited on?"

"Always wanted a few slaves myself."

"Maybe we shouldn't sell them after all," Roy laughed.

Holding his children still, Peter sat in the wagon, and coldly eyed the men and their guns. His head pounded; he wanted to kill.

Riggs suddenly said, "Okay, Johnnie, here's your gun. Take that white boy down and shoot him."

Everyone stopped what they were doing. The two white brothers stood up. The Indian emerged from the shadowy underbrush. Drawing up his pants, he paused and watched. Riggs had thrust a gun into the boy's hand.

"Don't look so scared, Johnnie. You heard what he said. He's a slave, like the rest of them," Riggs said and punched the boy's shoulder. "But he sticks out too much to go all the way with us. Understand?" He glanced at the Indian. "Right, Patches?"

In the daylight Peter saw that Nine Bears wore an odd assortment of colorful clothes, stitched together like quilt work.

"Don't know," said the Indian. "I come all this way to sell some slaves and make some money, that's all. If you want blood, make it come fair."

He walked to the side of the wagon and handed up a gun to Peter. Their unblinking eyes met, and held.

"We'll make it a regular duel," he said to Riggs.

Peter took the gun and stepped down from the wagon. Charity grabbed for the children behind him.

"This boy, Johnnie," said the Indian, "makes me think of you,

Peter Collins. I like the way things turn out sometimes. He ran away from home and came with us. Isn't that something? Everywhere I see stories. They begin and end, and end where they began."

"Shut up, Patches," Riggs snapped.

The Indian smiled serenely, stepping back to let Peter pass. Johnnie moved to the end of the clearing and stood with a hangdog look. His gun pointed to the ground.

"Come on, Johnnie," shouted Roy.

The boy watched Peter approaching, and there was no mistaking the desire in Peter to kill. It was in his pace and in his intense gaze. It made Riggs raise his rifle and point carefully at Peter.

"I can't," moaned the boy, as tears poured from his eyes. His head was bent.

"Throw down your gun, boy," Riggs said to Peter.

With a rifle aimed at him, the faces of his children, and Charity, Peter did as he was told. He understood with all his heart the boy's despair and sense of disgrace.

"Wait till I tell your parents, Johnnie," shouted Steve. "Wait till they hear about this."

"Little runt couldn't even kill a nigger-lover," Roy sneered.

The boy walked off into the woods. His hands covered his eyes. Peter returned to the campsite.

The white men and the Indian ate so much there was little left for the other seven. Crusts were given mostly to the children. The men talked about their plans and how they would enter Arkansas by the following morning, then stop there and seek out a decent slave auction in the area. The Indian sat quietly and then moved beside Peter.

"My sister, remember?" he said softly. "She's a whore now. Dodge City... Our parents were murdered, well, not very long after we ran into you. Been about, ah, how many years?"

"Near twenty," said Peter.

"Still a slave?" he said incredulously. "A big white man like you could be doing fine."

"Won't be long now," said Peter.

"Your woman could make a fine whore, too, bring home some money like that." He smiled to show brown, stained teeth. Peter saw in a certain dreamy fullness about his eyes the last traces of his boyhood.

"Well, let's get a move on," Riggs said, "else the War will be over before we get to Arkansas."

They gathered up their things and doused the fire. Peter was ordered to lay low in the wagon in case he would be recognized in the light. He faced the rear, where the boy and the Indian rode side by side. He had no fiddle now, but Wash began to sing. The others and the children joined him.

BY EVENING, they were all hungry. The sky was heavy and damp. Peter felt a familiarity with the climate, and realized he must be close to Collins's old plantation. The shapes of the hills were softer now. He wondered which way he would go to find the place, if Betty and Robert were there still, and if they would ever meet again. He rested his hand on Charity's ankle, stroking her gently.

They stopped on the outskirts of a small mining town, and Riggs and Roy rode in to buy some supplies. They seemed full of conspiracy, which excluded the Indian and the boy. Peter felt uneasy because he knew himself to be the brunt of most of their plots and abuses. Pretending to be at ease, he entertained the children by the campfire.

The Indian approached him from time to time.

"So you think you'll get your freedom?" he asked Peter.

"Think the War will be over soon?"

"What'll you do as a free man?"

Peter shrugged and said nothing. He sensed that the man had a certain moral code, which was different from other men's. It was strange, hidden, connected to his past. Even if he was in the business of selling slaves, he treated them politely. He seemed to view Peter's sudden arrival in his life as a warning or a supernatural event. "When someone comes out of the past, I have to understand why," he told Peter. "The pattern is confusing, but you've got to respect it."

"In such a pattern," Charity said, "isn't there always one strand that is left free, goes nowhere, just off into the wild blue yonder?"

"That's true, Miss. And I guess you know this because you're Osage."

6

THE NEXT DAY the group of eleven entered Arkansas. The mood of the party changed. The group knew it was on land committed to slavery. The air was a trifle warmer. The dread words—South and auction—were becoming a reality. Their captors believed they had pulled off a great coup in bringing these slaves down where they could easily sell them.

So they were high-spirited and jovial. The group in the wagon drew closer and quieter and no longer sang.

"And I do believe we can sell the white fella for a small fortune," Riggs chortled. "Now we're over the border, won't be no problem. Why, he's proud of being a slave!"

The men guffawed.

The land seemed infinite, so much of it unowned and untended, but ready for use. Peter scanned the western horizon and it seemed to recede from his powers forever.

At the day's campsite, Nine Bears, as Peter now insisted on calling him, announced he was leaving.

"What for?" asked an outraged Riggs. "We need you."

"I had a dream last night, and it gave me the pattern I was looking for," the Indian said in all his colorful patches. "I don't want to hang around with you now. Don't think there's any money in slaves. That's over. Too many white men want their jobs, but for money this time round. Waste of my time. West is where I'm heading."

The men were appalled. They had lost the boy, Johnnie. Now the Indian was abandoning them.

"But we don't know this part of the country like you do, Redskin," Steve said. "You told us you'd get us into a fine situation."

Nine Bears would not be persuaded. He smiled and mounted his horse. Gazing down at the group of slaves gathered by the fire, he saw Peter watching from their midst.

"We might meet again," called the Indian, "Peter Collins. Such surprises please me."

And he rode away toward the northwest across a stretch of empty prairie.

With profound dread, Peter watched him leave. Another link was broken. He was alone with these men. His friends and family were depending on him, and he was a captive. He could do nothing to vent his anger, and he would not show his grief.

THEIR DESTINATION turned out to be an empty schoolhouse on a desolate plantation. Saplings grew wild everywhere. Remains of battle and destruction littered the property. Once-rich fields of tobacco and cotton were now dark strips of weeds. Dandelions made the wild lawns yellow. Birds flew through windows and nested in mirror frames.

Peter and his family were put in the schoolhouse. One man kept guard over them in shifts, night and day, while the others went out to explore the area and take care of business. On a nearby farm lived an old judge, who let them use his well. Riggs and the brothers learned about the course of the War from him.

"Don't look good for our side, boys," he told them. "Nope. Don't look good at all. Might as well make yourselves comfortable over on the old Stock plantation. Be a long time before they come back and claim it."

Riggs told the judge he was a slave-owning man who had been

plundered up in Missouri. Even if the judge was supporting the Confederacy, Riggs didn't dare tell him the slaves were stolen. That was illegal under any system.

"Well, guess you've had hard luck then," the judge said, "and I've been pretty fortunate. Use my well. Have one of your boys come over any time and get the water. You can find your supplies in town about a mile down."

"Might have to sell my slaves," Riggs said, casually, "seeing as I'm flat broke. Any ideas?"

The judge, small and dapper in a clean-cut suit, gave Riggs a critical glance. "Nope. Better find yourself some employment instead. Nobody's buying slaves nowadays. Just trying to hold on to what they got already."

Riggs returned to the schoolhouse.

"Why don't we just move on?" suggested Roy. "Why don't we just forget these niggers and move on?"

"What for? Where to?" cried the angry man. "One place is as bad as the next... No. We're going to stick it out. Hold onto them. They're all we got, our only property. Now, just start getting things organized."

Tim and Wash were given the job of making vegetables grow in the old garden beside the big house. Charity was told to cook, and Ruth was sent to the judge's place to get the water. Peter was only allowed to leave the schoolhouse to go to the outhouse. The white men were determined to keep him invisible.

"We can't let him have a gun. Might go berserk. And if anyone sees him, white like he is, without one, they'll suspect something's not right over here," Riggs reasoned.

Peter passed through summer and into fall within four walls. Charity, growing huge with pregnancy, couldn't rouse him from his despair or make him feel good about himself. Ruth urged him to build a fiddle, and to sing, at night, with the others, but he hardly made a sound at all, returning to many of the patterns of his youth.

He hung his head, or stared into the middle distance. Bad memories came in flashes, he prayed for relief, his hair turned from golden brown to silver, he cursed himself for failing to escape when he had the energy, when Nora might have helped.

NO ONE in the schoolhouse knew the War was over. No one suspected that there would be an end to their long seclusion or their condition. On the old farm in Missouri, someone had to come to find them to let them know about emancipation.

Nick Nolland came to the farm before Thanksgiving, and found it occupied by Frank Howard and his family. Nick was back in civilian clothes, and only the furrows in his face showed signs of the war he had been through. Frank did not welcome him.

"What do you want of us?" he asked Nick. "Haven't you got all you want?"

"I promised Nora that I would watch out for Peter, and I want to keep my promise."

Nick stood on the steps below the heavy man, and let his gaze wander over the farm. There were desolate, overgrown fields and empty pastures. Frank warily watched Nick, following his gaze, and then said, "I don't know, Nolland. This place is a heap of rubbish. My old man is dead, alongside my mother. My brother? Well, the Lord knows where he is, dead or alive. And Bart's gone clear down to Texas, making a fortune off cattle . . . What can I say? I got his land, too. He could afford to hand it on to me. But look at it. I need help and can't afford it."

Frank invited Nick inside. The house was clean and orderly. Frank's wife and eldest daughter had that much under control. His wife offered Nick a cold drink of lemonade, and seemed impressed by his Northern manners and clothes. For another hour Frank was hostile toward Nick, asking questions about the War and what he thought of its outcome. Nick responded quietly, respectfully, forcing the larger man to soften his speech.

"Well, I guess it's all over and done with now," Frank sighed. "But I sure could use those boys—Wash, Tim and, well, Peter—out in the fields. It's a crying shame they been stolen south. Might have been sold, for all I know, and split up."

"Maybe," said Nick, "but I'd like to find out for sure. I did tell Nora—"

"She? She's dead... Maybe best to let sleeping dogs lie." His eyes slipped uneasily from side to side. "I don't relish Peter coming back a free man. All those stories in the Bible about branches and vines and grafting."

"What?"

"Well, he might be ignorant of his birthright, but you never know. Think I better look into the laws about bastard sons. You know what I'm talking about?"

"I do," said Nick pensively.

"Tell you what," Frank said abruptly. "Why don't the two of us head down the southern trail and see what we can uncover? Might be those boys aren't so far away after all. Too bad I can't sell them anymore. Imagine that. I could sell 'em and then, with the money I bought 'em for, pay them to do the field work. Ha!"

Nick did not appear amused. "I can do it alone. I have time. I'll look for them on my own."

"A city fellow like you?"

"I've got a couple of guns. It doesn't scare me to travel alone."

"Well, I don't know about that. I still think of them as my property, can't get used to thinking any other way." He looked off into space and added, "Peter's my big worry."

"Look. If Peter ever finds out where he came from," said Nick, "I doubt he'll do anything about it. He's been a slave all his life. What would he know about laws and birthrights?"

"Well, it sure would be worth it to me, if you found those boys. And I guess it's your time, not mine, spent looking."

"I want to know Bart Williams's address," Nick said and stood up. "He might know something, too. The grapevine travels a long way."

Frank complied. He had no faith that Nick would find the slaves, or "former slaves," as he must call them now. They were like so much dust in the wind.

7

THERE WAS one southerly trail. South, Nick knew, would be the way they would go. He had camping gear and food strapped onto his horse, and he was determined to do what he had promised Nora. Since learning of her death, his guilt had been an intolerable burden. That she had gone to her grave believing in a lie was more than he could bear.

Even with his determination, he was full of doubt. The country was enormous; the War had been devastating. In what pocket of land would he find any of those people? He was impetuous, operating on complete instinct. He might as well be blind. He moved on through a day and a night toward the Arkansas border, asking anyone he met if they had encountered a group of wandering people, black, and white.

"What kind of group is that?" he often heard with a clap of laughter.

Finally Nick came to a small town near the border. It was late afternoon. He needed more food and went to the general store to get some supplies. At the counter there was a horse-faced man, packing bullets in small boxes.

"Yep?" he asked, without looking up.

"Just want to buy some food," Nick said, browsing over the shelves. "And I wanted to ask you something, too. I'm looking for a group who might have passed this way a few months ago, with a white man."

"Stolen?" The man lifted his eyebrows and shook his head. "Didn't see no group like that."

"The white man," Nick persisted, "was someone you wouldn't forget. Dressed like a field hand, I'd guess, with a blond beard, light hair, blue eyes."

"How old?"

"Late twenties, early thirties." Nick set down some staples on the counter and looked at the man closely. "He was white, but he was a slave."

The man's face screwed into a smile.

"I know the one," he said slowly and thoughtfully. "Came here late one night. Reason I remember is he wasn't carrying a gun. He was in the company of darkies. Two white fellas were up behind him. They come in the store after he was gone. I was just cleaning up. They said, 'That was a slave you just saw,' and they stomped out of the place, full of laughs."

Nick smiled broadly.

"That must have been Peter. Did he look like I just said?"

"That's how he looked, but he sure talked and acted like an ordinary nigra. I always wondered what the story was."

Nick gratefully explained a portion of Peter's story to the man, and bought more than he needed. Rushing back to his horse, he continued his journey.

CHARITY LAY in a bed for the first time in her life. She held her new infant in her arms. The little girl was not well. She was born premature, and was having trouble suckling. The two lay in a little room behind Judge Potter's kitchen, and Charity could hear the judge shuffling around making her a bowl of hot sweet milk.

He was being kind to her so she didn't dare tell him what was on her mind. She was miserable in that comfortable room, because Peter wasn't there, and she didn't know how to tell him about Peter's existence. The judge was one of the nicest white people she ever met. He was a real person, a widower who took care of himself and now took care of her.

"Now Charity, my dear," he said, extending the bowl before her, "you must drink this, even if you don't want to. I know a little bit about birthing, you know. Three times I delivered an infant with my own two hands. Helped after, too...That baby needs lots of nurturing."

Charity placed the infant to her left side, and leaned up carefully to take the bowl and drink. Involuntarily, she gave a small sob.

"What's wrong?" the judge asked worriedly.

Tears sprang from her eyes at the tone of kindness, as if he had struck a spring on a lock.

"The baby will be all right. She's already made it through the first week," he said quickly.

"Oh, I hope so!"

"Then why are you crying so?" he asked and took the bowl from her weak hands.

"I want Peter," she wailed, "my husband."

"Well, where is he?"

"At home with my mother."

The judge, looking very baffled, said, "I know about Ruth and Wash. But who's Peter?"

"He stays inside all the time," sobbed Charity. "He can't go out."

She looked up into the judge's face and tried to restore her equilibrium. Rubbing the tears off her face, she hastily invented a story, which, she knew as she told it, was not altogether false. "He's sick, Judge, been sick since we got here. They keep him inside. But I want him!"

"Then I'll go get him for you," the judge said, simply.

"No," she cried, "they'll get mad over there. They didn't want you to know."

"Afraid a sick man would make me drive them away?" he inquired. "What's he got? TB?"

"I don't know what it is. I just don't know. But leave it alone, Judge, I'll be just fine."

"Poor Charity," he murmured. Then he smiled. "But I'm glad to know you've got a husband waiting for you. I was a little afraid—seeing how the baby's so light—one of those bosses of yours might have done it to you."

"No," she said and a smile turned into a laugh. "No!"

"All right, then. You just drink up and take care of your baby girl. Your mother will be over in the morning, and she'll be wanting to see you both strong. Understand?"

"Thank you, Judge."

He left Charity alone with her baby, whose lips puckered ever so slightly. She gulped down the milk, praying it would fill her and the baby. She could not bear to have a baby die and suddenly thought of Nora. *No wonder she was so sad and strange*, Charity thought as she pressed her baby to her breast, looking down into her soft dark curls. *Poor Miss Nora!* she cried. She cried and she cried, feeling all at one time the humiliation of their hiding in a foul place, buried in darkness, afraid of all they had learned on the road of lynching, stabbings, gangs of white men out to kill people just like them.

Was this freedom? she sobbed into her hand. Was freedom just about hiding, staying out of sight, not getting caught, not getting hurt? Was this what freedom really meant?

NICK AWOKE with thoughts of Nora the following morning. He looked at the broad prairie land stretching before him and wondered if he was mad to do what he was doing. Nora's face clearly seemed to swim before him as he remembered her begging him to make sure her slaves were free.

Since heading west, he had been alone a long time, and it was easy to carry on dialogues with himself and invisible companions. Riding, he often whispered conversations with Nora and explained to himself the reasons for making this journey. In his mind, he would often turn back, along the southern gulf, having failed to find those people.

Small farmhouses and larger plantations began to spring up around him, and Nick dismounted several times to speak to farmers or field hands, asking, "Could you tell me of any stray Negroes in this country, one of them white?"

"Nope. Can't say I've ever seen 'em."

"We got troubles enough without looking for more."

"Never heard of a group like that. Maybe you should put up in town, take a little rest."

Nick wondered if his tactics were wrong. Maybe he should describe Peter and the group in more detail, or say he was their owner, or only ask white men, or pretend he was from up in Missouri and fought for the Confederacy. Most of the field work around him was being done by blacks, so it looked as if no changes had come to that part of the land. The few white men he encountered were still giving orders to blacks and rode around like overseers.

He decided he would pretend to white men he was an old and embittered slave owner. To black men he would offer a piece of gold. A devious strategy might prove more fruitful than an honest one.

He rode by the Stock plantation, where the slaves were held in the schoolhouse, and on down the road for several miles. Then, at last, he came to another plantation where a kneeling old dark-skinned man was pulling up herbs.

Nick stopped and called to him. The old man moved slowly in his direction, his legs bowed, his back bent. Nick removed a gold piece from his pocket and got off his horse. He extended his palm to the old man.

"See this gold? I'll give it to you for some information," he said, anxiously exploring the man's ashy face.

"I don't go no place, nobody tells me nothing," the man replied in long slow tones, but his eyes sparkled over the piece of gold.

"How long have you been on this plantation?"

"I guess I was born here. Don't know, sir, just been here. Nobody tells me nothing."

"If you've been here that long, you'd know if there were strangers about, wouldn't you?"

"Don't know, sir."

"How about a group of slaves, men, women, children, in the company of one white man."

"How about it?" said the man.

"You want this coin?" Nick asked. "It's worth five dollars."

"Don't know, sir."

Nick's eyes reddened, and he slumped weary against his horse. The old man carefully eyed him through heavy-lidded eyes.

"You from the North?"

"But I'm heading south," Nick said, and turned to his saddle.

The man approached him softly and put his hand out before him; it was trembling.

"Turn back," he said. "Might' nigh four miles north. A bunch of darkies squatting in a schoolhouse. White men around. But don't tell no one, 'cause they very near kill old Bill if they knew I told you. Mean white men watching them."

Nick smiled, "No, Bill, I will never tell."

He handed the old man the gold coin, mounted his horse, and headed back the way he came.

The sudden sight of Ruth let him know that he had found them. She was carrying a heavy bucket of water through wide plantation gates and didn't see him. He knew it was Ruth at once, and his heart leaped up with joy. *Ruth!* he wanted to cry, but he held his tongue and reined in cautiously.

Now what would he do? If they were being guarded by a group of white men, he would be a fool to ride in alone. The plantation was circled by large trees. He could see a few buildings through the thicket. The other side of the road was open meadow, all the way to the next farmhouse. Nick quickly lost sight of Ruth. Dismounting, he decided to be as foolish now as he had been all along. His instincts had been correct and he had nothing but them and his guns to go on.

So he tied his horse in a wooded area and walked boldly through the gates Ruth had traveled through. He might pass for a simple stranger; no one would shoot him on sight. So he persisted and saw Ruth entering a red frame schoolhouse with an old bell tower on top.

In the shadowy grass beside the stoop, the figure of a man lay still.

His hat was pulled down over his face. A rifle lay across his belly. Nick moved stealthily around the area, near the back of the house, and heard voices inside. He saw Tim and Wash in a large vegetable garden east of the house. Nick's heart beat hard as he moved around to the front. He stood within feet of the man, who might not be sleeping.

Nick, rallying all his courageous energies, moved on ahead, till he hung right over the man. Then he knocked the rifle away from his stomach with the butt of his own and the man lurched up with a shout.

"Okay, you've had it," Nick said.

Steve was red-faced, terrified, and crouched back in the grass, asking, "Who the hell are you?"

"Just a friend of the people inside. Don't move."

Walking backward, Nick shoved his shoulder up hard against the door and it banged open. Ruth and Peter stood in a corner together.

Nick called, "Remember me?" and smiled to them.

The sudden shock of the encounter knocked all recognition from them, but Ruth after a minute understood who he was and that they were saved.

"It's Miss Nora's Nick," she said, and allowed her tears to flow for the first time in a year. "It's Master Nolland."

Nick looked at Peter with visible and sad wonder. Pale and gray-haired, his body was thin and he looked years older than he was.

"Peter," he said, "I've come to help you."

Peter straightened himself and pushed at his hair, but he had no words to say.

"You people are free now," Nick went on. "Yes, free. The War is over and our side won. Where are the others?"

Ruth, holding Peter's hand, anxiously explained where everyone was. The children were out back with Tim and Wash, and Charity was at the judge's place. Then she looked up at Peter and explained, "He's been locked up for many months, Master Nick, it's why he's so white and sickly looking. He's not sick, he just needs a little sun."

"Well, I thank God I found you," Nick said. "It was what I promised Nora. She made me promise I would see to it that you were free and well. And I've done it!"

He seemed to feel as much jubilation as they, letting out a hoot and aiming his rifle straight at Steve's head outside.

"Come on, Peter," he called. "Let's get the others. I'll need your help."

So Peter moved forward to stand beside Nick. The sun hurt his weakened eyes.

"Here's a gun," Nick said, placing one of his own six-shooters in Peter's hand. "Ruth, lead the way."

Ruth nearly danced out the door ahead of the men and up to the gardens where the four others were. Peter watched her rushing like a young girl through the tall grass and his eyes began to swim. He had forgotten what it was to be happy.

THE FOLLOWING HOURS were hard for Peter to believe. He witnessed the enactment of justice and stood back in awe. He felt as if he was part of an audience, watching a dance or a drama. The performance was beautiful.

The judge was appalled to discover that the three men he had been helping for months were common thieves, and he hustled them off to the jailhouse with the help of two deputies.

"Why didn't you tell me?" the judge kept asking Charity. And then to Ruth, "You must have known you were free now."

"We didn't know nothing of the kind," said Ruth. "You didn't tell us that, sir. Now, did you?"

He looked down at his boots, "No, I didn't, I just kind of assumed you knew."

Looking into Ruth's face, he acquired a guilty expression for he had spoken a half-truth, as she seemed to know.

"Of course, it's a hard thing, learning to treat you people normal, if you know what I mean, after so many years. I thought you knew, but didn't really think to discuss it with you neither."

"That's right," Charity said, holding her baby tight, "but no point looking back. You were real good to me and this little one. You were real good to all of us."

The judge looked inquiringly toward Peter, whose pale skin was ashen and drawn. Questions abounded on his face. Sighing, he said nothing and turned to go inside his home.

"Where you going now?" he asked Nick.

"On down south to Texas."

"Well, why don't you take my old wagon? I don't use it since the missus passed on. You can buy a team from Sam down the road. You'll need it."

He waved goodbye. Nick immediately took over, following the judge's suggestions, and asked Peter to accompany him wherever he went. Wash and Tim were confused by what was happening and were not quite ready to relax and enjoy the situation. Freedom was a big word.

Peter and the two women looked on the world with instant recognition of all the possibilities held out for them. By the time they were settled in the wagon and heading south, they already were discussing what they would do and where they would go. Nick listened carefully. Nuts from the brown and red branches overhead littered the trail.

"I still got Kansas on my mind," Peter said. "Don't know why, but there it is."

Nick said, "I think, with winter coming, we should head south and stop off at Bart's place. It will be warm in Texas, and you'll need some time to get yourselves organized. That was my plan, my idea—but you might not agree."

"No, that's fine," Charity said at once. The baby sucked her breast. "This little girl can't take no winter yet."

"That's right," said Ruth.

Peter looked anxiously at his other children. They silently watched the passing forests. "You sure Bart Williams won't take our freedom away?" he asked Nick.

"It's against the law, Peter. He can't."

Peter's shoulders relaxed, and he held up his face to the warm setting sun. He bathed in its rays and felt his whole body suffused with energy. *So you got us our freedom after all, and we're all together, like you promised we would be*, he said silently to Nora.

"Too bad she isn't here to see us now," he said aloud to Nick, who understood at once whom Peter was talking about. But he kept his mouth shut on his shame.

AFTER SEVERAL DAYS of steady traveling and increasing warmth, they arrived at Bart's new farm in the Red River Valley. The river charged the area with lush grass, ideally suited for cattle breeding. Bart's house was large and elegant, all his fields fenced or wired, and he raised only cattle. As the group rode in, they saw many familiar light and dark faces. As the word spread that they were coming, people ran from the house to greet them.

BART HAD KEPT HIS WORD and freed his slaves before the conclusion of the War. Most had stayed on, receiving pay for their labor and homesteading close in the area. Others headed east for the larger towns and cities. Sophie and Mary had remained on the farm, living in their own quarters, doing the housework for room, board, and a little money in exchange.

Bart was rich now. His children were sent away to expensive schools. He traveled a great deal. At home he entertained frequently. He was gone when Nick brought the people there, but was expected within a couple of days. Nancy took care of the arrangements and provided sleeping space for Wash, Ruth, and for Peter and his family. Within hours of his arrival, Tim moved in with Sophie. They locked themselves up inside her quarters and were not seen again for hours.

Peter, Charity, and the children were put in a gatehouse. Mattresses and cooking utensils were sent from the big house. They were tired from the long journey and the emotional upheaval, but Peter couldn't bear to go inside until long after the children were sleeping. The huge sky sparkled with thousands of galaxies. Lights blazed in the windows of the big house. He heard some of the people singing from across the meadows, where they had a little piece of land and a couple of houses of their own. He saw Tim looking up at the night sky as he always did.

His body began to grow strong again, though his hair would never return to its original color. He sat in the darkness. Watching and listening acutely, he sometimes felt almost electric with excitement. The arrival of freedom had been so long awaited, he wanted to cherish every minute of its newness. He wondered if freedom could ever lose its flavor and thought of the many white men he had known and how they had abused that luxury. Few of those men took responsibility for his liberty.

He had no one to model the rest of his life after—no father, no friend, no man with an equivalent history. He wondered what Robert was doing with his freedom, remembering him as a good and careful man, who probably could adapt to new conditions. Tim would be all right, he surmised, but his children would be better. Wash had always been confused, and might not know what to do now.

The old questions nagged at him again in the dark. Who was he? Where did he come from? Was he white, or was he black? How would he and his family be treated now that they were free? He knew he must get back his physical strength. It was a good thing they had this winter in Texas. Still he would be restless till the day he could drive away in his own wagon with his own team, his family beside him, and head for Kansas to make a home.

"You must tell Peter the whole story, Bart," Nick said two nights later. They were seated at the dining-room table, with after-dinner cigars and brandy. "I've wanted to do it myself, but now I think it would be better if you do."

"Why?" Bart asked with a smile. He had aged and thickened, but his face still wore its ruddy and humorous expression.

"I'm not very good at these things."

"It's that Northern training in being delicate," said Bart. "I never saw a Northern man say anything straight, but that's okay. It takes all kinds. Sure, I'll tell Peter."

"One thing, however, should be kept in mind. Frank Howard. He's afraid Peter will make some claim on a share of that property in Missouri."

"Ha. Why bother. It's all weeds, the way those people use it. They have delusions. Always did."

"Then you don't think Peter would bother?" Nick asked.

"He'd be a fool, and he's not a fool. I talked to Peter myself the other morning soon as I got back. He wants to do a little carpentry work for me here, over the winter, and then head up to Kansas to homestead. He's not going to be distracted. He never wants to see that piece of ground again."

Nick sighed and smiled slightly. "I'll take your word for it, but, for my part, I'd like to see him get some of that Howard land. It's only fair, especially when I think of Nora."

"Well, don't think too much. That's another Northern error. Instinct is better." Puffing on his cigar and looking as prosperous as he felt, he said again, "Sure, I'll tell Peter."

Bart went down to the gatehouse to find Peter in the the middle of the next afternoon. He was carrying some tools for carpentry work. Peter had already fixed up a bench outside. The air was cool, the sun bright in a cloudless sky.

"Hey, Pete," Bart said cheerfully.

Peter nodded and stood straight, looking him curiously in the eye.

"I got some tools and some good news for you," said Bart. "Come on over to the steps and sit down a minute."

Peter quietly followed him.

"Nick Nolland is leaving tomorrow," Bart said, "and he wants to give you the wagon and team you picked up in Arkansas. He's going home by way of the Santa Fe railroad. I'll be driving him down to pick up the train, so there's plenty of room for you to keep the team in the stables with the other nags. And now you got yourself a wagon."

Peter smiled and shook his head, "Well, that is good news," he agreed. "Don't know why that Mr. Nolland is so good to us."

"Yes, you do," said Bart.

He cleared his throat, feeling a little uneasy suddenly. He was determined to prove himself a more straightforward man than Nick Nolland.

"Peter, I got something else to tell you."

Peter was struck by the change of tone in his voice and quickly looked at him.

"It's about Nora," Bart said.

"Nora?"

"That's right." Again he cleared his throat, and looked off at the treetops. "Remember that little grave where her baby was supposed to be buried? Well, there wasn't no baby in there. Not hers anyway. Nora, when she was young, got knocked up by a Scots Irish fellow, some kind of surveyor."

"I know," Peter said. His eyes were still fixed on Bart.

"Well, the fact is, that baby didn't die. He was sent away by the Howard people to be raised by slaves... That baby, Peter, was you."

The entire universe seemed to pulse inside Peter's ears.

"Man's name was McCutcheon," Bart went on. "He did come back to marry her, but they drove him off, kind of."

Bart continued talking, explaining, filling the air with details which, at some level, Peter absorbed, and didn't forget.

During those moments Peter's attention was elsewhere, and he looked through Bart as through a ghost, watching the world open like a laughing mouth, then close again into an expression he had never seen before. The face of nature was transformed.

"... And we all felt kind of guilty, not telling you sooner, but we didn't think Nora could handle that information, being as sensitive as she was, if you know what I mean... and by then we thought of you—well, just as one of the slaves!"

He rambled on, rising to his feet, gesturing, apologizing, and finally backing off, leaving Peter there on the steps alone. His eyes explored space with a great intensity as if it might look back at him and engulf him with understanding. The rise and fall of the earth, the grass bowing before the wind, the crackle of leaves in a cold tree, these were all he could trust now. Wildlife, the ground and moving over it.

8

We stayed down in Texas through the winter. Then I hitched up the wagon and we said goodbye to Bart and Nancy Williams and all the folks down there. It was a great day when Grandma, Charity, me, and the three little ones—Jessie, Edward, and Maria—headed north the way we had come down. I'd say we sang our way along that trail.

It was when we got into Missouri that I got the urge to stop off on the Howard farm. Couldn't just keep going without one last look at the old place, especially now, as I thought of my true mother's grave being there, and her spirit, too.

Of course, we were free now, and Frank Howard knew it, and I had nothing to fear. I didn't tell him what I knew about myself and Nora, not right away, but agreed to work on the farm for twenty dollars a month, while Charity worked in the house for our board. Returning was something I had to do, in order to make peace with my past and my mother. Wages were a new experience for me. What was the value of labor without wages? I asked myself, and then how I worked for nothing all those years and still went on feeling my days were worthy. Did the wages actually equal the work done?

It was the land, I figured, because I loved that little piece of land and believed my work on it saved me from going crazy. The fences and pens I re-constructed and carefully hammered together, the fields I planted with my own hands, but especially the forests I tended where I felt I was finally alone, and the birds and rabbits were my friends, where I shaped and pruned and chopped—I felt the trees knew me and whispered welcomes when I returned. If I had been an artist, this would have been my work of art, my pride and joy. Strangely, it was the work that saved me, the woods themselves, the natural living creation that knew me like nobody else. I pray now that anyone who ends up enslaved, bullied, or in prison can find a natural place to work in peace.

During this time I realized that we always had to have some cash in hand, and that was the agreed-on way. So, strange as it seems, I worked on that land I knew as well as the back of my hand and can honestly say it would have moldered and festered into nothing, if we hadn't showed up right when we did. I knew every tree and stump and could almost hear their hearts beating. I took care of them and the gardens as if they were my own. Frank couldn't get a thing started. Once it was looking good again, and orderly, though, he got his energy back. I might should have stayed on then.

Sundays I made ox yokes for fifty dollars a yoke, and still played the fiddle for a dollar a night. Grandma took care of the children, and soon, pulling together, we had enough cash in our pockets to consider moving along. I hesitated before leaving my natural home, but I kept thinking of Kansas, free Kansas, out where a person could get some land and a real home. I didn't want to pay or receive wages so much as to have some dirt that belonged to me.

That was 1868. When it came time to leave, Frank Howard asked me what I called myself and my children, if we still went by the name of Howard. He wanted to know where and how to find us, he said. I told him right out that while I loved my mother, Nora, I hated her family, and would go by the name McCutcheon from there on. His face turned red, and he backed away, and was glad as could be to see us going. I said goodbye to my poor mother's grave before we left and felt at least I had pulled together the land she loved so well.

We started with two yoke of oxen to this Kansas territory. But when we got within ten miles of Topeka, little Maria got awfully sick and stayed sick a long time. We stopped our journey, rented some ground to farm, and we stayed there all of ten years. Those were hard times. We had two more children, and lost one in infancy, and that was the sadness that made us move on again, finally.

We took a homestead sixteen miles north of Elmsville, Kansas. I built a small land-claim house for the people around there, all of them homesteaders like us. But we were the only colored family in that country near Elmsville. The others were in Elmsville itself or a few miles away. And everyone was always making some remark on my color and asking me what I was doing with them people. I told them that this is what the Union was all about. As I said, those were hard times. The older children had to walk four miles to school. Our farm was all raw land, not a tree, or even a switch big enough to whip a child with.

Me and my oldest boy would break some new ground every year and try to raise some feed for that was about all the ground was good for. There wasn't much rainfall in those parts. We would have to go to a town almost fifty miles away to get grist ground. But after a time, the homesteaders began raising a little wheat, and there was a mill started up in Elmsville. Everybody was poor all alike, and it made some people dishonest. Sometimes you would take corn or wheat in town to have it ground and would almost have to fight for your sacks.

We started out with one cow; but after a few years we began to raise colts and calves and a few pigs and some chickens. In years the rain was good, I'd raise a load of watermelons and take them to town to trade for a sack of flour. Times were so tight, and everyone else so poor, it was not something you felt sorry for yourself about. We just did what we could, and kept on having those babies, as we had planned so many years before.

It took a few years, for sure, and we always lived on a small part of our quarter section, leaving the rest for pasture, but by the mid-eighties I had a herd of cattle, and was looking for more land. By then I was accepted by my neighbors, and they helped me the same as I helped them. We'd send teams back and forth to help plow the ground and hitch up a planter, on another man's land, and plant the ground that was plowed. We didn't think only of ourselves. We thought of the land and community as all one. Time had made me less self-conscious about my color and in truth I hardly ever gave it a thought.

I was known in those parts as a man who kept to himself, a family man. I was known pretty much the same as I had always been. Out in that part of the country, in those times, you could get lost, just ride for miles with nothing but the sky and the grass and that soft wind always blowing. Where you came from, or where you were going, well, it didn't much matter. I was always surprised I was alive and pretty much the same person all along. It was as if I was born to be myself and stayed that way.

9

When Peter was fifty, he needed more land, and a man in Elmsville had a quarter section to rent. The man told Peter to come to Elmsville and they would get a lawyer to fix up the papers for a five-year lease.

On a Saturday morning, Peter met Mr. Jacobs, and was introduced to the lawyer, John Freeman. Then Mr. Jacobs left, having filled out his part of the forms, and Peter sat across from the lawyer and explained he could not read or write.

"That's okay," the man said pleasantly, and took up the pen himself, "I can do it for you."

He was a fair-haired man in his thirties. Relaxed in his dress and manner, he eyed Peter with open interest.

"I've heard about you, Mr. McCutcheon," he said, "and how well you work your land out there. Big family, right?"

"Seven children," smiled Peter.

"I always wondered where you came from originally?"

"Jasper County, Missouri."

Freeman pushed the papers aside, and his face burned a little, his eyes lighting up.

"You won't believe this," he said, "but I'm sorry to say that I was the boy detailed to kill you when you were stolen so many years ago. Remember? I couldn't do it, and rode away from camp because I was ashamed."

Astonished, Peter stood up, and then sat down again.

Freeman continued. "It's incredible, isn't it? But then there aren't that many people in this part of the country, not yet...You know, I came from Missouri myself, and Jasper County, too. I know all about your people, the Howards.

"After I left that night, I was too ashamed to face my parents, so I headed west, and stopped right near here. I was lucky and fell into the hands of a doctor, who let me work for room and board. He got me educated. Made me into the man you see now. I was real lucky."

His gaze on Peter was kindly and full of concern.

"You know, when I first heard about you and your family, I thought it might be you. Not many white men running in the company of Negroes, not as family men anyway. But I heard, too, you were quiet and kept to yourself, working as hard as a man can. So I didn't want to bother you."

"Glad to meet you now," Peter said softly.

The man was silent for a moment and then said, "It just doesn't seem right, you know. Your people, the Howards, have made a fortune over the last twenty years. I remember, from my family, there was always some mystery over their white slave. The Howards were never popular."

"I'll tell you that mystery," Peter said, and proceeded to relate his personal history. John Freeman did not seem surprised, but his face deepened with concern.

"I tell you, it's just not right. Slaves never got what they were promised after the War. No half-acre, no mule. Look at the struggle. And here you are, disenfranchised, working your hands to the bone. No, it's just not right."

Peter did not quarrel with him, but he did not feel bitter or bear a grudge. To be alive and free were sufficient daily rewards for his labor. He didn't want to look back at the unjust side of his history.

The lawyer in John Freeman would not rest. The case was curious to him. He wished to pursue it with or without Peter's interest. Distractedly, he filled out Peter's forms for him and leaned back in his chair.

"I'm going to start legal action against the Howards, Peter," he announced. "It may take a long time. Those people are sitting on twelve hundred acres of land, while you're out here trying to buy a quarter section. We'll need verification of your identity, but I can probably track down Nolland without too much trouble, if he's still alive, and Bart and Nancy Williams.

"Meantime, I'm going to go through the law books and look up some cases relating to inheritance and illegitimacy. Must be some pretty interesting cases buried away there." Freeman smiled excitedly and held out his hand to Peter, who shook it warmly. "I feel good about this, Peter," he said, "partly because of what happened between us in the past and partly because it gives me a chance to work on an extraordinary case."

Peter stood up. He was eager to be alone with his thoughts.

Following him to the door, Freeman said, "I'll write to Frank Howard right off, and I'll keep you in touch with the proceedings."

He was as good as his word. Every week or so the lawyer got a livery rig and drove out to talk to Peter, Charity, and Grandma about the case. As he had predicted, it moved slowly. The hard part was tracking down Nick, who might well have been dead, for all they knew. Bart Williams responded to Freeman at once, but Frank Howard never wrote back.

Frank Howard's silence made Peter uneasy. In many ways the

whole case made him uneasy. Charity, her mother, and the children urged him to let John Freeman continue.

"Think what it would mean to the children," they said. "We'd have a little security at last."

Peter did not tell his neighbors what was going on, although word traveled about John Freeman's frequent visits to the farm. He worried in silence about it. The Howard men had always meant trouble to him, and he remembered them only in negative and cruel terms. Why bring it all back? He really didn't want to pursue it, but felt he had lost control. John Freeman was determined.

Sometimes he tried to soothe his mind with imaginings of the old farm in Missouri, of Nora, of returning to claim some land close to where she was buried. But the peaceful scene he tried to structure was always rimmed with a sinister line, a margin that grew narrower and narrower, squeezing out the picture at last.

Finally, Nick Nolland replied from Philadelphia, where he had moved. He was eager to see Peter and his family get their share.

"You see?" said Charity. "Even he thinks we should go through with this." She looked anxiously at Peter. "We got Bart and Nick behind us now, honey, so what's troubling you?"

His eyes gazed at her, straight and far from the past. "Something went out of me. I felt it leaving me when we were hiding away. It wasn't exactly hope. It was the natural outcome of my own temper since birth. I remember the feeling from when I was a boy on the Collins place. I can't put it into words."

"I know," she assented. "It silences me, too, the way we've been hurt, and when I think of those Howards like we knew them. Just want to be alone."

Still Frank Howard did not respond, nor did his brother who had moved in on the land with him. John Freeman wrote many people, inquiring about them, and was told they were still on the farm and raking in a small fortune off the fields Peter had restored for them.

"I might make a trip to Missouri myself," Freeman told Peter and his family one night, when he had stopped over for dinner. "I wrote and told the Howards to expect me any time—it may be soon before the winter comes."

"Maybe," Peter suggested, "we should just forget the whole thing."

"Forget it?" laughed Freeman. "Not a chance!"

His face glowed in the candlelight across the table. Peter saw the boy in him, the one who couldn't face him with a gun twenty years before. Peter was suddenly moved by this man's interest, accidentally triggered after so many years.

"Well, if you go to Missouri," Peter told him, "I'll go too. You'll need some company and protection."

"You think I'm still a coward, don't you, when it comes to guns," he smiled.

"No. I was just thinking of that Indian fellow and how he kept talking about what it means to meet someone from the past. That's all. Think I should stick pretty close to you."

Freeman stood up.

"I'll think about that, Peter, but in the meantime, I got some work to do back at the office."

He got in his rig. The family stood around him saying goodnight, and he rode off toward the black sky emblazoned with myriads of stars.

The next morning, John Freeman was found shot at his desk. His own gun lay at his feet.

At first the coroner pronounced him dead by his own hand, but then they discovered all the shells intact in his gun. There was money in his pockets and some in his desk drawer. His wife knew nothing of his legal business. No one could imagine who would have murdered him.

The sheriff stopped Peter before the funeral and asked him why John Freeman had been visiting him. Peter's voice came low and dry, though his eyes glittered.

"We were working on a land deal together, farther out west," he told the sheriff.

And he turned to look at his family gathered on the steps of their small house framed against the huge sky.

A FEW MONTHS after John Freeman's death, Peter and his family were seated around the house in the dusk and talking softly, when they saw, framed against the reddening sky, a small dark figure approaching on foot.

They all sat very still, observing this apparition, so unusual on the Great Plains. It was a very old woman, on foot. She carried a carpetbag in one hand.

She approached very slowly and hesitantly, placing one foot down deliberately after the other. Her brown feet were bare and dusty, and her brown face was dusty, too. By the time she had come to the gate, the sun had almost set.

"Peter? Is Peter here?" her voice called, high and anxious, as if she were blind.

Peter stepped forward, waving to his children to stay back, sit down, be quiet.

"Who is it there?" he asked.

"Peter?" she repeated.

She was very small. Her upturned face was deeply, finely lined, and indeed she did seem very nearly blind, the way she gazed up at Peter's face hungrily.

"Yes, I'm Peter," he said, and opening the gate, put out his arm to her.

She grasped it at once and, as light as a bird, leaned on him. "It's your mammy, Peter," she said in that same high voice. "It's Betty, remember? Now I paid my wages step by step just getting here."

Peter stopped and held her against him, rocking her like a small child. The rest of his family moved slowly out of the shadows around them and gathered close. She told him what had happened to her, how she had lost everyone and everything during the War, had made her way by stitching and cooking and even foraging, at times, like a wild rabbit, in the woods. She was looking for her children everywhere, north, south, east, and west, and finally went to the old Howard farm and heard from one of the women working there that Peter was here.

"You were the only one I could find, the only one," she said, "and I've come home to you to die, my boy. I told you I would see you first, now, didn't I?"

Peter took her in. Charity and Grandma washed her down. She didn't weigh more than eighty pounds. She died in Peter's arms not so long after.

10

I ALWAYS WANTED to put a lot of distance between me and Missouri, a lot of distance, and we kept on moving for some time then, three years till we settled outside of Topeka. People would ask me the same questions, every time, about my color, about whether I was Negro or white. But once we got involved in some work together, the questions would drop and the people would forget. All and the same, they rarely asked us over to their houses.

My dream was always with me, of a tribe of children and out of them all, one would be great, maybe long after I was gone.

As I grew older, I expect I looked more and more like my father, and there was no escaping it, but I stopped caring anyhow. My past was something I wanted to leave behind me, and that was easy enough. There was always plenty to do and worry about every day. The War brought freedom to my people, but it didn't bring any comfort, and we struggled like the rest of the pioneers out there, with the land.

I'd say we had to struggle a little harder, and more every year, because of the color question. I did what I could to protect my children, but they would have to fight harder still than I did. This is a fact that has hurt me, and makes me wish I would never die. I have become them, and our manners are all the same. I was the child of white people who wouldn't take care of me. And when I am gone, who will take care of my children, and theirs? That is the question I hold in my mind. Should I have fought harder for the farm where I was born? Everyone needs a piece of land. I was here in this country much longer than the men who want to take my land away.

PETER MCCUTCHEON died in his home in April 1907, the month of his birth, at the age of seventy-five years and a few days. He left behind him many friends in the community and a large family. Charity died in 1934 at the age of ninety-eight. They are buried beside each other in a cemetery a mile and a half east of Wabaunsee County, Kansas, as are several members of their family. The other members are buried within a radius of thirty or forty miles of Wabaunsee—at Alma, Manhattan, Eskridge, Newberry, and Chalk Mounds.

THE END

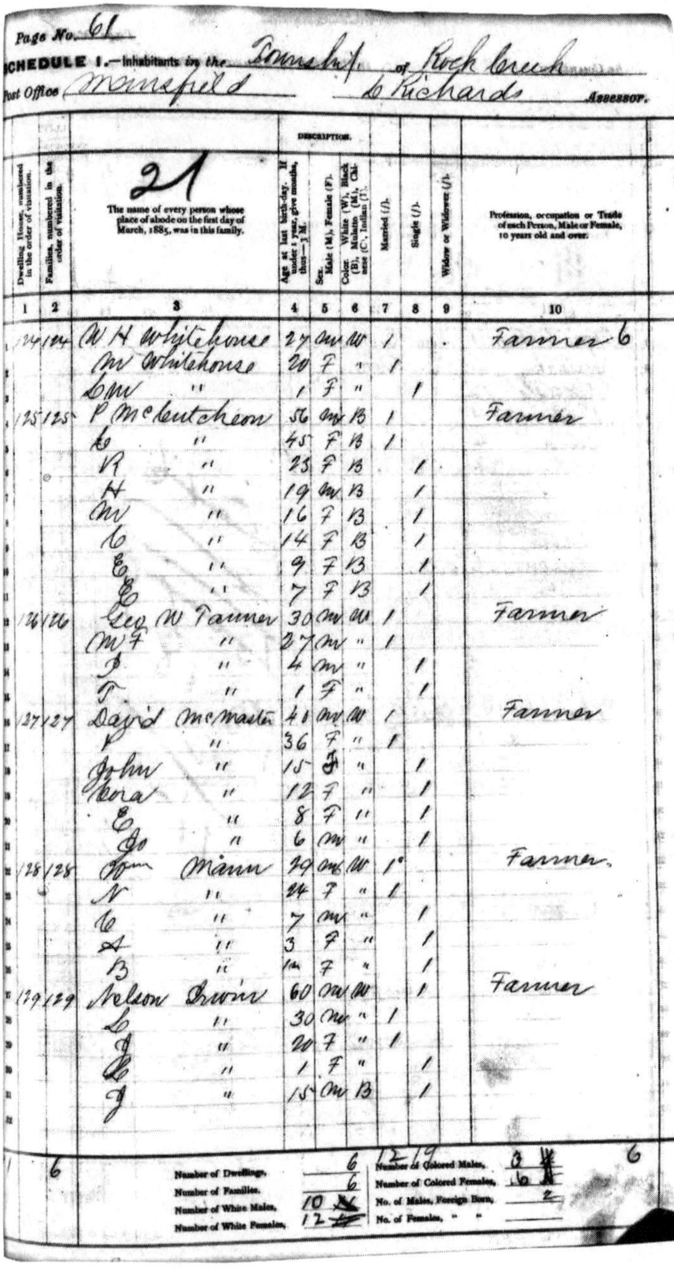
Page No. 61

SCHEDULE 1.—Inhabitants in the Township of Rock Creek

Post Office Mansfield — C Richards, Assessor.

21

Dwelling House, numbered in the order of visitation.	Families, numbered in the order of visitation.	The name of every person whose place of abode on the first day of March, 1885, was in this family.	Age at last birth-day. If under 1 year, give months, thus—3 M.	Sex. Male (M), Female (F).	Color. White (W), Black (B), Mulatto (M), Chinese (C), Indian (I).	Married (/).	Single (/).	Widower or Widower (/).	Profession, occupation or Trade of each Person, Male or Female, 10 years old and over.
1	2	3	4	5	6	7	8	9	10
124	124	W H Whitehouse	27	M	W	1			Farmer 6
		M Whitehouse	20	F	"	1			
		C M "	1	F	"		1		
125	125	P McCutcheon	56	M	B	1			Farmer
		C "	45	F	B	1			
		R "	23	F	B		1		
		H "	19	M	B		1		
		M "	16	F	B		1		
		C "	14	F	B		1		
		E "	9	F	B		1		
		E "	7	F	B		1		
126	126	Geo W Farmer	30	M	W	1			Farmer
		M F "	27	M	"	1			
		J "	4	M	"		1		
		T "	1	F	"		1		
127	127	David McMaster	41	M	W	1			Farmer
		[illegible] "	36	F	"	1			
		John "	15	F	"		1		
		Cora "	12	F	"		1		
		E "	8	F	"		1		
		Jo "	6	M	"		1		
128	128	Tom Mann	29	M	W	1			Farmer.
		N "	24	F	"	1			
		C "	7	M	"		1		
		A "	3	F	"		1		
		B "	1m	F	"		1		
129	129	Nelson Irwin	60	M	W		1		Farmer
		L "	30	M	"	1			
		J "	20	F	"	1			
		L "	1	F	"		1		
		J "	15	M	B		1		

Number of Dwellings,	6	Number of Colored Males,	3
Number of Families,	6	Number of Colored Females,	6
Number of White Males,	10	No. of Males, Foreign Born,	2
Number of White Females,	12	No. of Females, " "	

Work schedule for slaves on the Missouri plantation.

Facsimilies

Peter and Charity McCutcheon.

Charles McCutcheon and his sister Agnes Stewart.

Merton F. McCutcheon, brother of Charles and grandson of Peter.

Eden McCutcheon Tirl, great-great grandaughter
of Peter McCutcheon.

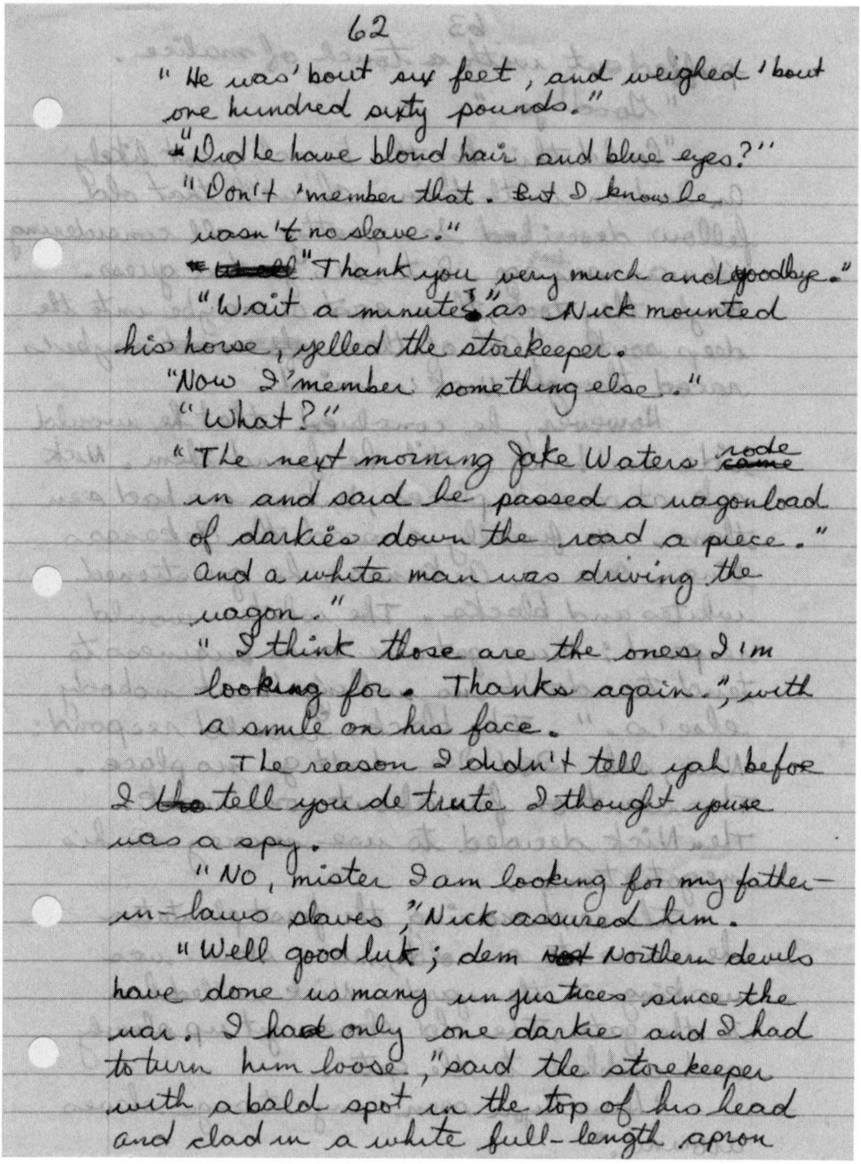
62

"He was' bout six feet, and weighed 'bout one hundred sixty pounds."

"Did he have blond hair and blue eyes?"

"Don't 'member that. But I know he wasn't no slave."

"Thank you very much and goodbye."

"Wait a minutes!" as Nick mounted his horse, yelled the storekeeper.

"Now I'member something else."

"What?"

"The next morning Jake Waters ~~came~~ rode in and said he passed a wagonload of darkies down the road a piece." And a white man was driving the wagon."

"I think those are the ones I'm looking for. Thanks again.", with a smile on his face.

The reason I didn't tell yah befoe I ~~tho~~ tell you de trute I thought youse was a spy.

"No, mister I am looking for my father-in-laws slaves," Nick assured him.

"Well good luk; dem ~~Nor~~ Northern devils have done us many unjustices since the war. I had only one darkie and I had to turn him loose," said the storekeeper with a bald spot in the top of his head and clad in a white full-length apron

The first full account written on lined paper in blue ink, by the young Charles McCutcheon.

McCutcheon page 1

Lee: Well now I*ll tell you. a— One thing--and I know you've told me this and I've forgotten. the White Slave was your grandfather?

Chuck: My grandfather.

Lee. U-huh. And he was--

Chuck: Scotch and Irish.

Lee: Scotch and Irish. And now he was your mother's or your father's father?

Chuck: Father's father.

Lee: And a now: One question. We made a list of some questions here. We'll call him Sam. That's what you called him in the story. What was his real name?

Chuck: Peter.

Lee: now His foster mother. You know the black woman that raised him. Did she ever know that Sam was not her natural child. Do you know?

Chuck: Oh, yes. She knew that.

Lee: Did she know that later on, or did she know that pretty much from the time that Sam was a baby?

Chuck: Well, you see, in slavery time a— when a--like the old boss's daughter. When she started to show got pregnant and she started to show why they locked her upstairs until she had the baby and they took it away from her before she come out from under it and they just took the baby and put it out in the slave quarters and let an old mammy take care of it him.

She nursed him.

Lee: Yes, uh-huh. But she knew right from. . .

JChuck: Yeh, the old mammy knew it wasn't hers, and she knew whose child it was but she wasn't allowed to say anything about it.

Lee: You know one thing that both Roger and I thought we would need to expand an awful lot were the details connected with this-this--what was his name? Mr. Howard's daughter getting pregnant--in other words, your — the white slave's mother. It comes through. You can infer from this what happend, but you don't have very many details. And I wondered what you could--I remember you mentioned there was a travelling salesman or something?

Chuck: Well, my grandfather was, his dad was a surveyor. He was surveying land for the railroad. And he stopped at this plantation and asked the old boss if he could keep him for two or three weeks or maybe

Excerpt of interview with Charles McCutcheon and Agnes Stewart transcribed by Lee Steinmetz.

THE WHITE SLAVE

ar of 1832 while slave[illegible] was at its height, there was a child
the world helpless [illegible] as[illegible] others, but there was
young mother [illegible] sweet moments, for
i from the [illegible] child was not there.
Chris [illegible] d that they
[illegible] taken and
[illegible] even if
[illegible] Of course

THE WHITE SLAVE

by

Charles McCutcheon

Afterword

by EDEN McCUTCHEON TIRL

MY GREAT-GREAT-GRANDFATHER Peter McCutcheon, though completely Caucasian, was a slave from 1832 until the end of the Civil War. After being freed from a ramshackle schoolhouse in the middle of dusty Arkansas with his burgeoning family, he made his way to Kansas. He had children and grandchildren, and as they grew he told them what he could about his life, and his son and grandson wrote down his story.

Growing up, my mother and her siblings had understood that their extended family had all died. My grandmother implored them not to go looking for them, as it was futile. But in 1985, while moving to Southern California, my mother decided to accompany me, and suggested we angle the trek in such a way that we would be able to visit the small town in Kansas where her father grew up. We had no idea what we would find there.

We pulled into town about midday, passing a modest cemetery on the left. The streets of Wabaunsee, Kansas, in 1985, were inert and forlorn. We slowed and pulled onto what looked like the main thoroughfare.

Not knowing what we were looking for, we wandered about, turning round and round in the center of the street like actors in a scene from the end of the world. We agreed we should start by going over to the graveyard we'd passed on the way in. It was an eerily beautiful day. The juxtaposition of the lifeless town, stunning blue sky, whispering breeze, and searing hot sun, felt almost supernatural.

We wandered around the tiny cemetery of no more than 100 headstones. I went to the left of the entrance, and became entranced with the flat, aged limestone slabs. My mother wandered to the right, looking for signs of family. Save for the occasional truck passing by, this dusty square of land was peaceful, no one around us but the dead.

I was on my haunches when I heard my mother audibly yelp. I saw she was in the corner of the cemetery, holding her mouth. I walked toward her quickly and called out, "What have you found?" She was standing in front of a rather large headstone. There, engraved in bold serif typeface: "Peter McCutcheon."

We realized this person must be a relative, but my mother had never heard his name before. We came prepared, and as I held a large piece of paper against the face of the headstone, my mother chafed over the lettering with a pencil. I felt her excitement, and I was happy for our discovery, knowing it was a piece of the family puzzle—how large a piece, we could not have imagined.

As we would eventually learn, Peter McCutcheon's experience as a slave is enigmatic in that he possessed no African ancestry whatsoever. In his early years, Peter believed what he had been told, that he was Betty's child. Later, when his skin tone failed to darken, he became overwhelmed with the need to know who he really was, and how he came to be.

The plantation my earliest family grew up on was remote in southwest Missouri, yet there must have been knowledge of other "white slaves." It was actually not unusual at all. After two-hundred-plus years of slavery, and many generations of interracial relations between black slave women and white plantation family members, "mulatto" or "high yellow" slaves were very common. This made the exchange of babies, and Betty's becoming Peter's mother, quite feasible.

In the Census Record from Wabaunsee, Kansas, in 1875, Peter

McCutcheon is listed as Black. In 1880, he is listed as Mulatto. In 1895, he is "Colored," and in 1900, he is Black again.

In 1905, he is listed as White, and in 1907 he died. His grave sits in that far corner of the Wabaunsee Cemetery, where we found it, under the protection of two large white oak trees.

Charity McCutcheon, Peter's wife, whose father was a Native American, is listed in the 1880 Census as Mulatto. In 1895, she is "Colored." In 1900, she is Black. In 1910 and 1920, she is Mulatto. In 1930, she is Negro.

All of their children are listed exactly the same as Charity until her death. And by 1930, all documents show their race as Negro. According to a Virginia law of 1662, if the mother of a child is a slave, her child will also be a slave. This was a law that adopted the ancient legal doctrine of *partus sequitur ventrem*, which held that the child follows the social status of the mother.

> Even after all visual characteristics of the African had long since disappeared, many generations of white people continued to be held in slavery because any child born of a slave mother automatically assumed slave status.

This was the primary legal principle used to perpetuate African American slavery from one generation to another, running contrary to the English tradition, which determined the status of children according to the status of the father.

During the Northern antebellum years, free people of mixed race were frequently considered white. Even if the person had one-eighth or one-quarter African ancestry, they were considered to be white. Certainly this was not the case with "Partus" slaves in the South.

Slaves were "free" after the Civil War. However, in 1910, in an effort to keep the bloodlines "pure" and the social status of blacks in check, the *one-drop rule* was established, asserting that any person with one drop of negro blood shall be considered black.

There was such rampant miscegenation; it is thought that this was the last straw for the antebellum North. Seeing people with such pale skin on farms and being sold at auction was far too much for many in the liberal North. And so they went to war.

I'M CONFIDENT Peter adored Charity. Loving her, confiding in her, learning about her culture, seems likely to have given him an affinity for the Native American people. He no doubt had learned that the state of Kansas, once home to such tribes as the Osage, Kiowa, Pawnee, and Wichita, was now increasingly occupied by often indignant European Americans, as well as the hostile US Army.

Peter must have heard, while living on the plantation, that Kansas was officially open to settlers in 1854. But abolitionist "Free-Staters" from New England and pro-slavery settlers from neighboring Missouri had begun rushing to the territory to fight a protracted and violent battle to determine whether Kansas would become a free or slave state—at the time, a territory still known as *"Bleeding Kansas."*

The abolitionists, led by John Brown and his sons, eventually prevailed, and on January 29, 1861, Kansas entered the Union as a free state—and the Civil War would begin two and a half months later.

MY GREAT-GREAT-GRANDFATHER'S DREAM, it seems, was to move to a free Kansas. The family was not fully settled until 1869–70, but the atmosphere that they found themselves in would have been distressing and unpredictable. As Harriet Tubman would say, "They were strangers in a strange land."

There was a huge backlash rising in the South against post-war Reconstruction, as pro-slavery Southerners could not handle black men being free and now claiming their rights.

The Ku Klux Klan, organized in Pulaski, Tennessee, in 1866, along with other "white supremacist" groups like them, were not centralized organizations, but local and regional throughout the South. They used violence to suppress and intimidate any attempts at racial equality, working nefariously to restore a system of radical white supremacy that continues today.

Southern local governments rarely protected black citizens from hostile whites. Progress and improvement were the goals of Reconstruction, but its attempts started some of the worst vigilante violence in American history.

White supremacist groups worked mostly at night, dragging people out of their beds to be tortured and often murdered. Beatings, burning of body parts, and lynching were all hallmarks of their forms of intimidation. *"Lynching became even more widespread beginning in the 1880's, and would remain common in the South until the 1930's."*

PETER MCCUTCHEON (1832–1907) was a farmer his whole life. He surely had solid knowledge of the land, its crops, and cattle breeding. The stories handed down in the family show him to be an uncommonly kind, enduring, and powerful man.

Early years farming in Kansas would have been erratic, as the soil had never been worked before. But Peter had plenty of experience with plowing that hard earth and clearing the trees. In time, things would progress, and the family would have small herds of cattle and hogs, and become quite self-sustaining.

My great-great-grandmother, Charity, lived to be 94 years of age (1840–1934). I continue to look for her people—we believe her to be from the Osage tribe. Charity lived in Kansas with my great-grandfather Edward, and his son Charles, until her death. Charity's mother, who, in the book is named Ruth, is Cyntha A. Nichols, who lived from 1819 to 1884.

There is little information about my great-grandaunts, Rhoda, born in 1862, and Ella in 1875. My great-granduncle Henry (1866–

1951) was the first child born free to Peter and Charity. He would also become a farmer and marry Nancy Bradley. They had one child together. Nancy was also of mixed race, like Henry. Her father was from Tennessee, and of African ancestry. Her mother was a Caucasian from Missouri.

Maria (1868–1910) would marry the handsome Richard Hiram Mitchell, also African American, and have three children together. My great-grandaunt Cyntha (1871–1890) died at the young age of nineteen.

My great-grandfather Edward (1877–1947) would marry Josephine Allen, a beautiful woman of mixed race. They would have five children together: William Levoid, born in 1902, would leave the small Kansas town he grew up in and become a sergeant in the US Army. He fought in World War II, married the lovely Dorothy D. Owens, and lived to be 77 years of age. He is buried in Denver, Colorado.

My grandaunt Agnes, born in 1900, and the only one to actually remember Peter and Charity, would marry Orville Douglas Stewart, a hardworking construction worker, also African American. In a 1930 Census, Agnes is listed as a "servant for private families." She would live until 1983.

My granduncle Charles (1911–1979), an ironworker, would stay in Wabaunsee, and marry his love Hope. He was the family member that recorded Peter's story as his father told it to him.

Grandfather Merten F. McCutcheon (1904–1957), youngest son of Edward, was a repairman who could fix almost anything from what I understand. He also had an artistic skill, whittling wood into various display objects, and writing uncomplicated, yet fervent notes and poetry to his wife, my grandmother, Lenora.

They too had five children together, my mother one of them. Our family continues to consist of a wide array of skin tones—we are a true American family, with a heritage reaching back farther than most.

I HAVE MADE considerable progress locating documents of the Rankin family that owned the plantation in southwest Kansas, where Peter was born. It is unsettling to see in print the reams of slave schedules from that time, to see my family members listed there, along with so many others.

I imagine my ancestors caged on the coast of West Africa, then shackled together in the putrid holds of the Middle Passage slave ships, finally to arrive in an unfamiliar, merciless, and incomprehensible world.

Growing up in the 70s, in a racially mixed urban Minneapolis, I certainly had knowledge of some fundamental issues. I had a long mane of wild, wavy hair, and skin that manifested a deep tawny hue in the summertime. I embraced myself in a way that felt natural and free, never questioning the significance of the well-anchored picture of the man that sat on top of the glass chiffonier in my grandmother's dining room—the suave, elegant black man, who watched over the house, yet no longer with us, was clearly connected to me.

The picture was cherished, an indication of great love. It too, was evidence of our family's lineage, the unknown stories of our ancestors, and the secrets of how we had come to be.

An ultimate and eternal thank you to my great-great-grandfather Peter—my love and gratitude are vast, immeasurable, and totally unwavering.

Acknowledgments

My deepest gratitude for their advice, friendship, and time in reviving this book: first and foremost the poet and editor William Corbett, the designer Michael Russem, and the invaluable Professor Roger Whitlow. Others who took time to read the new version are Colleen McCallion, Jennifer Tseng, Linda Norton, Penny Janeway, and Eden McCutcheon Tirl.